Jeff Gulvin was born in 1[illegible] and half English and has lived in various parts of the UK and for a time in New Zealand. He is the author of two previous novels featuring Aden Vanner, *Sleep No More* and *Sorted*. He lives in Norfolk.

Also by Jeff Gulvin

Sleep No More
Sorted

Close Quarters

Jeff Gulvin

First published in Great Britain in 1997
by HEADLINE BOOK PUBLISHING

First published in paperback in 1998
by HEADLINE BOOK PUBLISHING

A HEADLINE FEATURE paperback

10 9 8 7 6 5 4 3 2 1

ISBN 0 7472 5386 2

Typeset by CBS, Felixstowe, Suffolk

Printed and bound in Great Britain by
Mackays of Chatham plc, Chatham, Kent

HEADLINE BOOK PUBLISHING
A division of Hodder Headline PLC
338 Euston Road
London NW1 3BH

For Amy and Chloe,
my daughters

In researching this novel the author was accorded access to various units and specialist operations of the Metropolitan Police Service. He would like to thank those officers concerned for their assistance and confidence.

A special thanks to Andrew Seed, for the fag packet notes in Eureka

One

Rain fell in brittle rods that broke against the windscreen. Jessica drove sitting hunched forward in the seat with the wipers flicking back and forth before her eyes, mist on the inside of the glass. The clock on the dashboard read nearly seven thirty. She knew she would be there before him.

Cars passed her on the outside lane as she slipped off the motorway and dipped down the slope to the Cadnam roundabout. Headlights shone suddenly fierce in the mirror as a car braked hard behind her. She pulled onto the roundabout, followed the road under the motorway and turned left into the forest on the old B road. The car behind followed her.

She eased her way gently through the familiar village of Brook and snaked between trees to where the road forked right for Bramshaw. She kept left and the darkness opened up on either side of her. Her lights caught the eyes of a New Forest pony, grazing by the roadside. For a moment she was startled, knowing they were there but still not expecting to see one so near to the road. Behind her the car seemed very close and she slowed to let it past. For a moment it dropped back then gears ground and it accelerated hard and was gone.

She relaxed a little after that; nothing worse than a driver up your backside on roads smeared by the rain. It had fallen all day. In the office this morning the darkness seemed to close like a fist about the window. It lingered into the afternoon and beyond. The hours had dragged by. She had watched the clock, something she never did. As it turned out she was late getting away and crawled south out of London with rain falling like stones on the roof of her car. In front of her now the glow of the other car's tail lights bled to nothing.

Up ahead the car pulled off the road onto a dirt track. Lights out, door open, the driver stepped into the rain.

Jessica turned the music a little higher on the stereo and

really began to look forward to the weekend. There would be dry wood at the cottage and if she was quick enough she could get a fire going before he got there. She smiled to herself, and slowed where the road swept in an arc. To her right the flicker of somebody's house lights broke the depth of the shadows. Ahead the road was chipped and broken into hollows that brimmed with mud-flecked water in the sudden beam of her headlights.

A man stepped into the road and fell over.

Jessica cried out, stamped on the brakes and the car came to a halt with the back end swinging wildly. At the last moment she dipped the clutch and sat there breathing hard. She knocked out the gear and peered into the rain. The man lay on his side, facing away from her. He wore no jacket and his shirt was plastered to his flesh. She sat there. Far in the distance behind her she could see the glimmer of headlights.

Wait for the other car, she told herself. Wait for the other car. But she could not wait. The man lay too still. Opening the driver's door she got out and the rain thrashed at her. Quickly now she fetched her coat from the back seat and walked forward into the darkness.

She got almost to where he lay. 'Are you all right?' Her voice sounded very small against the night. Clouds blocked any light thrown down by the moon. Behind her the headlights were brighter.

'Are you all right?' she said it again, louder this time. Still the man did not move. He was twenty, perhaps thirty, yards ahead of her car. She walked quickly now; already the rain was soaking through the flimsy material of the coat she held over her head. Still he did not move, arms stiff at his sides. She bent and hesitated then reached out and touched him. She recoiled suddenly, almost falling over on the tarmac. His flesh was stiff and hard. Not flesh, plastic. A dummy.

She got to her feet, heart high in her chest. Behind her the car drew closer. And now she panicked, the darkness and the rain and a dummy in the road at her feet. She pushed it aside with her foot, staring into the gloom by the roadside. Darkness pressed back against her. Back to her car, she jumped behind the wheel. The car was right behind her now, lights on full beam. Jessica rammed home first gear and pulled away with a squeal from her tyres.

The car behind her hooted, but she shoved in second then third gear and tore up the road with the needle climbing the speedometer. Another horse close to the road shied away from her and she wrenched hard on the wheel to avoid it. She could feel herself trembling, moist palms, the steering wheel slithering under her grip. Behind her headlights shone full in her eyes.

The road trickled out in a thin line of grey under the weight of her lights. On either side naked New Forest moorland swept into the darkness. The car was almost on her bumper, horn blaring, headlights flashing and dulling, flashing again and then dulling. Again a little cry that stuck hard in her throat. Faster and faster. She held the gear stick and pressed her foot to the floor.

Seventy-five, eighty miles an hour with the tyres screeching on the bends. The lights from the solitary house were gone now and she was alone with the road and the rain and the car up close behind her.

Her hands were white about the wheel, the muscles taut in her face. Concentrating so hard she almost missed the turning when it came. Hale and Woodfalls and Little Woodfalls where the twin cottages were perched side by side set back from the road. Just a few miles now, just a few miles. And still the car pursued her, lights so high she could see nothing else. In the end she twisted the mirror to one side to stop herself being blinded.

She took the next corner hard and behind her the second car slewed, nearly skidded then righted itself. A little space now, a moment or two to breathe. She pressed her right heel into the floor and the car leapt forward.

But still the other car pursued her, lights duller then getting more and more fierce as the ground was swallowed up between them. But the village was ahead of her now, only two more turns and then the driveway. She made the first turn, her wheels half over the white lines just missing an oncoming car which swerved hard to avoid her. Still a gap between her and her pursuer. Who was it? Joy rider? Idiot with nothing better to do than chase lonely women through the forest at night? She took the right-hand bend and there was the cottage banked in darkness on her left. Braking hard, she hauled the wheel over and gravel hissed from her tyres. She drove to the garage doors and then stopped, lurching forward in the seat as the brakes bit. At the bottom of the drive she saw headlights.

And then her fear turned to anger, indignation that burned suddenly in her chest. She jumped out into the rain and stalked down the drive with her fists clenched at her sides. As she got to the road she saw a man climbing from the driving seat of a dark-coloured saloon car.

'What the hell d'you think you're doing?'

He did not speak, glanced at her once and then sprinted past her up the drive.

Jessica whirled around. He got to her car and she saw that the back door was open. The man stood there, panting and holding his side. He straightened and came slowly back down the drive to her. His hair was long and thin, face pinched and beaten about the eyes.

'Why didn't you stop?'

'What?'

'I was trying to get you to stop.'

'Stop? You must be mental. You scared me shitless.'

'You should've stopped.' He pointed back up the drive to her car. 'When you were out on the road just now – someone got in your car.'

Two

Vanner turned off the lane into the wide gravel driveway, and the Old Rectory lifted against the fingers of tree branches and above them the spread of the stars. He switched off the engine and glanced at Ellie, sitting next to him.

'My father's house,' he said.

Lights flooded the steps from the hall as the front door was opened. Vanner got out and grabbed their cases from the boot. Anne came down the steps to meet them.

'Aden. You made it. He'll be so pleased.'

Vanner held the cases. He bent and kissed her cheek. 'How is he, Anne?'

'He's okay.'

He looked into her face, eyes shadowed into her cheeks, hair pulled back as it always was, more grey than black now. She smiled at him then turned to Ellie, who stood self-consciously next to him.

'Sorry,' Vanner said. 'This is Ellie, Anne. Ellie, this is Anne. My stepmother.'

For a moment Anne looked at him. It was the first time he had referred to her as that. He knew it and he knew she knew it too. She shook Ellie's hand and slipped an arm about her shoulders. Together they crunched over gravel and up the steps into the wide wooden floored hall. Vanner followed behind with the bags.

Anne led them through to the kitchen where a fire burned in the grate. Ellie shivered, moved towards it and bent, rubbing her hands together.

'A fire,' she said. 'There's nothing to beat a fire.'

'The lounge is so big and cold,' Anne said. 'We sit in here these days.' She nodded to two wooden frame rockers with travelling rugs stretched over them that occupied the floor by the hearth. 'It's lovely just sitting in the firelight with the wind rattling the windows.'

'It's very windy up here,' Ellie said.

'Norfolk, my dear.' Anne plugged in the kettle. 'Nothing between here and Siberia.'

Vanner set the bags down on the floor. 'I've put you in the back bedroom, Aden. The one you had last time.'

Last time. That was a year ago when he had been recovering from stab wounds inflicted by Ninja, a low-life drug dealer's hardman. A year. He had promised them he would make it for Christmas but he hadn't. Somehow he never did.

'Where is he, Anne?'

'Upstairs resting.'

'Shouldn't he be in hospital?'

'Probably. But you know your father, Aden. Stubborn as the proverbial mule. He lasted all of three days.'

'Which hospital was it?' Ellie asked.

'Norfolk and Norwich. He just wouldn't stay in there.'

'Ellie's a nurse, Anne,' Vanner said.

Anne spooned coffee into thick earthenware mugs and poured boiling water. 'It's his second heart attack, Aden. Not like the one he had when he was still working but the doctors told him to take it as a warning. He just has got to start saying *No* to people.' She looked plaintively at Vanner. 'He does too much. He's supposed to be retired, but they will use him as a locum. Sometimes he travels half the bloody county to fill in for absent clergy.'

Vanner leaned on the sink. 'He'd only get bored if he didn't. Is he awake?'

'Why don't you go up and see?'

He climbed the stairs, listening vaguely to them talking in the kitchen. Ellie's voice, unfamiliar in this house. This was the first time he had brought anyone here since Jane left him eleven years ago. The stairs creaked under his feet, the runner getting threadbare, the board dusty on either side of it. Light showed under his father's door. For a moment he paused and thought about all the years that had passed between them. The years of strained silence, each of them unsure of his place in the other's life. It all came back to him now; the Yemen, his unremembered mother dying. The old photographs and his army chaplain father in khaki shorts and rolled-up sleeves, face burnt to a cinder by Middle Eastern suns.

He placed his hand on the doorknob but still he hesitated. In his mind's eye he could see him in younger days before his hair turned white, tall and thin and driving that battered Willis Jeep with no windshield. He opened the door and went in. His father lay on his back, the sheet tucked in about his chest, withered hands laid flat at his sides. His hair was thin now and his eyes were closed. Age hung in folds from his face.

Vanner closed the door. He leaned on it, hands behind his back. His father stirred, his eyes flickered and then registered. A thin smile creased withered lips.

'Aden.' His voice was low, husky, liquid in his throat. Vanner moved off the door and went over to the bed. He pulled up a chair and sat down. His father half-lifted his hand then lowered it again.

'Last time it was me visiting you in bed.'

Vanner smiled. 'How you feeling?'

'Been better, son. Been better.'

'Second time, Dad. You can't afford many more.'

'I'm seventy-three nearly. Not bad.'

'Anne says you're working too hard.'

His father smiled again.

'She'd be lost without you, Dad. You ought to take things easy.'

'She's younger than me, son. A lot younger. She's going to be without me.'

They were both silent for a while. Vanner could hear the wind lifting against the window.

'Raining?' his father asked.

Vanner shook his head. 'Raining in London, Dad. Raining everywhere but here today.'

'It'll get here.' His father half-closed his eyes again. 'It'll rain in the night. I like listening to rain in the night.'

He looked at his son then, lifted his hand, fingers stretching. Vanner looked at it, old and worn with age spots highlighting the skin that bunched over the blue of his veins. He reached out his own hand and clasped it. So much unsaid between them. The years rolled away once more and Vanner was a boy in a British army camp in some far-flung corner of the world, surrounded by the sweat of uniformed men, the straight-backed presence of a father and no mother.

'How's the job?' his father asked him.

'Okay.'
'What you working on?'
'Crack team. British blacks out of Harlesden.'
'Big time?'
'Big enough.'
'Will you get them?'
'If I have my way.'
His father closed his eyes again. 'And how are you outside the job? Got yourself someone at last.'
'She's downstairs.'
'Is she? That's good.' His father tried to move then. 'Lying in one position,' he muttered. 'Never could get used to it. Too many years on a camp bed.'
Vanner got up then and went to the window.
His father followed him with his eyes. 'What's she like – this lady?'
Vanner half-turned. 'Young.'
'How young?'
'Twenty-five.'
'Not so young.'
'Hell of a lot younger than me.'
His father grinned. 'Take after your old man don't you. Nurse is she?'
Vanner nodded. 'You remember the one who patched me up last year?'
'Vaguely. Not her is it?'
'Her friend. Same ward. I met them one night when I was out with Sid Ryan.'
'How is Sid?'
'He's okay. Got transferred to AMIP. Working with Frank Weir, the DI who replaced me last year.'
His father nodded. 'I want to meet her before you go.'
'We're here till Sunday, Dad.' Vanner moved back to the bed. 'You're knackered. Get some sleep now. I'll be here in the morning.'

Downstairs Anne and Ellie were seated in the rocking chairs, drinking coffee. Vanner made a cup for himself and went to the back door, where he lit a cigarette.
'You can smoke in here, Aden.' Anne smiled at him from the fireside. He shook his head. 'Bad for him up there.' He

looked at the glowing end of the cigarette. 'Bad for me.'

He went outside then and walked alone in the garden. He could see them both through the kitchen window. Anne used to remind him of Jane, but that seemed a long time ago now. Upstairs, light still glowed around the curtains of his father's bedroom. Vanner pictured him again, lying flat out, so still and pale he might have been dead. Wind toyed with the branches of conifer trees. The short cut grass was tight under his feet. He could smell the sea in the night air, east coast but a handful of miles away. He thought about the cottage then, perched so precariously now, all but on the edge of the cliff.

He walked and smoked and thought. His father, seventy-three. A second heart attack. He had been sat on a plot with Jimmy Crack and Sammy when Anne called him on the mobile. They were watching one of the posse Jimmy had brought to them. Little guy in a black VW, dealing out of the back of his car. Small-time player, well down the chain of command. He recalled how still he had felt when Anne mentioned the words heart attack and his father in the same breath. The past played out in slow motion and a lifetime of half-spoken words between them. What if he died, he had thought. What if he ever died?

He came to the kitchen door and dropped his cigarette, grinding it out on the path. Then he went inside, picked up his coffee and sipped at it. Ellie looked up and smiled at him. Vanner moved behind her chair and she caught up his hand in hers.

'Was he sleeping when you came down, Aden?'

Vanner glanced at Anne. 'All but.' He sat down on the floor and crossed his legs, staring into the low flame that licked its way around a fresh cut log. 'He looks old, Anne.'

'He is old.'

'I guess.' He caught her eye then and glimpsed the pain in it. But he was not sure whether it was pain for her or for him.

Jimmy Crack phoned The Mixer from his mobile as he drove home. Friday night, seven thirty already. It had been a long week and he was looking forward to a weekend with his wife and sons. They were supposed to be going out tonight, but there was one more thing he had to do before he went home. The Mixer answered the phone.

'Mixer, it's Selly.'

'What's happening?'

'You got anything for me?'

'Five grand this week.'

'I'm passing the shop. I'll toot my horn when I get round the back.' He switched off the phone and pulled off the North Circular road at Dudden Hill before heading up into Neasden. The Mixer ran an electrical goods shop which ran a Western Union money transfer office. The crack team Jimmy had been working on for over a year now thought they had him in their pocket. They were smurfing cash out to Jamaica in lots under the five thousand pound disclosure limit. Sometimes they took in as much as twenty thousand and The Mixer broke it into smaller amounts and it was sent out under five different names and addresses. But he had nicked The Mixer on handling charges years back and he had been informing on them for a year. If they ever found out they would kill him.

He pulled out of the circle and pushed the old Astra down into second gear where it whined in protest. Crap car, so obviously job. When would they finally realise and get him another? Still the car was unofficial and he supposed he was lucky to have it at all.

A broken-up alley stretched the length of the shops at the back. Jimmy bumped over the pot holes until he came to the black door behind the shop where The Mixer mixed and matched second-hand electrical goods until they were fit enough to sell on. Jimmy bounced his fist off the horn and wound the window down. Rain spattered the sill.

He had to wait barely a minute and then The Mixer was leaning at his elbow, chubby Indian face and thick silver-rimmed glasses. Greased grey hair fell over his eyes.

'How's it going?'

'Not bad, Selly.' The Mixer glanced to his left and right and then briefly at the windows of the flats that sat above the array of shops on the circle. He passed a roll of Western Union slips bound in a rubber band through the open window. Jimmy took them from him and leafed through them. 'Not one of ours,' he said, casting his eye over the first one. 'Nor this one or that one. This is.' He stared at the address. The address was wrong but he recognised the right post code. They often did that, false names, false address but the right post code. Difficult to think on your feet and come up with a suitable false one. They thought they'd get away with it. But they didn't. The slip was for three thousand pounds, the addressee in Kingston, Jamaica. There were four others for just under five thousand pounds a piece.

He passed the ones he did not want back to The Mixer and slipped the others up the sleeve of his sweatshirt. 'Top man, Mixer. I'll bring them back on Monday.'

'You won't photocopy them will you?' The Mixer always asked the same question.

Jimmy grinned at him. 'Course I won't.' He tapped the Indian man on the wrist. 'I'll bring them back and square up.'

Back on the North Circular he transferred the slips from his sleeve to the glove compartment of the Astra. He would look at them later and contact the Jamaican DLO on Monday. He yawned as the lights turned red in front of him at the Hanger Lane Junction. A car pulled up to his right and slipped into the space ahead of him. Black BMW with five-spoke alloy wheels. A black man was tapping to Soul music on the steering wheel. Jimmy stared at the back of his head, shaved high up the neck with mini dreadlocks dangling from the growth on top. Pretty Boy. He'd know that hairstyle anywhere. The BMW was a G Reg M3. Jimmy glanced at the battered interior of his own police Astra. The car on the inside lane moved forward as the lights switched from red to green and Jimmy dived for the gap. The BMW was still stationary and Jimmy came alongside. Pretty Boy was staring ahead of him, his long slim fingers rapping out a beat on the wheel.

Jimmy eyeballed him from the left. 'Come on you mother look at me.' Then the line of cars lurched forward and the BMW was ahead.

Jimmy was stuck in the inside lane when he wanted the outside one and the A40 for home. But Pretty Boy was going straight on, then suddenly Pretty Boy stuck his head over his shoulder and pulled directly across the traffic, his wheels spinning in the rain, and cut east onto Western Avenue. Jimmy looked once at the line of cars heading out west towards home and then he hauled the wheel over and drove after Pretty Boy.

They headed down Western Avenue, the BMW just cruising and Jimmy able to watch from three cars back. He unclipped the phone from his belt and called home.

The BMW left the dual carriageway at Horn Lane and then headed down into Acton. This was way off the patch, Jimmy had no addresses for this part of London.

'So where you going you bastard?' he said aloud. Acton on a Friday night. Friday night was mixing it up with the Irish in Biddy Mulligans and then the National on Kilburn High Road. But it was early yet. Who did he know in Acton?

Pretty Boy took a right at Acton main line station and headed west once more, running parallel to the railway lines. He passed the Haberdashers school and took a right turn across the railway lines. Jimmy followed him, no cars between them, but it was dark and all Pretty Boy would see was the yellow of headlights in his mirrors. The BMW followed Noel Road round and then pulled off into a road on the right. Jimmy noted the street name. Ahead of him brake lights shone red in his eyes and the BMW pulled over. Jimmy rolled slowly past and noticed something pasted on the inside of the rear near-side window. Pretty Boy was out, pulling on his jacket and shaking his locks in the rain. Jimmy pulled into a space and adjusted the door mirror. He could see Pretty Boy approach a house on the right and ring the bell. He could not see who opened it, but Pretty Boy disappeared inside.

Jimmy stepped into the rain and walked back along the pavement, nothing but his sweatshirt to protect him. Within a few seconds he was soaked. He noted the address though and lights shone from a curtained window on the ground floor. He paused and looked at the BMW, then he made his way into the road and stared at the poster affixed inside the rear window. It was a *For Sale* notice. Pretty Boy had his mobile phone number advertised for all the world to see.

Jimmy shook his head, memorised the number and walked back to his car, where he wrote it down. He took his phone from his belt once more and rang his wife. He told her he would be home in half an hour.

Vanner woke to the sound of Anne in the kitchen downstairs. Beside him, Ellie was still sleeping. He propped himself up on his elbow and gently eased gold-blonde hair from her cheek. Kissing her lightly, he slipped out of bed and reached for his clothes.

Sunlight filtered through the kitchen window, Vanner was tucking his shirt into his jeans when Anne looked round. She was holding a bread knife, thick slices from a fresh white bloomer on the bread board before her.

'Morning.' She smiled at him. 'Sleep well, Aden?'

Vanner placed his palm against the tea pot and took a mug from the cupboard. 'Can never get used to the quiet.'

'It's good for you,' Anne said. 'Restful. You should come up here more often.'

'I know,' he said. 'I should.'

He went out into the garden where the remnants of winter thickened the atmosphere. Again he could smell the sea and he closed his eyes for a moment and took great lungfuls of air. Childhood. This was a place of childhood. Norfolk, the sea and his father's cottage.

Anne came out behind him and handed him a piece of buttered toast and his tea. He thanked her and sat down on the dew-damp seat of the bench. Anne perched on the arm. Vanner looked about him, the neatly trimmed lawn and well manicured flower beds.

'You keep it so nice, Anne. Such a big garden too.'

'He's got one of those sit-on type mowers now, your father. I made him buy it. No good for his back all that bending.'

Vanner nodded. 'He always loved his garden.'

'Be the death of him if he doesn't let up. Too much physical exertion.'

'Doctor say that?' Vanner looked up at her. 'He was always very physical.'

'It's why he's so thin.' She grinned down at him. 'You're not much better yourself.'

Vanner sipped tea. 'What will you do if he dies, Anne?'

She looked into space then. 'I'll survive, Aden. I knew I'd outlive him when I married him.' She looked down at him again. 'More to the point – what will you do?'

Vanner stopped chewing and swallowed, the crust of toast harsh suddenly as if it was stale in his throat.

'Talk to him, Aden. Say all the things he wants you to say.' She rested the flat of her hand on his shoulder. 'Don't let him go without talking.'

Vanner sat forward and set his tea down on the lawn. A robin landed on the top of his father's garden fork where it was buried to the prong head in the damp earth of the flower bed. He watched it preening its feathers, head darting in tight jerky movements. It flew off and he was left staring at the empty fork.

'It was only a mild heart attack,' he said.

Behind him he heard her sigh and he looked up.

'He's seventy-three, Aden. There are things he wants to say.'

'He talks to you about it?'

'Of course he does.' She made a face then. 'He never used to. But he's older now. His time is precious and he spends a lot of it thinking.'

Vanner looked back at the fork. He took a cigarette from his pocket and cupped his hand around his lighter.

'He misses you.'

'He doesn't judge me does he.'

'Of course he doesn't. He's a lot like you, Aden. Kept his own counsel for most of his life. His view of the world and yours are not altogether different you know.'

Vanner thought about that then, sitting back with one hand tucked under his armpit, drawing on his cigarette and letting the smoke drift from his nostrils. A similar view of the world and yet his father a priest and he a soldier first then policeman.

'He has faith in something, Anne. I don't.'

'Don't you?'

He looked up at her. 'Only in what I do.'

'There you are then. It's the same for both of you. His God is rough and ready. You forget he's spent as much time around soldiers as you have.'

Vanner nodded.

'I suppose he just wants to see you at peace,' she said.

Vanner stood up, drew on his cigarette and pinched out the end between his forefinger and thumb. Peace. What exactly was peace?

'Ellie's a good girl, Aden.'

'She's young.'

Anne nodded. 'Maybe. Old head on her though.'

'Some maybe. She's not seen much of the world yet, Anne.'

'She's a nurse, Aden. She'll have seen a bit. She cares for you. I can see it in the way she looks at you.'

'You think so?' He looked at her. His ex-wife had cared

about him, but that was a long time ago, and that care had turned to fear.

'She knows nothing about my past, Anne.'

'So what? It's the past. Does she ever ask you about it?'

He shook his head.

'There you are then. Maybe she thinks that it's your past and not hers.' She took his hand between both of hers and squeezed. 'Give yourself a future, Aden.'

He smiled then. 'With Ellie?'

'Why not?'

They walked back into the kitchen and Vanner climbed the stairs. The door to their bedroom stood open. He poked his head around it and glanced at the empty bed. Steam rose from the open bathroom door. He heard voices from his father's room.

Ellie was sitting on the window sill in a white towelling dressing gown. Her shins glowed red from the shower and she rubbed at her hair with a towel.

'Hello early bird,' she said.

Vanner grinned at her and looked round at his father. 'How you doing?'

His father winked at Ellie. 'I'm doing just fine, Son. Pretty girl in my bedroom.'

'You're a priest, remember?'

'No longer practising am I.'

Ellie laughed then, slipped off the window sill and left them. She closed the door and Vanner walked over to where she had been sitting. He could smell her.

'She's a good girl, Aden.'

He looked back at his father. 'You think so?'

'I do, yes. She doesn't drink. She doesn't smoke. She doesn't eat foreign food. What more could you want?'

'I miss curries, Dad.'

His father laughed then and his eyes shone for a moment before settling once more in thought. 'You know you could do a lot worse. She's young and pretty and she's got a strong head on those shoulders. How long've you been seeing her now?'

Vanner pursed his lips. 'Three months or so.'

'Stick with it. She's good for you.'

* * *

Sunday night and Jessica Turner drove back to London with the breath of her lover clinging to her flesh. She glanced at the clock on the dashboard, nearly ten thirty now: she should've left much earlier. But the fire had been bright and the rug inviting and the touch of his flesh still warm. But now it was late and there was work in the morning and she did not know when she would see him again.

A car tore past her in the outside lane and for a moment she was reminded of Friday night. It seemed long ago now, that man in his car and the dummy in the road. They had driven out to the place where she thought it had been on Saturday morning but it was gone. But someone in the back of her car. Now she shivered and glanced a little fitfully in the rear-view mirror as if she half-expected to see someone watching her. She had wanted to go to the police, but that would've made things public and with Alec on his way back from Ireland she could not afford it. Alec. Guilt tinged her thoughts for a moment and she frowned. She reached to her bag on the passenger seat for a cigarette and pressed in the lighter on the dashboard. She lit it and rolled the window down far enough to feel the rush of night air through the crack.

Alec would be home tomorrow, back from his rugby tour with the lads. What was she worried about? The things he must've got up to. All those young Catholic girls. He would have had a wail of a time – he never called home when he was away on tour. Off the field then into the bar and whatever else they got up to. He had women. She knew he had women. Condoms in his jacket. She never mentioned it. They had their lives, they both knew it. Guilt was for other people. But would she leave him? Would her lover leave his wife? Did she even want him to? Lover, that was the word and that was what it was. Lovers – two people coming together once in a blue moon to make love, all night, all weekend in every room of someone else's house and then different cars and different routes back to different houses in two different places. That was the charge, the thrill, the total eroticism of it all. She liked him being her lover.

Again the chill of Friday night. There had been someone. She knew there had. Mud on the carpet in the back, mud from somebody's shoes. She shivered again and brushed the thoughts from her mind as she had brushed the mud from the floor.

And since then, bathing together, showering together, lying naked in front of a fire with candles dripping white and yellow wax and red wine in full-bellied glasses and cigarette smoke afterwards.

A joker, she told herself. Some jerk probably getting off in the only way his sad little mind would allow. Whoever he was he was long gone now, scuttling away like a suddenly discovered spider. Pushing her cigarette through the crack in the window she wound it up, and turned the heater full on. London lights beckoned. A few more miles and she would be home.

London. The woman drove slowly, feeding the wheel through long-nailed hands as she turned off Uxbridge Road and pulled over beside the church. Tall and imposing, its squared-off spire thrusting above the trees against the stars that lifted high above the city. No hint of rain, dry streets, dry grass and soft silent shoes. She switched off the engine and sat for a moment in darkness. The houses here were tall, expensive semis, three-storey affairs with dormer-windows in the attics. A little wind ruffled the uppermost branches of the trees on her left and in the mirror she glimpsed the angular lines of her face. Silent street, Sunday night late, with the pubs shut and people huddling against radiators with thoughts of bed and chocolate drinks and the fear of Monday morning. Beside her on the seat the cigar box looked small as she eased off the lid and lifted the gun still wrapped in clingfilm. It was small and black but heavy as she unwrapped the covering and slipped it back in the box. A holdall in a wardrobe, unzipped and inspected, then re-zipped and replaced.

The gun fitted snugly in the pocket of her short black jacket, unzipped now over the pink angora sweater. One glance ahead, one glance behind and she climbed out of the car and closed it without locking. Keys in her pocket then the walk to the corner and the upstairs lights of the houses opposite. At the end of the road she turned left and walked very deliberately past the side of the church to the next corner. The house loomed large and quiet on her left.

The front door was by the right-hand fence: beyond it the front door of the next house and once on the path she was unseen from the road. She studied the door and then the crazy paved area where once a front garden had been planted. The door was set back in a porch fronted by an oval arch. No light from inside.

She made her way along the front of the house, beyond the big bay window and into the shadows by the back gate. There she turned and waited.

Jessica yawned as she waited for the lights to change on Uxbridge Road and turned right towards Ealing. Almost home now and not yet midnight. She had made good time, though the Sunday-night traffic had been heavy on the M3 with people returning to the capital from weekend sojourns in the country. Her eyes were suddenly weighty, the movement of the car, the red and white lights of oncoming and passing cars. Only a mile or so now, enough time for her to collect her thoughts and prepare for tomorrow morning. There was nothing she needed to do, nothing until she got to the office. She could afford half an hour in the bath. Bath and bed, she told herself. One night alone before Alec returned tomorrow.

He would be full of it as he always was, like some overgrown schoolboy, injured no doubt in some way from his over-aged exertions on an Irish rugby pitch or an Irish bar in some Godforsaken hamlet deep in the back of beyond. He always came home with some kind of knock or other, then he would rub liniment on and stink out the whole house and tell her in graphic detail how he floored this winger, or was floored himself by the opposing fullback. None of it meant anything to her. Once and once only had she watched and that was only for half an hour before the mud and the mayhem bored her into submission. Let him have his games. She had hers after all.

In the shadow of the gate the woman waited, one hand in her pocket, fingers closed over the cold metal of the semi-automatic pistol. She lifted her head, pushing the hair from her eyes and looked above streetlights to stars. This was not how she had planned it, but experience taught her that things rarely go to plan. Too many people, but she knew what she was doing, had done it before and her exit route was planned. In and out. Short and sharp and effective. She would be gone before anyone knew what had happened.

* * *

Jessica drove past the familiar lights at the entrance to Ealing Common tube station and a few streets further on she turned left and pulled over into the space outside her house. She killed the engine, sighed heavily and opened the driver's door.

In the shadows the woman took out the pistol and worked a round into the breech.

Jessica collected her travel bag from the boot and slammed the lid shut. The air was frosted now and her breath came in steaming clouds. She moved quickly onto the pavement, into the gate and walked up the path, head down, fumbling in her bag for her keys. She had forgotten to leave the porch light on. Why did she always do that?

In the shadow of the gate the woman crouched, lips slightly parted, breath stilled into nothing.

Jessica was at the front door, head down still and then she had her key and was fitting it into the lock. The woman moved out of the shadows crossing before the window in soft-soled shoes that made no sound on the paving.

Jessica pushed open the front door, feeling for the light. And then something hard in her back and she stumbled into the hall.

In the house, door closed, the woman leaning on it and Jessica half on her knees, her bag tipped up on the floor. The woman sucked breath, arm straight out she fired. Once. Twice. A third time. Jessica fell forward. Her head thumped off the carpet and settled.

One moment, two; enough time to listen and then bend forward and smell spent blood and the stillness of the body about to go cold. The woman stepped over her in the darkness and was down the hall and into the moonlit space of the kitchen. Key in the back door, she turned it, felt a nail give on her finger and then the door was open and she was out and the door closed behind her. A short sprint to the back gate. Lights going on in the house next door. Fumbling now with the clasp of the gate. Something caught, her coat flapping open and for a second she panicked. Then she was through, leaving the gate to swing on rusty hinges and along the line of garages to the low wall of the church.

One foot up, her hands scrabbling briefly in the dirt and the gun slopping heavy in her pocket. She moved to the church wall, breathing hard. Then composing herself, stopping up her breath, she moved round to the other street and her car. Inside she started the engine and drove off up the road.

In the hall of her house Jessica lay very still, her eyes open and a line of spittle clinging in red to her teeth.

Three

Ryan heard the phone, opened his eyes and blinked in the darkness. Next to him his wife groaned and kicked her heel against his shin.

He sat up, flicked on the lamp and looked at the face of his watch. One o'clock almost. He lifted the phone from its housing.

'Hello?'

'Frank Weir, Sid. Get your clothes on and meet me at Hendon.'

Ryan sighed heavily. 'What's happening?'

'Somebody got shot in Ealing.'

He put down the phone and rubbed his eyes with the heels of both palms. He sat for a moment collecting his thoughts and then threw off the bedclothes. The room was chilly, they always slept with the window open, even in midwinter. He reached for his clothes and sat down on the edge of the bed to button his shirt.

'What is it?' His wife sat up, pulling the duvet up to her neck. Ryan buckled his trousers and reached for his socks.

'Shooting in Ealing.'

His wife sighed, shook her head and lay down again. 'When will you be back?'

'Whenever.' He picked up his jacket from the chair and moved to the door.

'Sid.'

'What?'

'Put Jenny on the loo before you go.'

Outside the sharpness of the night air took his breath. A fine frost lay across the windscreen of his Cavalier. Ryan turned the engine over and switched the heater on full; gradually it dissipated the mist from the windscreen. He lit a cigarette and reversed onto the road. Then he headed north for Hendon.

Frank Weir stood in his office chewing gum, smart suit even at this time of the morning, his camel-hair coat draped over his forearm. Fat-Bob Davies was collecting 101 forms from the cabinet as Ryan went in.

'Hello, Skinny.'

'Hello, Fatty.' Ryan went through to Weir's office.

'What we got, Guv'nor?'

Weir smoothed a hand over his all but bald head, what hair was left, black and shaved to his skull. 'Shooting, Sid. Close quarters. Upmarket address in Ealing.'

'Who found the body?'

'Neighbours.'

'When?'

'Midnightish. They heard the shots.'

The three of them took Weir's car and drove down the North Circular with the magnetic light flashing. Nearly two in the morning and still London did not sleep. Davies sat in the back.

'Fat-Bob Exhibits officer then, Guv'nor?' Ryan said.

Weir nodded.

'Make sure you write it all down, Bob. Not like the last time eh.'

Weir grinned at the pained expression that spread like a rash over Davies' features. Like Ryan he had little time for the man, thirty years in and just seeing out time. A dinosaur from the past.

'Make it a good one, Bob,' he said. 'Go out on a high.'

'Whatever you say, Guv'nor.'

They drove through red lights at Hanger Lane and Ryan rested the sole of his left foot on the dashboard. He had transferred to AMIP from the Drug Squad just after Christmas. This was the third major incident since then.

'SOCO on the move, Guv?'

Weir nodded.

'You calling the old man?'

'Have done.'

'Coming down is he?'

'I think we can handle things till the morning.'

'*That's* what I need to do then,' Ryan said, shaking his head.

'What?'

'Make Divisional Super – then I can get my beauty sleep.'

'And fuck knows you need it,' Davies muttered from the back.

Ryan reached in his pocket for a cigarette then remembered that Weir did not allow smoking in his car. He put his hands between his legs instead.

Grove Lane was taped off at the corner. Weir parked and they moved past the Ealing uniforms towards the lighted house with the church rising behind.

'Decent area, Guv'nor,' Ryan said.

Weir looked at the three-storeyed houses and grunted an acknowledgement. He walked with his hands in his pockets, the collar of his long coat turned up to the neck. A uniformed PC stood at the gate and next to him a WPC stepped onto the pavement. Weir took out his warrant card, flashed it at the uniforms and put it back in his pocket. Ryan flapped his open and slotted it into the breast pocket of his jacket. His tie was undone. He wore no overcoat.

The hall light was on. Two white-suited Scenes of Crime men were stooped over the body of a woman who lay away from them. Tendrils of blood spattered the walls in fine patterns like the ruined web of a spider. Ryan looked down at her, head half-gone, blood and mucus stretching from the top of her scalp to her collar. The pathologist was kneeling beside her. He looked up as Weir got to him.

'DI Weir. AMIP,' Weir said.

The doctor nodded and stripped off red-stained rubber gloves.

'What we got?'

'Three holes. Side of the face, neck and one shattering the collar-bone.'

'Time of death?'

'Don't know yet. A guess, I'd say a couple of hours ago.'

Weir turned to the uniformed WPC who hovered behind them. 'Who is she?'

'Name's Jessica Turner, Guv. Mrs.'

'Where's the husband?'

'Away. The neighbours found her.' She pointed over the gate to the lighted bay window of the house immediately adjacent.

'Somebody with them is there?'

She nodded again. Weir turned to Davies who was mopping

reddened features with his handkerchief.

'Take a look around, Bob. Then go and get some statements.'

Weir and Ryan stepped over the body, keeping close to the wall. Already Ryan could smell death in the air. It had its own distinctive odour, worse when it was old dead but it was always there, the sort of smell that clings to your clothes for days afterwards. Her hair was matted with blood, sticking to the carpet where the thick pool was darkening as it dried. Her hands were outstretched, the fingers of one scraping at the wall. Her eyes were open, one of them half-popped out of its socket where the bullet had shattered the bone. Ryan bent closer and looked at her.

'Clothes are expensive, Guv.' He nodded to the label sticking out of the top of her blouse at the back.

'Like you said outside, Slips. Good area.'

Ryan moved through the house to the kitchen, being careful to walk to the left of the hall; patches of blood were smeared on the floor. One of the Lab men moved past him and started taking photographs of the body. Another was in the kitchen studying the back door very carefully.

'What?' Ryan said to him.

'Unlocked, Slips.' He nodded to the key sticking half-out of the lock.

'Exit route.' Ryan looked about him.

The SOCO showed him a small transparent evidence bag. 'Found this.'

Ryan took the bag from him and looked at it. A painted false fingernail. He looked over his shoulder to where Weir was still looking at the body.

'Guv'nor.'

Weir turned and came through to the kitchen. Ryan handed him the bag. Weir looked at it, frowned and glanced at the SOCO. 'Where was it?'

'On the floor by the door.'

Ryan looked back at the body. 'Stepped over her. In the front door – bang bang bang – and out through here.' He glanced back at the mess in the hallway. 'Got sprayed everywhere didn't she.'

Weir went out into the garden and Ryan followed him. 'Got a torch, Sid?'

Ryan fished in his pocket for the flashlight he had collected from his desk in Hendon. He switched it on and handed it to Weir. Weir played the beam over the garden and picked up the gate, standing open in the stillness of the night.

'Went that way.' They walked to the gate, again being careful to avoid the obvious route. At the gate they paused and Weir shone the torch up and down its length. Then they stepped outside. A small patch of waste ground and a row of garages. Beyond the garages the church rose against the spread of the sky. Weir switched off the torch and turned back to the kitchen. 'We need to get floodlights set up.'

They made their way back through the hall and stepped over the body. The pathologist was organising two ambulancemen with the body. Weir went next door to find Davies. Ryan went upstairs.

The front bedroom was the master, very big, very neat with a reproduction iron bedstead in black with copper-coloured knobs on the four corners. The bed linen was white and two white dressing gowns hung on the back of the door. He opened the wardrobe doors and found an array of business suits, his and hers. The en suite smelled of perfume and the ceramic ware was white and scrubbed to a shine. He went through the rest of the house. Two more bedrooms on the first floor and a spacious attic study on the top. He looked out of the window at the flashing lights of the two-tones parked in the street outside. Across the road lights were lit in half a dozen houses, various people were looking out of their windows or standing in doorways. He hoped Weir would leave the house-to-house till the morning.

Downstairs the body was gone, only the darkly marked carpet and the smell to say she had been there. Nothing was disturbed anywhere. Her handbag was intact though spilled, purse unopened with over fifty pounds in cash and a fistful of credit cards.

Next door he found Weir drinking tea with an elderly couple who sat hand in hand looking pale and shrivelled on the settee. A WPC sat with them and Fat-Bob took notes from the other armchair. Weir introduced him and looked back at the old man.

'You say she'd been away, Mr Roberts?'

The old man nodded, kneading the hanging flesh of his neck between agitated fingers. 'All weekend. She'd only just got back.'

'You saw her?'

He shook his head. 'Heard. The car. I wasn't asleep. I have trouble sleeping.'

'You take tablets don't you, dear,' his wife added.

He nodded and looked again at Weir. 'We heard the shots, Inspector. I was in the army. I know the sound. There were three in quick succession.'

'What then?'

He shrugged his shoulders. 'I got up, looked out the front window.'

'Not the back?' Ryan said.

'No.' Roberts glanced at him. 'Our room's at the back but the shots came from the front. I know the difference.'

'What did you do then?' Weir asked him.

Roberts cleared his throat. 'I went downstairs and outside. I could see Jessica's car parked in her space. I looked over the fence but there were no lights. I was worried so I went round.'

'And?'

'Banged on the door. No answer so I looked through the letterbox. I could see her lying on the floor. Then I phoned you.'

Weir sat back. 'Have you any idea where she'd been?'

'No.' Roberts looked at his wife. 'We knew Alec was away. But not her.'

'Who's Alec?'

'Her husband. He's in Ireland playing rugby.'

'And Jessica?' Ryan asked him. 'She went away when – on Friday?'

'Five thirty. I saw her go.' Roberts smiled then. 'It's not that we're nosy or anything, just careful. It's a quiet neighbourhood,' he added.

Weir stood up. 'We'll let you get some sleep,' he said. 'We can talk again in the morning. Constable Davies here will write up your statements.'

Davies nodded and smiled. Outside Ryan said: 'Nothing moved next door, Guv'nor. She wasn't robbed.'

Weir scratched his chin. 'Close quarter. In – bang – and out.' He made a face. 'Doesn't make much sense does it.' They walked back to the car.

Sitting in his office at Campbell Row Vanner looked at the

fresh Western Union slips Jimmy Crack had got from The Mixer.

'Friday night?'

'On my way home, Guv. The post codes match two addresses I've flagged.'

Vanner pushed the slips away from him and Jimmy picked them up. 'I'll make copies and get them back to him. He gets paranoid when I hold them too long.' He folded the papers up again and stuffed them back in his pocket. 'Something else, Guv.'

'What's that?'

'I clocked Pretty Boy's M3 on my way home.'

'You follow him?'

Jimmy nodded. 'An address in Acton. I've run it through the PNC. It's four flats. I don't know which one he went into, but the occupant of the top one is a spade with form for dealing. Delbert Harris. Twenty-three. Did a stretch in Brixton for supplying Amphees.' He sat down in the vacant chair in Vanner's tiny office. Campbell Row was getting too small for them. Vanner was hoping the move to Hendon and formalisation of the Operational Crime Unit would come sooner rather than later.

'One other thing,' Jimmy said.

'What's that?'

'Pretty Boy's motor. It's for sale. Got a notice pasted up in it.'

'So?'

'Mobile phone number, Guv.'

Vanner grinned. 'Nice one, Jimmy.'

'I've requested the subscriber information but it'll take a day or two.'

Vanner thought for a moment. 'We can use it anyway, Jim.'

'How?'

'Bell him. Get him to think we want to buy the car. Set up a meet then get surveillance to follow him. If he's as clever as we think he is the phone will be listed to some business address, the arcades or the barbers' shop or something. Pretty Boy's a player isn't he.'

'Wants the top slot, Guv. Word is that Stepper's losing his grip. It's only Young Young that keeps him where he is.'

'The body armour?'

'Six feet six and an Uzi.'

Vanner lit a cigarette and shook his head. 'I want that one off the street before he kills somebody.'

Jimmy smiled then. 'Every fucker wants him off the street, Guv'nor. Harlesden nick are getting daily calls from small-time runners and dealers who want rid of him. He's messing up their plots big-time.'

'Then why doesn't somebody give him up?'

Jimmy made an open-handed gesture.

Vanner stood up then. 'Let me know when you get the subscriber info, Jimmy. I'll organise an IC3 undercover for the car deal.'

He went through into the other office where Sammy McCleod was typing up a report.

'What you got, Ginge?'

Sammy looked up at him. 'Bit of smack, Guv. Nothing to write home about. Friday night, the undercover buy.'

'Went well did it?'

Sammy nodded. 'Clockwork. The information was sound.' He took out a cigarette and lit it from the one Vanner was smoking. 'How's your old man?'

Vanner paused. 'He's okay I guess. Old though, Sam.' He looked beyond him then, out of the window and stared at the grey of the buildings the other side of the High Road.

'I hear Jimmy got Target 2's phone number. Result that, Guv.'

'That's the beauty of Jimmy,' Vanner said. 'If you're out there you see things. He's always out there.'

He went back to his office and flicked through pages. Jimmy had brought the crack team to his attention just before Christmas. He had been looking at them off and on for over a year, gradually piecing information together. Stepper-Nap, the Daddy, had been given to him by a snout last year, small-time information, but a Jamaican connection. Jimmy was the best crack man in London and by the time he brought the file to Vanner it was fifty pages thick.

The team were British blacks running in cocaine from Jamaica and washing it into crack to sell on. Stepper-Nap was the Don, the top man, the Daddy. He was protected by a six-feet-six hooligan called Young Young. So called because, surprise surprise, he looked young. He was a nasty bastard though.

The first time he was arrested it was because he had a penchant for stamping on Chinamen's heads. His father, also six feet six, had been a player in the seventies. Did time for various crimes of violence and finally got himself killed in a knife fight. It was Young Young's claim to fame and he milked it for all he was worth. The posse worked out of Harlesden primarily, but Jimmy had accumulated addresses and phone numbers in Neasden and Willesden as well as Wembley and Sudbury. The team were well organised, bossed by Stepper-Nap but Pretty Boy was his General. There were others, a whole stack of them, going from Stepper all the way down to the runners on the street.

The mobile number was a bonus. They had addresses for Stepper and a couple of the others, but Pretty Boy was a power broker who had connections with Tottenham Yardies and they desperately needed to house him.

Crack was not the problem that once they had thought it would be. The crack squad had been disbanded and a Crack Intelligence Officer had been assigned to the five Area Intelligence Units in London. Jimmy was the best there was. There was nothing he could not tell you about it. This team were bringing in kilos of coke at a time and somewhere there was a wash house where they were turning it into crack at twenty pounds a smoke. There were ten rocks to a gramme and twenty-eight grammes to an ounce. That meant there were 280 smokes to an ounce at twenty pounds a time. They were making a lot of money.

Jimmy had found out that the Jamaican connection was a nightclub owned by Stepper-Nap's brother. The Jamaican authorities knew about the club, but they could not get a handle on the coke being imported from Miami, or if they could they were being bought off somewhere. The end result was patsies swallowing coke and bringing it in to Heathrow or Gatwick. That meant that somewhere a doctor was tame enough to aid in getting it out of them.

Ryan parked his car in Grove Lane and got out. Paul Fuller, and two other Murder Squad detectives were with him. The tape had gone from the street and a uniform stood outside the front door of the Turner house. Ryan lit a cigarette and shifted his shoulders. He yawned. Might as well not have gone to bed for all the sleep he had had. He blew smoke into the wind that had lifted with the morning and now rustled through the leaves of the trees in the church yard. The SOCO team were working in the house. Ryan was here to meet the husband when he got home. He looked at the DCs as they moved onto the pavement.

'House to house, boys. You know the drill.' He grinned then. 'I'll be in number twenty if you want me.'

He left them then and went up to the front door of the Roberts' house. Mrs Roberts let him in, seated him down in the lounge and made coffee. He heard the toilet flushing upstairs and then her husband came down. He nodded to Ryan and sat down.

'Bad business this, Sergeant. Very bad.'

'You're right.' Ryan sat forward. 'Alec Turner's due back any time,' he said. 'Going to be something of a shock.'

'You can say that again.'

'He might need a bit of support, I mean our Lab team is swarming all over his house right now.'

'He can come here.'

'Good.' Ryan smiled at him. 'Good friends are you?'

'We're neighbours. Watch out for one another's houses, that sort of thing.'

'You know much about them – the Turners?'

Roberts half-moved his shoulders. 'Not much. They've lived next door about five years.'

'They got a family?'

'Not children. No.'

'Just the two of them then.'

'They're career people, Sergeant.'

'What do they do?'

'Don't know. He's in engineering I think. I don't know about Jessica.'

Ryan stood up. 'Nothing was stolen.' He nodded over his shoulder. 'Next door. Her handbag was untouched.'

'Not robbery then. Your motive.'

'No.'

'What then?'

'We don't know yet.'

Roberts stood up. 'It was all very quick, Sergeant. Three shots. That meant he meant to kill her. Head and neck wasn't it?'

Ryan nodded.

'Mark of a professional that. They must have gone out the back way. Car parked somewhere.'

'Did you hear a car?'

'I might've done. Can't really say. I was concentrating on her front door.'

Ryan looked out of the window. 'The other houses,' he said. 'Somebody might've heard something.'

He left the old man then and went next door. The SOCO team were busy. He found Weir talking to Chris Daly, the man who'd found the false fingernail the night before. He looked up as Ryan came into the kitchen. Ryan could see Superintendent Morrison at the back gate.

'Any word on when the husband gets home, Slips?' Weir asked him.

Ryan shook his head. 'The Roberts don't know. Old man's a sharp old buzzard though, Guv'nor. Already telling me this was a professional hit.'

'Oh yeah? Tell us why can he?'

Ryan made a face. He looked at Daly. 'What you got for us, Chris?'

'I was just telling the Guv'nor, Slips. The fingernail, false, glue on the back of it. Some kind of make-up fixative I reckon. We've got some pink wool from the catch on the back gate.'

'No prints on the door handle?'

Daly turned his mouth down at the corners. 'Not very clear ones. I might get something. We've found two black hairs on the front door. Maybe somebody leaned against it. They're very long hairs. Human I reckon, but we'll have to wait till Lambeth check them out.'

Weir jiggled a transparent plastic bag he was holding. 'Three shell casings. No doubt the pathologist will dig out the slugs.'

Ryan took the bag from him and looked at them. '9mm?'

'Look a bit small. 7.62 maybe.'

Ryan glanced at Daly who nodded. 'We'll need to check them out.' He handed the bag to him and followed Weir along the hallway. 'Long hair and a false fingernail, Guv'nor.'

'They could've been here already.'

'Pink wool?'

Weir shrugged.

Ryan heard the chug chug of a diesel engine and looking up

the path he saw a black cab draw up. 'Here we go, Guv'nor. Hubby's home.'

A tall man with short-cropped brown hair and large shoulders paid the cabbie and turned to the gate. Ryan stood there with Weir. For a moment the man looked at them, then beyond them to the uniform standing at his open front door.

'What the . . .'

'Alec Turner?' Weir said to him.

Turner looked at him and nodded.

'I'm Detective Inspector Weir, Mr Turner. I need to have a word.'

The three of them sat in the Roberts' lounge. Weir and Ryan side by side on the settee, Turner sitting hunched forward in the armchair, his hands clasped together between his knees. He stared into space, eyes widening and narrowing, a furrow cleft across the flat of his brow. His unopened bag lay at his feet. After a moment he spoke, moistening his lips and clearing the croak that opened his throat.

'I don't understand,' he muttered.

'I'm sorry, Mr Turner. Maybe we should leave you alone for a while.' Weir half-got up but Turner continued to stare blankly at the wall behind them. His eyes were glazed as if all thought had ceased in his head.

'Somebody shot her? Somebody shot Jess?'

'I'm afraid so.'

Turner looked hard at him now and his knuckles whitened over one another. 'In our house?'

Ryan nodded. 'Last night, Mr Turner. Round about midnight. They were waiting for her when she got home.'

'Who was? Who was waiting for her?'

'We don't know yet.'

Turner stared between them again and then he looked back. 'Wait a minute – what d'you mean – waiting for her when she got home? Got home from where?'

Ryan glanced at Weir. 'She was away for the weekend.'

'No she wasn't. She was home.' Turner jabbed himself in the chest with a thumb. 'I was away for the weekend.'

Weir slowly unwrapped a stick of gum, rolled it between his fingers and popped it into his mouth. He chewed slowly. 'Are you saying you didn't know she was away this weekend?'

Turner shook his head. Weir glanced at Ryan.

'I want to see her,' Turner said.

Weir shook his head. 'You can't see her just yet.'

'Why not?'

'Because we have to perform an autopsy. After that we'll need you to identify her.'

And then Turner's face crumpled and he burst into tears.

Outside they got into Weir's car. They had left Turner crying with the neighbours. Weir turned the car around and they headed back to Hendon.

'Over the side, Guv.'

Weir looked at him and nodded.

'He was pretty upset.'

'You don't think he ought to be, Sid?'

Ryan lifted his shoulders. 'I don't know, Guv. Yeah. He ought to be.'

'What're you thinking?'

Ryan gazed out of the window. 'I don't know what I'm thinking. But somebody really wanted to kill her didn't they. I mean we're not talking random here. We're talking about a planned, systematic shooting. Somebody knew exactly what they were doing.'

'Let's not jump to any conclusions till we know what we're dealing with eh?'

'Right, Guv'nor.' Ryan folded his arms.

Morrison was already back at the incident room in Hendon. He was freshly shaved, red hair cut close to his scalp in a marine-style flat-top. He was talking to Fat-Bob Davies, but came over as soon as Weir and Ryan arrived.

'Husband home yet?'

'Just got in, Sir,' Weir stated. 'He's staying with the neighbours. Have we heard from the pathologist yet?'

Morrison shook his head.

'I'll take a drive over there in a while.' Weir went into his office, stripped off his jacket and laid it over his chair. He sat down at his desk and scratched his head.

'What've we got so far?' Morrison asked him.

Weir told them about the Forensic finds and Morrison pursed his lips. 'Three shots.'

'To the head and neck. Cartridges are on their way to Lambeth.'

Morrison glanced at Ryan and sat down. 'Who was she exactly?'

Weir made a face. 'Still finding out, Sir. Jessica Turner, thirty-six, married to Alec Turner. He's an engineer. She worked for a marketing consultancy in the West End. Calderwood and Haynes.' He sat back and placed both hands on top of his head. 'Married for ten years, no children. Both of them in careers.'

Ryan leaned against the radiator. 'The husband didn't know she was away for the weekend,' he said.

Morrison looked up at him, then back at Weir. 'What does that tell us?'

'I think it tells us we're looking for another body, Sir. Whoever she was with.'

Morrison nodded. 'Have we released anything to the press yet?'

Weir shook his head. 'Body's not officially identified.'

Morrison stood up. 'I don't like shootings on my manor, Frank. Especially not this kind.'

'You mean assassinations, Sir.' Ryan rolled an unlit cigarette between his fingers.

'We don't know that's what it was, Sid.'

Ryan lifted his eyebrow. 'In – bang – and out. What else do you call it?'

Weir shook his head at him and Ryan went back to his desk. Davies came over to him and sat in the chair opposite, his bulk splaying out over the arms. Ryan cocked an eyebrow. 'Need to get you a bigger one don't we, sunshine.'

'Shut it, Slippery. What did the husband say?'

Ryan leaned his elbows on the desk and looked at him. 'What d'you think he said?'

Four

James McCauley lay in bed listening to the shouting of teenagers from the school playing fields across the road. Rolling onto his side he glanced at the scarlet digits of the clock and frowned. Nearly one o'clock and still she wasn't in. That meant he would have to deal with the children in the morning again. Why did they never see their mother till they got home from school?

He tried to close his eyes but he never could till she was home, and then it was hours after. He did not know why he even bothered coming to bed at all, except he could not bear to be there when she got home, never knowing which one of them she would be with.

He rolled onto his back and stared at the ceiling. Light played across its path in a white band that drifted from the street lamp. Outside he heard the rumble of an engine and then silence. He closed his eyes, furrowed his brow as he heard car doors opening, the giggle of a woman's voice and then her key being fitted in the lock.

More laughter, his voice this time, deep in his throat. The fat one, Stepper-Nap. James pulled the pillow over his face.

Downstairs, they moved into the living room and he heard music start up and then quieten. Didn't she care anything about the children? Getting out of bed, he padded across the landing to the girls' room at the back of the house. On tiptoe he pushed the door open and cast a quick glance at their beds. Blankets ruffled, Caran's foot sticking out of the side. James moved over to the bed and gently lifted the blankets so that she was completely covered again. He heard the living-room door open and he scuttled back to his bedroom. Eilish moved to the kitchen. He heard the chink of glasses and then the living-room door was closed again. He could feel the vibration of dance music through the floor.

Downstairs, his sister Eilish danced with Stepper-Nap. Petite in his arms, long red hair falling across her back. He dwarfed her, not as tall as Young Young but fuller in the figure, like a great black bear with his heavy jowls and nappy springing hair. Eilish looked up into his face, brushed his lips with hers and moved her belly against his groin. He gave a little moan and chewed all at once at her neck. She could smell the leather of his waistcoat.

He started to unzip her dress but she wriggled away from him. 'Not down here, baby.'

'Here,' he said, catching up her hand. 'I like it on the floor.'

'The bed's made up. I'm not getting carpet burns on my arse.'

His smile shallowed then and she moved fingers over his groin and squeezed, then she placed her arms about his neck and leaned her face into his. 'Take me upstairs and fuck me.'

James heard them on the stairs, a tiny giggle breaking from her as she stumbled against the wall. The weight of her feet, creaking with every step.

'Your baby brother in?'

'Ssshhh. Don't wake him.'

'Wake him. Little mother goes to bed the same time as the children.'

'He's good to them. We get to party don't we?'

They moved from the landing into her bedroom. James heard the door swing to then creak open a fraction. It never closed properly.

Eilish took hold of Stepper's belt and slowly unbuckled it. His trousers slipped to his ankles and his penis bulged in his boxer shorts.

Naked now she pushed him down onto the bed and traced lines on his belly with her tongue. Like his chest it was matted with kinky curls of black hair. She felt his fingers reach for her, ease between her legs and begin gently to probe. She opened her mouth a fraction. Moving herself around she straddled him. Stepper let go a gasp.

James carefully lifted his bedclothes, breath growing tight in his chest. He tiptoed to the door, eased it back and crossed the landing. Her door was ajar, light slipping over the bed from the gap between the curtains.

Stepper-Nap rolled Eilish onto her back and thrust his

weight into her once more. His fingers twisted her hair, half a beard nuzzling the tiny mounds of her breasts, tugging the nipples into peaks of crimson flesh with his teeth. Eilish wrapped her legs about his waist and squeezed. She could see James standing at the door, watching them. The past grew up in her mind. So long ago, but the same, only the man inside her was white and his hair was long and black and he had freckles on his shoulders and his arms and his eyes were the wild green of his mother. James was fifteen and then as now he stood at the door and watched them.

James heard Stepper-Nap leave at four in the morning. He was not asleep, lying on his back with one arm crooked across his face. Eilish went to the bathroom. He heard the car start outside and finally he closed his eyes.

The alarm woke him at seven o'clock and he felt the skin drag at his face beneath his eyes. His jaw ached with lack of sleep, mouth dry and husky. Next door the children were stirring. He threw off the bedclothes and reached for his jeans. Almost mechanically he pulled them on and stretched a T-shirt over his head.

Caran was getting dressed, nine years old, half-caste skin. She had never known her father. Kerry was the same. Different father, again she never knew him. James scratched his arm and yawned. He could smell the thick scent of Stepper-Nap on the landing. Kerry was watching him from under the bedclothes.

'Get dressed, Kerry. Come on, be a good girl like your sister.'

'It's cold.'

'I know it's cold, darling. But the sooner you're dressed the sooner you'll be warm.' He smiled at her. 'Come on, I'll make you breakfast.' He cocked his head at her then. 'Don't dawdle. I'm going to pour the milk so it'll be soggy if you take all day.'

Downstairs he plugged in the kettle and poured out their Frosties. He laid both bowls together with two spoons on the little kitchen table and took a mug from the rack. Half a bottle of red wine stood open on the side. He poured it down the sink.

Caran appeared pushing her long curling hair from her eyes and sat down at the table. Her tie was crooked. James straightened it for her. 'Your sister ready yet?'

Caran shook her head. James called up to Kerry from the

bottom of the stairs and she appeared, her shirt on but unbuttoned and her skirt at an askew angle. He could not help but smile. 'Come down, Kerry. I'll fix it for you.'

Caran spooned cereal into her mouth as James settled Kerry in the seat opposite her. 'Is Mummy going to take us to school today?'

James shook his head. 'No, darling. Mummy was out last night. I'm taking you.'

Kerry picked her nose, looked at it and sucked the end of her finger. 'Mummy goes out a lot doesn't she, Jamie.'

James did not say anything. He splashed cold milk over her cereal and took the sugar bowl from her. 'They've got sugar on.'

'That's why they're called Frosties, stupid.' Caran shook her head at her sister.

Eilish came to the top of the stairs as he opened the front door after delivering them safely to school.

'God, thanks, lover. I'd never had made it this morning.'

James just looked at her, stripped off his jacket and went through to the kitchen. He scooped up the dishes from the table and settled them into the sink. He heard the sound of the shower running above his head.

Eilish was getting dressed when the doorbell sounded. James wiped his hands on the cloth and tossed it over the tap. Then he answered the door. Mary-Anne Forbes stood there, hair long and black hanging against her shoulders. She smiled at him.

'What about you, James. Eilish in?'

James nodded to her. 'Hi, Mary-Anne. Come in.'

He held the door open for her and she stepped inside. 'You okay? You look really pissed off.'

'I'm fine, Mary-Anne.'

Mary-Anne went upstairs and James went back to the kitchen. He stood a moment in front of the sink and stared over the rumpled mess of the garden. He could hear them giggling above his head, just like they had done in the old days. He shook his head and dipped his hands in the sink.

Vanner sat in the passenger seat as Jimmy dialled The Mixer's number. They were parked in the Neasden circle in Jimmy's car. Vanner watched two black youths cross into Ska-Cuts

Barber's shop and eyeball them all the way. He shook his head. 'You've got to get another car, Jim. This is so much job you might as well be driving a two-tone.'

Jimmy was talking into the telephone. 'Mixer, it's Selly. You phoned me.'

'Where are you?'

'Parked outside in the Circle.'

'Come round the back. You can park at the top of the alley.'

'You sure?'

'Yeah. It's fine. I've got coffee on.'

'I've got a colleague with me.'

'It's all right. I've got more than two cups.'

They left the car and crossed to the second-hand electrical goods shop. 'Selly?' Vanner said.

Jimmy Crack grinned at him. 'Pseudonym, Guv. Easier that way. I know who they are when they call. First talked to The Mixer in a cell at Kilburn.'

Vanner glanced back at the car. 'When're they going to get you another set of wheels?'

Jimmy frowned. 'I know. Red bleeding Astra. I thought the furry dice might help some.'

'Did you,' Vanner said.

'Shouldn't really have a car at all, Guv. I'm not due one. This is a deal I've worked out with transport at Kingsbury.'

'Well tell them to get you a better deal. There must be an old SO11 car knocking about.'

The Mixer was brewing coffee at the back of the shop. He smiled at Jimmy and Jimmy introduced Vanner.

'You like sugar?' The Mixer asked him.

Vanner shook his head.

'Selly?'

Jimmy shook his head. 'The team been in again, Mix?'

The Indian man nodded and stirred sugar into his own mug. He indicated for Vanner to take one.

'Who?' Jimmy asked him.

'The big fat one.'

'Bigger Dan,' Jimmy said, half to himself. 'Or was it the littler one?'

'No. Not him. The big one.' The Mixer passed over the Western Union slips and Jimmy leafed through them. He raised his eyebrows and showed a slip to The Mixer. 'That the one?'

The Mixer nodded. Jimmy passed it to Vanner. It was made out for four thousand pounds in cash.

Vanner squinted at Jimmy. 'Tony Jones?'

Jimmy nodded. 'Bigger Dan, Guv. Second Tier, handles a bunch of runners for Pretty Boy. He's used the name before and I know the address.'

'This is good then?' The Mixer said.

'This is very good.'

The Mixer smiled through his glasses. 'I've got something else for you.'

He went into the back of the shop and came out with a packet of photographs. Vanner stared at him and he grinned. 'Little service I offer.'

Jimmy had the package open and was leafing through them. He could hardly believe his eyes. Virtually every member of the crack team was photographed. It looked like a party of some kind.

'They brought them in yesterday,' the Indian said. 'The other one, him with the funny hand.'

Vanner frowned.

'Thin Hand Billy,' Jimmy said.

'I made that set specially for you,' The Mixer said.

Jimmy beamed at him. 'If you weren't so ugly I'd kiss you.'

Back at Campbell Row Jimmy spread the photographs on Sammy's desk in the squad room. China was there and Anne.

'This the whole team, Jim?' Sammy asked him.

Jimmy nodded. 'Brit-Boy Massive. The whole bloody caboodle.' He looked at Vanner then. 'This is a result, Guv'nor. We've never had anything like this.'

The photographs were taken at night. Vanner could see the sea in the background. They were dated the Sunday before. He leafed through them and showed up one with a white woman in it, long red hair falling over her shoulders. 'Who's the BMW?'

Anne cocked an eyebrow and Jimmy grinned at her. 'Black man's woman, Anne. Status symbol.'

'You know her?' Vanner asked him.

'Never seen her before.' Jimmy laid out all the pictures and scrutinised them. 'Some kind of party,' he said. 'The whole posse's gathered. There's Stepper-Nap with the nappy hair. Pretty Boy looking serious as usual. This one's Jig. Stepper's cousin.' He pointed out Bigger Dan and then another man, smaller in girth but not much, his hair waxed and flattened, sporting a beard reminiscent of Barry White. 'Little Bigger,' he said. 'He's Young Young's half-brother. Same mother, different father.' He pointed to a picture of Stepper-Nap with Young Young towering over him. Black suit, black shirt, his hair cut short at the neck and flattened into a box on top. 'Shows doesn't it.'

'The sea,' Vanner said. 'Must've been an away-day.'

He moved to the window and looked out, then he turned again. 'Okay,' he said and sat down on the edge of a desk, moving aside a sheet of acid squares in a plastic bag. 'Jimmy clocked Pretty Boy's BMW the other day. We got his mobile phone number.' He looked over at Jimmy.

'I got the subscriber info,' Jimmy told him. 'The phone's registered to the Uxbridge Road amusement arcade.'

'One of their businesses?' China asked.

Jimmy nodded. 'The car was for sale, China. Pretty Boy's advertising it on the back near-side window. He left his mobile number.' He looked back at Vanner once more.

'We're going to buy it,' Vanner said. 'Or rather we're going to let him think we are. I've called in Level 1 Undercover. Black guy to do the number. He'll give Pretty Boy a bell on the mobile then set up a meet. We'll get surveillance on the plot and follow him. Our man'll um and ah about the price. No doubt he wants shitloads for it. It's a black M3.'

'Nice wheels for someone who's registered unemployed,' Sammy said.

Vanner looked at him. 'If we're lucky we'll house Pretty Boy.'

'He's a power broker,' Jimmy went on. 'Stepper-Nap is slipping. Getting old. Too many women. Too many kids. He's still got the Jamaican end sorted though, but Pretty Boy's young and smart.' He tapped the photos again. 'The only thing that stops him making his move is Young Young.'

'The bodyguard.'

Jimmy nodded. 'He's Stepper's insurance. I don't know how loyal he is but he likes shooting people. My snout told me that Young Young was responsible for the throat shooting at the dance last month.

'If we can house Pretty Boy we might get an OP set up nearby,' he went on. 'He's got contacts in other areas. The word is that he's sick of the way Stepper molly-coddles the Tottenham posse. His attitude is either join together or shoot them.'

Vanner looked at him then. 'You better explain, Jim.'

Jimmy sat down in Sammy's seat. 'Governor General Massive,' he said. 'Tottenham crack team. Not in this lot's league but getting there. Stepper's got a baby mother called Carmel. Ground-floor flat in Harlesden. The Tottenham team are bringing illegals in from Jamaica and Stepper keeps his manor clean by harbouring them.' He glanced at their faces. 'Immigration know about it. I've got Carver breathing down my neck to spin the place. But it's flagged to me and they can't move without my say so.'

'Plug?' Anne said.

'The same.'

'Mr Wannabe Copper.' Sammy shook his head.

'He's evil,' Jimmy said. 'Worse than some of these. The Jamaicans are scared shitless of him.'

Vanner moved off the desk. 'We'll set up the rolling plot,' he said. 'See if we can't find out where Pretty Boy lives.'

Ryan sat in the incident room at Hendon. Paul Fuller sat next to him reading a copy of the *Guardian*. Ryan stared at him and wondered why he had ever left the Drug Squad. Fuller was thirty-something, overweight with long hair and glasses. On the other side of him Tony Rob sat with his arms folded. Ex Regional Crime Squad. Face did not fit so he came back to AMIP. He was something of a dinosaur, still couldn't use the computer so he made all his notes by hand. Ryan liked him, his methods straight from the Jack Regan school of policing. Ryan himself had considered the Regional Crime Squad, but had decided against the move when Rob told him how they sat on plots for months on end and never nicked anyone. The problem, as he saw it, was that they always targeted the top man and then spent months trying to follow him. It never seemed to occur to them to chip away at the minor league players until the top man had nothing to stand on.

Weir and Morrison were at the front of the room, the rest of the Murder Squad team settled about them in plastic-backed chairs. On the board at the front, photographs of Jessica

Turner's battered remains were pinned. Morrison sat in a chair with his fingers pressed together. Weir stood with one foot resting on a chair. He smoothed a palm over the flat of his skull and chewed gum.

'Jessica Turner, victim,' he said. 'Thirty-six years old. Was married to Alec Turner. He was in Ireland playing rugby when the shooting happened.' He stood up straight then and put his hands in his trouser pockets. He glanced at the pictures then looked forward at his colleagues once more. 'The shooting was close quarter, inside the front door, the body a few feet along the hall. He or she, we don't know which yet, stepped over the body and escaped through the kitchen.' He paused again and his jaw worked the gum. 'Pathologist has confirmed the time of death at about eleven thirty on Sunday. Jessica had been away for the weekend, a detail that was big news to her husband. The neighbours, Mr and Mrs Roberts, reckoned she left on Friday at half-five and she had only just got back when the shots were fired.'

'Good weekend then,' Fuller said.

Fat-Bob Davies looked over his shoulder at him and grinned through red-flecked cheeks.

'There was no sign of any break-in,' Weir went on. 'The shootist was waiting for her. She got home. He was hiding. Pushed her inside and killed her. Three shots. The casings are with Lambeth now.' He looked from one face to another. 'Not a burglary. Her purse and handbag were left exactly where she dropped them. Fifty pounds in cash and all her credit cards intact. Nothing in the house was disturbed. The killer went through to the kitchen and got out the back door. So far SOCO have come up with the cartridges and a false finger-nail by the back door. We thought there might be prints but there aren't any we've seen before. Yesterday they checked the garden. We won't get anything from the grass but there was a snag of pink wool on the catch at the back gate. Angora so they tell me.'

'A woman?' Fuller sat forward.

'Possibly.'

Rob scratched thick grey hair. 'Anything else from outside, Guv'nor?'

Weir shook his head. 'Not so far. We've got somebody starting a car in Birch Street. That's the other side of the house, next road on running parallel. Beyond the church as you look from

Grove Lane.' He looked at Morrison then. 'We also have two black hairs found on the front door. Long black hairs.'

'A woman,' Fuller stated again.

'We don't know any of that yet, Paul,' Weir told him. 'We need to talk to the husband again but he's in no fit state. All of that could've been there. The nail, the hair, the thread.'

'Jessica's nails were long, Guv'nor,' Ryan reminded him.

'I know, Sid. Lambeth'll test everything but we'll have to wait. Hopefully the gun'll be quicker. You know the form, breech, firing pin, ejection marks. In the meantime we have her movements that weekend. If her husband didn't know she was away then we have to ask ourselves why.'

'Lover.' Pamela Richards spoke for the first time. The only woman on the team. She sat at the front facing Morrison. Ryan watched her from behind, her blonde hair bobbing about her jawline.

'Possibly. We don't know.'

'OTS, Guv,' Ryan said. 'Why else would her husband not know?'

Morrison stood up then. 'I'm going to ask Alec Turner for permission to release her picture to the papers,' he said. 'It's delicate but I think he'll agree. We can let the story out and see if we get a reaction. If she was seeing someone maybe they'll come forward. That way we can check her whereabouts for the weekend.'

'In the meantime we wait for Lambeth,' Weir said. 'I want the house-to-house finished. I want the pubs checked, the shops. Anyone noticing a car that shouldn't be there. This is a cosy neighbourhood and expensive. We're looking for a woman maybe, pink sweater, red nails, black hair. If her husband can account for the nail, the hairs and the sweater then we're looking for a man.' He sighed. 'Not much to go on but early days. This is a planned and clinical shooting. You all know how it goes – cradle to grave on Jessica Turner. Who was she? Who were her friends? Who would want to kill her?' He glanced at Sergeant Jones, the office manager. 'Jonesy's got your actions sheets so let's go to work.'

Vanner set up the plot for the meeting with Pretty Boy's car and then he went home. It was six thirty and dark outside, the London rush hour in full swing. He listened to the GLR news on the radio and heard Morrison being interviewed about the Ealing shooting on Sunday. They had nothing yet but their enquiries were progressing. He smiled to himself; at least Morrison would leave him alone for a while.

As he turned into his road he saw the lights in his downstairs windows and thought about all the years he had come home to darkness. Ellie had a flat in Acton Town but whenever he came home these days lights blazed out of every window.

Music greeted him as he unlocked the door. She had brought a CD player over from her flat. Up until then there had only been the radio and he only used that for the news. Ellie called to him from the bathroom upstairs. She had started cooking but not got very far. In the basement kitchen she had peeled potatoes and lamb chops sat under the unlit grill. No vegetables. She took vitamins instead of vegetables, something about being forced to eat them when she was a child. A glass of flat Coca Cola stood on the work surface. He switched on the grill and fetched a cold beer from the fridge. Flipping off the top he drank from the neck of the sweating bottle, then poured salt into water for the potatoes.

Ellie came down in her dressing gown, white towelling with a full collar. Her legs were freshly shaved and she padded around in bare feet. Vanner leaned against the work surface and watched as she inspected the food. He did not say anything, just watched the way she moved, blonde hair pushed back from her face, large green eyes that cast short glances in his direction.

'What?' she said at last.

'What d'you mean – what?'

'You keep looking at me.'

'I like looking at you, Elle.'

'Prat.' She flicked her fingernails against his chest, took a mouthful of Coke and pulled a face. She poured the remains down the sink. Vanner offered his beer bottle and she grimaced at him.

'You'll quit before I'm through,' she said.

'And smoking?'

'Definitely smoking.'

He smiled then and caught her by the sleeve, gently pulling her across the floor towards him. He kissed her full on the mouth, the softness of her face against his. She broke. They looked at one another and then Vanner switched off the stove.

Taking her by the hand he led her up to the bedroom.

Much later he sat in a chair at the window, feet resting on the sill. The curtains were drawn back, moonlight in the glass above the city. Behind him she was still save the soft burr of her breathing. Her clothes lay scattered on the stripped wood of the floor, her uniform left exactly where she had dropped it, dressing gown over the chair behind his head.

He could smell her and it pleased him. He had forgotten to phone Anne and ask about his father. He must remember to do it in the morning. Ellie lay so still, wrapped in the duvet with only her left foot extending beyond it. Vanner looked over his shoulder, only the foot and the breathing to let him know she was there. He sat more upright, drew breath and exhaled into the glass. It misted then faded and he could see himself looking back.

She brought a softness to the room, to the house. Lights on all over the place, music playing. It could almost have been a home. Outside, somebody walked past his parked car and kicked at a drinks can. He heard it rattle and bounce off the pavement. The walker had his hands buried in pockets, collar turned high against the cold. Vanner got up, slipped off his dressing gown and went back to bed. He moved gently so as not to wake her, so petite, elfin almost, curled into a foetal ball right in the middle of the bed. Her face was hidden in the duvet. He kissed the top of her head and stretched out on his back.

Pretty Boy had set up the meet on Pound Lane by the entrance to the Jewish Cemetary with glass set in concrete on the top of the wall. Difficult place to set up any kind of Observation Point. Maybe Pretty Boy was more careful than they thought. The undercover drove up in a Toyota Estate. Vanner did not know him other than he was Level 1 UC. He wore baggy jeans and a Rasta hat, dreadlocks wrapped up like a tea cosy. He had half a beard and smoked hand-rolled cigarettes, gold sovereigns on his fingers. Vanner sat with Jimmy Crack in Vanner's car on the High Road. They saw Pretty Boy drive up with his window down and dance music thumped bass from his speakers. Round the corner by the Cemetary a 4/2 from surveillance was sitting on his motorbike drinking coffee from a polystyrene cup and chewing on a bacon roll. He had panniers on the bike with a bogus courier company's logo emblazoned on them. He studied the map, spread out on his fuel tank.

The UC saw Pretty Boy arrive and got out of his car. The BMW parked behind him and Pretty Boy slipped out of the seat like a snake. Black rollneck sweater and black jeans. He toyed with a ring of keys on one finger.

'Yo.' The UC slipped him some skin and then began peering at the car, walking around it with his hands in his pockets, eyes bunched up in his face. He looked the bodywork over first and then the wheels, smoothing long black fingers over the alloy spokes.

'It's all there, brother.' Pretty Boy twirled keys.

The UC stood up and nodded briefly. 'Why you selling, man?'

'No reason. Fancy a change is all.'

Again the UC nodded. 'Lift the bonnet, yeah?'

Pretty Boy obliged and the UC took a good long look at the engine, very clean, well kept. He nodded and lowered the lid.

'Whizzer eh?'

'It moves, man.'

'I get to drive?'

'Leave yours here.'

'Ain't mine. Borrowed.'

Pretty Boy nodded. 'I want cash.'

'Sure.'

They went for a drive. When they came back the motorcycle courier was gone. A small white van was parked further along the street. A man outside fiddling under the bonnet. Pretty Boy climbed out of the passenger seat.

'I want my buddy to take a look. Mechanic, man.'

'When?'

'I got to call him.'

'So do it.'

'He's working. Later?'

Pretty Boy twisted his lip a fraction. 'You just wanted the drive right?'

The UC grinned and shook his head. 'That what you think, man?'

'It's what I think.' Pretty Boy moved round to the driver's

door. 'Don't fuck with me, man. I got buyers.'

'Hey.' The UC's face was still. 'Nobody's fucking with you, brother. I got cash. I'll make my call and I'll phone you later on.' He pointed at him, hand waist-high, finger stiff before him. Further along the road the van driver lowered his bonnet and got behind the wheel.

Pretty Boy was back in the car. 'Call if you want to. Can't say I'll be there.'

The UC lifted both hands palm upwards. Pretty Boy shook his head, spat out of the window and made a U-turn. The van had turned also and was waiting for him to move.

For a second Pretty Boy stared at the driver who drummed fingers on the steering wheel.

'Jessica didn't wear false fingernails.' Turner's voice was steady, his eyes fixed on Weir's face. Next to him Ryan shifted in his seat.

'You're sure?'

Turner looked witheringly at him. 'I was married to her for ten years. Don't you think I'd know?' He looked at Weir again. 'Why d'you want to know?'

They were seated in Turner's lounge. He had spent two nights with his neighbours but now he was back in the house. He looked much older than he had done on Monday morning, face drawn and pale, hair mussed on his head. He massaged the shoulder he had hurt playing rugby.

'We found a false nail in your kitchen, Alec.' Weir said it in a flat voice. Turner stared at him. 'So?'

'So we thought maybe it was Jessica's.'

'Well now you know it wasn't.' Turner pushed back his hair with both hands, dragging his fingers across his scalp. He sucked breath. 'Look, I've told your man Morrison you can have a picture. Shouldn't you be out there doing something?'

'We are doing something, Alec. But we've found a false nail, two black hairs and a piece of pink wool here at the scene.' Weir paused. 'Do you know any other women who wear false nails?'

Turner stared at him then. 'Meaning what exactly?'

'Meaning – do you know any other women who wear false nails?'

'You mean am I shagging anyone?'

'Are you?' Ryan cut in.

Turner flashed his eyes at him. 'I loved my wife.'

'Course you did.' Ryan lifted his shoulders. 'I love mine. We have to ask, Alec.'

Turner sighed then and closed his eyes.

'Okay, Alec,' Weir said. 'What about the weekend – where could she have gone? Have you any idea?'

'We don't know that she went anywhere.'

'The neighbours, Alec,' Ryan said gently.

'They could be wrong. So she went out on Friday. That's not unusual. She often goes out on Fridays.'

'Workmates?'

'What?'

'Does she go out with workmates?'

'Sometimes she does – yes.'

For a few moments they were silent. Ryan could hear the ticking of the clock on the mantelpiece. 'What's to say she didn't go out, come back and go out again. She told me she was shopping on Saturday.'

'You phoned her?' Weir asked him.

'She told me before I went away. But yes, I phoned her. Mobile from the bar in Cork.'

'What time?'

'I don't know. Six – six thirty.'

'Was she in?'

'No.'

Ryan stood up and took out his cigarettes. He showed the pack to Turner who nodded. Ryan lit one and put away his lighter. 'Look, Alec. We've spoken to your neighbours. They're adamant she was away from Friday night to Sunday night – late. Your Mr Roberts – he's a canny old buzzard. Doesn't miss a trick.'

Turner stared at the floor. 'Nothing better to do than sit around all day watching us all from his window. There's nothing goes on here that he can't tell you in advance.'

Ryan nodded slowly. 'So you reckon he might be right then.'

Turner rubbed his face with his hands.

After a few moments Weir said. 'Have you ever suspected she might be seeing someone?'

'No.' Turner snapped out the reply. 'Well, maybe. I don't know.' He looked from one to the other of them. 'Sometimes you get a feeling you know.'

Ryan touched his teeth with his tongue. 'Things she said. Things she did.'

Turner nodded.

'What things?' Weir said.

Turner looked back at him. 'Nothing specific. A couple of times I wondered. She went away once before.'

'When?'

'December. Said it was a work thing but that was the first time she'd ever had a work do at the weekend.'

'Did you check?'

Turner lifted his chin. 'No, I didn't check. Strange as it may sound I trusted her.'

They were still once more. Ryan sucked on his cigarette. 'No children.'

'What?'

'You don't have any children.'

'What's that got to do with anything?'

Ryan shrugged. 'Did you never want them?'

'I wanted them. Jess didn't.' He made an open-handed gesture. 'No big deal. I knew it when I married her.'

Weir looked at him carefully. 'Career girl was she?'

'Very much so. She was bright, Inspector. Going places.'

'Which of you earned the most?' Ryan asked him.

Turner again looked at Ryan, questions standing out in his eyes. 'Why?'

'No reason.'

'I do – did,' Turner replied.

Ryan paced over to the window. 'You've no idea who she might've been seeing – assuming she was that is?'

'I haven't got a clue.'

They drove back to the incident room, Weir musing, face twisted, fingers alive on the wheel.

'He knew she was over the side, Guv,' Ryan said.

Weir shot him a short glance. 'You reckon?'

'Yeah. Something else I reckon too.'

'What's that?'

'He's playing away himself.'

'You think so?'

Ryan nodded. 'He's got that just *had* guilty look.'

They drove on. 'Suppose he is. That doesn't put a bird in

the house and it doesn't give her false fingernails does it?'

'No.'

Weir looked at him then. 'So you reckon our shooter was a woman then?'

'False nail. Long black hair and pink wool. How many blokes d'you know like that?'

Weir nodded. 'And the angle of the shots gives us somebody between five-five and five-nine or else somebody crouching.'

'Spells totty to me, Guv.'

Back in the incident room Ryan gave his 50/20 form to the girls feeding information into Holmes. At the desk across from his own Pam Richards was leafing through the Turners' phone bill from the December quarter. Ryan leaned in front of her. 'You got this month's yet?'

Pam shook her head. 'I've been on to BT, Sid. It's coming. How's the husband?'

'So so.' Ryan sat down in his chair and glanced at the phone messages on the pad. 'Doesn't know anyone with false nails and his wife did not own any angora wool in pink.'

Pam turned her mouth down at the corners. 'Why would a woman shoot Jessica Turner?'

Ryan leaned forward. 'Why would anyone, Pammy?'

Vanner was looking at the selection of photographs of the Brit-Boy posse party. Jimmy was in the kitchen making coffee. They were waiting on a call from 2 Area Surveillance. Vanner pored over the photos, scanning every inch of Pretty Boy's face. It told him nothing. Jimmy Crack placed a mug of coffee at his elbow and Vanner grunted. Then he tapped a picture of one of the black girls seated at a garden table. 'Who's she?' Jimmy craned his neck to see. 'Carmel, Guv. She's Stepper-Nap's shagpiece. The one Plug's looking at.'

'Gets about a bit doesn't he.'

'They all get about. Babe mothers. It's a pride thing. More Yardie than Brit, but they're much of a muchness. Kids by different women, Guv. Baby mothers.'

Vanner looked at Carmel, a petite, pretty black girl with her hair stripped back from her face. 'She got kids by Stepper?'

'I don't know. I think he just likes her pussy.'

'What about the white bird?'

'Don't know who she is, Guv.'
'The Mixer not clocked her?'
Jimmy shook his head.
'And Stepper-Nap's married?'
'Three kids by the wife. He lives with her, but he's got other kids dotted here and there.'
'Must cost him a bloody fortune. No wonder he's washing crack.'
'He gets by, Guv'nor. Word is he's in the market for a Porsche.'
Vanner looked up at him. 'And he lives in a council house, right?'
'On the dole, Guv. Getting it from everywhere.'
'You ever eyeballed him, Jim?'
'Oh yeah. He doesn't know me though.'
'You sure?'
'He might know my car.'
'Change that car, Jim.'
'My life's work, Guv'nor. But I told you. I shouldn't have it in the first place.'
Vanner sat back and sipped coffee. He looked at his watch. 'Surveillance still got eye contact?'
'Last time I heard.'
'Taking his time,' Vanner said. 'To go home I mean.'
'We don't know where home is, Guv. That's the point.'
Vanner rolled his eyes. 'Go through the log with a fine-tooth comb.'
The doorway was suddenly filled by an immense frame behind them. Steve Riley, the Surveillance team skipper, stood there in a blue poloneck sweater that stretched over his massive chest. In his hand he held a little brown book.
'Guv'nor,' he said to Vanner.
'Steve. What you got?'
'Loss.'
'Shit.'
'Only for twenty minutes. 4/2 picked him up again on the Uxbridge Road. Parked outside an amusement arcade.' He handed the book to Vanner. 'Last address. Let himself in with a key.'
'Where?'
'Semi near Sudbury and Harrow Road.'

* * *

Friday night and Stepper-Nap sat with Young Young in the Dome at the National on Kilburn High Road. Young Young wearing a black suit, slouched in his seat, legs so far under the table they poked out the other side. He swirled spiced rum in his glass and watched the comings and goings at the bar beneath them.

'Where's Eilish?' he said.

Stepper gave him a laconic look and dabbed at the perspiration that gathered in sticky globules on his brow. 'Dancing.'

'Girl likes to dance.'

'Irish. They all like to dance.'

Young Young smiled slowly. 'She dance with you, fat man.'

Stepper wagged a finger at him. 'Don't call me fat man.'

Young Young drew breath through wide, flaring nostrils. 'I'm bored, man. This place sucks on a Friday.'

'Then take off, Young Young.'

Young Young drained his glass and ran a hand over his flat-top hair. He watched Little Bigger, his half-brother, come up the stairs with a tray of drinks in his hands. Behind him Pretty Boy stepped very deliberately with Jig moving beside him. They eyeballed everyone they passed.

Young Young sat up in his seat and gestured towards Pretty Boy. 'What you doing about him?'

Stepper looked where he looked and a steady smile played on his lips. 'I don't need to do nothing.'

'Word is he's after the action, Daddy.'

'What he's after and what he gets is two different things.'

'You think so?'

Stepper moved his bulk in the chair as Little Bigger set the tray on the table. His flattened hair gleamed with freshly pasted gel and gold flashed in his mouth. Pretty Boy and Jig had paused at the top of the stairs. 'I'm watching him, man.' Stepper went on. 'I got that nigger's number.'

Young Young lifted a fresh glass of rum from his brother's tray and lit a cigarette. 'You want him outa here you tell me.'

Stepper laid a hand on his arm. 'If I want I will.'

The girls came up the stairs, three black women and two white. Eilish with her red hair brushed back from her face, green dress off one shoulder.

'Who's that with Eilish?' Little Bigger asked.

'Name's Mary-Anne. Another Irish chick.' Stepper waved a hand at the women. Carmel smiled at him. Eilish looked at Young Young.

The girls sat down and Young Young stared at Mary-Anne. Older than Eilish with long black hair. She sat down, glanced a little nervously at him and nibbled on a fingernail. Little Bigger passed them each a drink. Carmel sloped behind Stepper-Nap and draped one arm across his chest. At the head of the stairs Pretty Boy and Jig were deep in conversation with a ginger-haired whiteman.

'Who's your friend, Eilish?' Young Young said.

Eilish glanced at him now, accepting a light for her cigarette from Little Bigger. 'Mary-Anne.' She looked at Mary-Anne and smiled. 'Meet Young Young, Mary-Anne.'

Young Young touched a fingertip to his forehead and pointed at her. 'Where'd you come from?'

'She's an old friend, Young Young. I've only just met up with her again.'

'Ireland was it?'

Mary-Anne nodded. 'We go way back.'

'I bet you do.' Young Young caught Eilish's eye then and grinned at her. Stepper caught the look and patted Carmel's arm still fastened over his shoulder.

Pretty Boy and Jig came over and stood before the table. 'You got time for a word, man.'

Pretty Boy looked at Stepper. Stepper looked back at him then shook off Carmel's arm. The two of them moved to the bar. Young Young stared at Jig. Jig looked away.

'What's happening?' Stepper said.

Pretty Boy lit a cigarette, inspected the end and blew smoke in a trail at the ceiling.

'Tuesday. Gatwick. I got two girls coming in.'

'We gonna need the doctor?'

'Yeah.'

'When on Tuesday?'

'Morning flight from Kingston.'

'Who you gonna send?'

'I figured Young Young's brother.'

Stepper half-nodded. 'He up to it?'

'He can drive can't he.'

Stepper sipped at a beer. Pretty Boy smoked, one hand in his trouser pocket. 'Who's that with the black hair?'

'Friend of Eilish.'

'Another Paddy is it?'

Stepper nodded.

'Don't know that I like the Irish.'

'They fuck real well.'

Pretty Boy laughed then and blew smoke rings.

'You sell your car?'

Pretty Boy shook his head. 'Not today, man. Had me a looker but he was just a fuck.'

'What you gonna buy?'

'Mercedes.'

Stepper nodded. 'I got a Mercedes.' He nodded to the ginger-haired man at the head of the stairs. 'You priming the man over there?'

Pretty Boy nodded. 'Let me know when and where for the doctor.'

Stepper smiled at him. 'You bring your women to me, man. I'll sort the doctor.' For a moment then they looked at one another, then Pretty Boy shrugged his shoulders. 'It's cool,' he said, and went back to the table.

Five

Ray Kinane sat at the breakfast table watching his two young sons spooning Coco-Pops into their mouths. Timmy, the younger one, dribbled milk down his chin and wiped it on the sleeve of his school pullover. He looked up guiltily at his father.

'Don't let your mother see you do that,' his father said. 'She's only just washed it.'

Timmy wiped the sleeve on the leg of his trousers and went back to his breakfast.

In the hall the letterbox flapped and Kinane eased back his chair. He went through to collect the post and the morning paper. Nice to have breakfast with the family. It was not often he could do it these days. Brown envelopes lay on the mat and a folded copy of *The Times* bulged out of the flap. Kinane scooped up the bills and slid the newspaper from the letterbox. He flapped it out and then stopped. A woman's face looked him right in the eye and a chill crept over his neck.

'What is it, love?' His wife's voice suddenly from the bottom step of the stairs. He had not heard her come down. For a moment he stared at her.

'Ray?'

'Nothing.' He folded the paper. 'A woman got killed in London. Shooting.' He shook his head. 'Shocked me that's all.'

His wife took the paper from him and scanned the headlines. Her brow furrowed. 'Good God. In her own home.'

Kinane went back through to the kitchen and laid the bills on the side. His sons had finished their breakfast and were flicking dried cereal at one another. 'Pack it in,' he snapped. 'Get your coats and I'll drive you to school.'

His wife followed him into the kitchen and laid the paper on the table. She poured herself some tea and settled down to read. In the hall the boys lifted coats from the pegs. Kinane picked up his briefcase and as he clasped the handle it slipped under the damp of his palm. He frowned, then looked up at his wife and smiled.

'See you later then.'

She took his arm and kissed him. 'Try not to be too late tonight. There's a Governors' meeting at school.'

'Six thirty.'

'Okay.'

He went through to the hall and slipped his jacket over his shoulders.

Pamela Richards showed the phone records to Weir. He had a copy of the *Express* on the desk in front of him, Jessica Turner's face lifting from the front page.

'Beaulieu,' Pam said. 'She called a number in Beaulieu. Either that or her husband did.'

She tapped the page. 'Three times. Once just before Christmas, again three weeks ago and the Monday before the weekend she was murdered.'

Weir picked up the sheet of paper and studied it. 'Ask Sid to get hold of the husband,' he said. 'See if he recognises the number.'

Ryan was in the outer office, standing by Davies' desk. A cigarette burned in the ashtray. Fat-Bob was reading an action sheet, his face very red this morning, tie undone and his weight spreading out from the chair. Ryan picked up the burning cigarette and tapped off an inch of ash. He handed it to Davies. 'Smoke,' he said. 'That way you'll get there quicker.'

'Fuck off, Slippery.'

Ryan grinned and patted him on the shoulder. 'Just my little joke, Fats. Just my little joke.'

Pamela gave him the phone records and told him what Weir had said. Ryan scanned the page and then laid it flat in front of him. He picked up the phone and dialled Alec Turner's number. The phone rang three times and then the answermachine clicked on. Ryan left a message and then put down the phone.

Weir came out of his office and beckoned to him. Ryan got up and went over. Weir was leaning with his fists on the desk. He looked up and motioned for Ryan to close the door.

'Guv'nor?'

'Phonecall just now, Sid. The Gun Room at Lambeth.'

'Oh yeah?' Ryan moved closer to the desk. 'What did they say?'

'The cartridges are from a Russian weapon. Tokarev. 7.62mm.' He picked up a sheet of facsimile paper and passed it to him. 'This is from Jane's manual. I got Lambeth to fax it across.'

Ryan took the sheet of paper and sat down: – *The TT-33 Tokarev is now obsolete in the Warsaw Pact countries. Production ceased in 1954 in its native country, although there is reason to believe it continued for longer than that in Yugoslavia and China. There are therefore many of these pistols to be met in the world and it is no longer safe to say their use is confined to the Soviet and former Soviet States. It was derived from the Browning design in the 1920's at the Tula Arsenal by Feodor Tokarev and he simplified parts of the design and modified others, but the basis was the model 1911 Colt.*

Ryan laid the paper down on the desk.

'It's rare, Slippery,' Weir said.

'Never heard of it, Guv.'

'Lambeth have.' Weir pursed his lips. 'They're sending it over to NIFSL.'

'NIFSL?'

'Northern Ireland Forensic Science Lab.'

Ryan felt the hairs lift on his arm. 'What're you telling me, Guv'nor?'

Weir sat back and drew audible breath through his nose. 'I don't know, Sid. But the only people who use Tokarevs in this country are the Provisional IRA.'

Ryan met Vanner for a drink in the Irish pub in Wembley. He ordered two pints of Caffreys and watched them settle. Vanner came in, damp on his clothes from the misted rain on the street. Ryan rolled licorice-papered cigarettes on the bar. Vanner sat down on the stool next to him and Ryan passed him a roll-up.

'Skint already, Slips?'

'Wife and three brats, Guv'nor. Unlike some.' Ryan lit his cigarette and held the match for Vanner. 'How's Ellie?'

'She's fine.'

'In love are you?'

Vanner ignored him and sipped the froth off his pint. 'So how's things with Weir?'

Ryan lifted his shoulders. 'He's got me minding for him.'

Vanner smiled. 'You're a good skipper, Slips. You might be a gobby git but you're not bad at your job.'

'Take that as a compliment shall I.'

Vanner took a long draught from his pint and looked around the bar. Apart from two old Irishmen playing dominoes they were the only ones drinking. 'What's happening with Ealing then?'

'Shooting.'

'I know that. How're you getting on?'

'Not very well.' Ryan checked to see who was behind him and then told Vanner what was happening. When he mentioned the gun Vanner frowned.

'That's a terrorist weapon, Slips.'

Ryan nodded. 'Lambeth Gun Room've sent the cartridges over to Ulster. They want to find out if the weapon's been used over there.'

'That'd make sense.' Vanner dragged on his cigarette. 'What does Morrison make of it all?'

'Same as the rest of us. Blank.'

'I saw the picture in the papers. You hoping someone'll come forward?'

Ryan nodded. 'She was playing over the side, Guv. Husband thought she was home all weekend but she wasn't. We need to know where she was.'

He pushed himself back from the bar. 'What you working on?'

'Crack team. Harlesden.'

'Jimmy's deal?'

Vanner nodded.

'Stepper-Nap.'

Vanner frowned at him. 'You know him?'

Ryan shook his head. 'Jimmy told me about him last year. British Black posse right?'

'Yeah.'

'I looked at the file but couldn't do anything with it then. It was bitty. Still an AIU deal really.'

'It's not now. They're about the biggest team in London. Jimmy's built up something of a dossier. He's got a connection in Jamaica and the DLO is feeding him information. We've got most of the team eyeballed, nicked a couple of runners, but we don't have a wash house.'

'Nobody talking?'

'There's one snout. They think they own him but we do. He's useful. They smurf cash through Western Union.'

'Nobody putting the finger on anybody?'

Vanner shook his head. 'We've got one possible. Ex-player doing time in Winchester. Got stitched up by one of the generals. He was over the wall for a while and ran with them. Got nicked by a PC writing out a stop slip. We're seeing him tomorrow. He reckons he can finger the doctor.'

Ryan made a face. 'Good luck, Guv. The black teams are always the hardest to crack. You're lucky if you get this much information.' He made a gesture with forefinger and thumb.

They bought more beer and Ryan rolled fresh cigarettes. 'How's your old man? I heard he had a heart attack.'

Vanner stared at himself for a moment in the mirror behind the bar. 'Mild one,' he said. 'He's recovering at home. I was there the other weekend. Took Ellie with me.'

'That'd be a first. You taking a woman home.'

Vanner nodded. 'She's a good girl, Slips.'

'Don't get hung up on her, Guv. She's young. The young ones always stiff you.'

They sat in silence for a moment then Ryan looked at his watch. 'I suppose I'd better get home. Haven't seen the missus for ages.'

'Weir keeping you late is he.'

'Murder Squad, Guv. You know how it is.' He finished his beer and pushed himself off the stool. 'Say hello to Ellie for me.'

In the morning Vanner drove with Jimmy Crack to Winchester to interview the informant. They left Campbell Row at eight thirty and headed out to the M25. Vanner drove, rain falling diagonally against the windscreen.

'Checked out the address for Pretty Boy, Guv'nor,' Jimmy was saying.

'Anywhere we can set up a plot?'

'I don't know. Difficult. There's two more addresses in that area flagged to me. It isn't going to be easy.'

'We can't get him tailed every day.'

'We need a drop, Guv. Somebody coming in.'

'Maybe your man today can help us.'

Jimmy lifted one eyebrow. 'Maybe.'

They got to the M25 and headed south for the M3. Vanner thought about his father. He had phoned last night and spoken to Anne. He was better but still bed-ridden. He asked for his son a lot. He thought about going up again at the weekend. Ellie was working and perhaps it would give them a chance to talk. A lorry pulled out right in front of them, hissing spray to confuse the wipers. Vanner flicked them to double speed and eased back on the throttle.

'You ever thought about trying to talk to Stepper's wife, Jim?'

Jimmy glanced at him. 'I thought about it yeah. Bumped into her at Tesco's once. I thought about telling her the whole bit there and then. You know, fronting her. Hi, I'm PC McKay. Did you know your old man's an international drug dealer?'

Vanner grinned.

'It's worked before, Guv. Sometimes with the Jamaicans – they marry British blacks to get citizenship over here. Then they take off with baby mothers or just treat them bad. I've had one or two shop the old man for going over the side.'

'Not this one though.'

'No. She likes the money too much.'

They drove on in silence, heater blowing warm air into the car. Vanner opened the window a crack and lit a cigarette. 'Who can we have a go at, Jim?'

'To spoil you mean?'

Vanner nodded.

'Immigration want to spin Carmel's place. I told you about Plug. He's working with a DC out of Willesden. Elsdon. Knife-in-the-back man. The smiling fucking assassin. Stick you between the shoulders if he thought it'd help his career.'

'Which one's Carmel again?'

'Radcliffe Road, Harlesden. She looks after the illegals I told you about. Part of the Daddy's politics, keeping the Tottenham Yardies off his patch. She's clean right now but I won't fend them off forever.'

'Does Carver know about the posse?'

Jimmy nodded. 'Seen my flag, Guv. But Elsdon thinks he can make a name for himself.'

'If he so much as steps on this plot I'll cut his legs from under him.'

'Stepper-Nap's canny, Guv. He'll know we're watching Carmel. He plays it very fine, just enough to keep things sweet in Tottenham.'

'Hell of a diplomat isn't he.'

'He's very smart. Much smarter than Pretty Boy figures he is. That one'll get himself burned.'

At Winchester Prison they parked and went up to the police interview room where they waited for the informant to be brought down.

'He was over the wall for a year, Guv'nor. PC with a stop slip picked him up again. The Crime Group let me know. He gave them an address which was flagged to me so I had a chat with him in the scrubs before he was transferred here. Name's Dion Rafter. Word is he's wanted in Jamaica for a shooting. He's terrified of going back. Reckons the police out there will kill him.'

'If they're anything like the ones I know – they will.'

They waited for five minutes before the warder knocked on the door and brought Rafter in. He was tall and slim, scars over one eye which looked to Vanner as though they had been made by a bottle. His hair was cropped short, criss-crossed with razor patterns. Jimmy gave him two packets of cigarettes and he sat down, loose limbed, watching Vanner carefully.

'This is DI Vanner, Dion. I'm working with him.'

Vanner nodded to him and Dion lifted one finger. He unwrapped one of the packets and Vanner offered his lighter.

'So how you doing in here?' Jimmy asked him.

Rafter half-smiled. 'Rather be out there.'

'You were weren't you,' Vanner said, 'for a while.'

'Not long enough, man. Was just getting amongst my women and you bastards nicked me.'

Vanner grinned at him. 'That's the game, Dion. Sometimes you win, sometimes we do.'

Rafter pulled on his cigarette.

'What you got for us, man?' Jimmy leaned his arms on the table.

'Couple o' things.'

'On the phone you said something about the doctor.'

Rafter slowly nodded. 'They got one of those, man. Need to get the stuff out you know. He sticks stuff up their asses to make them shit it all. Don't want to get caught with exploding bags in your butt.'

'Where?' Vanner looked him in the eye.

'You got money for my woman, man?'

Jimmy nodded. 'All squared away, Dion. If what you give us is good.'

'You know where to put the cash?'

'You told me.'

'The doctor, Dion.' Vanner took one of the cigarettes from the pack and lit it.

Rafter told them that the doctor the posse used had a surgery on Willesden Lane. He was an Indian man, in Stepper-Nap's pocket, they had been using him for two years on and off. He was tame and he was cheap. His surgery was a converted house in a street close to the Hindu Temple.

'Religious is he?' Vanner said.

'Oh yeah, man. Real religious.'

'What's the name of the street?'

Rafter blew out his cheeks. 'Can't tell you. I just know where it is is all.'

Vanner glanced at Jimmy. 'You got an *A-Z*?'

Jimmy shook his head.

'Listen, man. You don't need no map. The street right after the temple. It's all houses down there. There ain't but one doctor.'

Outside rain had stopped falling, but wind had risen from the southwest and it howled through the trees on the kerbside. Vanner cupped his hand to his lighter and smoke was whipped away from him.

'What d'you reckon?'

Jimmy shrugged. 'He's been good in the past, Guv. He gave us the last drop exactly.'

Vanner took his mobile phone from his pocket and phoned Campbell Row. Sammy McCleod answered.

'What you doing, Sam?'

'Setting up an undercover buy.'

'Do me a favour will you?' Vanner told him what Rafter had given them and Sammy agreed to take a drive and try to locate the address.

They were halfway up the M3 when Vanner's mobile rang.

Jimmy was driving, Vanner sat next to him, catlike in the passenger seat.

'Vanner.'

'Sammy, Guv.'

'Find it?'

'Yes. Doctor Jamani.'

Ryan phoned the Beaulieu number. He had spoken to Alec Turner who did not recognise it so they surmised his wife had made the phonecalls. He got an answerphone, a Mrs Holt so he left a message and hung up. He was at the coffee machine when Fat-Bob came into the corridor and told him the woman was on the phone. Ryan slopped frothy coffee over his fingers, cursed and went back to his desk.

'Detective Sergeant Ryan,' he said as he picked up the phone.

'Alison Holt, Sergeant. You telephoned me. I take it it's about Jessica Turner.'

Ryan was still for a moment. 'You saw the picture in the papers then.'

'I did. I was going to phone you but you got to me first.'

Ryan nodded to himself. 'Did you know her well?'

'No. I only met her once. She rented a holiday cottage from me in the New Forest.'

'When?'

'The weekend she was murdered. She had it from the Friday night till Sunday. It was the third time she rented it. Once last summer, once in December and the other weekend.'

'She booked it in her name?'

'Yes.'

'Nobody else's?'

'No. Why?'

'Just wondering.'

'She always paid by cheque. A week or so in advance.'

'Are you in for the rest of the day, Mrs Holt?'

'I am, yes.'

'I'd like to come and talk to you. I'd like to see the cottage as well if that's all right.'

'Fine.' She gave him her address and hung up.

Weir parked outside the huge Georgian house that overlooked the estuary and switched off the engine. Seagulls swooped over the marshland, chasing one another, their cries mournful, keening on the wind. The tide was on the turn, mud-coloured ripples bustling against the lean grass of the banks. Ryan got out of the car, buttoned his jacket and re-fastened the top button of his shirt. He could smell salt in the air. On a little jetty fixed into the mud a wooden dingy bobbed with the incoming tide.

Alison Holt must have seen or heard them as they crunched up the gravel sweep of the drive. A well-trimmed lawn bordered by dahlia beds butted up to the gravel and ran in a slope to the six-foot wooden fence. She was waiting in the porch as they approached.

Weir made the introductions and she led them into a high-ceilinged drawing room where a half-height inglenook fireplace lifted over freshly crackling logs. Ryan went over to the fire and rubbed his palms together.

'Beautiful house,' he said. 'Beautiful village.'

'We like it. Peaceful.'

Weir took off his coat and she took it from him and laid it over a chair. She motioned to a wide settee with tie-fixed arms and they sat down. She perched on the edge of a Queen Anne chair and clasped both hands on her knees.

Weir looked at her, about fifty, grey hair curled at the front and fastened with a long pin at the back. Her clothes were Harvey Nichols, blue Guernsey sweater over jodphurs and Chelsea riding boots.

'Is your husband in?' Weir asked her.

She shook her head. 'He's working.'

'What does he do?'

'He's a yacht broker. We have an office in Lymington.'

Weir sat back and put his hands in his trouser pockets. 'Thank you for seeing us, Mrs Holt.'

She hugged herself then as if she was suddenly cold. Ryan watched her face. 'Difficult for you.'

'I didn't know her well, but it's strange to think that after she left my cottage she was shot to death in her home.'

They were all three silent. Weir sat forward. 'We're trying to trace her movements during the time leading up to the murder,' he said. 'We knew she had been away for the weekend, her neighbours told us as much but before we spoke to you we had no idea where.'

'She rented a cottage,' Mrs Holt told him. 'I have a few. It's a sideline. Money left me by my mother. The yacht business can be precarious so I invested in bricks and mortar.'

'Where is the cottage exactly?' Ryan asked her.

'Not very far from here. It's just outside Little Woodfalls near Fordingbridge.'

Weir got up then and moved to the fire. He stood with his back to it, warming the palms of his hands. 'Cold day,' he said.

'The wind comes in off the water.'

He nodded. 'Was she on her own that weekend, Mrs Holt?'

'I don't know. I think so.'

'Did you go ever there at all?'

'While she was there?' Mrs Holt shook her head. 'No reason to. The cottage is self-contained. The key is kept with a neighbour. I only go over after to change the bedding and towels.'

'So you never saw her.'

'No.'

'But you have seen her. I mean you recognised her from the picture.'

'I recognised the name actually. But yes, I have seen her. The last time she was down here.'

'Was she on her own then?'

'No. There was a man with her. I went over on Saturday. There was a problem with the water.'

'The man,' Ryan said. 'Her husband?'

'I presume so. She didn't introduce him.'

'You've seen him before?'

'No. Only the one time. December last year.'

'Would you recognise him again?'

She smiled then and shook her head. 'I was only there for a moment.'

Weir nodded and scratched his head. 'This is delicate, Mrs Holt. We have reason to believe that she *was* there with somebody. A man. Not her husband. He was playing rugby in Ireland. He had no idea she was away.'

She looked between them then. 'I see.'

'Would the neighbours have said anything?'

She glanced up at Weir. 'You mean did they? Not to me.'

'The house,' Ryan said. 'It's detached?'

'All my properties are detached, Sergeant.'

'Stands on its own does it?'

She nodded. 'Hedges all round it. Pretty place really.'

'We'd like to see it now if that's all right,' Weir said.

They followed her Landrover Discovery along the B road toward Fordingbridge. This part of the forest was bare, moorland stretching flat on either side of the road. Ponies chewed at weak grass, their winter coats fluffed into rolls by the wind.

Mrs Holt led them almost to the village of Little Woodfalls and then indicated left before pulling up the driveway of a two-storey house just off the road. Weir turned in behind her and parked. Ryan got out. The drive was long enough to house three cars and the Discovery was fronting a garage with twin wooden doors. The garden was wide and laid to lawn with a hedgerow separating it from its neighbour. Mrs Holt came round the front of the Landrover jangling a set of keys in her hand.

The front door opened straight into a low-ceilinged lounge with a wood burner standing in the open fireplace. The house smelled of leather, two armchairs thrown over with white cotton cloths. A dresser stood against the far wall and freshly cut wood was stacked in the hearth.

'Feel free to look around,' she told them.

The lounge had a stripped pine door which opened into a narrow, beamed hallway which led off to the right. A door on the left opened into a study which smelled faintly of damp. To the right of the study the stairs climbed in a wooden sweep to the first floor. At the far end of the hall an open-plan kitchen was accessed by an arch.

Ryan climbed the stairs and found three bedrooms, two spacious and one box room. A bathroom on the left with a scrubbed suite and sloping ceiling. None of the beds were made up.

'She was the last person to rent it?' Weir said.

Mrs Holt looked at him and nodded.

'You strip everything?'

'Of course.'

Weir glanced at Ryan. 'The sheets,' he said.

'I don't look for stains, Inspector.'

'No. Of course you don't.'

She pointed through the open bedroom to the chimney pot of the house next door. 'You can speak to the neighbours if you want. They're retired. Almost always at home.'

Weir nodded to Ryan, who went back down the stairs. Weir looked back at Mrs Holt once more. 'I might want some people to look the house over.'

'Be my guest.'

Ryan met them both in the driveway. Mrs Holt locked the door and turned back to her car. Ryan nodded to Weir and they got back in his Scorpio.

'Neighbours clocked a car, Guv. Blue saloon. That's all they could tell me.'

'They didn't see a body?'

'Not a male one. Jessica collected the key. One thing though. They said she looked a bit shaken.'

'Shaken?' Weir studied his face. 'How shaken?'

'Just a bit stirred up. They asked her if she was okay and she shrugged it off. They didn't speak to her again until she dropped the key on Sunday night. She was happy as a pig in shit by then.'

'But they did see a car?' Weir backed out into the road and waved to Mrs Holt as she drove off ahead of them.

'Yeah. Saturday morning there were two cars in the drive. The neighbours went shopping and clocked them.'

They headed back towards the M27 and Weir took gum from his pocket, rolled it and popped it in his mouth.

'You still want a Lab team down here?'

Weir nodded. 'Its scrubbed cleaner than a swimming pool but you never know.'

'Local or ours?'

'Ours. I don't want anyone else involved.'

Ryan took the mobile phone from his belt and called the incident room in Hendon.

Eilish McCauley sat in front of her dressing table, legs crossed over the padded pink stool, and brushed her long red hair. Newly washed, newly dried, she could still smell the heat in it. From the table before her she took crimson lipstick and spread it across her lips. She eased them back over her teeth, pressed them together and pouted. Her mouth was red now, bright against the pale height of her cheekbones. Taking powder she brushed at the hollows of her cheeks until they coloured a fraction, accentuating the line of her face. As she bent forward to replace the powder one black lacy strap fell from her shoulder and her breast pushed against the material of her chemise. She saw her brother framed behind her in the mirror.

'Always creeping about, James.'

'I'm not creeping about.'

She looked back at him, a taunt on her mouth. The silent walker of landings. How many years had he done that? As if he knew what she was thinking, colour burned in his face and he pressed his gaze to the carpet. She laughed.

'Don't laugh at me, Eilish.'

She held up one hand. 'Sorry,' she grinned. 'I'm sorry.'

They looked at one another then and a lifetime passed between them. Brother and sister, each guessing at the other's thoughts as they had always done.

'Are you going out *again* tonight?' he asked her.

'*Again*, James?' She repeated the word with a downward sweep of her mouth. 'Yes, I'm going out *again*.' She looked at him as the muscles stiffened against the skin of his face.

'You weren't going anywhere were you?'

'No.'

'Then I can can't I.'

'The children like it better when you're in. They like to know you're there.'

'The children are asleep, James. It's neither here nor there.'

'They notice.'

She sighed then, placing her palms on her thighs. 'They don't notice.'

'How do you know? You're not here when they wake up.'

'I'm allowed a life, James.'

'Yeah. And so are they.'

She got up then and rolled black stockings over the cream of her thighs. He sat on the bed and watched her.

'Which one is it tonight then?'

'What?' She rested a fist on her hip.

'Fatty or skinny, Eilish? Does Stepper-Nap know you sleep with Young Young?'

She shook her head at him. 'You know one of these days you'll get a life of your own instead of criticising mine.'

'I might,' he said. 'Then what would you do for a babysitter?'

He sat down on the edge of her bed and shook his head. 'I'm sorry,' he said. Eilish sat a moment then got up and lifted her green Chinese dress from where it lay on the bed beside him. She ruffled the dark of his hair with pointed fingers. 'Don't let's fight, love eh?'

'I'm sorry, Eilish. I just worry about the girls.' He wrapped his arms about her waist then, like a child would its mother, and she smoothed his hair against her.

'You ought to get out, James. You know you really should. What about a girlfriend? Isn't it time you got one?'

'I know. I know.' He let go of her then as if her sudden proximity disturbed him. 'Dole cheques don't get you very far though do they.'

She bent to him then and rested the flat of her arms on his knees. 'I've got money if you need it.'

He stood up and went to the window. Street lamps bled yellow on the pavement. 'I don't want your money, Eilish. Don't worry about me. I'm fine.' He turned to face her again. 'You're right. We shouldn't fight. We're all that we have aren't we.'

'Yes, James. We are.'

The past clouded between them, each witnessing its dark reflection in the eye of the other. For a short moment they stared. Then, as if the knowledge was too deep, too painful, they both looked away. Eilish pulled her dress over her head and turned her back to him. 'Zip me up will you?'

He zipped her dress to the neck and fastened the tie. She stood before the mirror and smoothed hands over the flat of her stomach. 'Ready,' she said to her reflection.

'Eilish.'

She turned again and saw the light all at once in his eye.

'What?'

'D'you ever think about Tommy?'

For a second or so she stared. 'Of course I think about Tommy.'

Six

She sat with Stepper-Nap in the restaurant. He sipped white wine from a long-stemmed glass, incongruous in his chubby fingers. Eilish took his other hand and he paused, glass halfway to his lips. She smiled as he glanced at the other diners, such a big tough Daddy whom she could still embarrass when she wanted to. She turned his hand over in hers, the paleness of the palm contrasting with the thick brown skin on the back. His fingers, stuffed with rings, were well manicured; the nails clipped, cuticles pushed right back into the quick. He took the hand back, wiggled it and the heavy gold band slipped back over his wrist.

'Romantic tonight ain't you?'

She sat back and smiled at him. 'Candlelit dinner for two. I feel romantic.'

'I got a wife, babe. Three kids by her.'

'And another wife and two kids by her and God knows how many more. You're here with me and we've got no kids and I know how to please you the best.' She touched her teeth with her tongue.

He sat forward then and pushed his plate away. He put down the glass and rested his chin on his fists. 'We got business, first, baby. There's gear arriving. When you gonna do your stuff?'

'Whenever.' She sat well back in her seat, hands in the fold of her lap.

'Not whenever. When? That's a hole we got in the market, Eilish. Hole that I can fill.'

He leaned forward then and his flat face was serious. 'I need to fill the hole. Got to re-establish myself.'

'Pretty Boy?'

He nodded. 'Asshole thinks he's the man now. What he don't know is I'm three steps ahead of him.' He looked at her then. 'But I need you for that.'

She shook her head, leaned an elbow on the table and cupped her cheek with a palm. 'You really think it's that simple, don't you?'

His face clouded then, eyes very small in their sockets.

'Stepper, lover. How many others like you d'you think are out there.'

'There's none with contacts like I got.'

'You stupid black bastard.'

His eyes thinned into slits. 'Don't call me that. Don't ever call me that.'

'Why not? It's what you are.'

He stared at her then and reached for her hand. He took it, looked in her eyes and squeezed her fingers together. Her skin pinched and she tried to pull away. He squeezed all the more tightly. 'You're a good fuck, Eilish. And I like white flesh. But there's plenty more like you.'

He let her go then and she rubbed her fingers with her other hand. 'You hurt me.'

'Did I?' He shook his head. 'You dis' me, babe. Then you'll know I hurt you.'

She stared at her plate for a moment then gathered herself and lifting her stockinged foot from her shoe she placed it between his legs under the table. 'You should learn to take a joke.'

His eyes glazed as slowly she began to massage him with her toes. 'You should chill out, Stepper. You're too wired these days.'

'Don't play games, Eilish.'

She did not say anything, just pressed a little harder with her toes. She could see the muscles tighten across his face, and moved forward in the seat to release him.

'Pay the bill,' she said.

Ryan sat with Alec Turner in his office. Turner behind his desk, computer screen between them. They stared at one another. Ryan made a short gesture with one hand. 'She was seeing someone, Alec. I'm sorry.'

For a moment Turner stared at him. 'You don't know that.'

Ryan nodded. 'We do. She rented the cottage three times. Each time somebody was with her. Where were you on the weekends?'

Turner looked blank.

'Check your diary, mate. A monkey says you were away.'

Turner looked at the screen between them and slowly chewed his lip. 'Did anyone actually see her?'

Again Ryan nodded. 'The couple who live next door. They only saw the car this time but in December the woman she rented it from saw a man with her.' He scratched his jaw. 'It's a bummer, Alec. But you had to know.'

Turner sucked an audible breath, a rasping sound like sandpaper in his throat. His eyes puffed and he bit down on his lip.

'We need to find out who he is, Alec. He must know what's happened by now and he hasn't come forward. D'you have any ideas?' He took out a packet of Camels and shook two out. Lighting them both he handed one to Turner who drew heavily on it. He exhaled and looked at the glowing end. 'Non-smoking office,' he muttered. He looked sharply at Ryan then. 'Why hasn't he come forward?'

Ryan opened his hands. 'That's what we need to find out.'

'You think *he* killed her?'

'Maybe, although I don't know why he'd wait till she got back to London.' He shook his head. 'More likely he's married. Got kids.' He lifted his shoulders. 'Why mess up his life?'

'Bastard.'

'Probably.' He paused. 'Who could he be, Alec?'

'I don't know.'

'What about work? Most affairs happen at work.'

Turner sighed then. 'This is a shock, Ryan. You'll have to give me some time.'

'Friends, Alec.' Ryan stood up. 'Acquaintances. Mutual friends maybe. People at work she talked about a lot. Names coming up in conversation more often than others. Think about it will you? Bell me. You've got the number.'

Back at the incident room Tony Rob came up to him. 'How'd he take it?'

'How would you take it if your wife was playing away?'

'Not married, Slips.'

'You know what I mean.'

Ryan looked down at the pile of messages on his desk. 'We need to visit her workplace again, Tony. Talk to all the male colleagues she worked with. Married ones, I reckon. Kids maybe.'

'Right.'

Glancing up, Ryan saw Morrison sitting with Weir in the Investigating Officer's room. Weir had his hands on his head and chewed gum like a cow at the cud. He beckoned Ryan through.

'You see him, Sid?'

Ryan nodded.

'Any joy?'

'He's thinking about it, Guv'nor. Bit of a shock for him.' Ryan sat down and glanced at Morrison. 'He's going to bell me with a list of possibles. In the meantime we'll look at the married ones she works with.'

'Married?' Morrison looked at him.

'Yes, Sir. I reckon whoever it is must be married. Why else wouldn't he come forward?'

Morrison nodded. 'He's also a suspect, Ryan.'

'Of course he is, Sir.'

Weir got up and poured coffee from the pot behind him. 'There's something else, Sid.'

'What's that, Guv'nor?'

Morrison looked at him. 'We had a phonecall this morning. A man from Fordingbridge. Apparently he saw Jessica Turner on his way home from work on Friday night. He's very keen to talk to us.'

Weir handed them each a cup of coffee and Ryan stirred sugar. 'He's on his way in here now,' Weir went on. 'Photocopier engineer, works for a dealer in Camberley.'

'What's he got to tell us?'

Weir shrugged. 'Don't know yet. Said he was in London so he'd come down. Talk to us in person.'

The caller arrived at two that afternoon. Weir and Ryan put on their jackets and met him downstairs. They took him to the canteen which was all but empty. Ryan bought tea from Eileen at the counter and carried the tray over. The man's name was Case. Michael Case. Ryan put him at about forty, medium build with a bit of a paunch developing over his belt. His hair was long and thin, edging a pinched, pockmarked face.

'Good of you to come, Mr Case.' Weir passed him his tea.

'I was in London.' Case unwrapped a packet of sugar and tipped it into his tea. His manner was easy, relaxed.

'Up here on business?' Ryan asked him.

He nodded. 'I fix copiers. My patch is Hampshire and Dorset but I'm up here for a product launch.'

'Fortunate then.'

'Fortunate?'

Ryan nodded. 'Not far to come.'

'Right.' Case stirred his tea. 'We're always doing something or other. I'm in London quite a lot.'

Weir clasped his hands together and nudged the A4 pad in Ryan's direction. Ryan took out his pen.

Case told them how he had been travelling home on the Friday night in question, rain teeming down so hard he had to drive really slowly. He said he was aware of a car's tail lights far up on the road between the Cadnam roundabout and Woodfalls. It was only as he drew closer that he noticed it was stationary.

Ryan watched him as he spoke, meticulous in his pronunciation, eyes flitting from one face to the other.

'When I got closer I saw something very strange,' he said.

'What?'

'The car was parked, engine still running. There was this woman standing in front of it looking at something on the road. I could see her in the beam of her headlights. I thought she must've hit a fox or a pony maybe, they graze very close to the road on that stretch. No trees, more moorland than forest.'

Weir nodded. 'We've been there,' he said.

'Well anyway, I was about to pull over and help her when I saw somebody come out of the shadows and get in the back of her car.'

Ryan stared at him. 'What happened then?'

'She just got back in the driver's side.'

'Friend then? Getting in the back.'

Case shook his head. 'I don't think so. It certainly didn't look like it. He crept up to the door and opened it very carefully.'

'He?'

'It could've been a she I suppose. Coat. I couldn't see properly.'

'What did you do?' Weir asked him.

Case sipped at his tea and replaced the cup on the saucer.

'Well I didn't know what to do at first then I was sure she didn't realise so I drove up behind her and hooted, flashed my lights – you know – tried to get her attention.'

'What did she do?' Ryan asked.

'I thought she'd stop. But I think she must've panicked. Rainy night and everything. She took off, Sergeant, floored it, drove like a looney zig-zagging away from me.'

'And what did you do?'

'I went after her. I was sure then she didn't know. I couldn't just let her go.'

Weir glanced at Ryan. 'So you followed her.'

'I chased her really, as close as I could get without really scaring her badly. I flashed my lights and hooted. But she wouldn't stop.'

'I'd say you scared her pretty badly, Mr Case.'

He looked at the table top. 'With hindsight – I must've mustn't I.'

'She kept driving?' Ryan said.

He nodded. 'I followed her for about five miles then just before Little Woodfalls she turned into a drive.'

'What did you do?'

'I pulled over. She came running down the drive and had a real go at me, shouting and screaming she was. Like you say she must've been scared. Anyway, there wasn't time to calm her down so I ran up the drive to her car.'

'And?'

'Nobody there. The back door was open though.'

Weir stared at him. 'But you saw him?'

'Oh yes.'

'But when you got there he was gone.'

'There was time, Inspector. She was there before me. She came straight down the drive. He had time to get out.'

Ryan looked at the notes he had scribbled. Weir pushed away his empty tea cup. 'Why was she stopped in the road – did she tell you?'

Case sat forward then. 'That's the strangest thing,' he said. 'She said she saw a man lying there but when she stopped she found it was only a dummy. The kind you get in shop windows. Male, trousers and a shirt and a tie. All soaking wet.'

Ryan looked at Weir. 'Did you go back and look?'

'Not then. I wouldn't've found the spot. I drove the road in the morning though but I couldn't find anything.'

For a few moments a silence lifted between them then Weir said: 'You didn't report any of this – to the local police I mean?'

Case looked at him for a moment then lifted his palms. 'She said she would do it. It was her car after all.'

'Did you give her your name – your address?'

Case shook his head.

'She didn't ask you.'

'No. She didn't.'

Weir glanced at Ryan. 'Seems a bit strange. Did you offer?'

'I think I told her my name.'

'What d'you mean think – you either did or you didn't.'

'I did tell her, yes.'

'But she didn't write it down.'

'No,' he said. 'She didn't.'

Weir looked at him with one eye partially closed. 'She said nothing else.'

'No.'

'But you were absolutely sure there was somebody in the back of her car?'

'I'd put my life on it. I saw it, Inspector. Plain as I see you now.'

Weir scratched his head. 'Thanks, Mr Case,' he said. 'Appreciate you coming in. We might need to talk to you again. Is that all right?'

'Whatever I can do to help, Inspector.'

Upstairs again Weir said: 'Get on to the Lab team, Sid. I want them all over her car.'

Ryan nodded.

'One other thing.'

'What?'

'Find out all you can about Case.'

Young Young sat in his brother's flat, watching the NBA on Sky television. He sucked on a bottle of Rolling Rock, washing the pale beer around the inside of his mouth. A half-smoked cigarette burned in the ashtray on the table in front of him. Next to it a pile of cocaine like spilled sand from an hour glass. Seattle scored again and he grunted.

Little Bigger sat next to him, hair slicked back and shiny.

He stroked the mess of his beard.

'The Daddy know about this?'

'It's personal.' Young Young spoke without looking at him. Sitting forward he pressed the cocaine into a single, skinny line, before snorting it through half a straw. He blinked, sniffed again and flicked his head back. Then he sucked breath through his teeth.

Little Bigger touched his lips with his tongue and watched him. He shifted his weight and glanced at Carmel, who sat back in the other chair and watched Young Young's face. He caught her eye, held it for a moment before glancing back to the TV screen. He was long and lean in the chair, unblemished features pointed and sharp, lighted coal in his eyes. He wore leather jeans and black suede boots, a gold chain hanging loose at his neck. He rested his chin on a fist and the muscles tightened under the skin of his arm.

'Stepper don't want no trouble, baby.' Carmel's voice was barely more than a whisper.

Young Young ignored her. He stared at the clock on top of the TV set. He would give it till ten then he'd go.

'Pigs might be watching us, man,' Little Bigger said. He sat forward. 'I mean we don't know that they ain't.'

Young Young looked at him then, the pudge of his fingers, the swollen weight of his belly. He was much shorter than Young Young, squatter, with two chins bunching into his neck. Same mother, different father. Young Young's had been six and a half feet in his socks. Little Bigger was the elder by five years. He could remember Young Young's old man in the house, walking around naked half the time, his thing dangling between his thighs. He used to see him cross the landing, a lodger in his mother's house. In from Jamaica with nowhere else to go. A friend of a friend of a friend. That was in Brixton before Young Young was born. He had got his mother pregnant before moving on. Young Young had his build, his dick and his eyes, sharp points of coal that never joined his mouth in a smile.

Little Bigger fetched more beer from the kitchen, flipped the tops off and handed a bottle to Young Young.

'You can't go to Jimmy Carter's on your own, man.'

'You come with me then.' Young Young got up then, towering above him. For a moment Little Bigger looked up at him, then he dropped his shoulders and slowly shook his head.

They left Carmel in the flat and went down to the street. Starlit night with a chill on the air that set their breath in smoke. Young Young blew on his hands and felt in his pockets for car keys.

He drove, his brother silent in the seat alongside him. They trundled through Willesden Green and turned right on the High Road before heading north toward Cricklewood.

'Nobody bad-mouths me, man,' Young Young said very quietly.

Little Bigger glanced at him. Young Young was watching the road, his face still and cold.

A two-tone police car passed them at the lights and Young Young gave them the finger in the rear-view mirror. Then he grinned and punched his brother on the upper arm. 'Relax, man. I can take the fucker one-handed.'

'He'll have brothers with him.'

'So.' Young Young felt under his seat and brought up something black and heavy. 'I got mine don't I.'

Little Bigger looked at the cold steel of the Uzi. 'Put it away, man.'

Young Young tucked it into the seat behind him.

'Don't kill him. You kill him and we really are in the shit.'

'I ain't gonna kill him, man. Just mess up his face a little.'

'He won't be packing, brother. Not in Jimmy Carter's.'

'Carter's an Irish prick.'

'Yeah. But a tough one. He's got serious friends, man. Stepper'll go ape if you mix it up with him.'

'Listen.' Young Young jabbed out his chin. 'I ain't gonna let no Yardie fuck trash my name. You dig.'

Holden Biggs played eight ball pool in Jimmy Carter's snooker hall just off Kilburn High Road. Stocky, skinheaded black man with fists like hams that engulfed the cue he was holding. A second man stood next to him resting on his cue. Two more sat on stools at the bar. Along from them, pencil in one hand, ginger-haired and sweating, Jimmy Carter did his figures.

All the snooker tables bar one were taken. Men mostly, Irish. A couple of punky-looking white girls played on the second pool table.

* * *

YoungYoung cruised past the hall and spotted Bigg's 2.8 Capri. He was an illegal, one of the Tottenham team whom Carmel had put up as Stepper's favour to his neighbours. YoungYoung was around Carmel at the time and the word was that Holden Biggs was bad-mouthing him. Six feet six of brainless pussy was how it was told. Young Young thought about the word coming off the street as he parked further on. Biggs had had a big mouth even when he was at Carmel's. Big man back home so he told it. He was yappy and disrespectful. Young Young had already threatened to close his mouth for him in the flat. It was after, when Holden hit the streets, that the pussy cracks started.

He sat with the engine running, aware of the barrel of his gun against his back as he leaned over the driver's seat and sized up the two white men in penguin suits on the steps of Jimmy Carter's. Reaching behind him he lifted the Uzi and got out of the car. He pressed the gun into the waistband of his jeans and flipped his jacket down over it. His brother shifted across to the driver's seat.

'Spin it around. I won't be but a minute.'

Young Young started walking along the pavement back towards the snooker hall on the other side of the road. A woman walked past him and the scent of cheap perfume filled his nostrils. He felt an itch in his loins and smiled. He knew where he'd go after this.

Again he thought about Biggs. Stepper had told him to be cool. Chill out, baby, he had said. That mouth you're hearing is looking to get you killed. He had let it go. But the word kept coming up from the street and after a while he could not let it go any more. He was Young Young, the Harlesden Daddy's armour. He had a reputation to think of.

Then last Friday he had been out with a girl from the Archway. A pub close to Tottenham and Biggs there with his buddies. Then the cracks had been to his face and if there wasn't seven of them he would have done him there and then.

He nodded to the bouncers and pushed open the doors.

Jimmy Carter went behind the bar and poured Caffreys for a punter. He saw Young Young walk through the door, so tall he had to stoop to get in. Bobby Simpson, the crop-haired bouncer from downstairs came in behind him and glanced toward the bar.

Biggs was bending for the five ball, chalk freshening the end of his cue. Young Young saw him and his eyes seemed to glint in the overhead lights. He pushed between two snooker tables, his gait long and loose and easy. As he got to the pool table he felt the adrenaline begin to rush and the gun was hot at the base of his spine. Biggs had not seen him, concentrating now on the six ball. Young Young moved to the wall and picked a cue from the rack.

In one smooth, uncluttered movement, he brought the heavy end down over Biggs's head. It bounced off bone and jarred up his arm. Biggs's head thumped the table and blood flew in a spurt from his nose. The second player took one pace and Young Young flat-footed him in the stomach. Biggs was holding his head, crying aloud and spitting bloodied teeth onto the blue baize of the table. Young Young grabbed him by the collar and hit him again with the cue. It snapped against his face and then Young Young threw him against the wall.

One of the other blacks was off his barstool and feeling for the knife in his pocket. Young Young rolled his eyes and hit him roundhouse style, knocking him against the bar. Biggs was a crumpled sack on the floor, blood and mucus dripping from his head and nose. Young Young took the Uzi from his belt and waved it at the bouncer who was all but on him now.

'Whoa!' The bouncer jumped back, palms out in front of him. 'Hey. Hey. Take it easy.'

Young Young was breathing hard.

The bouncer took three steps backwards and then Carter came round the bar. 'You stupid black bastard.' His lips were curled over his teeth. Young Young stared at him.

'Guns in my club is it?' Carter seemed oblivious to the weapon that Young Young was pointing at him. 'You want me to tell ye about guns?'

Young Young stepped towards him now and Carter hesitated. The black's face was the still cold of a killer. Dead eyes, flat in their sockets like a shark before it bites.

Young Young paced towards Carter, who was back against the bar now. Young Young stopped. Slowly he reached out with his empty hand and squeezed Carter's features together. Then he lifted the Uzi and poked the barrel into his nostril. 'Guns is it?' He mimicked the Irishman's accent. He stroked the trigger with his index finger. 'All I got to do is squeeze and you're all over the paintwork.'

For a long moment he stared into Carter's eyes and he could smell the fear in his pores. Young Young smiled, only not with his eyes, then he shoved Carter into the stools and emptied the magazine in the ceiling.

Outside, Little Bigger threw open the passenger door of Young Young's Rover and he piled in. They drove off, the back end slewing wildly and the tyres screeching on tarmac.

'I heard shooting, you fuck. Who the hell did you shoot?'

'Relax, brother.' Young Young was laughing. 'I wasted furniture is all.'

'Biggs?'

'Busted his skull with a pool cue. Carter fancied it till I shoved my gun up his nose.'

They got back to the flat and Young Young leaned across his brother and pushed open the driver's door. 'Out.'

'Where you going?'

'Pussy hunting.'

'Now?'

'Yes, now. I need an alibi. So do you. You was shagging Carmel. Got it?'

Little Bigger gaped at him. 'Stepper's gonna love me for that.'

'Fuck Stepper-Nap. This is me and you, brother.'

His brother stared at him. 'You're crazy, man.'

'Out.' Young Young slipped into the warmth of the driver's seat and wound the window down. 'Later,' he said and drove off.

Eilish was getting ready for bed. James was downstairs watching TV. She was bathed and warm and about to step into the silk of her nightdress when she heard a car outside. Downstairs, James heard it too and he moved to the window. Not Stepper-Nap. He knew the sound of the Mercedes. No, it was the other one, midnight-blue Rover. He felt his heart slowly sinking. The tall one with the evil look in his eyes and the children were sleeping upstairs.

Young Young parked the car and walked up to the front

door. Sweat crept on his flesh now and the pump of his heart was stiller. The night freshened the skin of his face and he felt the familiar ache in his loins. No Merc. The Daddy was home with his woman and his young ones like he always was on a Wednesday. He was Thursdays and weekends if he got lucky. Midweek was for other takers. He pressed a long finger into the doorbell.

In the lounge James had switched off the TV and was sitting on the edge of the chair with his hands deep in his armpits. He heard the bell, swore softly to himself then heard his sister's feet on the stairs.

Young Young walked into the hall and looked down at Eilish.

'I wasn't expecting you, baby.'

He lifted her right off her feet and marched her backwards into the kitchen, closing the door behind him.

James sat where he was, listening to her moaning. Had she no shame? Her children upstairs and everything. His face buckled and he bit down on his lip. Then he got up and went quietly upstairs.

In the kitchen Eilish pushed Young Young away from her. 'Not here,' she said. He kissed her face and her neck, lips bruising hers and she could feel him against her. 'Quietly,' she said. 'The children are sleeping and there's my brother.'

'Fuck your brother.' Young Young hoisted her against the sink.

Later, in her bedroom, Young Young lay on his back as she ran her fingers over the tight knots of his flesh. She could hear James on the landing. She closed her eyes and the past grew up in her mind.

Lonely nights, years before, Tommy in her bed with his wild green eyes and his shock of black hair that danced on her face as they made love. She could feel him now, pressing his body into hers while James hovered outside. Words like *I love you* in her ear, and then thoughts of Tommy's wife and his four tiny children in front of the TV or in bed but oblivious to her husband, their father, in the arms of a nineteen-year-old girl with fire-coloured hair.

'Anyone ask, I been here all evening. Tell your brother too.' Young Young's voice was low in his chest and it shook her from threads of the memory.

'Why?'
'Never mind why. Just remember is all.'

Vanner came off the phone to his father and Ellie watched him from the lounge doorway. She held a glass of Coke in her hand. He looked at her then, hair caught in the lamplight, frizzing away from her head. The velvet-green of her eyes.
'Don't look at me like that.'
'Like what?'
'That.' She made a face and then smiled. 'I don't know. Concentrating.'
Vanner moved towards her. 'I like concentrating on you.'
They moved back into the lounge and he sat down on the settee, crossing his ankle on his knee. Ellie sat close to him, her hand on his thigh, fingers gently kneading the muscles.
'How is he?'
'Not bad. He's downstairs now. Anne's made up a bed in the study so she doesn't have to keep going up and down the stairs.'
'Did you talk to him?'
He nodded. 'He wants me to go up again.'
'Why don't you?'
He turned to face her then, looking in her eyes. 'I thought I might go this weekend.'
'Fine.'
'You're working aren't you?'
She nodded.
'I will then.'
They sat for a moment then Ellie got up and put music on. She knelt down by the small table and selected a CD from the pile. Her CDs, her CD player. Vanner realised that he did not own anything. This house had been bare before she came. She put Wild Wood on and rocked back on her heels as the strains of Paul Weller drifted into the room.
'I saw them in 1978,' Vanner said.
Ellie looked over her shoulder at him. 'Paul Weller?'
'The Jam.'
She nodded. 'Another snippet of your past I don't know about.'
He glanced at her. 'I saw The Jam, so what?'
'Not what I meant.'

He looked away from her.

'You never tell me anything about before I knew you.'

'I do.'

'No you don't. Not really.'

Vanner shrugged. 'There's nothing to tell you, Ellie.'

She sat down next to him again, drawing one foot under her backside. 'What d'you mean – nothing to tell? You've got a whole history, a whole past life that I know nothing about.'

Vanner looked at her then. 'Ellie, I've spent too much of my life thinking about a past. I don't want to do it any more.'

Pain in his eyes: she could see it though he himself was not aware that it showed. Gently she cupped his cheek with her palm and kissed him on the lips.

'Even so,' she said. 'I'd like to know.'

He reached for a cigarette and she flicked his lighter for him. He sat hunched forward now, wrists resting on his knees.

'You know everything there is to know about me, Aden.'

'That's because you wanted to tell me.'

'And you don't want to tell me?'

He sighed. 'Not that I don't want to – just that I don't see the point.'

She shook her head and laughed. 'God you're a cripple aren't you.'

Her words stung him and he looked up. 'What d'you mean?'

'You find it so hard to feel.'

'Do I?' He drew harshly on the cigarette and exhaled a stream of smoke. The music seemed louder now, plaintive almost in his ears.

'Talk to me, Aden. I want to know all there is to know about you. Your father. You have such a strained relationship with him and he's such a nice man.'

Vanner sat back again. 'You talked to him?'

'You know I did when you were outside with Anne.'

'What did he say?'

'He asked me about myself.'

'And you – what did you tell him?'

'Everything. Why not? He was interested.' She waved away his smoke and reached for her glass of Coke. Vanner crushed out the cigarette and lifted his beer bottle from where it gleamed on the carpet. He held it in both hands, rolling it between his palms.

'You grew up without a mother.'

He nodded. 'My father was a chaplain in the army. I was born in the Middle East and then we moved to Africa, Germany, Cyprus, Gibraltar. When I was twelve he got a job as a priest at Norwich School so I went there.'

'Did they take the piss – the other boys?'

Vanner glanced at her. 'You mean because he was a priest?'

'Yes.'

'Some of them did, yes.'

'Did it bother you?'

'Yes, it bothered me.'

'What did you do?'

'I became a boxer, Ellie. I got in the ring and punched people.'

She looked carefully at him. 'And after that?'

'They didn't take the piss any more.'

She was quiet for a moment. 'You keep a picture of your wife in the bottom drawer in the kitchen.'

Vanner sat very still. 'I don't have a wife.'

'I was looking for a tea towel. I found it by accident.'

He looked at her now. 'I don't have a wife.'

'Ex-wife then. She was very pretty.'

'Yes, you're right, she was.'

'What happened?'

'We got divorced.'

'Why?'

'Oh Christ, Ellie.'

Vanner finished the beer and got up. He moved over to the window, one hand in his trouser pocket. A couple came out of the Greek restaurant on the corner and scuttled through the rain to the door of the pub opposite.

'She decided she couldn't cope with my kind of life. She went off with my best friend instead.'

'I'm sorry, Aden. I shouldn't pry.'

'No,' he said. 'You shouldn't.'

Later, when they were in bed she lay away from him, naked, but her back to him. He could make out the knots of her spine in the half-light through the window. Her side rose and fell with her breathing. He did not know whether she was asleep or not. They had not made love.

Seven

Jimmy Crack was waiting for him in his office at Campbell Row the following morning. When they woke Ellie had been awkward for the first time since Vanner had started seeing her. He walked in and caught Jimmy's expression.

'The doctor?'

Jimmy shook his head. 'I'm still trying to set up an OP, Guv.'

'What then?'

'Jimmy Carter. Somebody shot up his snooker hall last night.'

'Did they?' Vanner moved past him and pulled back his chair. 'So what? That's a Crime Group deal, nothing to do with us.'

'It was Young Young, Guv'nor.'

Jimmy drove, Vanner sat thinking alongside him. 'Kilburn got the call about ten thirty last night,' Jimmy said.

'Who called?'

'Mr Nobody.'

'Well there's a surprise. How do we know it was Young Young?'

'Description. Very tall, very slim, young looking. He beat up some spade with a pool cue then shot up the ceiling.'

Vanner looked sideways at him.

'Carries an Uzi. I told you.'

'Where did a shit like that get an Uzi?'

Vanner knew Jimmy Carter of old. He was old-school Irish, Silverbridge-born with long-time connections in Belfast. His time had been the seventies and these days he was definitely a non-player, but connections never die and Carter's place thrived off Kilburn High Road. Vanner knew him from his days in Special Branch with Neville Standish. Carter was mean, very mean, and he was about as fond of Old Bill as a Rottweiler was of lettuce leaves.

Vanner glanced at Jimmy again as they headed up the High

Road. 'Kilburn haven't nicked him then.'

Jimmy shook his head. 'Scarpered before anyone got there.'

'Has Carter made a complaint?'

'What do you think?'

Vanner thinned his lips. 'Do we know the black that got hit?'

'Nobody's giving a name, Guv.'

'In-fighting then. Must be some kind of prat to use Carter's place for a venue.'

They parked outside the main doors to the snooker hall and climbed the maroon-carpeted stairs. A doorman in jeans and a sweatshirt stopped them at the top. He was short and stockily built with gelled spiky hair. He looked them up and down. Vanner flipped open his warrant card.

'Where's Jimmy?' he said.

'You're too late, mate. Plod's been and gone.'

'Well he's back again, mate.' Vanner looked in his eyes. 'You go tell Daddy that Vanner wants to see him.'

For a moment the bouncer looked back at him then he dropped his chin and turned to the inner door. 'Wait here,' he said.

They did not wait. They followed him through the curtained swing doors into the main hall. All the blinds were pulled and the only light showed over the bar, where another man in a white collarless shirt was wiping down the wood. The bouncer looked back at them. 'Wait,' he said. 'I'll get Jimmy.'

He disappeared through the doors at the back and Vanner and Jimmy Crack made their way through the silent snooker tables to the bar. The cleaner looked up at them and looked away again. Jimmy pointed to the holes in the ceiling; bits of plaster and dust still clung to the lip of some of them. The cleaner looked up again as Vanner sat down on a stool and laid his cigarettes on the bar.

Carter came through the doors at the back, followed by the bouncer with the short spiky hair. Vanner looked over his shoulder and their eyes locked. Carter paused for a fraction of a second, sleeves pushed up. He scratched the curling hair on his forearm then half-smiled and sauntered over. Vanner held his eye until he was alongside then he nodded to the ceiling. 'Had a little accident, Jim.'

Carter glanced from him to Jimmy Crack and back again.
'DC McKay,' Vanner said.

Carter did not nod or smile. 'Mr Vanner?' he said. 'The police have been and gone.'

'I told him that, Mr Cart . . .' The bouncer started to speak but Carter stilled him with a wave of his hand.

'You want coffee, *gentlemen*?'

Vanner looked him in the eye. 'That'd be very nice.'

Carter sent the bouncer away to make coffee and settled himself on the stool next to Vanner. Vanner lit two cigarettes and handed one to him. They watched each other like two cockerels in a farmyard.

'Been a long time, Jimmy.'

Carter nodded.

'Still see the old faces?'

'I'm not looking these days, Mr Vanner. You know that.'

Vanner smiled without moving his eyes. He drew on his cigarette and tapped ash into the freshly polished glass of the ashtray.

'So what happened here then?'

'Nothing I can't handle.'

Vanner nodded. 'I'm sure. Trouble is – the way you handle things I'd have to come back again wouldn't I?'

'Would you?'

'Oh, I think so.' Vanner looked again at the ceiling, then he noticed the bloodstains not yet scrubbed from the wall. Getting up from his stool he crossed the floor and paused at the spoiled baize of the pool table. He glanced down at the mess and then looked at the wall once more. 'That'll need painting,' he said. 'And the ceiling? Don't know what you're going to do with that?'

'I'll manage.'

Vanner nodded and moved back towards him. 'Sure you will, Jim. But somebody'll have to pay for it won't they.'

He sat down again as the bouncer came in with a tray of coffee. He set it down on the bar and some of it spilled into the saucers. Jimmy hissed and took a beer towel to the spillage. He waved the bouncer away and passed a cup each to Vanner and Jimmy.

'Young Young,' Vanner said as he sipped. 'The black with the shooter, Jimmy. His name is Young Young.'

'Yeah? I wouldn't know now would I. Don't mix with the blacks.'

'Course not.' Vanner looked sideways at him. 'Dealer. Crack. Nasty nasty bastard. Well . . .' He motioned to the ceiling again. 'You know that already.'

Carter finished his cigarette and buried it in the ashtray. He looked keenly at Vanner. 'Is there anything else you wanted?'

Vanner nodded. 'I want Young Young, Jimmy. I know you want him too now, but I want him really bad. I'd like to get him before you do. In fact you could save yourself a whole bunch of trouble by giving him up to me.'

Carter laughed then. 'Now I'd never thought ye'd go soft in the head, Mr Vanner. Not you, what was it – soldier from Belfast in the old days. You remember the old days, Mr Vanner?'

Vanner leaned one arm on the bar. 'Oh, I remember, Jimmy.'

'Then you know you're wasting your time.' Carter pushed himself off his stool. 'I don't know the name, Mr Vanner. And if I did I wouldn't give it to you. Now,' he looked at both of their faces. 'If ye don't mind I've got a ceiling to fix.'

Outside, Jimmy unlocked the car. 'Laid down a marker if nothing else, Guv.'

Vanner looked up the steps to where the crop-haired bouncer was still watching them.

'Not that it'll do us any good.' He got back in the car. 'If Carter finds Young Young he's history.'

Jimmy made a face. 'Young Young's mean, Guv.'

'No.' Vanner shook his head. 'Carter's mean, Jim. Young Young's just an amateur.'

'Balls to go in there though.'

Again Vanner shook his head. 'Lack of brains, Jim. Just lack of brains.'

He talked as they drove. 'Jimmy Carter ran the Belfast brigade of the IPLO in the late seventies. I knew him when I was a soldier over there. I did a tour when I was eighteen, before I went to Sandhurst. Carter was big news, though more to do with organised crime than politics. IPLO were gangsters. I mean real gangsters, not like this posse we're chasing. Their outfit went to war with PIRA and got wasted. Carter played both sides against the middle and shipped himself over here. He's still a hardman, Jim. And I mean the *Irish* meaning of hardman.'

* * *

Back at Campbell Row Jimmy went down to his desk in the AIU and found Tim Carver from Immigration there with DC Eldson from Harlesden Crime Group. Carver, Plug to his back, being tall and skinny like the character out of the Beano, was Mr Wannabe Copper and Jimmy Crack despised him. He sat there with his arms folded, waiting for him.

'Holden Biggs,' he said.

'Who?'

'Holden Biggs. The black who got slapped in Jimmy Carter's snooker hall.'

Jimmy moved papers on his desk. 'What about him?'

'Young Young hit him.' He smiled, showing his crooked teeth. 'I got my snouts, James.'

Jimmy folded his arms and sat on the edge of the desk. 'Young Young's flagged to me.'

'Yeah and Biggs is an illegal alien. I want him out of the country.'

'Then go and get him, Tim.'

'I will.' Carver stood up. 'He's running with the Governor Generals in Tottenham. He was holed up at Carmel Connolly's flat.'

'Was he?'

'Yeah. He was.' Carver stepped closer to him. 'Just came to tell you, James. Next time I get a line on Carmel – she's mine.'

Young Young twirled an unlit cigarette like a mini baton between long fingers. He lounged in the chair in Carmel's ground-floor flat and looked at Stepper-Nap looking back at him.

Carmel came in from the kitchen and Stepper flicked his hand at her. 'Close the door behind you.' She disappeared and Stepper glowered at Young Young. 'A fuckin' Uzi. Where the fuck you get off, man?'

'Pussy.' Young Young half-closed his eyes.

'What?'

'Called me a fuckin' pussy.'

'Oh wow, baby.'

'Messing with my name, man. Messing with my name.' Young Young shook his head.

'You is a black twat, Young Young.' Stepper got up out of the chair and looked down at him. Young Young drew back his lips.

'I ain't looking for no war, man.' Stepper levelled his hand at him. 'Not from Tottenham. And certainly not from no Jimmy fuckin' Carter.' He shook his head. 'You really fucked up, baby. I don't know that I can fix it.'

'Then don't. I ain't scared of no Irishman.'

'No? You should be. Carter'll kill you, baby. Kill you really slow.'

Young Young snorted. 'Not if I kill him first.'

Stepper sat down again and blew out his cheeks. 'Names, man. Where you get off worrying about names?'

'I get off all right. I just get off is all.'

Stepper shook his head. 'I tell you, man. You lay low till I think about this.'

'I ain't scared, Daddy.'

'I ain't talking about scared. I'm talking about my business. The business that buys your suits, that puts gas in your car. I got plans, Young Young. You ain't gonna mess them up.' He got up again. 'You lay low and you lose that shooter you hear. I hear you been fucking with me – I fuck you. You got that.'

For a moment the silence was brittle. Stepper-Nap stood there with his hands by his sides, looking down at the coiled form of his bodyguard.

'Don't say those things to me, man.' Young Young's voice was a whisper.

Stepper curled his lip. 'Listen to you, man. Just listen.' He leaned very close to him then, their noses all but together. 'I'm the Daddy, remember. I pay your wages. You. You is just a soldier.'

Frank Weir addressed the briefing, nine o'clock in the morning. Ryan sat at his desk with Tony Rob perched on the edge of it and Pamela across from them. Fat-Bob Davies sat squeezed into the seat alongside. The rest of the team were silent as Weir flicked through the Holmes report. Pictures of Jessica Turner with half her head missing were massed on the wall behind him.

'We have a body,' Weir said. 'And we have a cottage in the country where she went OTS for the weekend. We don't have a lover yet. What's happening with that?'

Pamela stood up. 'We're covering her workplace, Guv. But so far we don't have any possibles.'

'Nobody?'

'Everyone's alibi'd,' Pierce said.

Weir glanced at him then back at Pamela. 'What else?'

'We're checking the Turners' social circle.'

'And?'

'Nothing so far.'

Weir sat down on the edge of the desk and looked at Morrison. Morrison cleared his throat. 'The gun – we know was a Tokarev,' he said. 'Eastern Europe. You know that Lambeth have sent it over to Ulster for checks.'

'Guns get about, Sir,' Ryan said.

Morrison looked at him and nodded. 'They do, Sid. But Lambeth are right to check.'

'How long till we know if they find anything?'

'Not long now. A week or so maybe.'

Weir took over again. 'We had a call from a man who claimed to have seen the subject on the Friday she went away. New Forest,' he said. 'Quiet road on the way to Fordingbridge. The cottage is just outside Little Woodfalls.' He went on to tell them all that he and Ryan had learned from Michael Case. 'Lab Liaison have done the business on the car again,' he added. 'It was clean. No sign of anyone being in the back who shouldn't have been there. Swept and hoovered. She was obviously very particular.'

'And nothing was reported?' Morrison asked.

Weir looked round at him and shook his head. 'Case told us that Jessica was going to report it. He claims to have given her his name, but she didn't write it down.'

Ryan flipped open his A4 pad. 'Case lives in Cadnam. It's near Southampton. He's forty years old and lives with his mum. He also owns a shotgun.'

Silence. Tony Rob looked at Weir. 'What about the dummy?'

'There wasn't one. Or at least there isn't. Local boys did a sweep of the road for us and found nothing.' He paused. 'Somebody could've been there though. The road is open, ponies wandering about – that kind of thing. There could've been another car. Plenty of places to pull off unnoticed, especially in weather like it was that night. There could've been a third body.'

Pamela made a face and Weir caught her eye. 'Pam?'

'Just wondering, Guv. Why would Case come forward with

a story like that if it wasn't true?'

Weir looked briefly beyond her, then he caught Ryan's eye. 'Good point. He read about it in the papers. He's a loner who lives with his mum.' He made a face. 'He's probably telling the truth but we all know it happens. How many callers did Yorkshire get claiming to know the Ripper?'

Fuller stuck a hand up. 'Forgetting Case for a moment, Guv'nor,' he said. 'If the gun's Russian – maybe we should talk to Interpol.'

Weir looked at him. 'Why?'

'Maybe there's some kind of Eastern European Crime Register we can look at. Gun could've been used somewhere else.'

Ryan started to laugh and everyone looked round at him.

'What's funny, Sid?' Fuller's face flushed red.

Ryan lifted a hand. 'That is. There is no European Crime Register. They're not *quite* that sophisticated. Mate of mine from SO13 was sent over to Yugoslavia a couple of years ago. Bomb went off in Slovenia, long before any of this Bosnian shit hit the fan. Some old toad sat on it, blew bits of him everywhere. Crime scene a mile square.'

'What's your point, Sid?' Weir broke in on him.

'I'm just saying, Guv. Sophisticated they ain't. Old Bill over there rounded up a bunch of possibles for the bomb. They got a sniffer dog to walk up and down and nicked the first geezer he barked at.'

'All right, all right.' Weir made a calming motion to curtail the laughter. 'We don't have very much. We know that. But what we do have is some hair, a broken nail and some pink wool. Pathologist has confirmed that – given the angle of trajectory – the height of the shootist is small enough to be a woman. Turner has told us that his wife owns no angora sweaters. She didn't wear false nails and she didn't have black hair. Unless he's hiding a bit on the side himself we're looking for a woman.'

'So Case is just a waster then?' Ryan said.

'Maybe. Maybe not. I want him re-interviewed.' He looked at the faces of the others. 'I want the lover found. And I want the husband to tell us about anyone he knows who wears false nails and has long black hair. I want the house-to-house done again.'

They groaned in unison. 'That's the way it is. We've done it once and got nowhere.' Weir broke off and looked at them. 'I also want Turner himself looked at. I want to know if he was playing away. I want to know what state the marriage was in. I want to know about money, life assurance, the whole bit. Come on, people. Let's go to work shall we?'

Tim Phelan was nervous. He sat in his front room, watching the lunchtime edition of Home and Away on the TV. Angel was stealing money from Alf. Stupid Australian rubbish. This was his life now, watching bronzed complete bodies on the TV; all shiny with sweat and the surf. Smiles and long hair and earrings and too many characters to get a grip on. But this was his life, every day he would sit here, trying not to look down at his own shattered body and compare it with the whole ones that lived and loved on the screen.

Every morning he would wake to the silence and after a while drag his half-body from his bed, press it into ill-fitting clothes and spend the day dreaming of life and limbs and the time that was lost to him now. But that was until Thursday. Thursday he had seen her for the first time, sitting out there in the park on the children's swings with her tight little body and her long black hair.

At first the image had been pleasing. He could still be stirred even now, with no legs and half an arm. His one clean hand, good only for changing channels and masturbating. On the TV the images seemed to blur and he felt the nag of his bladder, ever-present almost these days: he hated himself for his weakness. Reaching for the remote control he flicked the set off and pressed his chair into motion. At the specially lowered window he looked out over the park.

March wind chipped at the day, the sky a haze of cloud like rippled sand. The woman sat on the swings, head down, long black hair dripping over her face. For the second time in as many days a chill crept into his veins. She looked up and for an instant their eyes met, then she got up and walked away.

Instinct. Years of training; every morning searching under his car, sidearm wherever he went. Till one day he looked the wrong way and stepped on a booby trap. And then he was down, watching his legs cartwheeling away from him. No pain, just shock and a sense of disbelief; the emptying of an unfilled bladder and a vague sense of embarrassment. And lying there thinking that semtex explodes at seven thousand metres per second. He wondered if they would find his legs four miles away. Booted feet sailing over buildings or crashing through a window or just disintegrating into a mush for all the good they were now.

In the hospital he had wanted to die. That was after the morphine had worn off, the cheery fool's optimism that came with a filling up of the drug. The first time his wife (long gone now) had visited, tears in her eyes and him white-faced with his jaws clamped, fighting a desire to scream at her. The ambulance and the pain, still conscious. Blood loss. He had begged them to slow down, turn off the bloody siren, dim those flashing lights and amble along till his blood dried up and he could slip into the oblivion that by rights should have been his. But they saved him. That's what they called it. He looked down at himself now and felt the tingle of fear as the woman paused and looked back at him.

Thin Hand Billy sat with Bigger Dan and watched Ginger Bill wash crack out of fine-grained cocaine. A single light bulb glowed above the stove; black cloth curtains, fastened to the sills, blocked all light from the windows.

He stood in black jeans and a T-shirt, red hair spiked straight up from his head, a roll-up cigarette dangling in the corner of his mouth. He hummed to himself as he worked, spooning three parts coke into two empty Lucozade bottles and then pouring them two-thirds full with water. On the stove, two huge pots used for jam-making slowly heated water. When the water in the pans came to boiling point Ginger Bill added the Bicarbonate of Soda to the bottles. Solution fizzing, he placed the bottles into the water. They frothed bubbles up the neck and he added a touch more of the baking powder.

Thin Hand Billy lit a cigarette and clutched it between the fingers of his withered hand. He had been born with it, named as a kid and it stuck. He and Bigger Dan cut the crack into rocks and weighed them on Tanita scales. Once weighed they wrapped them into individual smokes with cling-film.

Bigger Dan yawned and lit a cigarette, waving the smoke from his face. 'How's it going?'

Ginger Bill glanced round at him and shrugged. 'Fine. These the last two?'
'For tonight yeah?'
'You taking those?'
Bigger Dan nodded and looked then at Billy who took his knife to the mound before him.
'Get the weight right, shithead. We ain't giving it away.'
Billy swore at him and concentrated on the solidified solution.
On the stove the water was dying in the bottles, the fizz still gurgling but with less ferocity now. In a few minutes it would cease completely and the ready-made rock would sink to the bottom of the bottle. Then Bill would pour off the residue of the water and the crack would be ready for cutting into single smokes at twenty pounds a time. A single smoke and you're hooked. He didn't smoke it himself. Thin Hand Billy was a crackhead and look at the slime ball he was.
Bill sat on the stool and watched the solution. Bigger Dan got up and came over to him. 'I could do that.'
Ginger Bill grinned to himself. 'Go on then,' he said.
When the last of the solution was ready and all the cocaine used up, Ginger Bill opened a beer and looked at the pile of merchandise as Dan and Billy separated it into paper bags.
'Who's coming for it?'
'Pretty Boy. We're meeting him downstairs.'
Bill went to the blacked-out window and eased the curtain aside. Cars moved up and down the main road outside and he could make out the lights in the flats opposite.
'You heard about Young Young, man?' Dan asked him. Bill let the curtain drop again and looked back at him. 'Fuckin' nutter ain't he.'
'I wouldn't tell him that.'
'No. But true all the same.'
'Goes his own way. Step's really pissed off. Young Young shouldn't dis' the Daddy like that.'
Bill nodded. 'Pretty Boy know?'
'Yeah.'
'What's he saying?'
'He don't give a fuck. He don't know Jimmy Carter.'

Detective Chief Inspector Westbrook took the phonecall at his desk in the offices of the Anti-Terrorist Branch at Scotland Yard. He had been flicking through what they had so far on the South Quay bombing the month before.

'Westbrook.'

'Ops room, John.'

'What is it?'

'Just took a call from over the water. DPOA in Belfast. They've had a call from an ex RUC Special Branch man in Yorkshire. Wheelchair case, medicalled out in '86.'

'What about him?'

'Reckons he's being looked at.'

Westbrook frowned. 'Got a number for him?'

He came off the phone to Tim Phelan and left the office. He was a big man, six four and built like the number eight he had been. DI Johnson came out of the squad room.

'Word from Box, Guv. Possible.'

'Anybody we know?'

Johnson nodded.

'Be with you in a minute.'

Westbrook walked down the corridor and went into the Bomb Data Centre. Tania Briggs had the heavy-duty battery open on the desk before her. Jack Swann from the squad room squatted next to her, turning a Mark 15 timing device over in his hands.

'What you got, Tania?'

Briggs looked up at Westbrook. 'Cunning bastards, Guv'nor.' He indicated the bottom of the battery when it had been cut and welded back on. Safe but still packed with yellow-coloured semtex. 'Mercury tilt to set off the timer. Eleven hours fifteen minutes later it's sat in the cage all nicely primed.' He pointed to the second mercury switch with the end of his pencil. 'Somebody picks it up . . .'

'And bye bye fifteenth floor.' Swann pursed his lips.

Westbrook looked at Swann. 'Box've come up with a nominal.'

'You want me in the squad room?'

Westbrook shook his head. 'Got another job for you.'

Swann squinted at him.

'Where's Webb?'

'Throwing sherry, Guv'nor.'

Westbrook looked blank. 'What?'

'Los Remos Bar. His Spanish drinker. They've got some promotion on. He's a dab hand with the long spoon.'

'You mean there's Spanish totty there.'

Swann grinned at him.

George Webb threw sherry. He stood on the chequer-board parquet floor with his feet slightly apart as he spooned the sherry high and dropped it in the glass. For the umpteenth time tonight he did not spill a drop. The Gonzalez Byas rep watched him, a broad smile on crimson lips; thick dark hair ebbed against the shoulders of her waist-length braided jacket. Skintight leggings and boots. She looked as though she had just come from the Bull Ring.

He woke next to her in the morning and tasted stale sherry on his breath. She lay on her back, hair scattering over the pillow, the duvet gathered just above her pelvis. The dark swell of her nipples was easy.

Webb groaned and rolled over. He should have gone home last night. He really should have gone home. From the pile of his clothes on the chair his pager bleeped. He rubbed his eyes and sat up. Drink swelled in his belly and he burped, then rubbed his eyes again. His head thumped as he moved to the pile of clothes and looked at the face of his pager.

He put on jeans and stretched his polo shirt over his head. Maria was still sleeping and he fought the urge to bend and kiss her one last time. Instead he sat on the floor, took the phone from the table and dialled SO13. He got the Ops room on the sixteenth floor.

'George Webb, Harry. Put me through to Westbrook will you.'

The line clicked and then the ice of Westbrook's voice bit into his flesh.

'Where are you?'

'Wasted, Guv. Show me a day's self-inflicted.'

He heard Westbrook laugh. 'No chance, Webby. You don't have days off for hangovers. Get your arse in here. I've got a job for you.'

Webb sat where he was and gazed longingly at exposed Spanish nipple. He sighed and hung up the phone.

Vanner spoke to the Drug Squad team at Campbell Row. He

and Jimmy had driven by the amusement arcade on Uxbridge Road and spotted both Stepper-Nap's Mercedes and Young Young's Rover. They had got nowhere with the doctor so far. That morning Jimmy had been on the phone to his informant in Jamaica who told them that Stepper-Nap's brother was organising another shipment. So far he had no date or carrier but the word was on the street. He would call when he found out the times.

'He that good – your snout, Jim?' Sammy McCleod asked.

'Not let me down so far.'

'So we need a plane, an airport and a patsy.'

Jimmy nodded. 'Pretty Boy organises the collections. He'll send Jig or someone to pick up the girls.'

'We'll set up a rolling plot,' Vanner said. 'Pick them up and follow them wherever they go. The snout in Winchester gave us the doctor. If they go there then Stepper'll get involved.' He looked at Jimmy. 'That right?'

Jimmy nodded. 'Likes to supervise those himself.'

China grinned. 'Maybe he likes to watch.'

Vanner tapped the photograph of Young Young sitting with Carmel they had blown up on the copier. 'We might get another angle,' he said.

'Somebody giving him up?' Anne asked.

Vanner shook his head. 'Not Young Young. I doubt we'll get to him before Jimmy Carter does. No. The girl, Carmel. She's got a ground-floor flat on Radcliffe Road.' He looked at Jimmy.

Jimmy stood up. 'Stepper-Nap,' he said. 'The Don. He's a diplomatic bastard for all his other faults. He's been at pains to keep the Governor Generals, that's a Yardie Massive from Tottenham, out of his patch. He's a British Black but his Jamaican connections are good. His brother organises the coke coming over from his nightclub in Kingston. The local plod is on to him but he pays them off.

'He uses Carmel's flat to house illegal Jamaicans as a favour to the Tottenham posse. That keeps them sweet and his manor is left alone. The lad that Young Young smacked at Jimmy Carter's is Holden Biggs. He's an illegal that immigration are trying to catch. He stayed at Carmel's for a while when he landed. That's where he got wrong with Young Young. I don't know what went down between them but it doesn't take much. The hammering he dished out will cause Stepper a problem.

How big I don't know, but it'll be problem.'

'Anne looked blank. 'What's this got to do with Carmel?'

'Plug is looking to bust her,' Jimmy went on.

'Carver?' Sammy curled his lip.

'The same.'

Jimmy grinned at Vanner as Sammy sat shaking his head. 'He wants to spin Carmel's flat the next time he gets word that she's holding. If Stepper's looking to sort things with Tottenham she might be doing that sooner rather than later.'

'Walks a fine line this Daddy,' China said.

Vanner leaned on the desk. 'Immigration can't do a turn on Carmel without us knowing. The address is flagged to Jimmy and I've had words with the AIU Guv'nor who's had words with Plug's bosses. They won't move without us knowing about it.'

'So we sit in on it, Guv?' Anne asked.

'Yes. When they nick Carmel we'll have words with her – see what kind of a deal we can do. In the meantime we keep tabs on the word from Jamaica and keep up the OP at Pretty Boy's address.'

Stepper-Nap sat in his front room with his youngest child on his lap. He swirled the ends of his fingers through the boy's matted, curling hair and looked at the TV screen without seeing it. Pretty Boy had been on the phone asking about the load due from Jamaica. Ginger Bill had made up the final batch now and it was already on the street. Pretty Boy was anxious to move. Stepper sat now in the semi-stillness of the room while his son wriggled on his lap and giggled at the antics of the cartoon characters on the TV. Stepper's big flat face was still, though lines edged his brow in a frown. Pretty Boy troubled him, gathering his own troops in the background. Young Young had made that situation much worse and he had to move on the new market soon. But Young Young, the brainless prick, might've fucked that up for good. Holden Biggs was a turd with a mouth and Young Young ought to know better. Jimmy Carter of all people. Why couldn't it have been a pub or the street or something?

He did not need trouble from Tottenham and he certainly did not need any from Irish Jimmy Carter. He placed his son on the floor and told his wife he was going out.

* * *

Eilish sat across the table from him, one leg swinging over the other and clicked her tongue. 'This is going to cost you, baby.'

Stepper grinned his sloppy Eilish grin and inclined his head. 'Special favour, honey. Special reward for special favours.'

'Very bloody special.'

'So you can do it?'

She threw back her head then and looked down the line of her nose. 'I can do it. If I want to.'

'And you want to?'

'You make it worth my while and I want to.'

'Then do it.'

'When?

'Tonight. Carter'll already be planning who'll get Young Young's head for their birthday.'

James put the children to bed and read them a story. He could hear Eilish and Mary-Anne talking in the kitchen downstairs. Funny how Mary-Anne should show up again after all these years. When the children were tucked up he went down and found the two women smoking cigarettes in the kitchen. Mary-Anne smiled at him and bit her nail. Long black hair and pale skin like his sister's.

'You okay, Mary Anne?'

She nodded. 'Doing well so I am.'

'Where you living now?'

'Fulham.'

'Nice.'

'Not bad.'

'You working?'

'Aye.'

'Good job is it?'

'Cleaner, Jamie.'

He grinned at her.

When she had gone he followed his sister upstairs and watched her get ready to go out.

'Where you going tonight?'

'Just out, James. I'll not be late.'

'Don't bring the mean one back.'

She looked at him then, her chin high. 'I'll bring back who I want.'

James let breath go in a hiss. 'Why d'you let them both into your bed?'

'I like them both.'

'Why black?'

'What's wrong with black? You're not racist are you, Jamie?' She fastened her dress and studied herself in the mirror.

'What's wrong with our people, Eilish?'

'Like your Irish girlfriend you mean?'

He looked away. 'Don't.'

'Then *don't* me either.'

He sat on her bed and she slipped on black high-heeled shoes. 'There was only ever one of our people,' she said softly. 'You know that, Jamie.'

He looked beyond her to the mirror and caught the light that flared in her eyes. 'Yes,' he said. 'I know that.'

He left her then to finish her make-up and went downstairs to the lounge. There he stood in the silence and stared at the photograph of their mother. It had been taken years before, part of a family set when she was still young and their father was still one of them. He was long gone now and their mother was back across the border with her family. He wished they were back there. Things had been different then. If they had stayed then maybe things would still be different.

He had been seven when their father left. Eilish eleven and already headstrong and going her own way. She had kept going ever since, too much like her father so their mother told him. He was more like her, dark-haired and gentler than the fire that seemed to bleed from their father. Not once had he made contact. Australia or New Zealand or somewhere, no doubt remarried with other children to call his own. Their mother had struggled when he left but the neighbours were kindly and the priest was a good one and they managed. But when Eilish was nineteen their mother vacated the flat and headed south to be with her own sick mother. Tacitly Eilish took on the flat and James had had the choice to stay with her or go south with their mother. He had chosen to stay with his sister and he had been with her ever since.

Eight

Eilish took a cab to Kilburn and left it outside Biddy Mulligans on the corner of Willesden Lane. From there she walked the short distance to the side road and Jimmy Carter's snooker hall. Her heels sharp against rain-washed pavement, she came to the doors of the club, where the spiky-haired bouncer looked her up and down. His face was red and bloated like a bull frog, the collar of his trench coat turned up over a black bow tie.

'Yeah?'

'I want to see Jimmy.'

He leered at her. 'Jimmy don't want to see you.'

'Yes he does.' She stared at him, one leg protruding through the gap in her coat. 'Tell him Eilish McCauley is here.'

'You got an appointment?'

'I don't need an appointment.'

Jimmy was in his office behind the main hall. Eilish passed between the snooker tables and smelled fresh paint on the ceiling. He was working on his accounts, sitting at his desk behind the glass of the door, hair oiled flat, sleeves pushed up and a crystal tumbler at his elbow.

He did not look up when she went in, chunky fingers of his right hand punching the keys of a heavy, desktop calculator. Eilish stood before his desk watching the polished crown of his skull where it showed pink through the slicked rash of his hair. After a few moments he steepled his fingers and looked up at her out of piggy eyes that coiled into the flesh of his face.

'Eilish McCauley,' he said quietly. 'For a good Catholic girl you hang out with the wrong kind of people.'

They stared at one another for a long moment then Eilish glanced at the vacant chair on her side of the desk. Jimmy nodded and she sat down.

'You know why I'm here, Jimmy.'

'Do I now?'

'I think so. Young Young. He was acting on his own. It had nothing to do with Stepper-Nap.'

He sat back then and looked at her, a crooked smile on his face. 'Is that a fact?'

'You know it is, Jimmy. Stepper wouldn't fuck up like that.'

'Wouldn't he? I never know with blacks. How come you keep such company, Eilish?'

She did not reply, crossed her legs and placed both hands on one exposed knee. Carter watched her, his eyes flicking a line between her legs and her face. He touched his lips with his tongue.

'Stepper doesn't want trouble with you, Jimmy. It's the last thing he wants what with the deal and everything.'

'Deal is it? That's what you're calling it now.' He shook his head, sitting back with the weight of his belly pressing against the strained buttons of his shirt. Suddenly he sat forward and jabbed his index finger at her. 'Your man ought to keep his mutt on a leash.'

She nodded. 'I know it. He knows it too.' She paused then. 'He didn't know it was going down, Jimmy. If he had known Holden Biggs was here he'd have sent someone.'

'To stop Young Young?' Carter shook his head again. 'Only one way to stop him.' He squinted at her then. 'Does Stepper know you're screwing him, Eilish?'

Eilish looked away from him and he laughed. 'Course he doesn't. Seems like everyone else does though eh. That's the way of it isn't it. Always the last one to know.' He sat back again and rubbed his stomach with his fingers. 'Young Young's got an attitude, girl. Thinks he's tougher than he is.'

Eilish moved in her seat, the air brackish between them. She could smell his sweat, the whiskey, the taint of cigar smoke on his breath. He looked between her legs.

'Stepper doesn't want trouble,' she said again. 'He wants to make things right.'

His face clouded then and he stared at her. 'Listen, lady. That black bastard walked into my club with a gun. He wasted a head then shot holes in my ceiling. You think I'm just going to sit here and take it?' He laughed again only there was no hint of merriment in his voice. 'You walk in here with your skirt split to the hip and tell me that your crack man wants no trouble. You talk about deals, Eilish.' He pinched his lips together then, nostrils flaring. 'Maybe there aren't any deals. I could give him plenty of trouble if I want to.'

'He knows it, Jimmy. Why d'you think I'm sat here?'

Again he sat back and again his eyes wandered her flesh through her clothes. 'And what exactly have you got to offer me? What can you do for me that'll stop me cutting Young Young off at the neck?'

She could feel him undressing her and she moved in the chair, perspiration sticking to the seat of her dress.

'Stepper wants the deal to go through, Jimmy.'

'You're not answering my question, girl. What've you got that I want?'

And then she steeled herself, hated herself for it, thought momentarily of Tommy and his wild green eyes and slowly hitched up her dress.

She watched his mouth open a fraction, felt the sudden heat of his breath as his eyes moved to her breasts, swollen now against her dress and then to her belly and her thighs as the dress crept further up them. She wasn't wearing any knickers and a few seconds later he knew it. She opened her own mouth, letting breath trapped in her throat exhale in a hiss. Carter's eyes stalked and he shifted in his seat. He looked her in the eyes then.

'Think that'll do it do ye?'

Eilish stared back at him. 'I think so, Jimmy. Don't you?'

Afterwards he re-fastened his trousers and Eilish smoothed away the creases in her dress. She did not feel as dirty as she thought she would, but Stepper owed her big time. Carter was quiet, chastened almost; as if the Catholicism of his past had finally caught up with him there in that office in Kilburn. He lit two cigarettes, passed one to her and poured fresh whiskey into glasses.

He sat back in his chair and rubbed a finger under his nose. 'What else do I get?'

'If you smooth the way for me, Jimmy, you get a cut.'

'I want half.'

She shook her head slowly. 'You won't get half.'

'You're in no position to bargain.'

'Come on, Jimmy. Stepper won't give up half.'

He looked at her and smiled.

'I want to meet with Cahal,' she said quietly.

He swallowed whiskey and wiped his mouth. 'A lot of people worry about Cahal, Eilish. Not as reliable as he was.'

'Is that right?'

He nodded. 'How long since you've been home?'

'A while.'

'You're out of touch.'

'Am I?' She sat forward then and placed her glass on the desk. 'Look, Jimmy. Stepper doesn't want a war but he will fight you. He'll lose but he will fight. You might lose some. This way you lose nothing and you get a slice of anything that goes on.'

'Diplomat now are you.'

'Five grand, Jimmy. Five grand to make a phonecall.'

'Two phonecalls,' he said. 'Ten grand.'

'I'll have to talk to Stepper.'

'No you won't – you'll tell him.'

She shook her head. 'Come on, Jimmy. Five off the top and their cut? No point in doing business at all.'

'You let me worry about their cut, Eilish.'

'And Young Young?'

He looked at her then, brows drawn into lines in the thick skin of his face. 'He'll take a beating. I can't let it go. What would people think?'

'How bad a beating?'

'It'll still work, darling.'

She stood up then. 'So I can tell Stepper.'

'You can tell him.'

She turned to go.

'Eilish.'

She looked back again.

'I've got AIDS.'

'Fuck you, Jimmy.'

Webb and Swann from the Anti-Terrorist Branch drove up the A1 to Yorkshire in Webb's Cavalier. His bomb gear was stowed in two bags, one in the boot with his ballistic helmet and body armour, the other on the back seat. The detachable blue light filled the doorwell in front of Swann's feet.

'So tell me about Conchita, Webby.'

'Conchita?'

Swann grinned at him. 'The Spanish bird.'

Webb chuckled then, remembering crimson nipples in darkened flesh. He shifted his weight in the seat and grinned at him. 'Where d'you think I was when the Guv'nor bleeped me.'

'You old bastard.' Swann looked through the windscreen and shook his head. 'I'm much better-looking than you.'

'Yep.' Webb overtook a lorry in the outside lane.

'So how d'you do it?'

'Some of us've got it, Jack.'

'But not you.'

Webb tapped his skull at the temple. 'Baby blues, buddy. Paul Newman eyes. Gets them every time.'

Swann squinted at him then and was caught by the look he got out of piercing blue eyes. 'Bollocks,' was all he could think of to say.

Swann was attached to 4 Investigation Squad, George Webb, an Exhibits Officer, the second call out man for any bomb blast in London and first for anywhere outside London. Crime Scene Manager. Both of them had worked on the Heathrow Airport attacks. They had been looking for mortars on the ground with only minutes to go before the airport was due to re-open. Swann standing there asking Webb what they looked like with one upended in the turf all but between his legs. Webb had never let him forget it. Between them they had rigged up the Canary Wharf road sign on the wall of the Exhibits office after the ceasefire officially ended in February.

Webb drove quickly, Swann scouring the map. 'Pickhill,' he said. 'I think it's the Thirsk turn off.' He glanced at Webb. 'What else did Westbrook tell you?'

Webb made a face. 'Only what RUC told him. Ex B Squad man from the eighties. Got blown up pretty badly. Reckons someone is taking a look at him.'

'The woman in the park with no kids.'

Webb nodded. 'Three separate occasions.'

Swann lifted an eyebrow. 'Why would PIRA take a gander at an ex RUC who they'd blown up already?'

'The Paddy factor, Jack. Why do they do anything?'

They left the A1 and made their way to the tiny village of Pickhill. On the right they passed The Nags Head pub and Webb looked wistfully through the window.

'Theakston's,' he muttered to himself.

'I thought you only drank Spanish beer.'

'Mate, I'll drink anything.'

They found the house that fronted the park at the far end of the village and Swann turned his collar against the wind that lifted from the east. 'Always was cold up here,' he said.

'Remember that hide we found?'

Webb nodded and locked the car door.

The house was a bungalow with unusually low windows. There was no doorstep, just a ramp. Webb pressed the doorbell. 'We should've brought him a bottle or something.' Through the glass they saw a wheelchair approach the door and then it was opened and half a man with thin black hair looked up at them, trousers dangling empty where his legs should have been.

'Tim Phelan?' Webb said.

The man nodded. Webb flipped open his warrant card. 'DS Webb. DS Swann,' he said. 'SO13.'

Phelan smiled then, his whole face lighting up. 'Come in, lads. Come in.'

He laid his only hand on the operating knob of his chair and made a one hundred and eighty degree turn. Webb and Swann followed him into the hall. They closed the door and went through to the lounge. Swann went to the huge flat window and glanced out. He could see a children's park with swings. The park was empty. Phelan parked his chair in front of the silent TV screen and looked at them both. 'Good of you to come, lads. Cup of tea is it?'

Webb nodded. 'Tea'd be good, Tim. Yeah.'

Phelan made tea and wheeled it in on a tray balanced on what remained of his knees. Swann took the tray from him and set it on the coffee table.

'So what's happening, fellas?' Phelan said. 'You got anyone for the Docklands yet?'

Webb grinned at him. 'Miss it do you?'

'Course I miss it. My life for twenty years.'

Webb nodded. 'We're looking at nominals, Tim. You know the form.'

Phelan shifted himself in the chair. 'Knew it couldn't last,' he said. 'The ceasefire.'

Webb looked at Swann. 'We've never stopped working, Tim. Since '94 we've been busier than ever.' Webb passed him a mug of tea. 'What's the story here? Word from your mates back home is that someone's taking a look at you.'

Phelan's face darkened. 'Sounds stupid doesn't it. I mean what would anybody be wanting with me when they've more than got me already.'

Webb glanced at his shattered body. 'Shit happens, Tim.'

'You're right. It does.' He looked down at himself then smiled. 'I knew the risks when I joined the reserve.'

Swann stirred sugar into his tea. 'Tell us about this bird in the park.'

Phelan told them all he could then, the fact that he had seen her three times, sitting on the swings apparently watching his house. As far as he could tell she was a stranger in the village and she had no children with her. He shook his head. 'Probably nothing, lads. But when you've been in the job twenty years you get to know the feeling.'

Swann's face was serious. 'What did she look like?'

'Not very tall. Dark hair, quite long. I couldn't see much of her face.' He shrugged. 'It was on those swings out there. Must be all of fifty yards.'

Webb took his tea to the window and looked the length and breadth of the park. It was empty, the swings rattling on their chains in the gathering pace of the wind. 'You saw her three times you say?' He looked back at Phelan then, who nodded. 'Different days?'

'Two different days. Twice the first day, then the following morning.'

'Last week?'

'Yeah.'

Swann placed his empty mug on the table and sat back in the chair. He glanced above the fireplace where an old photo of Phelan, able bodied, in uniform, looked down on the room. 'What did she do?'

'Nothing. She just came across the park, sat on those swings there and watched.'

Swann glanced at Webb.

Phelan looked from one of them to the other. 'She could've been anybody. Probably just my nerves. Shot to fuck like the rest of me.'

There was silence after than then Webb said quietly: 'You were right to make the call.'

Phelan nodded. 'DPOA,' he said. 'Lot of disabled RUC's like me. Good of you blokes to come all the way from London.'

'The job, Tim.'

'Right.' He moved the wheels of his chair with a little humming sound from the electric motor. 'You looking at any female nominals right now?'

Webb pulled a face. 'We're always looking, but nobody in particular.'

He crouched by the table and patted Phelan on his withered knee. 'We'll make a few calls, Tim. Got mates up here. If she's about – and something is going down – you'll have nothing to worry about.'

They left him then and went back outside. He sat in his chair with the front door open and watched them till they were both back in the car. Webb started the engine and Phelan closed the front door.

'Poor bastard.' Swann shook his head. 'I wouldn't want to live like that.' He glanced at Webb, who chewed the end of a fingernail. 'What d'you reckon?'

Webb shrugged and put the car in first. 'I don't know mate. Maybe it's nothing. Cracks beginning to show. Must get pretty paranoid living up here on his own in that state.' He glanced back at the house. 'Let's make a few calls.'

Ryan sat at Jessica Turner's old desk and went through her client list. She had been a marketing consultant, out and about a lot. Clients. Maybe she was sleeping with one of them. An effeminate man hovered in the doorway and looked from Ryan to Pamela Richards who was flicking through a computer printout.

'Can I get you coffee?' the man asked them.

Ryan grunted and looked back at the list in front of them. 'CableTech,' he said to Pamela.

'What?'

'Security firm in Bournemouth. Her biggest account.' He looked from the listing to the open A4 diary Jessica had used. 'She went down there a lot.'

Pamela raised her eyebrows. 'The other side of the New Forest. You want to pay them a visit?'

* * *

They parked their Mondeo in the carpark of CableTech Security, a large square building built in red brick on the industrial estate on the outskirts of Bournemouth. Ryan flipped away a cigarette and looked up at the building. 'Johnson?' he said to her.

Pamela checked her notes and nodded. 'Marketing Director.'

'Come on then.'

From the upstairs window Ray Kinane watched them from his desk. The car, their clothes, the conversation he had had with Johnson earlier. He swivelled his chair around and tapped a pencil on his desk.

Ryan and Pamela sat on a cloth-covered couch in reception while the blonde-haired girl behind the desk paged Paul Johnson for them. Ryan flicked through a copy of *Country Life* while they waited. Five minutes, then the glass-panelled door to the right of the desk swung open and a man in his late thirties breezed through. Brown loafers with tassles and cream-coloured chinos. His multi-coloured tie hung at the open neck of his denim shirt.

'Paul Johnson,' he said, offering his hand. 'Managing Director.'

Ryan introduced them both and they followed him to the corridor. They made their way through an open-plan office and up a flight of metallic stairs to his office. His desk was in black wood and shaped like a boomerang. A flat computer screen at one end and an Apple Mac laptop in the middle of it. He moved behind the desk and gestured to the chairs opposite.

'Jessica Turner,' he said when they were all seated. 'Unbelievable.' He lifted his hands, 'Just unbelievable.'

Ryan sat forward. 'You knew her well?'

'Pretty well, yes. We worked together for two years.' He leaned his elbows on the desk top. 'We re-structured two and a half years ago. Management buyout. The consultancy was recommended. Jessica in particular. She was very good. This department exists largely because of her.'

Pamela scribbled notes on her pad. 'What exactly did she do for you?' she asked him.

'Do?' He sat back. 'Christ. What didn't she do? She devised our whole marketing campaign when we split from our US parent.'

'Security,' Ryan said, glancing round the room. 'What kind of security?'
'CCTV. Alarm systems, that kind of thing.'
'Personal?'
'What?'
'For homes?'
'No. Corporate sector. Defence we specialise in. We're MOD-approved thanks to Jessica.'
'MOD.'
'Yes. We've tendered for air bases, that kind of thing. You know, sensitive installations. BNFL, that kind of thing.'
'And Jessica helped you with that. Was she qualified?'
'Excuse me?'
'Had she had experience of the market?'
'Now you come to mention it – I don't know. She must've. She was very good, Sergeant. I can tell you that much.'
Ryan stroked his chin. 'Did you know her personally?'
Johnson looked at him then. 'No,' he said slowly.
'You never met her outside work?'
'Once or twice maybe. We did promotional work at hotels now and then.'
'Just the two of you?'
Johnson lifted his eyebrows. 'We led the things but there were others, some of my colleagues, occasionally some of hers.'
Ryan studied him then. He wore an identity bracelet on his right wrist, no rings on his fingers. 'You married, Mr Johnson?'
'What's that got to do with anything?'
Ryan glanced at Pamela who laid her pad down on the desk. 'The weekend Jessica was murdered,' she said. 'We know she spent the Friday and Saturday night with someone. She rented a cottage in the New Forest. We believe she was with a man.'
'Not her husband,' Ryan added. 'He was in Ireland playing rugby.'
'You mean she was having an affair.' Johnson's face was colder now.
'We think so. We appealed for anybody who saw her that weekend to come forward but whoever she was with chose not to.'

Johnson smiled then. 'Hence the marriage question?'
'Pretty good reason to keep quiet. Wife and kids in the background.'
'But she was killed. Surely any reasonable man would come forward.'
'Maybe.' Ryan was watching him closely. 'Funny old world though isn't it. *Are* you married, Mr Johnson.'
'No, Sergeant. I'm not.'
'You're in a relationship though.'
Johnson sucked air through his teeth. 'I don't know that's relevant. If you're asking me whether I was having an affair with Jessica – the answer is no.'
Ryan sat back again. 'Fine,' he said. 'That's all we wanted to know.' He looked at Pamela. 'Thing is, Mr Johnson – we've been through her friends, workmates, the usual sources for these things and so far we've drawn a blank.'
'So you figured you'd look at her clients.'
'Your firm was the biggest,' Pamela said.
Johnson sat back and swivelled his chair from side to side. He looked from one to the other of them.
'You liked her?' Ryan asked him.
'Yes.'
'Attractive?'
'I suppose.'
'You didn't fancy her though?'
Johnson coloured again. 'I've told you. I wasn't having an affair with her.'
Ryan looked at him. 'Does happen though. Client relationship like that. Pretty woman. Good-looking bloke like you, working closely together.'
'I'm sure it does.' Johnson's lips were compressed. 'But not with me.'
They were quiet for a few moments then Pamela said, 'D'you mind telling us where you were the weekend of the 11th and 12th, Mr Johnson?'
'I can tell you exactly where I was. I was working at home.'
'On your own?'
'I live alone, yes.'
Ryan watched him carefully. 'This office is pretty close to the New Forest, Mr Johnson. You can see why we're interested.'
'Yes, I can see that.'

'Who else here would she speak to besides you?' Pamela asked him.

'Christ,' Johnson said. 'The marketing team. The sales force. The installation consultants.'

'Who?'

'Technical bods. She talked to just about everyone.'

Ryan sat forward and made an open-handed gesture. 'Look,' he said. 'We're just trying to figure out what went on. Playing away with another bloke's wife isn't a crime. But we need to talk to anyone who might've seen her that weekend.'

'And because I was on my own that makes me a suspect?'

'Not a suspect. No.'

'But a possible? Is that what you call it?'

Ryan sat back again.

Johnson seemed to steel himself then and sat forward. 'Okay,' he said. 'It's none of your business but I'll tell you.'

'Tell me what exactly?'

'Why it wasn't me with her that weekend.'

'And why was that?'

'Because I'm gay, Sergeant.'

Back in the incident room they saw Morrison and Weir deep in conversation in the IO's office. The door was closed. Fuller got up from his desk. 'Any joy with the client, Slips?' Ryan shook his head and flicked through the information sheets on his desk. 'Only real possible was the marketing director and he turned out to be a shirt lifter.'

Weir opened the office door and called to him. Ryan left his desk and went through. Morrison's face was dark, brows knitted heavily together.

'No joy with CableTech, Guv'nor,' Ryan said. 'Johnson turned out to be gay.'

Weir ignored him and motioned to the empty chair.

'What's going on?' Ryan said.

Weir sat down again and clasped his hands together. 'We've had a call from the Gun Room in Lambeth, Sid.'

'And?'

Weir did not reply; instead he glanced at Morrison.

'Gun's been used before,' Morrison told him. 'July 1994. An off-duty Special Branch Officer was killed in Northern Ireland.'

Ryan stared at him.

'They found him floating in Spelga Dam with a Tokarev slug in his rib cage.'

Nine

Vanner drove back from Norfolk very early on Monday morning. He had meant to be back on Sunday night but his father was weaker so he phoned Ellie and told her he would stay another night. He left before it was light, his father still sleeping. Anne got up to make him a sandwich which he knew he would not eat. He drank coffee then stepped outside onto a frosted gravel drive and scraped ice from the windows of his car.

'Nearly April,' he muttered. 'You'd've thought it would be warmer by now.'

'Cold up here, Aden. Always was.' Anne hugged her dressing gown closely about her.

'Don't catch cold, Anne. Go inside.'

She smiled at him. 'Thank you for coming. I know how much it meant to him.'

He paused then, and flicked frost from his fingernails. 'I thought he'd be better than he was,' he said blankly.

'Don't worry too much, dear. He's stronger than he looks.'

But he had looked so pale, so thin in the face, the skin all loose and sagging about his neck. The deep coal of his eyes had dulled to a liquid lead and his hair was weak and loose on his scalp. 'Shouldn't he be in hospital?'

'Maybe.' She half-lifted her shoulders. 'You know what he's like, Aden.'

'But he's had a heart attack. He should take more care.' Vanner opened the driver's door. 'I'll come again soon,' he said.

Driving back he was plagued with the kind of memories he had dismissed for years. Thoughts of his childhood with no mother, when there had been just him and his father and the army for company. It seemed so long ago and yet this weekend, sitting with his father, still so much unsaid between them, he was haunted by images of the past. His father tall in dust-covered khaki, moving more easily amongst his men than any man of the cloth had a right to. The way he drove the battered Willis Jeep with no windscreen. Even now, driving back down the M11 with the dawn lifting to his left he could hear the crashing of the gears and the whispered curses as dust caught his father's face.

That face was old now, worn out almost. They had talked but not as either of them intended. The odd word, 'How's that girl?' his father had said.

'The same. Still doesn't drink or smoke.'

'Or eat foreign food.' The old face had cracked in a grin.

'She doesn't even eat vegetables. Takes vitamin pills instead.'

His father had lifted one gnarled hand then and gripped his with it. 'Look after her, lad. She's a good one.'

And that was all that had really been said between them, a father's worry for his son. A son whom he had watched alone for too long. Too caught up in the past. And now as he drove Vanner missed Ellie. He missed her like he had not missed a woman since Jane. And that missing had been painful like a bitter taste in his mouth. This was different, a fondness he had thought himself incapable of. He could see the green of her eyes, the way she half-looked at him out of the corners when she smiled. He missed the warmth of the bed they now shared. Maybe he could talk to her.

Ryan chewed a stick ofWeir's gum and watched the red bristles on the back of Morrison's head. He had that gnawing feeling in his gut as they parked on Victoria Street just up from Westminster Abbey. They were on their way to the Yard. That morning Morrison had phoned the Anti-Terrorist Branch.

'Just what we need,' Ryan muttered. 'SO13 stomping all over the plot.'

Morrison craned his neck. 'The gun's been used in Ulster, Sid. We don't have any choice.'

'I know. I know. But I've worked with them before, Sir. Nicked this geezer trying to run dope to Belfast. They sent a body down, he went through all my files and waltzed back up here with them. I never saw them again.'

Weir glanced in the rear-view mirror. 'Don't worry, Sid.

They'll keep us informed on this one.'

They passed the armed uniform standing on the corner and made their way behind the DTI building. Morrison led the way into the foyer and Ryan glanced at the eternal flame as he always did. They all had their warrant cards flipped open in the pockets of their jackets. Morrison spoke to the uniform behind the desk. Ryan took his gum from his mouth and pasted it under the counter, then the lift doors opened and George Webb came out into the foyer. He looked at Ryan and grinned.

'Hello, Slips,' he said. 'Long time no see.'

Ryan introduced Weir and Morrison to him and they stepped inside the lift. 'So where do you two know each other from then?' Weir asked Ryan.

'Paddington. Uniforms together years ago.'

Weir glanced at Webb. 'How long've you been with the branch?'

'Seven years, Guv'nor.'

Ryan glanced at Webb then. 'You getting close to anyone for Canary Wharf?'

Webb just smiled at him.

Outside the lift, Webb swiped his card through the magnetic slip and the door opened. He led the way past the Commander's office. The Commander glanced up at them from where he talked on the phone. Webb paused outside the Superintendent's office and stuck his head round the door.

'AMIP team, Sir,' he said.

The door opened fully then and Superintendent Finch appeared, a bull of a man with all but no neck and hair grazing his skull like Morrison's. They shook hands. 'Andrew,' Finch said. 'How goes it in 2 Area?'

'It was fine till this thing blew up,' Morrison said to him. Finch glanced briefly at Weir and Ryan. 'We'll use the DCI's office,' he said.

He led the way round the corner and they walked past the squad room. Jack Swann appeared and nodded to Webb. Beyond the Special Branch cell, Webb went into the DI's office. The rest of them went to the next room where Finch held the door open.

Two desks stood empty and Finch motioned for them to sit down. Ryan wandered to the window and gazed out over the city. Behind him Webb came in with Westbrook, the DCI.

'Come in, John,' Finch said to him. Westbrook grinned at Ryan. 'Hello, Slippery. Looking for a transfer?'

Ryan shook his head. 'AMIP, Guv'nor. I already had one.'

Westbrook nodded. He had been Ryan's DI at the Drug Squad before Vanner took over.

Finch sat forward in his seat. 'Okay,' he said. 'What've you got?'

Morrison spread fingers on his thighs. 'The murder in Ealing on the 12th March,' he said. 'Close-quarter shooting. Three shots to the head. Jessica Amanda Turner. The cartridges came from a Tokarev.'

Webb lifted one eyebrow.

'Gun Room at Lambeth sent them over the water,' Morrison went on. 'NIFSL came back with a killing in the Mountains of Morne in July 1994. David Quigley. RUC Special Branch. Off duty.'

Nobody spoke for a few moments. Westbrook ran a hand through his hair. 'What've you got so far?'

Morrison looked at Weir, who sat forward. 'Not a great deal. Married. No kids. Husband was playing rugby in Ireland when it happened.'

'Ireland?' Westbrook cocked his head to one side. 'Where in Ireland?'

'Cork somewhere.'

'He got any Irish connections?'

Weir looked at Ryan.

'Haven't asked him, Guv.'

'Ask him,' Westbrook said. He looked at Webb and then Finch. 'We haven't had a PIRA close quarter over here for years.' He sat back. 'Are you looking at anyone?'

'Not yet.' Weir shrugged off his jacket. 'We know she was away from the Friday night until Sunday. She got back at about midnight and the killer was waiting for her.'

'Where was she over the weekend?'

'New Forest,' Ryan said. 'OTS, Guv'nor.'

Westbrook looked closely at him. 'You know that?'

Ryan nodded. 'We haven't got the other body though. Made an appeal for witnesses. One came forward but not the bloke she was shagging.'

Weir told them about Michael Case and the dummy in the road, the story about somebody getting in the back of the car.

'And you've only got his word for that?' Westbrook said when he had finished.

Weir nodded. 'No other witnesses, nothing to suggest anyone in the back of the car and no dummy.'

Westbrook scratched his head. 'Hell of a story to make up.'

'Case has got a shotgun licence,' Ryan told him. 'He lives with his mother. Fixes photocopiers for a living.'

'Is he telling the truth?'

Ryan shrugged. 'Seems plausible enough but we're digging.'

Webb stretched his arms above his head. 'Those two things could be totally unconnected. PIRA don't do that kind of stuff. The shooting – ' He made a face. 'Toky. In and out very quickly. What've you got from the Lab team?'

Weir squinted at him then. 'False finger nail, two strands of black hair from an IC1 female and a bit of pink angora wool.'

'A woman?' Webb looked from Westbrook to Finch and back again.

Morrison cleared his throat and spoke to Finch. 'How do you want to play this, Sir?'

'We'll look into the Ulster shooting, Andrew, and get back to you.'

'We'll carry on with our investigation then. Try to locate the lover.'

'Fine.' Finch stood up. 'I'll get you an accounts manager. Webby?'

Webb nodded and looked at Ryan. 'I'll come down in the morning and take a look at the crime scene.'

Downstairs, Ryan thrust his hands into his jacket as they walked outside. 'If PIRA had shot Jessica Turner they'd have said so,' he stated.

Weir took gum from his pocket and looked at him. 'Not necessarily. I want you to give your man Webb all the help he needs, Sid.'

'Team are going to love having him on the plot.'

'Got to be done all the same.'

Back on the fifteenth floor Webb and Westbrook drank coffee in the squad room. 'A woman?' Webb said. 'That'd be a first for PIRA.'

Westbrook stroked his chin. 'I've got a meeting with Box, George. I'll leave this to you.'

Webb went back to his desk in the Exhibits office. Tania Briggs was there with Jack Swann.

'Ealing?' Swann said.

Webb nodded. 'Weapon was a 7.62 – Tokarev. Personal protection weapon.'

'PIRA wouldn't use that for a hit.'

'I know.'

'They looking at anyone?'

Webb shook his head. 'Initial forensics suggest it might've been a bird.'

Briggs looked round then. 'PIRA don't have any close-quarter shootists who're women.'

Webb grinned then. 'Makes it interesting doesn't it.'

He sat down at his desk and lifted the telephone. He called the local RUC station where the murder of David Quigley had been investigated. They confirmed the ballistics report that had been sent over to Lambeth. They also told him that nobody claimed the murder and they never got a body for it. He put the phone down and drummed his fingernails on the desk. Nobody had claimed the shooting in Ealing either. If it was PIRA they would've issued a statement – unless of course they hit the wrong target – and if that was the case, who was the right target?

Young Young parked his Rover outside Carmel's ground-floor flat and locked the door. He could see his brother's Golf parked further along the road. Darkness clung to the street, only meagre light from the lamps spilling onto the pavement. He shook himself against the cold and looked for a moment at the two-storey houses shouldered into each other.

Somebody moved behind him. He heard the sound, distinct, a foot scraping the kerb. He stood still, then drew himself up to his full height and turned. A figure stood by his car, just outside the fall of yellowed light from the street lamp. Young Young could not see his face, shorter than he was but broader. Then he heard another footstep, the other side of him this time. A second man stepped across the road towards him. And then he felt the adrenaline began to pump and for an instant he was visited by an unseen image of his father, in the yard at the back of the pub where he stacked barrels as a cellarman. Young Young flared his nostrils and felt for the blade in his pocket.

The first man moved closer, white, the bouncer from Jimmy Carter's place. Young Young balled one fist and drew the flick knife from his pocket. And then more footsteps, hurried, the other side of the road. From the corner of his eye Young Young spied two more of them coming straight for him. Spider's legs moved on his spine and he felt the cold burning his cheeks. The man in front of him brought something short and heavy from his coat, sticklike. Young Young flicked open his knife. The crowbar whistled through the air, missed him and cracked the pavement like a gunshot. And then he was bending and bringing up the blade. A foot in the back of his knee. He buckled and dropped the knife. He heard himself curse as blows rained down on his head. He shuffled away, for a moment free of them, and then someone kicked him hard in the ribs and he rolled onto his side.

He woke up with something cold and hard pressing against his tongue. For a moment his mind wandered and he could not place himself. Darkness, save a dull glow to his left. The street: he realised he was lying on the street. The hardness against his tongue was the grit of the pavement. And then as his senses regained themselves, pain throbbed through every quarter of his body. His right cheek was like ice and he moved his hands so that his palms were under him. He pressed and pain shot through his ribs. He groaned, the noise a pain in itself. A metallic sensation filled his mouth and he spat blood and teeth. Again he tried to get up but his limbs would not work. And then he heard the sound of feet, walking at first and then running towards him along the pavement. Now he forced himself up and pain tore at his chest. He got to a half-sitting position and spat a glob of blood from his mouth.

'Young Young, baby.' Little Bigger, his brother.

Young Young let go another groan and blood filled his mouth. He spat and it rolled down his chin. His eyes focused on his brother's round and bearded face.

'Jesus, man. What happened?'

'I walked into the lamp post. What the fuck you think

happened?' He felt the tearing sensation against his ribs once more and he winced.

'You got to go to a doctor, man.' Little Bigger was crouching now, one arm about his shoulder, a hand under his chin.

'Fuck doctors. Get me into Carmel's.'

Little Bigger half-dragged, half-carried him into Carmel's front room and she eased him out of his jacket. It was soaked with blood and spittle and the leather was torn at the sleeve. He breathed in scarlet bubbles.

Carmel looked down at him, shock standing out on her face. 'That his chest or just in his mouth?'

'I don't know.' Panic in Little Bigger's voice. 'I want to call a doctor.'

'No.' Young Young seized his sleeve with stiff fingers. 'No doctors.' He tasted bloodied gums where his teeth should have been. 'My teeth. They kicked out my teeth.' Again he gripped his brother's arm. 'How many teeth I got?'

'Your teeth are fine, man. Your chest.'

'Fuck my chest. How many teeth?'

Little Bigger knelt down then and gripping Young Young's cheeks between his fingers, he gently prised open his mouth. His eyes bunched in his face.

'What?' Young Young mouthed.

'Three. You lost three.' Little Bigger counted again. 'Yeah. You got three gaps.'

'Where?'

'One in the front. Two on the side.'

Again Young Young touched his gums with his tongue and pain seared to the roof of his mouth. He felt Carmel begin to dab at him with warm water.

'Who was it?'

'Only saw one face.'

'How many?'

'Four.'

'Brothers?' Little Bigger said.

'White fuckers. One from Jimmy Carter's.' Speaking was hard, his lips swelling with every blood-filled word.

Little Bigger stood up then and looked at Carmel. 'Can we get him through to the bedroom?'

'What? You think I want blood on my sheets.'

'Fuck your sheets, Carmel. This is bad.'

She slopped the cloth into the bowl of water, splashing it over the floor. 'No way. No way, man. The big bastard was asking for it. I ain't having blood on my sheets.' She stood with her hands on her hips. 'You see to him, man. I'm going to bed. Lay him on the couch if you have to. But if he makes a mess he pays for it.'

Frank Weir addressed the briefing the following morning. Ryan sat on the edge of his desk next to Pamela. Webb and Westbrook from the Anti-Terrorist Branch stood by the door to Weir's office. Morrison was speaking to Westbrook. He broke off and made his way to the front of the room. The chatter dissipated until there was silence save the hum of computers from the Holmes suite.

'Okay,' Morrison said brusquely. 'Let's get on with it. In case it's escaped anyone's attention we've been joined by DCI Westbrook and DS Webb from SO13. The Tokarev used to kill Jessica Turner was also used to kill an RUC officer in the province just before the ceasefire.'

'I've spoken to the husband, Sir,' Ryan said. 'And neither of them had any connection with Northern Ireland. He's been there once. Jessica never as far as he knows.'

'What about family members?' Westbrook asked him. 'Anyone in the services?'

Ryan looked at him and shook his head.

'We don't have any answers to the *why* questions yet,' Morrison went on. 'But the weapon link indicates some kind of terrorist involvement.'

'Nobody's claimed the killing,' Ryan said.

Morrison looked squarely at him, then Westbrook stepped forward. 'Look,' he said, 'we appreciate this is difficult for you. You're midway through an investigation but –' he lifted a finger and looked at Ryan – 'we're on the same side. This is still an AMIP investigation. DS Webb and I are here merely to assist you.'

Ryan folded his arms. 'If it was PIRA they would claim it though right?'

Webb stepped forward then and grinned. 'Not necessarily, Slips. There hasn't been a shooting like this on the mainland in years. The ceasefire only ended last month. We can expect the unexpected.'

Ryan made a face. 'But they normally claim their killings. They claimed South Quay didn't they.'

Webb nodded. 'It's unusual, but not that unusual.' He looked at Morrison.

'DCI Westbrook is right,' Morrison said, 'I want this thing sorted as quickly as possible. If it is terrorist then it's an SO13 bag. That's the deal. We assist them in everything.' He smiled then as if to break the air of suspicion that clouded the room. 'There are advantages. It makes this a category 1 murder. That means priority with Lambeth, with forensics, with everything. DCI Westbrook and DS Webb have access to everything.'

'Yeah,' Ryan muttered, 'and give us nothing.'

Webb shook his head slowly from side to side. 'Hey, Sid,' he said. 'You ever had a job blow out on you?'

'Course.'

'We haven't.'

'Exactly.' Weir flattened Ryan with a stare. He looked at Westbrook and Webb.

'Where'd you want to start?'

'The files so far,' Westbrook said. 'I'll take copies back to the Yard. George'll want a look at the crime scene.'

Ryan drove Webb to Ealing with Pamela sitting in the back. Webb sat sideways in the seat and hummed to himself. Ryan shook his head at him. 'Don't give us any shit, Webby. Play it straight.'

Webb grinned at him. 'You know your trouble, Sid. You're paranoid.'

They went a long way back. Uniformed PC's together in Paddington from years before. They used to patrol at night in a van, eat Kentucky fried chicken and drink red wine out of glasses they rested on the dashboard. They chased women together. But Ryan had a thing about secrecy and the needs of the Anti-Terrorist Branch. Pamela sat in the back and sensed the suspicious friendship between them.

'I take it you two know each other.'

'Unfortunately.'

'Yeah,' Ryan said. 'For me.'

They parked outside the house and Webb got out. The wind had died and the air was clean and cold. Turner was not at home but Ryan got the key from the Roberts' house next door.

He walked up the path with Webb alongside him and Pamela just behind. 'We reckon she was hiding there,' he said, pointing to the gate on the other side of the bay window.

'She?'

Ryan nodded. 'Female black hairs, false nail and pink wool, Webby.'

Webb smoothed fingers over his moustache and moved towards the gate. He stood in front of it and scanned every inch in turn. The bottom was chipped and the unpainted wood was rotting. Bending, he scoured the concrete at the base. Then he turned and looked at the path. 'The woman came up the path?'

Ryan nodded. 'Killer must've gone in after her.'

Webb went back to the road and looked up at the street lamp that stood above the wall at the front. He looked back at the house and gauged in his mind how far the light would have fallen. Then he went back to the gate and looked more closely at it.

'Lab team?'

'Serious Crimes Unit.'

Webb looked back at the gate. He noticed that the paint was soft and peeling at shoulder height. 'What did they do here?'

'I don't know. The usual.'

Webb nodded. 'I'll want this gate off, Slippery. I'll need it back at the Yard.'

'The gate?' Pamela stared at him.

'Yeah.' Webb looked back at Ryan. 'Was it locked or unlocked?'

'Unlocked.'

'Straight through to the garden?'

Ryan nodded.

'Why d'you want the gate off?' Pamela asked him.

Webb looked at her then and grinned. 'It's peeling,' he said. 'The paint here at shoulder height. The light from the lamp out there would reach almost to here. If the body was standing here for a while, which presumably she was – she would've leaned against it.' He smiled again, showing the white of his teeth. 'There's things I can do to it.'

'Then you'll want the front door as well,' Ryan said. 'We found the hairs on that.'

Webb stroked his moustache. 'Is there a back gate to the garden?'
Ryan nodded. 'Patch of ground beyond it and a few garages.'
Webb took a few paces backwards and looked up at the church spire which lifted above the trees. 'Church is right beyond the garages, yeah?'
'Right. It fronts the road directly parallel to this one.'
Webb walked back to the gate and bent down, inspecting the surface once more, his hands upon his knees. 'Did you find any fibres here?'
Ryan shook his head. 'The pink wool was caught on the back gate.'
'I'll take a look in a minute.'
They traced the killer's steps to the front door and Webb stopped again. 'Killer hiding by the gate. The body walks up and opens the front door?'
'Yeah. Then she gets pushed inside and the door is slammed.' Ryan fitted his key into the lock and twisted. Webb saw the brown stain on the carpet. 'Did you know only thirty per cent of head shots are ever fatal,' he said.
Ryan cocked one eyebrow. 'When they're this close they are.'
'Generally yes. Who got here first?'
'Neighbour. Saw her through the letterbox. He's ex-army and recognised the sound of the shots.'
'Three.'
'Yes.'
'Powder burns?'
Ryan nodded. 'Cheek and neck.'
Webb looked back at the carpet once more and measured the distance from the doorstep to the bloodstains in his head. He spoke as if to himself. 'Up behind her, shoved inside and door slammed.' Again he looked at Ryan. 'The body's on the deck?'
'Hands and knees.'
'Three shots.'
'One after the other.'
Webb pursed his lips. 'In – bang – and out.' He scanned the length of the carpet to the open kitchen doorway. 'Who got here first – after the neighbours I mean?'
'Uniforms from Ealing. Broke open the door.'

'Where did they tread?'

Ryan grinned then. 'The side. They were careful, Webby.'

'That's a first for uniform.' He stepped over the stain to the side of the carpet and squinted. 'They kept well out of the way of the main tread?'

Ryan nodded.

'Did the Lab team do an ESLA lift?'

'Not that I know of.'

'I want one.'

Pamela folded her arms across her chest. 'Why? The Lab team were very thorough. SOCO and the SCU have been right through the place.'

Webb grinned then and looked at her. 'I still want an ESLA lift. With the best will in the world, Pam, SOCO are minimalists. They're good but they're still minimalists. When you're used to looking for things that go bang you learn to be a maximilist. If the ESLA lift shows up anything I'll want the carpet up.'

Ryan cocked an eyebrow. 'Maximilist. That's a technical term is it – like bollocks.'

Webb laughed and went out to the garden.

He traced the killer's movements across the grass, the most direct route to the garden gate. Here he stopped and again scrutinised every inch of it. Ryan watched him and rolled a licorice-papered cigarette. Webb opened the gate then and stepped outside. The waste ground was about twenty feet long, running from the side road to the garages, with a low wall separating them from the church yard. The bulk of the church itself ran behind the garages and the path was shaded with trees. He nodded to the path. 'That way.'

Ryan nodded. 'The path runs round to the front.' He flicked ash from his cigarette.

'We've checked with the houses behind. Somebody reckons they heard a car start up and pull away.'

'Quickly?'

'Not especially.'

They followed the path around the church then, Webb walking slowly, checking the ground, checking the wall of the church. At the front he moved onto the pavement and walked up and down the road, looking in the gutter.

'Been a hundred cars parked there since, Webby.'

Webb looked back at the church.

'We talked to the vicar,' Ryan told him. 'See if he heard or saw anything.'

'And did he?'

'He was away that night. But about a week before he remembered seeing a woman on her own in one of the pews. Church door is always open.'

'Did he talk to her?'

'Just to say hello. Thought she needed her privacy.'

Webb nodded slowly. 'Description?'

'He couldn't really remember. Scarf over her head.'

Webb glanced at the church once more. 'Take a look shall we?'

They went inside. A single aisle with rows of pews either side. At the far end the pulpit lifted with a gilded lectern set over it. The altar was covered in white cloth with gold stemmed candles set at either end. A stained-glass window depicting an image of St Andrew shouldering a ship was fixed in the far end wall. They walked the length of the aisle and the vicar came out of the vestibule. He recognised Ryan and smiled.

'Hello again,' he said.

Ryan introduced Webb as a colleague.

'Have you had any joy?' The vicar's face was lined, mouth set in an arc, grey hair swept back from his forehead.

'We're making some progress.'

'The woman you saw,' Webb asked him. 'Two weeks beforehand?'

'About that yes.'

'Did you speak to her?'

'Just a few words. She looked as though she wanted to be on her own.'

'Had you seen her before?'

'No.'

'And since?'

The vicar shook his head.

'Any accent?'

'Not that I noticed.'

Webb nodded. He glanced to the vestibule door and then back the length of the church. At the far end two bell ropes dangled over the font. 'Did you see a car?'

'Not one that I noticed specifically.'

'Certain people in the street said they saw a red Toyota on

the Friday before Mrs Turner was killed,' Ryan said.

'I'm afraid I don't remember. I wasn't around much that day.'

Webb looked again at the ropes and nodded to the metallic spiral staircase that lifted alongside them.

'The belfry?'

'That's right.'

'There's a window up there isn't there. I noticed from outside.'

'A very small one yes. Very grimy I'm afraid. We don't get much call to go up there.'

'I'd like to take a look.'

The vicar smiled and waved his hand. 'Be my guest, Sergeant. There's a trap door. Be careful though, the boards are a bit creaky.' He cast a short glance over Webb's stocky frame. 'There's not much room up there.'

'I'll manage.'

Ryan and Pamela waited at the bottom of the steps while Webb climbed on his own. They were very narrow and curled tightly arc after arc until his head was below the dusty wooden trap door. Holding the rail with his left hand he pushed on the trap door and was surprised at how easily it lifted. A woman could have done it.

The door leant against its own hinge in the vertical and Webb pressed his frame through the hole. The boards were indeed creaky and he could see the floor through the gaps in them. He climbed up and knelt in the dust, shining his pencil-light torch into the gloom. Getting his bearings he saw the twin bells. He clambered on until he was upright.

Below him the vicar stood with Ryan and Pamela. 'I need to know the last time anybody was up here,' Webb called down to them.

'Goodness. Weeks ago.'

'How many weeks?'

'I couldn't say.'

'Before the weekend of the murder or after?'

'Oh, before I would say. Yes, definitely before.'

Webb looked into the floor space, no more than six feet at the most. Footprints in the dust, messy, as if somebody had moved around to get comfortable. There was one that was reasonably clear. He estimated the shoe size in his head. From the angle he was standing he could tell that the window looked out over the Turner house. He had his observation point.

On the ground once more he looked at the vicar. 'Under no circumstances can anyone go up there,' he said. He looked at Ryan. 'You got any tape in the car?'

Ryan shook his head.

'I can make up a sign if you like,' the vicar offered. 'What is it?'

'Somebody's been up there,' Webb told him. 'I can't tell how recently yet. But I'll get my gear.' He grinned at the vicar. 'Do that sign for me eh?'

Outside, Ryan lit a cigarette and breathed out heavily. Webb grinned at him. 'I'll get to work up there,' he said. 'Then I'll organise the ESLA lift. After that I want to talk to the pathologist.'

Young Young lifted uneasy fingers to the swelling of his jaw and swore very softly. He stood in the bathroom at Carmel's flat and looked at his bruised and battered face. 'So damn pretty,' he muttered. Pain shot through his gums as he peeled back swollen lips to inspect the gaps in his teeth. Little Bigger had told the truth at least, one in front was missing and two molars on the left. Bloodied holes, shattered nerves in white where the teeth had broken off. His shoulders sagged as he closed his mouth again and stared malevolently into half-closed eyes. His ribs pricked him every time he breathed and each step was agony. Turning on the tap, he splashed cold water over his face and left blood on the towel as he dried it. From the floor of the living room he collected his ruined coat and went out to his car. From across the road Jimmy Crack watched him.

He followed at a distance as Young Young drove south on Old Oak Lane before cutting left under the railway and down past the scrubs. He parked on East Acton Lane and limped into the amusement arcade. Jimmy slowed and slipped his sunglasses over his eyes as he cruised past. Young Young stood in the doorway with the lad who gave out change from the booth.

Vanner met Jimmy in the Irish Pub near Campbell Row. He was sitting at the bar sipping Caffreys and thinking about his father. Jimmy came up behind him and tapped him on the shoulder.

'Hi, Jim. Miles away.'

'You looked it, Guv. Things on your mind?'

Vanner shifted around on his stool. 'This and that. What's happening?'

'Young Young. Somebody gave him a battering.'

Vanner ordered him a beer. 'Jimmy Carter's boys.'

'I reckon, yeah.'

'War with the Irish in Harlesden?'

'What, Stepper-Nap?' Jimmy shook his head. 'Not if he can help it.'

'What then?'

Jimmy sipped lager. 'I don't know, Guv'nor. Young Young went after Holden Biggs on his own. Biggs was bad-mouthing him. It was personal. He just picked the wrong venue to slap him.' He licked the froth from his moustache. 'Maybe Stepper gave him up?'

'Young Young?'

Jimmy shrugged. 'Maybe they came to an arrangement. Stepper's got enough trouble with Pretty Boy, the last thing he needs is someone like Carter on his back.'

'A deal then?'

Jimmy shrugged. 'You told me yourself – shooting up Jimmy Carter's place is enough to get you killed. Young Young only got a kicking. Something must've gone down.'

'Maybe we ought to watch Carter.'

'We haven't got the manpower.'

Jimmy finished his beer and ordered two more. 'There's something else, Guv. Immigration belled me this morning – Plug and the smiling assassin are going to spin Carmel's gaff. She's holding for Stepper again.'

Vanner lit a cigarette and thought about it for a moment. 'If they're going to spin her we might as well take the opportunity to have a word.'

Young Young made his way through to the back room where Stepper-Nap sat with Bigger Dan. Stepper drank thick, black coffee and chewed on chocolate biscuits. 'You ain't so pretty no more.'

Young Young leaned in the doorway and held his ribs. 'It

took four of them with bars, man.'

'Yeah?'

'Yeah.'

Stepper sat forward in his chair and dipped another biscuit in his coffee. 'You should've left Biggs alone.'

'Biggs had a mouth.'

'He did. But that don't mean you close it in Jimmy Carter's place.'

Young Young touched his cheek. 'I don't give a fuck, man. Who's Carter anyway? I'll kill him when I'm fixed.'

Stepper-Nap shook his head, a sneer twisted on his face. 'You a fool, man. You real fuckin' stupid.'

Young Young thinned his eyes.

Stepper glanced at Bigger Dan who filled a seat, his hands stretched over the weight of his belly. He looked back at Young Young. Young Young said: 'When I'm fixed up I want us to go after Carter.'

Stepper-Nap stared at him. 'You what?'

'You heard, man.'

'You really that fucked up?' Stepper tapped his skull. 'You stay away from Jimmy Carter you hear. We stay away from him. Think yourself lucky a kicking's all you got.'

He shook his head. 'You trying to fuck up everything I been working on. You got no brains, Young Young. And you don't listen.' He stood up then, six inches shorter, but broader, flat faced with dark snarling eyes and wide, flaring nostrils. 'I been working this gig for years. I got me a fine operation. I got all the connections, man. I got Jamaican brothers in my pocket and I got the Irish in my pocket. We don't need no wars, baby. Can't you get that through your stupid fucked up head?'

And then Young Young knew what had happened to him. Stepper-Nap had handed him to Carter. They had a deal going and he was part of it. He shallowed his eyes and clutched at his ribs through his jacket. 'I'll see you around, man,' he said. Then he turned and shuffled out of the door.

George Webb sat with Jack Swann in the Special Branch cell on the fifteenth floor of Scotland Yard. The SB sergeant scrolled through images on the computer. Nominals. Webb sat with his legs crossed under the chair. The sergeant looked at him.

'You sure it's a woman?'

'They are. False nail. Black hair. Pink angora wool. I haven't seen the pathologist in person yet but I've read the report. Could easily be a woman.'

Swann sniffed. 'PIRA don't have close-quarter shootists who're women.'

'No,' the sergeant said. 'They don't. And they haven't popped anyone over here for years.'

'Who's possible?' Webb said. 'We need some definite maybe's. The weapon was a Toky PPW. Been used over the water.'

'Different shootist,' Swann said.

They looked at the screen as the DS went through the most likely female names on file.

'What did the body have to do with Ulster?' he asked.

'Nothing,' Webb said. 'As far as the AMIP team can tell anyway.'

'What're they doing?'

'Trying to trace the party she was shagging the weekend it happened, but he won't come forward.'

'Obviously married then.'

'Obviously.'

Swann looked out of the window. 'PIRA haven't claimed this, Webby?'

'No.'

'Mistake.'

Webb nodded, then he looked at the Special Branch sergeant. 'Who were they really after?' he said. 'And why use a woman?'

The DS sat back again and let go of the mouse. He sipped from his mug of cold coffee. 'False nails and pink wool.'

'Between five-six and five-nine. Shoe size between five and eight. That's big for a woman.'

'Long black hair.' Swann squinted at the computer screen and Webb looked up at him.

'The bird in the park in Pickhill.'

Outside he bumped into Westbrook, who was coming out of the DCI's office. 'What's happening?' Westbrook asked him.

'SB're looking at nominals, Guv'nor. They'll get on to Box and RUC SB and maybe 90 Section.'

'She had no connection with Ulster.'

Webb made a face.
'So who were they really after?'

Ten

Ellie moved about the ward, administering medication to ageing, saggy men in striped pyjamas. She hummed as she worked, thought about Vanner and felt withered eyes on her flesh. She was used to it, part of the daily routine. At least it gave them something to look forward to. One old man gaped dejectedly into the plastic tablet container.

'Come on Mr Wilkins. You have to take them.'

'I don't want to take them.'

'Come on. They're not that bad.'

He thrust the little cup at her. 'You take them then.' He folded his arms and looked at her out of liquid blue eyes, the veins broken up in his nose. Ellie shook her head at him.

'If you don't take them I'll grind them up and inject them.' She cocked her head to one side. 'Needle in your bum.'

The old man looked beyond her then and she turned and saw one of the new cleaners leaning on the shaft of her mop. Black hair and high cheekbones, a little over-done with make-up. She smiled at Ellie and then at Mr Wilkins. 'There's two of us now,' she said.

He scowled, shook his head and swallowed the pills.

Ellie pushed the trolley back to the nurse's station and the cleaner went back to her mop. They exchanged a wink and a smile.

Later in the canteen Ellie sat drinking tea and staring at the wall. She was thinking about Vanner again, this past weekend. His father was weaker than before and it troubled her. She had seen the fear in Vanner's eyes. They had only been together a few months but she could tell he was disturbed, a sensation in his face as if time was all at once running out.

'Penny for them.'

She started, then looked up at the face of the cleaner. 'Sorry,' she said. 'I was miles away.'

The cleaner smiled and nodded to the empty chair on the other side of the table. 'Mind if I sit down?'

'No, of course not.' Ellie sat back in her chair and the woman sat down opposite her.

'Glad to get the weight off my feet.' She had a hint of an Irish accent.

'You're new aren't you.'

'Relief. I've only been here three days.'

'Ah right. The contract.' Ellie shook her head. 'You all seem to come and go so much.'

'That's the way of it these days. They don't pay very much.'

'Tell me about it.' Ellie finished her tea.

The woman offered her hand then. 'I'm Anne,' she said. 'Mary-Anne actually. But everybody calls me Anne.'

'Ellie.'

'That's a pretty name. Short for Elizabeth?'

'Eleanor.'

'Even prettier.'

'Everyone calls me Ellie.'

Anne sipped at her coffee and Ellie noticed her hands, short-fingered with bitten-down nails. As if suddenly self-conscious Anne placed her hands in her lap.

'You're Irish,' Ellie said quickly.

'You noticed. I've lived so long over here I thought I'd lost my accent.'

'They say you never do – lose it I mean. If you move when you're an adult. Children, they lose theirs but not adults.'

Anne smiled. 'Have you got any children?'

Ellie shook her head.

Anne sipped again at her coffee. 'You live in the nurses home?'

'Flat in Acton.'

'That's a long way to travel every day.'

'Not far on the tube. I was in Hammersmith before.' Ellie finished her tea. 'Anyway I spend most nights at my boyfriend's.'

'Where's that?'

'Camden Town.'

'Just down the road.' Anne finished her coffee and smiled. 'Oh well, I better get back to it.'

'See you about then.'

'I hope so.'

* * *

Ray Kinane met Paul Johnson, the marketing director of CableTech Security in the carpark. He was on his way to a customer in Camberley. Johnson had just arrived and was lifting his artwork case from the boot of his car.

'Delta?' Johnson asked him.

Kinane nodded. 'Site assessment. They like the price in principle. It'll depend on the configuration.'

'You think there'll be any problems?'

'Logistically,' Kinane shook his head, 'nothing I can't handle.'

'Good. Let's hope we get it then.'

Johnson shouldered his bag.

'Those two coppers the other day,' Kinane said. 'Jessica Turner?'

Johnson nodded. 'They think she was with somebody the weekend she was murdered. Somebody who wasn't her husband.'

'You?'

Johnson grinned. 'They thought it might be. We spent a lot of time together.'

'And was it?' Kinane cocked his head to one side as he said it.

Johnson smiled quietly. 'No,' he said. 'It wasn't.'

'They coming back?'

'Unless they want to talk to just about everybody in sales, marketing and your department I don't think so.'

Kinane watched him walk to reception. He thought briefly of his wife and children and then he got in his car.

At eleven o'clock that night Young Young sat in his Rover outside Eilish McCauley's house. He was parked on the school side of the road, nursing his bruises and his hatred of Stepper-Nap. They had some kind of a deal going with Carter. And the only way Stepper could swing that kind of thing was to use Eilish so the bitch must be in on it too. He was glad now that he screwed her. He hoped Stepper-Nap knew, the fat bastard. He drummed fingers on the steering wheel for a moment then he got out of the car.

James opened the door the length of the chain. Young Young leered at him through the gap. 'Where's your sister?'

'Not in.'

'Where is she?'

'Away.'

Young Young pressed a hand against the chain. 'Open the door.'

'No.'

'Open the fuckin' door.' He kicked at it and James jumped back.

'Okay,' he said. 'Okay.'

Inside, Young Young stalked into the living room as if he expected to find Eilish hiding from him. She was not there. He looked round at James and showed him the gaps in his teeth. 'Where is she?'

'I told you,' James's voice was calm, 'she's gone away.'

'Since when?'

'Since this morning.'

Young Young glanced at the stairs.

'She's not in.'

'When's she coming back?'

'I don't know.'

'She out with Stepper-Nap?'

'I don't know.'

'You're a liar.' Young Young took a pace towards him. James backed up against the door. 'She ain't out with him. Where is she?' He grasped a handful of James's T-shirt. 'It's eleven o'clock on a Wednesday, man. Don't dis' me. Where the fuck is she?'

James prised himself out of his grip. 'She's gone home for a few days.'

'Home?' Young Young looked about himself. 'This is home ain't it.'

'Ireland. She's gone home to Ireland.'

Young Young tasted the spittle on his lip. 'Yeah? That figures don't it.' He thought for a moment. 'When she gets back you tell her Young Young's looking for her.'

Eilish sat in the alcove with the door shut. The gas light burned above her head and the last few drinkers were noisy out in the bar. She glanced at her watch. Ten to eleven. He was late, very late. The Crown in Belfast city centre, years since she had been here. She fingered the tattoo on her thigh through her jeans and sipped white froth from the Guinness before her on the table. Not as white as Dublin but better than the awful brown you got in London. She never drank Guinness in London.

She lit a cigarette, glanced at her watch once more and waited. He wasn't coming, the unreliable sod. And then the door clicked and a man stepped inside and sat down opposite her. He placed his pint on the table and looked her up and down.

'Hello, Cahal,' she said.

'Hello, Eilish.'

'You're late.'

'Got held up so I did.' He smoothed a black-nailed hand through stringy hair and took a cigarette tin from his pocket. His face was as lean and pinched as she remembered. His eyes were greyer and hollows crawled beneath them. He must be fifty now, she thought, wearing the same faded Levi's and leather waistcoat he always had before.

'Long time since I saw you, Eilish. You were no more than a girl.' He sat back then. 'Christ, you're wearing well. What're ye – thirty?'

She nodded. 'You've not changed yourself.'

He smiled. 'Oh I have that. Not so much hair these days.' He drank his beer leaving a film of white on his upper lip. Voices lifted from the other side of the booth.

'Closing time,' she said.

'We've a while yet. How's your mother, Eilish?'

'Haven't seen her.'

'Still in the South is she?'

'Aye.'

Eilish pressed her cigarette to the ashtray and leaned forward. She watched him watching the thrust of her breasts. 'Jimmy Carter sends his best, Cahal.'

'Does he now?'

'He does.'

He narrowed his eyes and licked the paper on the cigarette he was rolling. 'Something I can do for ye, Eilish?'

Vanner and Jimmy Crack sat in the briefing room in Harlesden. It was chilly, the inadequate heating barely raising a murmur from the radiators. Outside, night strangled the city. Vanner glanced at his watch. Two thirty in the morning.

Ralph Elsdon was taking the briefing. Tim Carver from

Immigration sat in the chair next to him in jeans, Timberland boots and a lumberjack coat like a Drug Squad copper. Elsdon had penned a map in the black marker pen on the revolving SASCO board.

'House is on Radcliffe Avenue,' he was saying. 'Ground-floor flat on the right as you're looking from the street.' He tapped the box he had marked with the closed end of the pen and glanced at Carver. 'Two illegals, Tim?'

Carver nodded. 'IC3. Jamaican. Been here a week already. Links with the Governor General massive that run out of Tottenham.' He stood up and looked at Jimmy Crack.

'Stepper-Nap, who runs the Brit-Boy posse over here lets the Jamaicans use Carmel's gaff to keep the peace between himself and Tottenham.' He took a bundle of photographs from the plastic wallet on the desk and passed them back. Vanner took two from a TSG officer sitting in front of him. The two men in the photos were young, early twenties, one with shortish dreadlocks and the other with his hair cut very close, a leather peakless cap on his head.

'DI Vanner and DC McKay are here from the Drug Squad,' Carver went on. 'This address is flagged to them.'

'AIU,' Jimmy corrected him. 'I'm from the AIU, Tim.'

Carver coloured and looked back at him, unsmiling. 'AIU,' he repeated. 'You want to give your bit now?'

Jimmy stood up. 'Stepper-Nap is the Daddy of the posse Tim told you about. He keeps his favours topped up with the Tottenham team. Right now there's bad blood between them. His body armour smacked one of theirs in Jimmy Carter's snooker hall off Kilburn High Road. I imagine Carmel's busy so soon because no-one wants a war.' He looked again at Carver. 'I've been working my end of the deal for eighteen months and I reckon we're looking at the biggest crack team in London.' He paused then. 'So I don't want anyone sassing with Carmel about the Brit-Boys. As far as she's concerned this is your average immigration spin.' He scanned their faces, then he looked at Elsdon. 'When's she's back here DI Vanner and me want a word.' He looked again at Carver who pushed out his lips and said nothing.

Elsdon took up his pen again. 'We take up the forward position at the corner of Radcliffe and Leghorn. The TSG'll jump off at the corner with Wrottesley. As far as we can gather from the Recee there's no tension indicators other than the Sunrise Club. A black late-night drinker on Wrottesley. We've had a drive by and it's quiet. We've no reason to believe that the illegals are armed.' He glanced at the uniformed Territorial Support Group. 'TSG'll put the key in the door and we'll need two at least round the back.'

Jimmy Crack drove the car, following the TSG troop carrier. He glanced at the dulled neon sign of the black drinker as they passed it on Wrottesley Road. 'I don't trust Plug, Guv. And I trust Elsdon less. If there's gear in the flat, which there might be, he'll want the collar for that.'

'I'll talk to his Guv'nor, Jim.'

Jimmy pulled over as the TSG van stopped at the jump off point at the junction with Radcliffe Road. Four in the morning now, the houses were dark and silent. Carmel's place was three buildings down on the right. Officers climbed out of the troop carrier and the second van stopped in the road ahead of them. Plain-clothes PCs from Harlesden piled out and three of them went for the back of the houses. Vanner and Jimmy waited. Sitting in the dark with the heat blowing over his legs, Vanner thought about the grey of his father's face. It made all of this irrelevant.

Two TSG officers made their way up the path with the red battering ram between them. Vanner opened his door. He watched them. One good swing and they piled into the hall. He heard a second crash and then the sound of a woman screaming. He lit a cigarette, glanced at Jimmy and tossed away the match. 'Give them a minute to sort it,' he said.

The flat was compact, made even more so by the TSG and the struggling Jamaicans they pulled from the second bedroom. Carmel stood in the hall in her nightdress, hugging herself with her arms. Elsdon moved past Jimmy Crack. 'Hiding under the bed,' he muttered.

Jimmy grabbed his arm. 'I want Carmel in the interview room at the nick.'

'After we charge her.'

Vanner wagged his head. 'Before,' he said quietly.

Just then the illegal with the dreadlocks broke free of the TSG officer trying to cuff him. Vanner stepped into his path and crashed him against the door. The man cried out, head bouncing hard off the wall. He crumpled at Vanner's feet.

'Put your hands behind your back,' Vanner spoke through his teeth. The man groaned, and slowly lifted his hands to the small of his back. Vanner knelt on his neck. 'Interlock your fingers.' He placed one of his hands over the locked fingers and gripped. The TSG officer slipped plastic handcuffs over his wrists.

They moved back into the front room. Carver was standing with Carmel. 'Get dressed,' he told her. Vanner looked at her, naked under the nightdress, the points of her breasts sharp against the flimsy material. Elsdon came in then with a pair of jeans and a T-shirt. He tossed them to her. The WPC in uniform came over, took her arm and ushered her to the TV set, then stood in front of her as she pulled the jeans up under the nightdress.

In the interview room Vanner handed Carmel a Marlboro and lit it for her. He watched her eyes, weary yet defiant. She sat with her arms across her chest and stared between him and Jimmy Crack as if she did not see either of them. The WPC stood by the door.

'D'you want tea or anything, Carmel?' Jimmy asked her.

She did not reply, just continued to stare across the space between her and the magnolia paint on the wall.

'Coffee?'

Jimmy sat back and looked at her. 'This is informal, Carmel. Nobody's charged you with anything yet.'

Somebody knocked on the door and the WPC opened it then turned to Vanner. He scraped back his chair and went out into the corridor. One of the plain-clothes PCs held up an evidence bag containing three toothlike rocks of crack wrapped in clingfilm.

'Where'd you find it?'

'Under the mattress in the spare room.'

'Where the illegals were sleeping?'

The PC nodded. Vanner made a face and pocketed the bag. 'I'll bring it back in a while.'

Jimmy had her talking when he went back inside. 'Immigration'll charge you, Carmel. You harbour illegal immigrants for Stepper-Nap,' he stated quietly. 'We know them, Carmel. They end up running with the Tottenham posse.'

'Don't know anything about that, man. Those two is just friends. They're only staying one night.'

Vanner laughed then. 'What – like Holden Biggs?'

Carmel made a face and sucked on the cigarette.

'Young Young gave him quite a kicking,' Vanner went on. 'Hardman is he, Young Young?'

'He'd eat you for breakfast.'

Vanner smiled. 'And what about Stepper – would he eat me too?'

She stubbed out the cigarette.

'How often does Stepper sleep over, Carmel?'

'Ain't none of your business.'

'Once a week. Twice?'

'I ain't talking to you. Those two is just two guys I met who needed a place to crash.'

Jimmy lifted one eyebrow. 'Just now they were your friends.'

'I make friends easy.'

'So we've heard,' Vanner said.

He shook his head and brought the evidence bag out of his pocket and laid it casually on the table. 'You talk a lot of shit, Carmel.'

Carmel stared at the bag.

'Three rocks. Found in your flat.'

'It ain't nothing to do with me.'

'In your flat, Carmel.'

She shook her head. 'I don't do that shit. It's not mine. Must be those other two.'

'In your flat, Carmel. That makes it your possession.'

She swore under her breath.

'Gets worse doesn't it,' Vanner said. 'Now you're looking at a possession charge as well as illegal harbouring. You're in trouble, girl.'

She looked between them again, lips pressed into her face. 'Maybe you ought to talk to us.' Vanner fingered the bag. 'Then maybe we can talk about this.'

'I don't know nothing.'

'We think you do.'

Jimmy sighed then and drummed his fingernails on the table. 'Ever been in a women's prison, Carmel? Ever been to Holloway?' He glanced at Vanner. 'They say it's much worse than a men's prison. Women can be so much crueller.' He sat forward again and looked at the crack. 'All kinds of weird women inside. Old ones, thin ones, fat ones. Child killers. Man killers. Gay killers. They love the new girl on the block, especially when she's black and pretty like you.'

Carmel shook her head. For a second her lip trembled and then stilled again. Jimmy looked at Vanner and they got up.

'Well don't say we didn't try, Carmel,' he said. They went to the door and the WPC moved toward the table.

'Wait.' Carmel looked up at them. 'I don't want to go down.'

Vanner sat down slowly. 'You want to talk, Carmel?'

She hunched up her knees and gripped them with her arms. 'I don't know much.'

'What do you know?'

She shrugged. 'I don't get told nothing.'

'The team, Carmel. Tell us about the team. Where do they wash the crack?' Jimmy leaned a fist on the table.

She shook her head. 'I'm just Stepper's Friday girl. I don't know nothing.'

'Stepper brings in coke from Jamaica right?'

'I don't know.'

'Come on, Carmel.'

'Maybe. I said *I don't know.*'

'Course you do.'

'He don't tell me nothing.'

'What about Tottenham?'

'I don't know nothing about Tottenham.'

Vanner sat back then and lit a cigarette. 'So what do you know, Carmel? How come Young Young only took a beating from Jimmy Carter?'

She shifted her shoulders, eyes fixed on the floor.

'Jimmy Carter doesn't just hurt people, Carmel. He kills them.'

'I don't know him. You ask Eilish. She knows Jimmy Carter.'

'Eilish?'

'Eilish McCauley. White bitch with long red hair.'

Ryan drove with Webb to see the pathologist. Webb had worked on the belfry and come away with a footprint. The sole was the same size as the one they had got from the ESLA lifts. Ryan smoked a cigarette as he drove. 'You got any ideas, Webby?'

Webb lifted his shoulders.

Ryan smiled to himself. 'That's what I like best about SO13,' he said. 'So free with their information.'
'You're doing it again, Sid.'
'Am I. And there's me thinking about teamwork.'
'We're on the same side. What you need to know – we tell you.'
'You talked to the blokes in the Gun Room.'
Webb looked sideways at him. 'What do you think?'
'They tell you anything?'
'Nothing they haven't already told you.'
Ryan nodded. 'The killings connected then?'
'I don't know.'
Ryan drove on. 'You told me once that PIRA don't let anyone use the same gun more than once.'
'True.'
'So this is a different shootist then?'
'What do you think?'
Ryan exhaled smoke at the windscreen. Webb waved it out of his face and dropped the window still further. 'Is there anywhere you don't smoke?'
'Lifts,' Ryan said after a moment. 'Them and the Guv'nor's car.'
They parked the car and went into the mortuary. Ryan showed his warrant and they went down to the pathologist's office. 'How many cells are you looking at with women in them?'
Webb shook his head. 'I'll tell you one thing, Slips, okay. PIRA don't have any close-quarter shootists who're women.'
'You know?'
'We know.'
Ryan laid a hand on the pathologist's door. 'You want to know what I think?'
'What?'
'This has got nothing to do with PIRA.'
'Why?'
'Because Jessica Turner had no connection whatever with Northern Ireland. They kill political targets. They don't shoot women in their homes.' He looked at him then. 'So either one of their guns went walkabout or they got the wrong person.'
Webb grinned at him then. 'You ever thought about a transfer, Slippery?'
Ryan shook his head. 'I'm a street man, Webby. Crash bang

wallop sort of copper. Find them, watch them, then bosh bosh bosh – nick them. Your firm – I couldn't stand the waiting.'

The pathologist was flicking through papers on his desk when they went in. Ryan closed the door. 'This is DS Webb,' he said. 'SO13.'

'Ah.' The doctor stood up. 'Heard you were involved. Tell me, have you got anyone for the Docklands yet?'

'Which bomb?'

'Either. Both.'

Webb just smiled at him.

The pathologist sat down again. 'Crime scene manager?'

Webb nodded.

'Accounts manager for our little deal,' Ryan said.

Webb stroked his moustache. 'I want to know about the shooting,' he said. 'The body was already on the floor?'

The pathologist pushed his hair from where it fell across his forehead. 'Not prostrate. Hands and knees.'

'Pushed over.'

'There's a contusion on her shoulder which indicates some contact. Yes, a push maybe.'

'And the shots hit where?'

'Side of the head,' he touched his jaw. 'Under here beneath the left ear. The others were in the neck and the top of the skull here.' He motioned above his eye. 'That one deflected off.'

Webb nodded. 'Angle of entry – straight arm? Bent arm?'

'Powder burns. Two feet away max. Straight arm. Forty-five degrees.'

'The killer standing?'

'Over her, yes.'

'Leaning on the door?'

'Possible. Probably two-handed.'

'Gun pointing down.'

The pathologist nodded and took a selection of photographs taken at the scene and passed them over. Then he took some more from the mortuary slab and passed them across as well. Webb had seen the first batch in the incident room. He flicked through them again. 'I think the killer was leaning on the door. Not enough room otherwise. Stability. It would make sense.' He looked up again. 'How tall?'

'Difficult to say. He/she could have been crouching. They probably were.'

'How tall?'

'Between five-six and five-nine I would say.'

'Definitely female?'

'I can't tell you that. But you found hairs which were definitely female.'

Vanner and Jimmy Crack trawled slowly through Harlesden. Vanner was weary, fatigue plucking at the corners of his eyes. He had not slept since yesterday. He had not seen Ellie. He knew he should phone his father. They trundled up the High Road and got snarled up in traffic. In the square by the lights a large sweating black man brandished a Bible and shouted at passers-by to redeem themselves. Jimmy watched him through the window.

'Think it makes any difference?'

'What?'

'What he does?'

Vanner caught the rolling eye of the black man. 'To him maybe.'

By the mobile phone shop on the corner two black kids in bomber jackets and red bow ties handed out 'Final Call' newspapers. Jimmy looked beyond them to 'Ska Cuts' the barber's shop. 'Run by Jig,' he said. 'Stepper-Nap's cousin.'

'He cuts hair?'

'Not him. Others. A front, Guv'nor. Cash business. The Western Union money goes back to Jamaica to pay for the coke. That place,' he nodded across the road again, 'the arcades, just fronts for the cash.' He stopped talking as Pretty Boy walked out of the barber's shop. He wore a black suit over a white silk granddad shirt.

'Look at it,' he muttered. 'And kids look up to him.'

Pretty Boy was oblivious to them. He walked half a dozen paces and climbed into his car.

'How many mobile numbers have you got?' Vanner said to Jimmy.

Jimmy pulled his mouth down at the corners. 'YoungYoung's. Pretty Boy's. Couple of others.

'Who do they call?

'Each other mostly.'

They drove up Craven Road, past Harlesden nick, then headed up Church Road towards Willesden.

'Any fresh word from Kingston?' Vanner asked.

'I'm talking to the DLO. They watch Stepper's brother over there but can't get close to him.'

'What about Rafter?'

Jimmy looked at him then. 'He gave us the doctor didn't he. I want to go see him again, Guv. One of his girls is a runner for the posse. He might be able to organise a trip for her from inside. If we pay him enough we might set up a plot and follow her when she gets home.'

'The doctor?'

'Yeah. She'll carry internally.'

They drove on and passed the Willesden Community Hospital. 'Eilish McCauley,' Vanner mused.

'The BMW in the photos.'

'You reckon Stepper's got something going with Jimmy Carter?'

'Young Young got hammered instead of killed didn't he?'

Vanner scratched his head. 'Carter worries me, Jim. He's big-time in the real sense of the word.'

They came to the slip road by Roundwell Park and pulled in. The park stretched away from them, uncut grass matted by the breeze. Vanner wound the window down and lit a cigarette. Jimmy pointed to the houses on the right of the street directly opposite the park.

'Brown pebble-dash council,' he said.

Vanner flicked ash over the sill of the window and looked at the houses. 'Third one in, I reckon,' Jimmy said. 'You want to take gander?'

'Drive by in a minute.' Vanner glanced at his mobile phone on the dashboard.

'You got to make a call, Guv?'

Vanner looked sideways at him.

'You just keep looking at it.'

Vanner smiled. 'My father,' he said, 'had a heart attack last month.'

Concern lifted in Jimmy's eyes.

'Second time,' Vanner went on. 'He's old you know.'

'Bell him then.'

'Later.'

They looked again at the houses. A smallish man with dark hair was walking down the street with two half-caste girls on either side of him. They were young, swinging off each hand as if to pull his arms from their sockets. He crossed the road in front of them and the girls skipped away from him into the long, wet grass. Jimmy hunched into the door.

'If we can get Rafter to set something up with his girl we might get a result.'

'We need one, Jimmy. We got nothing on Pretty Boy and even less on the Daddy.'

A car pulled up in front of them and a woman got out. She was petite, dressed in blue jeans and a padded leather jacket. Her hair was tied in a ponytail but it was long and red and hanging over her shoulders. Vanner looked at Jimmy.

Eilish had spotted James with the girls in the park as she was about to turn into their road. She pulled over into the slip road and got out. James had not seen her, chasing the girls in circles with his back to her. She made her way across the grass towards them. Caran saw her first and shouted. James looked round then and she smiled at him. The girls rushed up to her and jumped into her arms.

Vanner and Jimmy watched from the car. 'Stepper-Nap's kids?' Vanner offered.

Jimmy shrugged.

'Who's the bloke then?'

They watched the greeting, the girls in their mother's arms. The man hung back, hands in the pockets of his jeans. Jimmy looked at Vanner. 'Pissed-off boyfriend he looks like.'

Eilish kissed the girls then produced a bag of sweets for each of them. They skipped away again and began to compare the contents. Eilish looked at her brother. 'They been good have they?'

'Fine.'

'Anybody call for me?'

James hunched his shoulders into his neck. 'The other night,' he said. 'Mary-Anne came round.'

'What did she want?'

'Didn't say.' He kicked at a tuft of grass.

'Anyone else?'

'The tall one. Young Young. Somebody beat him up.'

Eilish shivered as she thought of her night with Jimmy Carter.

James was watching her. 'How's our mam then?'

'Not too bad. She sends her love.'

James nodded. 'I'll go next time.'

'Whatever.'

He looked beyond her to the two men sitting in the car with the window down. Eilish came up to him. 'I'm tired,' she said. 'And I need a bath.'

He nodded. 'Mam any closer to getting a phone?'

'She hates phones, Jamie. You know that.'

'Don't call me Jamie.'

She looked at him then. 'Your dad called you that didn't he.'

'Don't remember.'

'She still goes on about him you know. Even now.'

'What did she say this time?'

'The usual – what a useless waste of space he was.'

'She's right.'

'Aye. So she is at that.' She yawned then. 'I'm going back. Bring the girls when you're ready.'

Vanner and Jimmy watched her get back in her car and drive across the road. She parked outside the third house on the right and walked up the path.

Webb sat at his desk in the Exhibits room and put down the phone. He had been talking to the Disabled Police Officers Association in Belfast, seeing if they had had any more word from Tim Phelan in Yorkshire. All was quiet they told him. Swann sat opposite him. 'It was just the cracks then.'

Webb pulled a face. 'Had a good look didn't we.'

Swann nodded. 'You've not heard anything from your mates up there?'

Webb shook his head.

'Cracks then.'

'He probably just misses it.'

The door opened and the sergeant from the Special Branch cell came in. Webb swivelled round in his chair.

'What's happening?' the sergeant asked him.

Webb shrugged. 'I told you we got a print from the belfry in the church. Matches the size from the ESLA lift. Flat woman's shoe, size seven I reckon.' He rested clasped hands behind his head. 'I talked to the pathologist yesterday. He confirms the subject's five-six to nine.'

The sergeant squatted on the edge of the desk. 'Doesn't make any sense, Webby.'

'Tell me about it.'

Swann made an open-handed gesture. 'Maybe they just want to make us think it's a woman.'

Webb wrinkled his brow. 'They don't go to that much bother.'

'I've checked the body, Webby,' the sergeant said. 'Word's gone out through Box and no-one knows anything about her.'

'Wrong target,' Swann said. 'We knew that already.'

Webb stood up and went to look out of the window. When Canary Wharf blew they could all but see it from here. He looked over Westminster Abbey, where people thronged on the pavement. 'Any ideas on the right target yet?' he said without looking round.

'We're looking.'

'Snouts,' Swann said.

The SB sergeant nodded. 'Box are looking at it, Jack. There's a few nervous women out there.'

Webb grinned. 'Should keep them on their toes then. We got any close to Ealing?'

'Hammersmith's the nearest.'

Webb scratched his nose. 'What about possibles for the shooting?'

'A couple of nominals. They're based over the water.'

'Maybe PIRA have changed the rules,' Swann said, 'sending hardcase babes instead of volunteers.'

Webb ignored him. 'Who've we got?'

'Two definite maybes,' the sergeant said. 'One from Belfast and the other from Silverbridge.'

'Silverbridge. Now there's a fine friendly place.' Webb sat back at his desk.

Eilish lay in bed with Stepper-Nap. His breathing grew harsh in his throat and he exhaled stiffly. Then he rolled off her and lay on his side. She lay flat on her back, resting her palm on her stomach. For a few minutes he lay facing away from her. She could hear James creeping back to his room and the past grew up in her head. Seeing Cahal had done it, sparked off memory that had freshened and freshened until Tommy's face burned in her mind. In that moment she hated Stepper and all she had become.

Stepper broke in on her thoughts. He lifted himself to one podgy elbow and looked at her through the darkness. She could see the white of his eyes.

'Carmel got busted,' he said.

'What for?'

'Holding two Jamaicans.'

She laughed. 'Oh Stepper, lover. That'll teach you to spread your wings so far.'

He looked at her. 'I'm a diplomat, baby. I like to keep things sweet.'

'Too sweet ends up making you sick.'

He touched her nipple with his fingertips. 'Never mind about that. What happened?'

She looked at him again. 'What I said would happen. I made the contact, lover. Don't worry, he's an old friend and he trusts me.'

He grinned then, showing the white of his teeth. 'Jimmy came good then.'

'Jimmy put in a word. But this contact is mine.'

'Whatever you say, baby.'

He sat up, lit two cigarettes and handed one to her.

'How's Young Young?' she asked him.

'Pissed off. But's he's alive.'

'How bad was the beating?'

'Bad enough. Ribs, I think. Couple of teeth.' He squinted at her then. 'You're not worried about him are you?'

She did not say anything.

He blew smoke through his teeth. 'Young Young's history anyway.'

'You losing him?'

'When I'm ready.'

'What about Pretty Boy?'

'Baby, I can take care of Pretty Boy. He's just a jumped-up nigger. I don't need Young Young for him.' He paused then and inspected the glowing end of his cigarette. 'So you reckon we're on then?'

'They want a kilo and a half.'

'Already.'

'A tester. They want it in powder first.'

He pushed away the bedclothes and walked naked to the window, the thickness of his waist sagging over his buttocks. Young Young was built so much better.

'I want you to carry, babe.'

'Somehow I thought you might.'

He turned and looked back at her. 'You can do it. They never check the ferry. You told me that yourself.'

She drew smoke in through her nose. 'I'm taking all the risks.'

'Yeah.'

'I don't know I like it much.'

'You earn don't you?' He gestured to the open wardrobe doors. 'You reckon the social pays for this?'

'I know I earn, Stepper.'

'And your little brother – keeps him in smarties don't it.'

Eilish sat up then and stared at him. 'He looks after the kids.'

Stepper looked back at her. 'Whose kids are they anyway? The little one looks like Young Young.'

Eilish got up then and went through to the bathroom. James's door was closed and the silence lifted from within. She flushed the toilet and walked back across the landing. Stepper was getting dressed. Eilish lay down on top of the duvet. He squinted at the Gaelic inscription tattooed across her thigh. 'What does that mean? You never did tell me.'

Eilish touched the blue ink with her fingertips. 'You really don't want to know.'

He finished dressing and looked across the landing towards her brother's bedroom. 'Tell me something, baby?'

'What?'

'How come your little brother gets to watch us fuck.'

She stared at him.

'I heard him on the landing. What is it – gets his kicks that way?'

'Leave him alone.'

He held up a palm. 'I'm just asking, baby.'

Eilish sneered at him then. 'Go home, Stepper-Nap. Go home to your wife.'

When he was gone she climbed beneath the duvet and drew her knees up to her chest. James moved onto the landing and started for the bathroom.

'Come in, James,' she called to him.

He pushed open the door and stood there framed in the half-light. He looked vaguely lost, standing in T-shirt and boxer shorts. Eilish threw back the bedclothes and beckoned him. He hesitated and then climbed into the bed alongside her. She drew his head to her chest and smoothed fingers over his brow.

'You all right?'

He did not answer her.

'I do love you you know.'

'I know.'

'And I'm grateful for all that you do.'

James eased his head into her shoulder. 'Did you see Cahal, Eilish?'

She did not reply right away. 'Yes, love. I saw him.'

'Did he say anything?'

Webb and DCI Westbrook sat down in the incident room with Weir, Morrison and Ryan. Ryan smoked. Weir chewed gum. Morrison looked at Westbrook. 'Well?'

Westbrook shifted in his seat. 'You know about the print. The ESLA lift separated it from the others.'

Morrison nodded.

'The lift gave us something we could compare with what we found in the church. Now we know the size and roughly the sole pattern.'

'A woman's shoe,' Weir said.

Webb nodded.

'The same woman the vicar saw in the church.'

'We don't know do we.'

Morrison sat forward in his seat. 'So who is she and why are the IRA suddenly using women to do their close-quarter stuff?'

'And why Jessica Turner?' Ryan twisted the end of his roll up. 'It's more likely to be a jealous wife with a gun.'

Webb shook his head slowly. 'PIRA personal protection weapon? Don't think so, Slips.'

'So who then?' Morrison repeated.

'We don't know yet.'

'Who might it be?'

Webb glanced at Westbrook. 'We're looking at a couple of nominals.'

'Over here?' Weir asked.

Westbrook shook his head. 'Not at the moment. But we're checking to see if they were.'

Ryan drew smoke into his lungs and Morrison wrinkled his nose. 'I thought this was a non-smoking office.'

'Sorry, Guv'nor.' Ryan smoked on regardless. He looked at Webb. 'Who did they mean to hit, Webby? Because it certainly wasn't who they got.'

'What makes you say that?' Westbrook asked him.

'Because I'm not fucking stupid – Sir.' Ryan looked back at him. 'Jessica had nothing to do with PIRA. And they never claimed the killing.'

Webb scratched his thigh through his jeans and said nothing.

Ryan looked at Weir. 'I reckon this is bullshit,' he said. 'What about the dummy in the road?'

'We don't know there was one.'

'Case reckons there was.'

'It doesn't make it connected.'

'It's a hell of a coincidence.' He looked back at the Anti-Terrorist officers. 'Webby, PIRA wouldn't ponce about like that.'

'No. They'd do exactly what they did do. In – bang – and out.'

Silence then. Ryan breathed deeply and stood up. 'I'm out of here,' he said. 'I finished hours ago.'

He met Vanner and Jimmy Crack for a swift one in the Irish pub on Wembley High Road. Jimmy grinned as he came through the door, collar up, unshaven, roll-up cigarette flapping in the corner of his mouth. Vanner drank Caffreys and looked him up and down. 'I thought AMIP wore suits.'

'Lager,' Ryan said. 'Tall and cold and you're paying for it.'

'Not Guinness then?' Jimmy said.

'Fuck your Irish beer.' Ryan slumped onto a stool and slapped his cigarette tin on the bar.

'Good job is it then, Sid,' Vanner asked him, 'working with Frank Weir?'

'Weir's all right, Guv'nor. It's 13 that get up my nose.'

'Rattled your cage did they?'

'They don't tell you anything. I mean I thought we were on the same side.'

Vanner laughed then. 'National security, Slips. Positive

vetting and all that. You only get told what they think you need to know.'

'It's our investigation.'

'Not any more it isn't.'

Ryan took a long draught from his beer. 'It's worse than the bleedin' Flying Squad. They don't talk out of the side of their mouths – they keep the bastards closed.'

'Get a transfer then, Slips. I could do with my minder back.'

'You don't need him, Guv. Morrison is on my back.'

Morrison. Vanner had hardly seen him this year. But they went way back and as always Morrison liked to watch him.

'What're you doing in here anyway?' Ryan said. 'I thought you'd be tucked up with your totty.'

'You mean Ellie?'

'The nurse, right?' He looked at Jimmy Crack. 'I thought you'd have warned him about nurses.'

'Tried to, Slips. But she's a babe and twenty-five and you know – he wouldn't listen.'

Vanner laughed at the sullen expression spreading across Ryan's face. 'She's got big green eyes, Slips. And her cheeks dimple when she smiles. And you know what? I think she loves me.'

'That'd be a first.' Ryan shook his head. 'Impossible, Guv'nor. You're too much of a bastard.'

They moved to a table and Jimmy fetched more drinks. Vanner looked at Ryan. 'I wanted to talk to you.'

'What about?'

Vanner nodded. 'Your snout on Shoot up Hill?'

Ryan furrowed his brow. 'You mean The Coalman?'

'Right.'

'Haven't seen him in ages.'

'He's still on the books?'

'I never took him off.'

'You got a number?'

'Somewhere maybe. Why?'

'He's top man in Kilburn right?'

'He was. Well, he knows every pub if that's what you mean.'

'And every club?'

'Most of them yeah.'

'Jimmy Carter,' Vanner said.

Ryan stared at him now. 'Had his snooker hall shot up.'

'Right. Young Young did it. He's the body armour for the posse we're chasing. By rights he ought to be dead. He only got a kicking. I want to know why.'

Eleven

Young Young sat in his flat. The ashtray on the coffee table brimmed with gold-filtered butts and a bottle of Rolling Rock sweated on the arm of the chair. He scraped fingers over the glass and dabbed his forehead with his fingertips. No music played. Outside somebody shouted and he heard the clink clink of a can rolling in the gutter. His jaw was stiff and ached when he tried to chew. The swelling had receded under his eye, but the missing teeth troubled him. They changed the way he looked, left his smile crooked and empty. On the floor at his feet his gun lay broken in pieces.

He lit another cigarette, exhaled lazily and thought through it all once again. The hint of betrayal, bitter now on his tongue. Stepper-Nap and Eilish and the Irishman – Jimmy Carter. They must think him really stupid, some dumb fuck to kick over and leave in the dirt. The amount of times he had stood in front of Stepper when shit was going down. The amount of heads he had broken on account of that fat bastard nigger. Stepper's problem was he liked to mix it up too much, the Jamaicans in Tottenham, giving them little sweeteners instead of sorting it once and for all.

The cold of the beer hurt his teeth but he swallowed from the bottle anyway. It wasn't over, not by a long way it wasn't. But his ribs still ached and every now and then when he coughed he spat blood. His teeth needed fixing but one day soon he would be ready. He thought of his brother then, Little Bigger, dodging between Stepper-Nap and Pretty Boy depending on who he thought might be winning. He thought of their mother, the first time in a long while. He ought to go visit her. Little Bigger went now and then but he didn't. He missed Eilish, white flesh in his bed. The best part of that was she was Stepper-Nap's woman.

* * *

James dressed Kerry for church, like his mother used to dress him all those years ago. Sunday morning, Eilish still asleep after rolling in at four o'clock in the morning.

'Is Mummy coming with us, James?' Caran tugged at his arm and he realised he had not noticed her come in. He looked down at her, clear dark skin with her hair rising in crinkles from the top of her head. He had to admit she was pretty. Both of them were pretty.

'Will she?' Caran asked him again.

'Will she what?'

'Come to Mass with us?'

James shook his head.

Outside the sun was in his eyes and the first hint of spring scented the air. The girls were wrapped up still, scarves about their necks but Caran's gloves hung from the elastic James had sewn in her sleeves. The sky glistened, emerald almost in colour and the air would be clean if it was not for the exhaust fumes of buses. They walked, James holding each of their hands. A group of lads kicked a ball about in the park and they crossed the grass behind piles of coats laid out for goal posts. For a moment James was reminded of the past, playing football with Tommy.

Ten o'clock Mass with Sunday school for the girls. He took them as often as he could although it was not every week. He did not know quite why, he doubted if he really believed, but it was something he and Eilish had done with their mother.

He dropped them at the church hall door then took his place in the pew at the back and stared at the statue of the virgin alongside the pulpit. Christ hung battered and bloody amid the crystal of the stained-glass window. James stared at him and for a moment he seemed to stare back through the blood that dripped in his eyes. Tommy, a memory. Once he had seen him in church, seated in a pew during the week; head in his hands, as if atoning for the things undone in his life. James looked to his left and the memory became the present. Mary-Anne Forbes smiled at him.

After the service he collected the girls and was walking out to the street when Father O'Halloran called to him from the door. James waited while the priest said another goodbye and then he walked back up the path. O'Halloran bent to the girls. 'And how are you, my beauties?' he asked.

Caran giggled, tugging at James's hand. The priest stood straight again and smiled at him.

'What about you, lad?'

'Fine, Father. Just fine.'

'And your sister – how's Eilish?'

'She's fine too.'

'Home is she?'

'Aye.'

O'Halloran stuck his hands under his robe and nodded. James knew he was feeling for cigarettes but would wait till everyone was gone before lighting up. 'You thought any more about what we talked about?'

'I have, Father. But I'll need to talk to Eilish.'

The priest nodded. 'You've not had a chance yet then.'

James looked at him. The girls' first communion. 'She's been away, Father. Went home to see our mother.'

'How's she doing?'

'Not too bad. Been a bit poorly mind.'

The priest looked at the girls and winked, then he laid a hand on James's shoulder. 'Talk to her, lad. Eh?'

'I will, Father. I will.'

James led the girls down the path and saw Mary-Anne waiting for him on the pavement. She chewed the end of her fingernail.

'What about ye?'

'Not bad, Mary-Anne. You?'

'Fine. Your sister home is she?'

'Aye. Got back the other day.'

'I'll walk on back with you then.'

At the park the girls ran off and James walked with Mary-Anne. The sun was warm on his face and for a second he closed his eyes.

'Nice day,' Mary-Anne said.

'So it is.' James glanced at her then, slightly smaller than he was but not much. He wasn't tall himself. Her black hair hung about her jawline and she looked lithe and fit in her sweater and jeans.

'What was it like inside, Mary-Anne?' He said it before thinking. She stiffened a fraction, did not reply, then just shrugged and looked at him. 'I'm out now, James. I don't think about then.'

* * *

Vanner watched his father sleeping, face twitching every now and then, the skin loose at the corners of his mouth. Sunlight streamed through the window, setting the dust particles dancing. The house was quiet, Anne and Ellie taking a walk in the garden. His father's bed was made up in the study, warmer than the draught of their bedroom. Vanner thought how old and pale he looked and he knew then he was not going to get any better. Weak, the doctor had said. That's the trouble with a man of his age.

Age. Years, so many of them. All his lifetime, the only certainty Vanner had known; with no woman to soften the space between them. His father had known it, more than once he had spoken of it. Then Anne had come along when he was sixteen and after that – Jane, his former wife. Ellie had found the single last photograph of the two of them on honeymoon in Calvi when he had watched French Legionnaires on manoeuvres in the bay. He had destroyed the picture. The past. He no longer needed to be reminded of the past. He glanced to the bed once more and his father's eyes were open.

'Where were you?' Even his voice had lost all its strength. Vanner felt the life dribbling away before his eyes and he fought to quell the panic that reared in his gut.

'I don't know.'

'Thinking?'

Vanner nodded.

His father rolled his head to one side and craned to see the window. 'Sun's shining, lad. You should be outside.'

Vanner said nothing.

'Where's Anne?'

'Walking with Ellie.'

His father looked back at him and his voice was firmer than before. 'Good girl that.'

'Yes.'

'Fond of her are you?'

Vanner looked beyond him.

'Come on, son. I'm your old man. You can tell me.'

Vanner smiled then. 'Yes, Dad. I'm fond of her.'

'Ever tell her?'

'What?'

'Do you ever tell her? Women need to hear it from their man, Son. Makes them feel worthwhile.'

Vanner got up and moved to the window. He could see them, Ellie with Anne talking together under the sycamore tree. His father moved and cursed under his breath. Vanner looked back quickly. 'You okay, Dad?'

'Not used to being in bed, Son.'

Vanner sat down again. 'You've never been in bed. You spent your life wandering through deserts, trying to make soldiers think beyond their bayonets.'

His father grinned then. 'Is that what I did? And which bayonets d'you mean?'

'The sharp ones.' Vanner chuckled. 'Both. Whatever.'

'And did I do a good job, Aden?'

'I don't know. Did you?'

'I'm asking you.'

There was an edge to his father's voice as if he knew now that his time might be short and he really needed to know. Looking back over life attempting to piece together whatever sense could be made of it. How many people talked of lying on their deathbed and thinking over their days. His father's eyes, though liquid at the edges, were still dark and they still had the power to penetrate.

'You did a good job, Dad.'

His father grunted, half-closed his eyes and opened them again. 'And you?'

'Me?'

'What about you – did I ever make you think?'

Vanner pushed out his lips. All at once he had a craving for a cigarette. 'You made me think, yes.'

'What about?'

'Everything.'

His father smiled. 'Well that's something then.'

Vanner shifted his hard-backed chair closer to the makeshift bed. His father's hand lay on the coverlet and Vanner wanted to lift it. He did not though. Instead he folded his arms and said: 'What about you, Dad – did I make you think at all?' As he said it he realised he was talking in the past tense.

His father gazed at him then. 'Yes you made me think.'

'About what?'

'Lots of things.'

Vanner stared at him for a moment. 'Am I what you thought I'd be?'

His father half-shut his eyes as if he was fighting with sleep. He blinked a few times and looked evenly back at him. 'You're just about what I thought you'd be. How could you be anything else?'

'You're a priest.'

'Yes. And you're a soldier. Oh you might wear a different uniform these days, but fundamentally that's what you are. How could you have been anything else, Aden? The army. Men fighting wars. It's where I brought you up.'

'Why did we move to Norwich when we did?' Vanner had often wondered what the answer to that question was but this was the first time he had asked it.

His father fluttered his eyes again, then his gaze fastened once more. 'You needed some stability. You were twelve then, Aden. Twelve years of Africa and the Middle East and Germany. Army camps. Raucous foul-mouthed men. When the Norwich School post came up it was time to hang up my khaki.'

'For me or for you?'

'Both of us. It did you a lot of good that school. Probably kept you on the straight and narrow.'

Vanner laughed then and thought about hitting a suspect two years previously. He thought about the other men he had hit or wanted to hit in his life. Now, as he sat there he bunched his knuckles into a fist until they whitened against his thigh. 'It was where I learned how to punch.'

'Box,' his father corrected him. 'Boxing, son. Nothing wrong with that. Boxing has rules. Nothing at all wrong with that.' He chuckled then, a liquid sound in his throat. 'Heck, you were pretty good at it.'

'Light heavy, Dad. I might've been a contender.'

They both laughed then and Vanner told him about boxing in the Met Lafone championships. He had never articulated it before. He had won the title in 1987. A year later he defended against Jimmy Crack, who was three years his junior. It had been a great fight, biggest turnout in years. Vanner was the ex-soldier, only five years' service under his belt. The loner, SB recruit with the Sandhurst education. Jimmy was an ex-builder from the Isle of Wight and master of the sucker punch. He used to spar against Super heavyweights and the only way he saved his face from a mashing was to lean into the jab and deliver the killer blow right under the rib cage.

Vanner had danced and boxed and jabbed for eight rounds, watching for Jimmy's special. Then in the ninth just as he thought he had him, Jimmy looked him in the eye, leaned in close and took him under the ribs. Vanner saw it coming and closed up his elbows but the punch got through. He didn't go down at first, then Jimmy piled in with two left hands and a right hook that almost took off his head. He woke up with smelling salts under his nose and Jimmy wearing his belt.

'Always someone tougher than you are, Son,' his father said.

'Jimmy isn't tougher. He just punches in the right place.'

His father cracked a grin. 'What happened to him?'

'Nothing. He's in the Area Intelligence Unit. I'm working with him now.'

'So you don't hold it against him then?'

Vanner grinned. 'Only when he pisses me off.'

He drove back to London that evening more at peace with himself than he ever felt he had been. Ellie sat next to him with her hand resting against his thigh.

Webb and Swann from SO13 had a Sunday night drink in the Spanish bar where Webb had met the dark-eyed beauty from the sherry company. They had been working all weekend, a cell gone live in West London. The call to stand down had come only an hour ago. Swann yawned and swigged from his bottle of beer. The chef came through from the kitchen with a plate of steaming chicken pieces soaked in garlic and placed it on the bar between them.

The barman set up two more bottles and snapped off the tops. Beer bubbled up the necks and frothed over the lip. Webb dusted one bottle with his finger and felt his paper vibrate at his waist.

'Here we go,' he said. 'Gone live again.'

Swann watched him go to the telephone by the steps that led up to the street. Webb dialled the office and was put through to the Special Branch cell on their floor. The sergeant answered.

'Where are you?'

'Licensed premises where I always am.'

'Thought you'd gone home. Your wife must wonder who this stranger is that shows up once in a while.'

'What you got, Harry?'

'Thought you'd like to know – Silverbridge possible.'

'Yeah?'

'Word just came in from Box. They've got a snout who saw her on the 11th. She was over the water, Webby. She's alibi'd.'

Webb sucked breath, the weariness of another weekend without sleep. It was time he went home. 'Okay,' he said. 'So now we're down to just one.'

'She's a ringer, Webby. And the word is she gets about. She's over our side right now.'

'Got a plot on the roll have we?'

'We have. I'll let you know as soon as I can.'

Webb hung up and went back to the bar.

Swann was putting on his coat. 'What's the story?'

'Job's still off. That was SB. Ealing. Dervla Finn's alibi'd.'

Sid Ryan should have been at home. Frank Weir had organised a seven-thirty briefing for Monday morning. SO13 were silent and their own inquiries were about as tight as a three-year-old's knitting. But he was not at home: he was drinking Irish whiskey in a hotel room off Brompton Road with The Coalman, his informant from Shoot up Hill.

He had brought the bottle of Jameson's. The Coalman's favourite tipple. Ryan hated Irish whiskey but he drank anyway. The Coalman always insisted. He had arrested him four years ago, only a month or two after he started with 2 Area Drug Squad. He was a Belfast man, transplanted to London. Ryan had nicked him for selling gear out of a bedsit near Brondesbury Park station. The Coalman had prattled on about his erstwhile wife and seven children living in a rancid council house in west Belfast as Ryan cuffed him and placed him in the back of the troop carrier. Later, he found out the man had never been married; instead he left a string of Catholic girls in his wake. The only reason he was in London at all was because the brothers of one pregnant sixteen-year-old were looking for him with hurling sticks.

The Coalman was Ryan's age, but short and chunky with heavily calloused hands. His day job had been delivering coal to the house in west and north Belfast and even now his fingers were black under the nails. The Coalman was the pseudonym he had taken when Ryan set him up as a snout. He had been good for a year or so and then he dropped out of sight. But Vanner was right about him: he was known in every dive and drinking hole from Maida Vale to Cricklewood. He had even shown up one Christmas at the Flying Squad do in the Trade Hall because he heard the beer was cheap.

Now he sat in the only chair with his legs crossed and half a tumbler of Irish in one hand and a burning cigarette in the other. He studied the Camel insignia on the end as Ryan placed the packet back in his pocket.

'Still smoking this Turkish shit are ye?' he muttered.

'It's either that or a roll-up, Coal. You're lucky it's not late in the month.'

The Coalman took a long drag and blew smoke rings. 'So what is it you're after, Mr Ryan? I heard that you'd moved on.'

'I have,' Ryan said. 'This is a favour for a mate.'

'I'm not sure I'm in the business any more.'

'You're here aren't you?'

The Coalman nodded. 'That I am, Sir. That I am.' He swallowed all of his whiskey and poured three fingers more. 'What is it ye want?'

Ryan crossed one leg under him, sitting where he was on the bed. 'Eilish McCauley,' he said.

The Coalman squinted at him.

'You know her?'

'I might. What does she look like?'

Ryan handed him the photograph Vanner had given him, one of the ones from the party that Jimmy Crack had obtained from The Mixer. The Coalman took it, drank more whiskey and looked thoughtfully at it. 'Not bad,' he said. 'Red hair. I like 'em with red hair.' He laughed then. 'You know the song, Mr Ryan. *Takes a redheaded woman* . . .'

Ryan nodded. 'Bruce Springsteen. I heard it, yeah.'

'True enough so it is.' The Coalman looked again at the picture and he closed one eye. 'Who's this lot she's hangin' out with?'

'The fat one's the Daddy of a Harlesden crack team.'

'Jamaicans?'

Ryan shook his head. 'British.'

'Don't know them.'

'What about her?'

'Not seen her.'

'You sure?'

'Aye. I'm sure. B'Jesus, I'd know if I had.'

Ryan put out his cigarette and took the picture back. 'My old Guv'nor on the Drug Squad reckons they might have some kind of deal going with Jimmy Carter. The geezer that shot up his snooker hall is the body armour for the Daddy there.'

The Coalman's eyes clouded. 'Jimmy Carter. Now you're talking about a serious man so you are.'

Ryan sat down on the bed once more. 'Can you do some digging for me – see what you can find out?'

The Coalman sank the rest of his drink and weighed the empty glass in his hand. He glanced about the room. 'Paid for is it?'

Ryan stood up. 'For tonight yeah.' He grinned as he wrote his mobile number on a slip of paper and handed it to him. 'Give some Jack'n'Danny a tug. Call it old times' sake.'

In the morning Weir sat with Morrison while the AMIP team gathered in the incident room. Monday, early, rain lashing at the windows and the investigation hampered rather than helped by SO13 and apparently going nowhere.

'We're hamstrung,' he told Morrison. 'PIRA haven't claimed the killing yet it was definitely their weapon.'

'Mistake,' Morrison said.

Weir nodded. 'If it was them at all. If 13 think it was a mistake, they'll be wondering who they were after.'

Morrison smiled and made a calming motion with the flat of his hand. 'Meaning they'll be taking more notice of that than this.'

Weir scraped a hand across his skull. 'Meaning I don't know what, Andrew.'

Morrison glanced through the window at the team gathering outside. He saw Ryan come through the swing doors spilling coffee and cursing. He looked at Weir once more. 'Frank, if this is PIRA, 13 will do everything to get who did it. Webb was right when he talked about no jobs going wrong on them. Since 5 became the lead agency for UK source gathering it's worked bloody well. They win more than they lose.'

'I know all that, Guv. But it's the way they swan in here with their mouths shut and their bloody positive vetting.'

'Got to be that way, Frank. Tongues wag don't they.'

'I know. I know.' Weir stood up. 'We better get to it. I'm starting to sound like Ryan.'

They moved outside and Weir addressed the briefing. He told the team that SO13 were due in the incident room that morning but not until later.

'They've got something to tell us at last.' Ryan said it without any conviction in his voice.

Weir shrugged his shoulders. 'We'll find out when they get here.'

'I think it's bullshit, Guv'nor.'

Weir soured his lips as he looked at him. 'You got anything more helpful to say, Sid? Because if you haven't keep it shut.'

Ryan wagged his head from side to side. 'It isn't PIRA. It's a hit all right. But it isn't PIRA.' He looked at his colleagues, then beyond Weir to the board with the pictures pinned up. 'We've checked every avenue there is,' he said, 'and we haven't got one iota of evidence to suggest that PIRA were after Jessica Turner.'

'Security installations,' Weir commented.

'Yeah, but bugger all to do with anything they'd be interested in. The only security deal she worked on was CableTech, and they only do CCTV.'

Weir looked at the others then back at Ryan once more. 'So what're you saying?'

Ryan sighed heavily. 'I'm saying we're looking in the wrong place.'

'And the right place?'

'What about the husband?'

'Alec Turner?'

Ryan nodded. 'Jessica was well insured, Guv. He's going to collect a packet.'

'How well insured?'

'Couple of hundred thousand.'

Silence. Weir thinned out his eyes and glanced at Morrison. Morrison moved off the desk. 'Tokarev pistol, Sid. You know how rare that is in any form of shooting?'

Ryan looked at the floor. 'Guns go walkabout, Sir. It happens all the time.'

'But this gun we know was used to kill an RUC officer in Ulster.' Morrison shook his head. 'It's too much of a coincidence.'

Weir took the floor again. 'SO13 think it was PIRA,' he stated.

'Maybe.'

Again he looked at Ryan.

'Meaning?'

'You've heard it from them yourself, Guv. They don't have any shootists who're women. They never have had. Not over here. Not close quarters. Those guys are in, bang and out. They don't use sleepers.'

'We come back to the weapon, Sid.'

Pamela looked at Ryan then. 'What's your point about the insurance, Sid? You think Alec Turner knew she was OTS and imported some other bird to shoot her while he was in Ulster?'

'It wouldn't be the first time.'

'He had no money worries.'

'No. But he wasn't rich either.'

Tony Rob spoke then. 'There is another angle to all this. Maybe Jessica Turner didn't have any connection with Ulster, but perhaps whoever she was seeing did. He hasn't come forward has he.'

Again silence. Weir could hear the rain on the window. 'The lover,' he said.

Rob nodded.

Ryan lifted his eyebrows. 'It's possible.'

Morrison looked doubtful. 'Unlikely,' he said. 'If PIRA have a target they go after them.'

Weir placed both hands on the top of his head and looked at all of their faces. 'Whatever it is we need the lover. We need to know why he didn't come forward. If we find him we might get somewhere. Find him,' he said.

Webb arrived then with DCI Westbrook and they stood at the back of the room. Weir put the lover connection to them and Webb scratched his head. 'The only way they'd do that is if she was involved in something. PIRA kill their targets. Apart from the innocents in bombings they're selected for military or political reasons. Jessica Turner would need to be in it up to her neck to become legitimate enough for them.'

'And they never claimed it,' Ryan finished the sentence for him.

Webb glanced at him and nodded.

'Which means one of two things,' Ryan went on. 'Either it

wasn't them or they got the wrong person.'

Webb nodded. 'That's about the size of it yeah.'

Morrison stood up then and spoke to Westbrook. 'Have you got anything?'

Westbrook looked at Webb. 'We had two definite maybes,' he said flatly. 'One of them is alibi'd.'

'How?' Ryan knew the answer but wanted to voice it anyway.

Webb just looked at him.

'Come on, Webby. How?'

'Ryan.' Morrison snapped at him.

'You know the game, Slips.' Webb grinned at him. 'If I tell you she's alibi'd she is.'

'What about the other?' Weir said.

Webb looked back at him. 'We're still looking at her, Guv'nor. You'll know if we find anything.'

After the briefing broke up Webb came over to Ryan's desk and sat down. They looked at one another. Ten years had passed since they had worked together. Webb grinned at him. 'Still paranoid then, Slips.'

'Fuck off, Webby.'

'You could always get a transfer. Always looking for good coppers on the fifteenth floor.'

'What's the plonk like?'

'Plonk's good, Sid. Brains as well as looks.'

'Never cared about brains. Just as long as they've got a pulse.'

Pamela overheard them. 'Ryan, you're a dinosaur. You know that?'

Ryan looked over his shoulder at her. 'My best quality, Pammy.'

He looked at Webb again. 'We have to find the lover.'

Webb nodded. 'You need him.'

'Got no background without him. He hasn't come forward. It might just be because he's got a wife and kids but it might be something else.' He finished rolling his cigarette and looked at it. Then he looked at the rain rolling in rivers down the window. He put the cigarette in his shirt pocket. 'You reckon it's them but a mistake, yeah?'

Webb nodded.

'So who were they after?'

Webb smiled. 'We'll find out.'

'Snout?'

'Maybe. they're paranoid about snouts. We make sure of that.'

'Misinformation?'

'Shit happens, Slips.'

Vanner addressed the Drug Squad at Campbell Row. They were gathered in the cramped confines of the squad room and again Vanner was grateful for the mooted move to Hendon.

'We've made a little progress with the posse,' he was saying. 'Immigration gave Carmel Connolly's address a spin and arrested two illegals. They found three rocks under one of the beds. It's the illegals' gear but we were able to use it to lean on Carmel a little.'

'You setting her up, Guv?' Sammy sat forward in his chair.

Vanner shook his head. 'You know what blacks are like, Sammy. They don't give up their own. We did get something though. The white girl in the photos we got from the snout.'

'The BMW?' China said.

'Name's Eilish McCauley. Lives near Roundwell Park in Willesden. Got two half-caste kids and a brother James. They're Irish. Jimmy and me eyeballed them in the park. I don't know if they're linked to Stepper-Nap, but we know from Carmel that he sleeps with her.'

'White baby mother.' Sammy lifted his eyebrows. 'Make him look fine on the street.'

Vanner rolled up his sleeves and sat down on the desk. 'We know that Young Young beat up an illegal in Jimmy Carter's snooker hall. Holden Biggs, from the Tottenham team that Stepper does his diplomatic routine with.' He thought for a moment. 'By rights Young Young should be propping up some flyover somewhere. Jimmy Carter is old school. Gangster outfit from over the water. He never takes prisoners.' He glanced at Jimmy Crack. 'Funny thing here though is Young Young's walking around. He's beat up but he's breathing. Not at all like Carter.'

'So Stepper's talking to him?' Anne said.

'Maybe.' Vanner looked at her. 'He doesn't want a war. Maybe he bunged him a few grand. Maybe not. But when we pushed Carmel about the Brit-Boys she told us to ask Eilish McCauley.'

Quiet slipped over the room while everyone digested his

words. Vanner said: 'Maybe there's more to it than just avoiding a war.'

'Like an Irish crack connection?' Sammy said.

Vanner made a face. 'Crack's a black drug.'

'Coke isn't. And they're having hassle over there. More now than ever. I've got a mate on the Antrim Road. Ever since the ceasefire things have got worse.'

'PIRA control all drugs to Ulster,' Vanner said. 'They get a rake-off from everybody. Maybe Jimmy's doing our posse a turn. If he is then Eilish McCauley's the connection.' He looked behind him as the wind rattled against the loose-fitting window. He pushed his sleeves down again. 'I've had a word with Slippery. He had a snout over on Shoot up Hill.'

'The Coalman,' Sammy said. 'I knew him, Guv.'

'Reliable?'

'In his day yeah. Not much happens in Kilburn that he doesn't hear about.'

'How come he slipped out of sight?'

'Slippery moved over to AMIP. Before that things were pretty quiet.'

Vanner nodded. 'Slips phoned me this morning. They had a meet last night. The Coalman's going to put his ear to the ground for us – see what he can come up with.' He stood up. 'In the meantime we're setting up a pick-up in Jamaica. Dion Rafter, the snout down in Winchester wants a move back up here.' He looked at Jimmy.

'Rafter's bird is a runner for the posse,' Jimmy said. 'He can set something up so she doesn't know we're watching. Hopefully we'll tag her all the way through. Meet her when she gets back and follow her, maybe to the wash house, maybe to the doctor. Either way we get a little on Stepper-Nap.'

Jimmy Carter played three-card brag with Billy Hammond and Carl Lever, two of his cronies from Finchley. They sat around a circular, felt-topped table in the upstairs room at the club. Bobby Simpson, the stocky bouncer who had organised the hit on Young Young stood by the door, his features wrinkled like a bulldog chewing a wasp. Money going down on the table, moisture gathered in a cluster of droplets on Carter's brow, an open bottle of Tequila beside him. He always drank Tequila when he played cards. It helped his concentration. It helped him now. He held a pair of twos and Lever was raising him nicely, a match fixed like a miniature wedge in the corner of his mouth.

'Good hand, Carl?' Carter watched as the fifties were laid on the pile of notes between them.

'Lay your dosh down and I'll show you.'

Carter smiled then, poured another shot from his bottle, downed it and rubbed the red hair on his forearm. It reminded him of Eilish McCauley and his smile widened considerably. Billy Hammond sat back in his chair, hands over his belly where it squashed against the buttons of his shirt. He had folded already, his cards laid face down on the table.

'What d'ye reckon, Billy?' Carter asked him. 'Your man winding me up?'

Hammond lifted one corner of his mouth. 'Don't know why you're asking me, Jim. I'm a monkey down already.'

Carter looked back at Lever who smiled thinly. 'Time marches on, Jim. What's it gonna be?'

Carter lifted four fifty-pound notes from his stake and pressed them over those placed by Lever. 'There's yours, Carl. And here's some more for luck.'

Lever's face fell. 'You're not seeing me then?'

'Does it look like I'm seeing you?'

Lever hunched forward now, tongue pressed to his lips and concentrated on the curled cards in his paw.

'Time marches on, Carl,' Hammond said.

Young Young turned off the High Road and cruised past the lighted front of the snooker hall. Music thumped at him from the stereo as he spun the steering wheel with the flat of his hand. One doorman. The blond one, not the fat bastard who'd jumped him. He stood blowing on his hands, a crombie overcoat covering his penguin suit. Fifty yards further on, Young Young glanced to his left and spotted Carter's Bentley in the small carpark beyond the twelve-foot-high gates. He pulled into a parking space on the right and switched off the engine.

He sat quietly now, watching the illuminated hands of the dashboard clock. Ten thirty. The club shut at eleven during the week. An hour after that Carter would come out, walk to the carpark and get his car. He knew. He had watched him. Leaning over the seat, Young Young took his gun from the floor in the back.

Upstairs, Carter scraped the pile of money towards him with both hands as if to accentuate Lever's loss. Lever sat, poker-faced with his elbows on the table. Hammond sipped iced whisky.

'You should know I never bluff,' Carter was saying, 'ace high for Christ's sake. Who d'you think you are – Henry bleeding Gondorf?'

'Who's he?' Hammond said. 'That fella we played with the last time?'

'It's a film, you prat,' Lever said through his teeth. 'Paul fucking Newman.'

Hammond took up the cards and squeezed them into a shuffle. Lever looked at Carter. 'If we're playing on I'll need to cash a cheque.'

'You want to play on then?'

'Course I want to play on. You've got all my money.'

Carter snapped his fingers at Bobby Simpson who came over. Lever was scribbling out a cheque with a gold-nibbed fountain pen. Carter handed Simpson the empty Tequila bottle.

'Get another,' he said. 'And get Carl a grand.'

Simpson weighed the bottle in his hand. 'I'm driving then, Boss.'

'Looks that way doesn't it.'

Young Young watched the clock tick beyond midnight and shifted himself in the seat where his trousers stuck to the leather. The adrenaline pumped through his veins and his backside was loose with the tension. He glanced again in the mirror behind him. The club was closed. The car beyond the one behind his was gone. The steps of the club were empty. Again he looked at the clock.

He sat deep in the seat and forced himself to relax. He could do this. He could do this easily. He thought of his old man, long dead but a player when he was alive. He would've done this. He wouldn't take shit from nobody, not Carter or Stepper-Nap or any of them, jerks like Pretty Boy for instance. Who the fuck was Pretty Boy? He ate people like Pretty Boy. In the distance through the mirror the High Road was emptying. A black cab, a joy rider maybe. Cold night and midweek and people going home. He knew he was not really ready, his ribs still hurt but he no longer spat blood and he could not wait any more.

He had lain very low since they hit him. No woman, no white Eilish McCauley. But he'd have her one last time after this was done. He'd have her so hard for setting him up. He was bigger and better than Stepper-Nap. She only fucked him for the money. That made him smile. The saggy-arsed nigger shit. With his big belly and his fat freaky face. As if to remind himself he rubbed his fingers over the flattened ridges of his own belly and smiled. She *fucked* him because she liked it. Again he thought about his father. Little Bigger remembered him better than he did; Young Young had only been ten when he was killed. But he could see him all right, with hands like shovel heads and arms as long and strong as tree branches. Black eyes, a mass of kinky hair and that scar running from his ear right to his lip.

He picked up his mobile phone and pressed in a number. A woman's voice answered, sleep on her tongue.

'Baby.'

'Oh, man. You know what time it is?'

'What you doing?'

'Sleeping. What you think I'm doing?'

'I'm coming over later.'

'You called me to tell me that. You got your key don't you?'

'Yeah I got my key.'

'Then don't wake me up when you get here. The children is playing me up.'

'Later, baby.' Young Young pressed End and put down the phone.

They were all against him now, Little Bigger on the Daddy's side or Pretty Boy's side depending on who came out on top. He had tried to give him all of that big-brother shit, the hand on the shoulder and the *stay cool* chat lines. Young Young had nodded and patted him on the arm and given him the finger when his back was turned. He wondered what it would be like in prison.

Upstairs they wrapped up the game. Carter handed the bundle of money he had won to Simpson to lock in the safe. Then he got Lever's coat for him and draped it about his shoulders. 'Some game, Carl,' he said. 'You've should've quit when you were ahead.'

Lever looked at him, lips curled as if he had just bitten into an apple and got a maggot. 'When was I ahead?'

Hammond grinned and steadied himself with a hand on the back of a chair. 'Luck of the bloody Irish,' he said.

Carter winked at him and picked up the Tequila bottle from the table.

Simpson came out of the office with Carter's coat and gave it to him. 'See the lads out, Bobby,' Carter said. 'I'll finish up here. Bring the car round when you're done.' He tossed him the keys and sat down behind his desk.

Young Young watched the doors open and saw three men come down the steps. He craned his neck so he could see them and once again his ribs seemed to tear at his flesh. The fat bouncer and two others. No Carter. Where the hell was Carter? The two men got into the Jaguar that was parked across the road and Young Young heard the engine fire. The bouncer started along the pavement towards the carpark gates. Exhaust fumes coughed from the back of the Jag and it lurched forward with a squealing of tyres. For a moment Young Young panicked. The gun in his hands now. Where was Carter? Where the hell was Carter?

The bouncer came alongside him and disappeared behind the iron gates of the carpark. Still no Carter. Young Young heard the engine start on the Bentley and then headlights washed over the wall. A moment later the Bentley swung onto the road. Young Young looked back toward the club and saw Jimmy Carter locking the door at the top of the steps.

Then he was out of the car, the night clinging to the skin of his face. The bouncer drove the car along the wrong side of the road and pulled up in front of the club. Young Young moved towards them. Carter teetering down the steps. Young Young marched, gun down at his side, breath coming in smoke. He passed the remaining parked cars and came alongside as the bouncer got out of the driver's door. Carter looked as though he was having trouble standing. The bouncer steadied him, guiding him around the length of the bonnet and then leaving him with his palms flattened on the paintwork as he opened the passenger door. Young Young stepped onto the road. Out of the corner of his eye he saw a woman at the bus stop on Kilburn High Road.

Carter reeled again, shaking his head and the bouncer helped him towards the passenger seat. Young Young took one more step and lifted his gun to waist height.

'Hey, fuck pig,' he called.

Carter looked round. The bouncer looked round. Young Young levelled the Uzi. 'Remember me?' For a second he saw Carter's eyes ball in their sockets and he felt his bowels suddenly loosen. He squeezed his finger into the trigger. The weapon kicked in his hands as it sprayed off the rounds. He raked them, Carter, the bouncer and the side of the car in one sweep of his arm. Carter doubled then flipped back, arms flailing on either side. Young Young saw blood spit from little rips in his shirt and he was thrown back against the car. The bouncer went down like a tree.

Young Young stood for a second, steam rising over Carter's body. And then a scream rose from the High Road. Running now, back to his car. He leapt inside, throwing the empty gun ahead of him and started the engine. Reverse. The Rover leapt back and crunched into the car behind.

First gear and spinning the wheel with both hands and lurching into the road. He pressed his right foot flat to the floor. Left and right, he disappeared into the warren of houses.

Twelve

Vanner lay in bed with Ellie. Through the uncurtained window the darkness still banked against the city. Ellie was sleeping, her head on his chest. Vanner lay against the pillows with one arm crooked behind his neck listening to the softness of her breathing. She was warm against him, her breasts pushed into his side. Gently he stroked the softness of her hair. The muscles strained at his shoulder, a pain in his side. He wanted to move, but at the same time he did not want to disturb her. He delighted in the closeness, moments like these, the sort of moments he had not allowed himself in a long time. He glanced at the clock by the bed.

The phone rang. Ellie stirred, muttered something unintelligible and rolled off him, dragging the duvet with her. Vanner swung his legs over the edge of the bed and picked up the receiver.

'Vanner.'

'Guv'nor, it's me. Jimmy Crack.'

Vanner rubbed his eyes with the heel of his hand. 'What's up?'

'Jimmy Carter's been shot.'

Vanner met him at the crime scene off Kilburn High Road. He parked the car beyond the blue and white tape and stepped out into drizzle. He lifted his collar, flashed his warrant card at the uniform and strode towards Jimmy who was standing beside a silver Bentley with DI Keithley from 2 Area AMIP, one of Weir's cronies, but older, less edgy. Keithley nodded as Vanner stepped up to them.

'What you got, John?'

'Automatic weapon.' Keithley pointed to the smattering of holes in the car.

Vanner nodded and bent to a patch of blood on the road, all but washed clean by the rain. He could feel the drizzle chill against his neck. He looked up at the holes. 'Slugs'll be in there,' he said.

Keithley nodded.

'Jimmy Carter.'

'You knew him?'

'Dead then.'

'Very.' Keithley pulled his unzipped anorak more tightly about him and sniffed. He took a soggy handkerchief from his trouser pocket and blew his nose with it. 'Bloody weather. I'll never make old bones.'

'The bouncer got hit too, Guv,' Jimmy said. 'The fat, black-haired one.'

'Bobby Simpson,' Keithley said.

'Dead?'

Keithley shook his head. 'Took one in the chest but it went clean through him.'

'Will he make it?'

'Don't know yet.'

Vanner looked up and down the road. 'When did it happen?'

'Two thirty this morning.'

'Witnesses?'

Keithley lifted his eyebrows. 'Surprisingly, yes. A woman waiting for the night bus on the High Road down there.'

Vanner gauged the distance in his mind. 'Sixty yards. What did she see?'

Jimmy looked in his eyes. 'IC3, Guv. Male. Very tall and thin.'

Vanner felt something crawl on his spine.

A Granada Scorpio pulled up and Morrison got out. He spotted Vanner, frowned and moved towards them, hands in the pockets of his coat. Vanner left him to Keithley and Jimmy Crack and walked up the road to where two blue-suited SOCO's were bending beside a parked car. As he got to them Vanner could see they were scraping broken tail-light glass from the road. He looked at the dent in the cream-coloured Escort and frowned. From his pocket he took a pen and scraped in the groove. Dark blue paint came away. He passed the pen to the officer who deposited the paint in a plastic evidence bag.

As Vanner stood up Morrison came up behind him.

'What're you doing here, Vanner?'

Vanner lit a cigarette and looked down at him. 'We're looking at a spade called Young Young,' he said quietly. 'Part of the Brit-Boy posse from Harlesden. He shot up the club there with an Uzi. Crime Group pulled a slug from the ceiling.' He nodded towards the Bentley. 'I'll bet my pension it matches.'

Morrison smiled thinly. 'Pension? You think you'll last long enough to collect it?'

Vanner blew smoke in his face. 'You know what,' he said. 'One of these days you'll say something funny.'

He went back to Jimmy who was still talking to Keithley. Vanner took him by the arm and they stepped to one side. 'SOCO over there found blue paint and a broken tail light.'

'Young Young's Rover.'

'Tall and thin and black. It doesn't take a genius.'

'What's Morrison saying?'

'The usual.' Vanner looked round at Keithley. 'I want Jimmy Crack seconded to your firm, John.'

'You sure about this Young Young?'

'Very.'

'Okay.' Keithley looked at Jimmy. 'You any idea where we can find him?'

Jimmy blew out his cheeks. 'I can make a couple of calls.'

'Do it.' Keithley looked at Vanner. 'What did SOCO pick up over there?'

'Blue car paint. He backed into the Escort in his rush to get away. Young Young drives a midnight-blue 820.' He turned to Jimmy Crack. 'Jim, the club normally closes at eleven. If it was him he must've been sat there a while. You might want to do a cell-site analysis – see if he used his phone.'

'Okay.'

Vanner turned to Keithley again. 'You going to use Hendon or Ruislip?'

'Frank Weir's working out of Hendon. But if we have a body this might not take very long. I'll square it with him.'

'Be a bit crowded on Holmes.'

'Such is life.'

Vanner patted him on the shoulder and went back to his car. Morrison caught up with him.

'I want details of this crack team, Vanner. On my desk this morning.'

Vanner dropped his cigarette in a puddle. 'Okay. Jimmy Crack's seconded to the Murder Squad. He knows Young Young better than anyone. I'll let his Guv'nor know.'

'Fine.' Morrison watched him as he drove away.

George Webb sat with the Special Branch DS in the cell on the fifteenth floor. They worked through nominals on the computer.

'Here we go,' the DS said. 'Michelle Moran. Sleeper. Born in Crossmaglen.'

Webb looked at her face in the scanned image on the screen. 'Black hair, long to her shoulders, thin face.' He looked at her statistics. 'Right height. Right pedigree.' He sat back. 'A definite maybe then.'

'Yeah.'

'What does she do over here?'

'Works for the council. She's been here six years, Webby. Not so much as a sniff. We reckon she's carried weapons but she's been very quiet since she's been here. We've never had anything on her but Box reckon she could've been Mullery's donkey.'

'The Quarter Master? Very possible then.' Webb stroked his moustache. 'What about the real target – any word from Box?'

'There's one possible. Lives in Hammersmith. Same age as your body in Ealing.'

'Description fit?'

'Not exactly. But she drives the same kind of car.' He sat back. 'We've organised a rolling plot. If it is her they wanted they might move again soon.'

Eilish washed her hair. James had taken the children to school. She stood half-naked in the bathroom and showered the suds into the basin. Downstairs the doorbell rang very savagely. Eilish jumped and swore. She turned off the taps and wrung out her hair. The doorbell sounded again. Wrapping a clean towel about her she went downstairs and opened the front door. Stepper-Nap pushed past her. 'Where's Young Young?' he demanded.

'What?' Eilish closed the door.

'Young Young. Where is he?'

'How the hell should I know, Stepper? I'm not his keeper.'

He looked malevolently at her then. 'You were screwing him weren't you?'

His words stung. She tried to keep her face still but it showed.

Stepper smiled without using his eyes. 'When was he here last?'
'I don't know.' She looked away from him. 'Ages ago.'
He moved into the sitting room. 'You got a drink in here?'
'It's eight thirty in the morning.'
'I didn't ask you the time.'
He followed her to the kitchen and she fetched a beer from the fridge. He took the can from her and tore off the ring pull. She watched his throat convulse as he swallowed. 'What is it, lover?'
He looked at her then, eyes glazing. 'YoungYoung. The fucker killed Jimmy Carter.'
They sat in the living room, Stepper-Nap sunk into the chair. He finished the beer and wiped his mouth. 'I deal crack,' he said. 'I don't kill Irishmen.' He slapped the arm of the chair so hard dust rose. 'Christ. The stupid nigger fuck. I should've let Carter kill him.'
'You couldn't. How would it look to the team?'
'Eilish, we needed Carter.'
Eilish smiled then. 'We did. But we don't any more.' She sat back and crossed her legs. 'So Jimmy Carter's dead. So what. I've got all the contacts you need. All we had to get from Jimmy was an intro. We got that didn't we?'
'But the Irish. Carter's people.'
She shifted her shoulders. 'Give 'em YoungYoung.'
He looked at her then and smiled. 'Yeah,' he said. 'You're right.' His face clouded again. 'But I don't know where he is.'
'Get hold of his brother.'
'I'm looking for him. He don't answer his phone.'

Vanner sat in his office on the phone to Jimmy Crack. 'We're looking for him, Guv. The witness gave a pretty good description considering how far away she was.'
'Can she pick him out from his photo?'
'Not that good.'
'What about the cell-site analysis?'
'Result. He bounced a call off Beacon 501 at one thirty this morning. That puts him within half a mile of the club.'
'Nice one, Jimmy.'
'We've got two slugs from the car. Another from Carter's brain.'
'You mean he had one?'

'Apparently, Guv. Just his heart was missing.'

Vanner chuckled. He thought for a moment and then he said, 'Young Young'll dump the gun. Even he isn't that stupid.'

'He won't if he's worried about his health.'

'You mean Carter's team.'

'They'll be very pissed off.'

Vanner sat back. 'He's holed up somewhere, Jim.'

'I know. I'm trying to get hold of a snout. You remember that bird I told you about who used to hang out with him. She fingered him for me in the first place. I nicked her for intent to supply. Remember?'

Vanner did remember. Sandra somebody. An old Rasta car dealer got himself a whole load of crack when he broke the heads of two of the Governor Generals when they were extorting protection money from him. He beat them up, took their guns then tied them up and pistol whipped them senseless before dumping them from the back of his van. He dealt the crack himself and Sandra had been arrested with five thousand in cash in her handbag.

'You think she'll know?'

'She's my best shot, Guv'nor.'

'Has Keithley got SO19 on standby?'

Jimmy paused. 'Not yet. He wants a positive ID on Young Young first.'

Vanner furrowed his brow. 'And how does he plan to get that?'

'Bobby Simpson.'

'The bouncer. He isn't going to say anything.'

'He might with what Keithley's got planned.'

Vanner sat back once again and lifted his foot to the desk. 'What about the car?'

'No sighting.'

'If he's smart he'll get the light fixed.'

'We're checking the likely gaffs.'

'Good. Keep me posted, Jim.'

Vanner put down the phone and then dialled Ryan's number in the Hendon incident room. Ryan answered almost immediately.

'Sid, it's Vanner. What's happening?'

'Oh the usual. Us looking – finding nothing. 13 looking and telling us nothing.'

'Anyone ever tell you you're a cynic.'

'My wife. My kids. You.'

'You heard about Jimmy Carter?'

'Just now. Morrison was down here panicking. Two of his AMIP teams fighting over the Holmes suite.'

'Give him something to think about.' Vanner stood up and looked out of the window.

'The shooter for Carter's flagged to Jimmy Crack.'

'You know who he is already?'

'Young Young. The Harlesden Daddy's body armour.'

'Keithley's in for a result then.'

'When he nicks him. Nobody knows where he is.' Vanner pressed the phone closer to his ear. 'Listen. Any word from your snout?'

'Not yet.'

'Now's the time, Slips. With Carter blown away – tongues'll wag in Kilburn. Get him on the phone. Tell him to put it about.'

Keithley, his skipper from AMIP and Jimmy Crack stood in the hospital corridor and gazed through the glass panel of the intensive care ward at Bobby Simpson's bed. His eyes were closed, face bereft of colour, a tube protruding from his mouth. The doctor came out and stripped off rubber gloves. Keithley, short, grey-haired, blue eyes, stood up straighter.

'Will he live?' he asked the doctor.

The doctor made a face. 'The bullet missed his heart, but his left lung is collapsed. He's got a large hole in his back.'

'But will he live?'

'Yes, I think he'll live.'

'Does he know it yet?'

The doctor stared at him. 'He hasn't come round yet.'

'When will he – come round?'

'I can't say. A few hours. Tomorrow maybe.'

Keithley took a card from his pocket and passed it to him. 'Will you do me a favour, doctor?'

'If I can.' The doctor inspected the card.

'As soon as he wakes up page me on that number. I want to talk to him before anyone else does.'

'As soon as he's fit enough you can.'

'One other thing.'

'What's that?'

'It would be really helpful if you didn't tell him he wasn't going to die straight away.'

'I'm not going to lie to him, Inspector.'

Keithley smiled. 'I wouldn't ask you to. If he doesn't ask – just don't tell him that's all. He can identify the gunman, but he might not want to – if you follow me.'

The doctor grinned then and nodded. 'Soon as he wakes I'll page you.'

'Thank you.' They shook hands and the doctor walked off down the corridor.

Young Young stood under the lamp, inspecting the fresh paint and new tail light on his car and nodded his appreciation. The mechanic with the dreadlocks wiped his hands on a rag and they brushed knuckles. 'Respect, Lonny. I owe you.'

Lonny grinned and took the wad of cash. 'See you around, yeah.'

'You haven't seen me at all.'

'Seen who, man?'

Young Young drove to Harlesden, watching for police cars. He got as far as Roundwell Park without seeing any and parked in the slip road across the street from Eilish's. Leaning over the back seat he picked up the carrier bag with the gun in it, then he opened the door. It was raining hard now and he zipped his jacket to the neck. He looked in both directions, crossed the road and made his way up to Eilish's house.

The night pushed against the city, the cloud cover complete and weighted with the rain that spattered off the pavement. Young Young paused under a street light by the school and studied the lighted windows of Eilish's house. He was cold and for a moment he imagined her inside, warm and wet and inviting. Shadows crossed the thin curtains in the front room and he could hear the wail of the TV.

He moved across the front of the house and ducked down the side to the unkempt garden. Light, harsh and unshaded, flooded half the garden from the kitchen. He paused, then picked his way carefully over the discarded children's bicycles. He moved around the edge of the lawn being very careful to keep in the shadows. He could hear the clatter of pans from the kitchen and he looked up to see James at the sink.

'Pussy,' Young Young mouthed and moved further round

the garden till he came to the coal bunker. Lifting the rotten top, he peered inside and saw bits of wood and concrete. Moving aside the first layer of debris, he placed the bag with his gun inside between two pieces of stone and covered it up again. Then he looked back at the house. The bathroom light was on and he saw the naked outline of Eilish frosted against the glass.

His loins ached all at once and he realised how long it had been since he had had any. White flesh and red hair. She was good, for all her other faults. But like all white girls she was two-faced and unreliable. Give him a black mother any day. In the bathroom Eilish smoothed the towel over her breasts then down her belly to her thighs. Young Young sucked in a breath.

Her baby brother was still at the kitchen sink and Young Young watched him drying up. Rain fell on him and he shivered. He took one last look at the bathroom and then moved back round the edge of the lawn, being careful to stay in the darkness. James did look up and he stepped back to the road. He turned for the park and stopped. A two-tone police car was parked by his car with its lights flashing.

Young Young swore and walked the other way.

At the end of the road he phoned his brother's number.

'Yeah?'

'Little Bigger.'

'Young Young. Where you at? Every mother's looking for you.'

'Yeah – who is?'

'Stepper-Nap is. Pretty Boy is. Everyone's asking me where you at.'

'And what did you tell them?'

'Nothing. I mean I don't know do I.'

'They there now?'

'No.'

'Where's you at?'

'Carmel's?'

'She there?'

'In the bedroom.'

'You getting amongst it?'

'Later maybe. Young Young, man. What you want to go shoot the Irishman for?'

'He had it coming.'

'But Jimmy Carter, man.'
'You think I'm scared of him?'
'I didn't say that. But his boys'll be looking for a six-foot-six nigger with half his teeth missing.'
'I don't give a fuck.'
Little Bigger was silent for a moment. 'Where you at?'
'On the street. I just lost my car to the pigs.'
'Where you going?'
'Somewhere. Somewhere even you don't know, man. I ain't never told you.'
'I need to know, baby. You're my brother.'
'You got my number. Phone me. Oh, and brother.'
'What?'
'Give Stepper the finger for me.'

Vanner was just leaving the office when Jimmy Crack called him from Hendon. It was eight o'clock and he was meeting Ellie for dinner. Anne had phoned. His father was getting worse and he was debating whether to drive to Norfolk.
'We found the car,' Jimmy told him.
'Where?'
'Roundwell Park. Near Eilish McCauley's house.'
'Somehow that figures. I don't suppose he was in it.'
'No.'
'Is Keithley giving her a spin?'
'No. We're setting up an OP over the road. He wants to watch for a while.'
'He's a cautious man, Jim.'
'Tell me about it.'
'Maybe just as well though. We don't want to upset our own plot.'
'We're leaving the car tonight, Guv. We've got spotters in the school. If he doesn't show in the morning we'll tow it in.'

The following morning Jimmy Crack was at the second Hendon incident room when Keithley's pager vibrated against his midriff. They were talking about Young Young's car. He had not been back for it and there was no sign of him at Eilish McCauley's house. This morning both she and her brother had left early. The spotters were convinced the house was empty, so they towed the car in. Keithley upturned the face on his pager. 'The doctor,' he said. 'Let's go.'

As they went up in the lift at the hospital Jimmy Crack looked at Keithley. 'If we do nick Young Young me and Vanner want a word, Guv,' he said. Keithley glanced at him. 'You can have all the words you want, Jim. But we have to nick him first.'

They walked the length of the corridor, Keithley with his hands in his coat pockets. 'I'll do the talking,' he said.

Bobby Simpson was awake. He still lay prostrate in bed, a tube in his nose and a drip feeding him from a plastic bag on a pole. His eyes were dull and blurred, yellow at the edges as if he had been taking steroids. Keithley stood at the end of his bed with his coat flaps pushed behind him.

'How you feeling, Bob?'

Simpson did not appear to see him. The nurse standing beside the bed checked the movement of the drip in his arm. Keithley glanced at her and smiled. 'You couldn't give us a minute could you?'

'Just one then. He really shouldn't be talking.'

The movement as she went out seemed to stir Simpson in the bed and his eyes thinned then focused on Keithley's face. He swallowed, a liquid hiss in his throat. He was naked from the waist up, black-haired torso swathed in crêpe bandage. Redness seeped through the gauze on his chest.

Keithley pulled up a chair and looked at him. 'My name's Keithley, Bobby. Detective Inspector. You know Jimmy's dead.'

Simpson stared at him, said nothing then looked at Jimmy Crack.

'Took three in the chest,' Keithley went on quietly. 'One more in the head. Same bullets that shot up the ceiling of the club. It was Young Young wasn't it, the crack dealer from Harlesden.'

Still Simpson did not say anything. He half-lifted his hands as if he meant to lay them on his chest, but pain weakened his eyes and he laid them flat again.

'You took one right in the chest, Bob.' Keithley glanced at the floor as he said it. 'You must've looked him right in the eyes.'

Simpson cleared his throat again, tried to move but pain stiffened his features. Keithley sat more to the edge of his seat. Simpson's eyes were closing. Gently Keithley squeezed his arm and he opened them again. 'Young Young, Bobby.'

'I ain't talking to you.' His voice was weak, wheezing, a rasp of moisture gagging up in his throat.

Keithley sat back, folded his arms and nodded. 'You've got one lung down, Bobby, and half your back is missing.' Fear then in Simpson's eyes. Keithley sat forward and nodded. 'You want him to walk?'

'He won't walk.'

'Oh, he will.' Keithley sat forward once more. 'You're not going to get to him, Bobby. He's probably in Jamaica already.'

Simpson pursed his lips then, water in his eyes.

'You want to go out knowing the guy who shot you is on his way to Jamaica?'

'I don't give names.' Simpson coughed then and pain stood out in his eyes.

'Course you don't. But this is different. By the time you get the word out, that's if you ever do . . .' Keithley let his eyes drift to the heart monitor bleeping faintly behind the bed. 'He'll be long gone. One long holiday – back home with his women and his kids and his beer. He'll just kick back and get all the drinks he ever wanted. Just imagine their faces when he tells his mates how he killed Carter and his bouncer.' He stood up then and leaned over the bed. 'We know where he is, Bobby. If we don't move on him soon it'll be too late.'

The nurse came back in then. 'That's it, gentlemen.'

Keithley stilled her with an upraised palm and looked into Simpson's face. 'Come on, Bobby. Do yourself a favour. Do us all a favour. Your mates'll do him inside.'

Simpson's eyes widened then and he half-opened his mouth. The nurse moved forward.

Jimmy stepped in front of her. 'One minute,' he said. 'This is really important.'

'You can't touch him, Bobby,' Keithley was saying. 'Even if you do walk out of here you'll never mind a door again let alone take on someone like Young Young. *Tell me*,' he said. 'It was him wasn't it?'

Simpson looked into his face.

'Young Young. Yes?' Keithley said.

Simpson pursed his lips. 'Yeah,' he muttered. 'Yes.'

'Good lad.' Keithley laid a hand on his arm.

Outside he stalked along the corridor, Jimmy abreast of him, still feeling adrenaline thump in his muscles. 'Nice one, Guv'nor.'

'Your snout, Jimmy. Find her. Find him. I'll get SO19 on standby.'

Little Bigger met Stepper-Nap and Pretty Boy in the amusements on Uxbridge Road. Pretty Boy was standing, oiled dreadlocks shiny against his scalp. His eyes, as ever, were cold. Stepper sat squashed into his chair and looked up at Little Bigger.

'Well?'

'I talked to him.'

'When?'

'Last night.'

'Where was he?'

Little Bigger shrugged. 'Don't know. Wouldn't tell me. Sounded like he was on the street somewhere.'

Stepper looked at him then, as if sizing him up. Little Bigger took a step backwards and bumped into Pretty Boy.

'Is all, Step. I swear. I don't know where he is.'

Stepper looked through him. 'Where would he go?'

'I don't know, man. He ain't in his flat. I ain't seen his car.'

'His car got towed away.' Pretty Boy spoke then. 'I seen it, this morning. Near Eilish's place.'

Little Bigger looked round at him. 'So they know he done it then.'

Pretty Boy flickered his eyes. 'Looks that way don't it.'

'I want him.' Stepper slapped his palm on the desk, making Little Bigger jump. 'He got a baby mother someplace I don't know about?' He stood up then and looked down his nose at Little Bigger.

'I don't know, man. He said he was going someplace no-one knew about. I reckon, yeah he got one.'

'Where?'

Little Bigger lifted his hands. 'He told me I got his phone number. He told me to call him.'

'Then call him. Find out where he is. Tell him you got his car or something.'

Little Bigger shook his head. 'He knows about his car.'

'Well tell him something else.' Stepper-Nap pushed his weight against him. 'Tell him anything, man. I need to know where he's at.'

When he was gone Pretty Boy clasped his hands behind his back and leaned on the door frame. 'That's you fucked with the Irish.'

'You reckon?' Stepper looked at him. 'Man, I'm just beginning.'

Pretty Boy shook his head. 'You shouldn't mix with the Irish, man. They ain't brothers. They blow people up.'

'You dumb fuck. You really that stupid. I know them, man. I got connections.'

Pretty Boy snorted. 'White pussy's what you got.'

Stepper stood up again and they looked one another in the eye. 'I'm ahead of you, man. You can't keep up with me.' Stepper stroked fingers over Pretty Boy's face. 'You may be pretty, but you ain't in the big league.'

Pretty Boy pushed his hand away. 'We'll see, my man. We'll see.'

Eilish met Stepper-Nap at the door. His face was bright, fresh from his words with Pretty Boy. James was at the job centre, determined it seemed to make some kind of start on his life. Eilish had been expecting Stepper, but not this soon. He carried a plastic shopping bag which he passed to her. Gingerly she took it, then opened it and withdrew a tupperware sandwich box.

'That's a kilo and a half, baby. Don't you lose it now.'

Eilish turned away from him. 'You sure this is a good time, lover? I mean with everything that's happening.'

'They expecting you, girl. We gotta show good faith. Show them we had nothing to do with Carter getting hisself shot.' He moved into the lounge and sat down. 'The kids at school are they?'

'Course they are. Where else would they be?'

Eilish sat across from him, the sandwich box on her knees. 'What about Young Young?'

'What about him?' Stepper stared at her. 'What's with you, girl. The other day you was saying how we don't need him, how we don't need Jimmy Carter.'

Eilish ignored the jibe. 'I've only just got back.'

'So you go again.'

She sighed then and sat back. 'When?'

'This afternoon. I booked you on a boat.'

'This afternoon? I can't go this afternoon. What about my kids?'

'Your brother can look after them like he always does.'

'But what will I tell him?'

'Think of something.' He sat forward then. 'They ready for this, girl. We need to show faith. I don't need Irish nutters on my back.'

Eilish stared at him then. 'I'm not going this afternoon. There's no-one to pick up my kids.'

'Where's your brother?'

'He's out – looking for a job. He won't be back in time.'

'I'll get Jig to get your kids.'

'No you won't. I don't want that slime ball anywhere near them.'

Stepper's face furrowed. 'Jig ain't into kids, baby.'

'I don't care, lover. He's not going anywhere near them. Book me another boat.'

He stood up then and shook out his hands. 'Oh, for Christ's sake. I booked it already.'

'Then unbook it, Stepper.' She placed the box very firmly on the floor beside her chair. 'Either that or you take it yourself.'

He stared very coldly at her then, fist clenching and unclenching at his side. 'You watch yourself, babe.'

'No, babe,' she mimicked. 'You watch yourself. Without me you haven't got a deal.'

'You white bitch.'

Her eyes stalked then and she stood up. 'You listen, Stepper-Nap. You think you're such a hardman. Let me tell you about hardmen. Real hardmen. I was hanging out with hardmen when I was half your age. Men that'd dip you in their tea. I saw one shot dead by soldiers. I saw others shoot soldiers dead. So don't give me your macho black guy routine – you worthless piece of shit.'

He stared helplessly at her then, eyes boiling with frustration. 'What is it with you people. First Pretty Boy then Young Young and now you. Who runs this operation?'

'You do, Stepper. For now. But you need me and I'm not going today. So change the fucking ticket.'

Ellie wrote up her notes at the nurse's station. She was half-concentrating, half-watching Anne swabbing the ward floor with her mop. The patients were taking their afternoon rest. A television set buzzed in the background. Anne leaned on her mop, looked over at Ellie and rubbed her back. Ellie laid down her pen.

'Fancy a cup of tea?' she said.

They sat in the staff room, Anne holding her cup in both of her hands. She smiled a little wearily.

'Hard work,' Ellie said.

'Pays the bills.'

'Does it?'

'Just about.' She looked at the floor. 'Must be nice – living with your boyfriend – only half to pay?'

Ellie thought about that. 'I've still got my own flat to pay for. Not that I spend much time there.'

'Like to be with him do you?'

Ellie grinned. 'Yes,' she said. 'I do. Mind you – I don't seem to see him much.'

'Works shifts too, huh?'

'Sort of. He shouldn't. He's a Detective Inspector with the Drug Squad. It's supposed to be regular hours but it never seems to work out that way.'

'A policeman, eh?' Anne sat back. 'What is it with nurses and policemen – the uniforms?'

Ellie laughed. 'Aden doesn't wear one, Anne. Detective. Plain clothes.'

'Of course. Anne sipped her tea. '*Aidan*. That's Irish isn't it?'

'ADEN. Different. He was born there. Somewhere in the Middle East.'

'The Yemen,' Anne said.

'Is it?'

'Yes. The capital.'

'I think I should've known that.' She smiled. 'You got a boyfriend, Anne?'

Anne shook her head. 'Not any more.'

'Walked out on you did he?'

Anne's face clouded. 'Sort of. He got killed, Ellie. In Ireland. A long time ago.'

'I'm sorry.'

'Don't be.' Anne held up a hand. 'Like I said – it was a long time ago.'

'What happened to him?'

She looked at her then, as if she saw her and yet did not. Her eyes had darkened a fraction. 'He got shot, Ellie,' she said quietly. 'Shot dead by policemen.'

Ellie was stunned. She put down her cup and then picked it up again. 'My God,' she said. 'I'm really sorry, Anne. I shouldn't have asked.'

'They thought he was a terrorist, but he wasn't. He was unarmed. They shot him down like a dog.' She smiled then. 'Policemen. Not always what they seem.'

Jimmy Crack and Keithley inspected YoungYoung's car. Vanner was with them, bent on his hands and knees. 'Rear light's new,' he said. 'Look at the screw. They forgot to put the rusty one back.'

'Paint's fresh too.' Jimmy was flicking through his electronic notebook.

'Snout?' Vanner asked him.

'Sandra, Guv. I can't get her. I've got another number somewhere.'

Vanner looked at Keithley. 'You been to the McCauley house yet, John?'

'Spotters left this morning. We're going over now.'

Vanner nodded. 'Take Jimmy with you eh?'

Keithley chuckled then. 'I'm old school, Vanner. I'm not going to spoil your plot.'

Vanner grinned and apologised.

'Got it.' Jimmy tapped the little screen with his fingernail. He took his mobile from his belt and dialled. Three rings then an answerphone. 'Sandra. This is Lofty,' he said. 'Phone me please – soon as you can. It's urgent.' He switched off the phone and placed it back on his belt.

'Result you reckon, Jim?' Keithley asked him.

'He was shagging her, Guv. If anyone knows she will.'

Vanner went back to Campbell Row. He looked at his watch as he parked. He must phone his father. He climbed the steps from the High Road as the darkness fell. Not long now till the clocks went forward again. Ellie was off at five. He really ought to get home soon after. He smiled at himself as he punched in the combination and went upstairs. A long time since he had rushed home to a woman.

Sammy met him at the top of the stairs. 'Message for you, Guv'nor. Slippery.'

Vanner nodded, went into his office, thought briefly about the report that Morrison wanted and picked up the telephone. 'Sid, it's Vanner.'

'Hello, Guv'nor.'

'What you got for me?'

'The Coalman. He belled me. I'm meeting him at a hotel off Old Brompton Road in an hour.'

'I'll meet you at the Trade Hall,' Vanner told him.

Ryan was sheltering from the wind in the porch of the Cricklewood Trade Hall. He wore a lumberjack coat over his suit. Vanner hooted his horn and Ryan trotted across the road. 'Old Brompton Road,' he said as he got in. 'There's a hotel round the corner. You got the bottle?'

Vanner nodded to the back seat and spun the steering wheel one hundred and eighty degrees. Old rain water hissed from the tyres as he pulled out into traffic. They drove the length of Kilburn High Road and on to Maida Vale. The traffic bunched and Vanner drummed his fingers on the steering wheel.

'Why Old Brompton Road?'

Ryan lit two cigarettes and passed one over. 'Gives him a night out I suppose. He won't come anywhere near a nick.' He sucked hard on the cigarette. 'Used to be a bird puller, Guv. I think it reminds him of the old days.'

They headed into the West End, skirting Hyde Park before swinging the loop into Knightsbridge. Vanner half-opened his window and the smoke zig-zagged from his cigarette.

'How's the bird then?' Ryan said.

'Fine, Sid. How's Frank Weir?'

'Frustrated.'

'Inquiry going cold?'

'You could say. Sharing it doesn't help.'

'They found anyone yet?' Vanner asked. 'Got to be a mistake. They took out the wrong party.'

'That's what they reckon yeah.'

'Takes time, Slips. But they're good.'

'That's what Webby keeps telling me.'

They parked outside the Cleveland Hotel and Vanner took

the bottle of Jameson's from the back seat. He flipped it over in his hand and looked up at the windows. Rain was falling again, grey against the white of the building. Vanner shook the moisture from his shoulders and they went inside.

The Coalman was waiting for them in a bedroom on the second floor. He opened the door in his socks, took the bottle from Vanner without speaking and fetched glasses from the bathroom. He poured two, splashed some more into a coffee cup which he handed to Ryan. He raised his glass to Vanner. 'Here's to swimming with bow-legged women.' He knocked it back, sucked breath and poured another.

He stretched himself out on the bed and crossed his legs at the ankle. Ryan sat in a chair, Vanner stood by the window and sipped at the whiskey. He took cigarettes from his packet and threw one at The Coalman who caught it smartly and clamped it between his teeth.

'This is my old Guv'nor,' Ryan said. 'DI Vanner, Coal.'

The Coalman's eyes shone for a moment. 'I've heard of you so I have.'

'All bad I trust.'

The Coalman smiled thinly. 'Bad as it gets,' he said.

Vanner looked at him, then glanced at Ryan before looking back again. He tipped the last of his drink down his neck and placed the glass on the table. 'Where'd you know Jimmy Carter from?' he said.

'Knew Jimmy Carter.'

'Whatever.'

'Same place as you I reckon.'

'Is that so?' They looked at one another. 'Got himself in a fight back home.'

'Naw.' The Coalman shook his head. 'He switched sides long before that fight started.'

Vanner stood up straighter. 'So what do you know?'

The Coalman poured more whiskey. 'Enough.'

'What d'you know about Carter and Eilish McCauley?'

The Coalman smacked his lips together and lit a second cigarette from the end of his first one. 'Eilish McCauley,' he said as if tasting the name on his tongue. 'Bonny wee thing she is. Red hair, just how I like them.'

Vanner glanced at Ryan who made a calming motion with the flat of his hand.

'She's bright too, even if she has taken to hanging out with the wrong colour o' company.' He sat straighter and fixed his eyes upon Vanner. 'She had a little deal going with Jimmy. Jimmy knew certain people who knew certain other people.'

'Over the water,' Vanner said.

'Aye, over the water. It was those people she was interested in.' He looked at Ryan then, and back again at Vanner. 'Your black man from Harlesden – the big fella – he's using her to set something up back home.'

Vanner was still. 'Set what up exactly?'

'All I know is she was in Belfast the other week having words wi' a fella from the past. In The Crown it was. Remember The Crown? Nice pint in The Crown.'

'Crack,' Vanner said. 'In Belfast?'

'Not crack. Cocaine. Pure as the driven snow. The white stuff, Mr Vanner. Never tried it myself but they say it kicks like a mule.'

Thirteen

Vanner dropped Ryan off back at the Trade Hall and asked him to speak to his contact in the Anti-Terrorist Branch to see if he knew anything about Eilish McCauley. Ryan nodded, closed the door and walked through the rain to his car. Vanner drove home, late. He called Ellie but got the engaged tone.

When he got there the house was in darkness. It disturbed him, the first time he had not come home to lights in three months. She had left him a note in the kitchen, telling him that an old friend had called and they were having a drink in the pub across the road.

The silence of the house seemed to resonate inside him like an empty noise in itself. He shook the feeling away, sat down on the couch and thought about phoning his father. Instead he dialled Jimmy Crack's mobile number. The sound of children crying emanated down the line.

'Vanner, Jimmy. You're obviously at home. Sorry.'

Jimmy laughed. 'Twilight zone, Guv.'

'What?'

'You've never had kids have you.'

'No.'

'The twilight zone. Sort of lost time between four thirty and seven thirty. They're tired but not tired enough to go to bed. I'm told it gets better.'

'Right.' Vanner stared at his reflection framed in the darkened glass of the window. 'Eilish McCauley, Jim. She's a patsy for the posse.'

'Slippery's snout?'

'Yeah. She's been over the water just recently. He reckons Stepper-Nap's trying to supply them with coke.'

'That's serious, Guv.'

'Indeed.' Vanner heard the children's noise subside as a door was closed. 'What happened at the house?'

'Got her brother. He told us Young Young hadn't been there.'

'And Eilish?'

'Gone home to visit her mother.'

Vanner gripped the phone that little bit tighter. 'Where's home?'

'Ireland.'

He phoned his father and got Anne. His father was resting. Anne told him he wasn't any better but he wasn't any worse. Vanner said he would drive up again at the weekend. Anne told him his father would be glad to see him.

'He's dying isn't he, Anne?'

She was silent for a moment. 'Yes, I think he is.'

A crushed feeling in his chest as he put the phone down. He had been hungry when he came in but now a knot filled the space in his stomach. Father dying. He stood up, rationalised with himself and paced the room in the half-light thrown out by the lamp. He lit a cigarette, smoked it quickly and lit another. He looked out of the window, across the empty street to the lights of the pub on the corner. He wanted to see Ellie, needed her suddenly to hold him and hated himself for his weakness. He exhaled heavily, crushed the second cigarette and unscrewed the cap on the bottle. He thought of the Coalman's eyes as he splashed whiskey into the glass.

For a while longer he sat on the couch, smoked a third cigarette and memories of unfulfilled childhood wove images in his head. He thought about the black and white photograph of the mother he had never known and wondered what regrets he would have when his father finally died. He would die. There would be no getting better from this. He could feel it, a sense of dread he had not experienced since Jane had left him, when he had travelled home on a grim flight from Aldergrove twelve years earlier. The dread of unlooked-for certainty. A feeling that crept in his bones.

Getting up he shook himself, set his mouth in a line and went out. He crossed the road, rain water splashing up his legs from the puddles. The pub was half-full, warm, cigar smoke drifting in a swathe from a fat man at the bar. Ellie was sitting in a booth with Valesca, the girl who had introduced them, the girl who had sewn the thirty-seven stitches that marked his back to this day. Ninja's sword. The gypsy. A year ago now. He bought a round of drinks and sat down on a stool. He had the distinct impression he had interrupted something. Girl's talk. Ellie reached across the table and squeezed his hand.

'You look tired,' she said. 'Where've you been?'

'Brompton Road.' Vanner sipped Caffreys and licked the froth from his lips. 'I tried to call you. Sid Ryan's snout. The deal we're working on.'

'I thought Sid was in the Murder Squad.'

'He is. Old contact from his Drug Squad days.' Vanner looked at Valesca. Hers had been the first face he had seen when he woke up after the beating he took last year. 'How're you?' he said.

'Fine.'

Vanner looked at Ellie, who sipped Coke with ice but no lemon. 'I phoned my father, Ellie. I think I need to go up this weekend.'

He knew she could see the fear in his eyes. He did not say anything. She did not say anything. Vanner swallowed beer and got up. 'I think I'll go home,' he said. 'Not much company tonight.' He glanced down at Valesca. 'Good to see you again.'

'You too,' she said and she smiled. Vanner glanced at Ellie across the table and left them.

Sid Ryan took George Webb to one side after the AMIP briefing. Webb was there with Westbrook again. Nothing to report. The AMIP team still had no idea who Jessica's lover might have been. They were re-checking all the people they had spoken to – but so far all they had was a blank.

'My old Guv'nor, Webby,' Ryan said. '2 Area Drug Squad. He thinks he's got a donkey carrying over the water. Eilish McCauley. You know her?'

Webb made a face. 'No bells ringing. I'll check when I get back to the Yard. If we know her I'll give your Guv'nor a call.'

Weir came up to them. 'So no joy with number two subject then?'

Webb shook his head. 'Not so far.'

'But you're looking.'

'We're always looking, Guv'nor.'

'What about the real target – I mean if this was a PIRA mistake?'

Webb grinned at him. 'We're looking.'

Weir glowered at him and Webb made an open-handed gesture.

Webb went straight to the Special Branch cell when he got back to the Yard. He bought two coffees and placed one at the DS's elbow.

'Eilish McCauley,' he said.

'What about her?'

'Nominal?'

The DS turned to his computer and punched in the name. Nothing came up. He looked round at Webb. 'What does she do?'

'I don't know. But 2 Area Drugs Squad thinks she's a runner for a crack team working out of Harlesden.'

'There's not much crack over the water, George.'

'I know that. She's running coke.' He lifted his shoulders. 'Maybe they make the crack themselves.'

'Or maybe they sell coke.' The DS looked again at the screen. 'She's a non-player, Webby.'

'What about RUC or 90 Section?'

'I'll have a word.'

Webb got up. 'I'll bell the DI at Wembley – see if we can get a handle on her movements.' At the door he paused. 'Any more word from the DPOA about your man in Yorkshire?'

'Not a whisper.'

Webb nodded. 'Must've just been the cracks.'

'Comes to all of us, George.'

Vanner spoke to the Drug Squad officers working on the crack posse, Sammy and China and Anne. 'Slippery's snout gave us Eilish McCauley,' he said. 'Stepper-Nap seems to have done a deal with Jimmy Carter before Young Young blew him away. Carter had serious contacts in Belfast. It seems that Eilish is a donkey for the Brit-Boys. They're ambitious, very ambitious, trying to start up a route to Ulster.'

Sammy entwined his fingers on his knee. 'Crack in Belfast,' he said. 'Antrim Road won't know what hit them.'

'If it *is* crack. It might just be coke.'

'Either way it makes our Daddy a player.'

'Tell me about it,' China said. 'What with the Tottenham team and now this.'

Anne looked at Vanner. 'He must be stretching himself very thinly, Guv.'

'Let's hope so, Anne. It might mean he makes a mistake.'

Sammy got up then and leaned on his desk. 'PIRA control all drugs in Ulster.'

'They get a kickback, Sam. Yeah.'

'SO13?'

'Slippery's speaking to a mate of his there. I've asked them to check on Eilish. If she's running coke one way who knows what she's bringing back.'

'Let's hope it's just the coke, Guv. The last thing we need is 13 all over the manor.'

Vanner grinned at him. 'You sound like Slippery, Sam.' He looked at the pictures of the posse on the chart behind his head. Taking down one of Eilish he scanned the contours of her face. 'She's over there now,' he said. 'Supposedly visiting her mother.'

'Where does she live?'

'In the south, Sam. Trouble is – Eilish took the night boat from Liverpool to Belfast. It's a ninety-mile drive to the border.'

They were quiet then Sammy said, 'Have you spoken to Antrim Road, Guv?'

'First thing this morning. They've got spotters watching for her.'

'They going to pull her?'

Vanner shook his head. 'I've asked them not to for now. We need to get to Stepper-Nap. I reckon this'll be our best shot.'

'He's sleeping with her?' China said.

'Yes. And without her his Irish deal doesn't work. They won't deal direct.'

'Hang on a minute,' Anne said, a troubled expression creasing her brows. 'Surely Young Young shooting Carter messed this up.'

Vanner opened his hands. 'Obviously not.'

'What're we going to do?'

'I'll get Liverpool to put a tail on her when she gets back. Antrim Road'll let us know when she gets on the boat. We pick her up at South Mimms and follow her.'

Sammy smiled. 'Getting somewhere at last. About bloody time.'

The phone was ringing in Vanner's office. He left them then

and went through. 'Vanner,' he said as he lifted the receiver.

'George Webb, Guv. SO13 Reserve.'

'Ah.' Vanner sat down. 'Sid Ryan spoke to you.'

'Slippery. Yeah.'

'You know her up there?'

'No.'

'Non-player then.'

'Apparently.'

'What d'you want to do?'

'About her? Nothing right now. We've got the word out over the water. Somebody might tag along for a while.'

'Have a word with the Drug Squad on Antrim Road,' Vanner said. 'She's over there now.'

'Thanks,' Webb said. 'I'll do that.'

'We're letting her be for the time being, George. She's very close to the main man and we've been waiting for something like this.'

Webb chuckled. 'We won't tread on your toes then.'

'I'd appreciate it.'

Jimmy Crack waited for Sandra in the carpark by the playing fields in Sudbury. It had taken her till this morning to call him back. She had been very jumpy and even now he wasn't sure she would show. When he had arrested her last year he had no idea she was in Young Young's bed. That had been a bonus. She had been bailed and for a time fed him little snippets of information on the posse, but then she and Young Young had a fight and she had all but disappeared.

He sat in the silence, engine off, April cold creeping into the car. Idly he flicked at the furry dice he had hung from the rear-view mirror in the vain hope it would make people think it was not a job car.

A group of lads kicked a football about in the cold. Jimmy looked at his watch, then illuminated the screen on his phone. He put the phone down again and waited. Ten minutes later, half an hour after she should have shown up, he saw a car turn off the road and trundle over the ramps raised in the tarmac. He sat up straighter and stared. He could not see who was driving. One person it looked like but he could not be sure. She might set him up. She had been very nervous earlier. The car got closer and he knew he should have told somebody where the meet was. It was too late now. The car drew closer and he saw a black face, hair straightened and pulled back from her head. He shifted himself in the seat.

She parked at the other end of the carpark, got out and pulled the hood of her jacket over her face. Carefully she looked around her and then made her way slowly to where he was parked. Reaching across he opened the door and she slid into the seat alongside him.

He could smell her, the sweet scent of skin that black women had. He flared his nostrils and smiled. She looked at him, flat face, white teeth against heavily reddened lips.

'How you doing?' he said. 'Long time no see.'

'I ain't got much time, Lofty. I didn't ought to be here.'

Jimmy nodded. 'We need to talk, Sandra. Where've you been? I had a hell of a job getting hold of you.'

'I been working. I got me a job.'

'Right. Good. Good.' He smiled at her, the tingling sensation in his hands, the flutter in his chest that he always got when he spoke to an informant he hardly knew. He had to be so careful what he said.

'You're looking good.'

She grinned then and took out cigarettes. Jimmy lit one for her and she sucked smoke through her nose. 'What you want, man?'

'Young Young.'

Her mouth closed and she drew her lip back with her teeth. 'I don't see that fuck no more.'

'Hurt you did he?'

'Hurts everybody.'

'He killed Jimmy Carter, Sandra.'

She shivered. 'Never heard of him.'

'Irishman. Very bad. Everybody's looking for Young Young. Us, Stepper-Nap. The Irish.'

'He's had it coming a long time.'

'You're right.' Jimmy looked out across the park. Next to him Sandra flicked her gaze left and right and now and then behind the car. 'You shout if a black face shows up,' she said. 'I didn't ought to be here.'

Jimmy nodded and swivelled round in his seat so he could look at her. 'You know where he is, Sandra?'

'Uh uh.' She shook her head.

'I really need to find him.'
'I don't know. I ain't seen him in ages.'
'What about the others – Pretty Boy. Bigger Dan . . .'
'Ain't seen none of them.'
Jimmy looked forward again. 'Where could he be, Sandra? He's not at Carmel's. He's not at his brother's and he's not in his flat. Who else does he know?'
She drew her lips in again. 'He got a baby mother.'
Jimmy felt his pulse quicken a fraction. 'Yeah?' he said casually.
She nodded. 'Bitch stole him from me.' She made a face then. 'Okay so she had his kids already but she stole him back from me.'
'Where?'
She looked forward again, watching intently as a black lad on a mountain bike cycled across the grass in front of them.
'You know him?'
She shook her head. 'Just a kid.'
'Where's the baby mother live, Sandra?'
'Hackney.'
'Where in Hackney?'
'Don't know exactly.'
Jimmy felt his heart sink again.
'I know it's by a canal. Some fancy new flats or something. Park across the road.'
Jimmy fumbled across her to the glove compartment for his weathered *A-Z*. He flicked through the pages till he came to east London. Sandra watched him turn the pages then she stabbed a finger. 'There,' she said. 'Hackney Marsh.'
Jimmy looked at the page, found the canal running under the Eastway and looked at her. 'You said a park across the road?'
She nodded. He found Hillington Park and the canal and, between them, Hillington Road E9. He looked at her once more. 'You haven't got an address?'
'Nope.'
'Phone number?'
'Nope.'
'Could you find one?'
'Address, maybe.'
'How come you found out about her?'

'She phoned him one time on his mobile. Fucker was sleeping with me at the time. He told me about her, about the kids. I didn't mind so long as he don't go back with her. Bastard went back with her.' She opened the car door. 'I got to go now.'

Jimmy laid a hand on her arm. 'Thanks, Sandra. If you can find out the address, I'll get him off the street.'

Keithley had already begun the afternoon briefing back at Hendon when Jimmy Crack arrived. He bumped into Ryan in the corridor. 'Piccadilly Circus,' Ryan muttered. 'Holmes working overtime.'

Jimmy grinned at him. 'If I have my way we'll be out of your hair in no time, Slips.'

Ryan cocked his head at him. 'Result?'

'I think so.'

'Jammy bastard.' He shook his head and swung his coat over his shoulders.

Keithley was talking to the AMIP team. 'The target is definitely Young Young,' he was saying. 'We have the car and the paint scrapings from the Escort match. The light is new but so is the screw and we know from the cell-site analysis that he made a mobile phonecall from within half a mile of the club at one thirty on the morning of the shooting. We also, unbelievably, have a positive ID. The bouncer, Bobby Simpson has fingered him for us.' He looked up then as Jimmy slipped into the back of the room. 'I've been on to Old Street and given SO19 the SP. They're fully briefed on the background, pictures etcetera and the MO. They're on stand by waiting to move.'

Jimmy put up his hand. 'I might be able to house him, Guv'nor.'

He told them what he had found out from Sandra. 'I haven't got an exact location yet but I've got the area. I think the snout'll come up with the rest. She knows the address – she's just not sure she wants to give it up.'

'What if she warns him?' Richard Hall, one of the AMIP detectives looked up at him.

Jimmy twisted his mouth down at the corners. 'No chance. She's pissed off, Rick. The baby mother took him off her. You know what they're like. As far as she's concerned that's over the side. She isn't going to warn him.'

'What d'you want to do?' Keithley asked him.

'If he's laying low he'll be there a while,' Jimmy said. 'I'll drive over tomorrow and see if I can house him. I'll keep on at the snout till she gives up the address. If I house him where I think he is we might be able to set up an OP on the canal bank. Plot someone up with fishing rod, put him to bed and let an SFO team dig him out.'

Vanner toyed with his food and watched Ellie, quiet, across the table from him. Candles dripped wax between them.

'You okay, love?'

She smiled at him. 'Tired.'

'You want to go to bed?'

'I said I'm tired, Aden.'

He sat back, lifted his wine glass and rolled it between his palms. 'You're very quiet tonight.'

She hunched her shoulders. 'Are you going to Norfolk this weekend?'

He nodded. 'Will you come with me?'

'Can't. I'm working.'

'Right.' He looked at his plate. 'What's up, Elle?'

'Nothing's up.'

'No?'

'No.'

He nodded again. 'I don't want any more of this.' He pushed his plate away and lit a cigarette. She watched him flap out the match. 'I wish you didn't smoke.'

'I know.'

'So why do it?'

'I smoke, Ellie. I always smoked.'

'Right.'

'Oh, for God's sake.' He stood up and gathered up the plates, then dumped them in the sink. Upstairs the phone rang and he went up and answered it.

'Jimmy Crack, Guv. Sorry to bother you at home.'

'What's happening?'

'I think I've found Young Young.'

Vanner sat down on the top step and settled the telephone beside him. 'How?'

'Snout came good. Sandra. The bird I nicked for intent.

She's housed him in Hackney. Baby mother.'

'Nice one, Jimmy.'

'I don't have the exact location yet, Guv. But I will. I'm going down there tomorrow to check it out. If I can put him to bed I'll set up a plot with my fishing rod. It's down by the canal on Hackney Marsh.'

'You want company, Jim?'

'Like fishing do you?'

'Never tried it.'

'I'll probably get surveillance.'

'Let them catch cold.'

'That's what they're paid for, Guv'nor. What's the word on Eilish?'

'Still over the water. Antrim Road Drug Squad have a spotter on her tail. Liverpool will pick her up this side and we'll take it from the M25.'

'Good. Speak to you tomorrow then.'

'Right. See you.' Vanner put down the phone.

When he went back downstairs Ellie was still sitting at the table. 'Who was that?'

'Jimmy Crack. He thinks we've found the killer from Kilburn.'

'Oh.'

Vanner looked sideways at her. 'It's my job, Ellie. It's what I do.'

'I know.'

'I don't do anything else.'

'I know that too.' She was quiet then. Vanner looked down at her and she glanced up. 'What will you do if your father dies?'

'Bury him,' he said.

She lay away from him in his bed. Tonight it felt like his bed. Not their bed. There was a coldness about her that he did not recognise. Not in her anyway. But he did recognise it and it chilled him. He could feel the old stifling sensation that he had put behind him. For the first time in months he thought about Lisa Morgan, a prostitute he had helped ruin last year and he wondered how she was. Throwing back the bedclothes he stepped naked onto the cold, wooden floor and walked to the window. Ellie lay very still in the bed. He leaned his forehead on the window and looked over the silent street. Nothing moved, parked cars, a fine layer of frost on the windscreen. He imagined his father lying in the made-up bed in his study with frost on the windows and frost on the lawn and frost on the fingered twigs of the sycamore tree in the garden.

Fourteen

Jimmy Crack drove along Victoria Park Road towards Hackney Marsh. Ten thirty, Thursday morning. He cursed his old Astra as it jumped out of third gear for the umpteenth time that morning. At the junction he turned onto Eastway and passed under the flyover before turning left onto Hillington Road with the canal on his right. He slowed as he came to the asphalt football pitch in the park. To his right a complex of modern town houses bordered the canal, separated by concourse parking areas with lock-up garages. At first glance they looked fresh and clean and well kept but as he looked more closely he caught sight of rusting cars and dustbins over full with rubbish.

Parking the car he sat for a moment and looked the complex over. Then he took his mobile phone from the dashboard and dialled the informant's number. To his surprise she answered immediately.

'Sandra,' he said. 'This is Lofty. I really need that address.'

He heard her sigh.

'You on your own?'

'Yeah.'

'I really need it. I'm on Hillington Road now but there's a dozen or so blocks and I can't check them all.'

She hesitated. 'What if he ever found out?'

'How can he? I'm not about to tell him.'

'He'll get put away?'

'For life.'

Again she hesitated.

'Sandra?'

'Hang on then.'

She put down the phone and Jimmy heard her rummaging through a bag, then the phone was picked up again.

'It's Block K. Flat 2.'

'Nice one, Sandra. I owe you.'

'Yeah, you do.'

Jimmy pressed End and then made another call to the incident room at Hendon. 'DI Keithley,' he said as it was answered.

Keithley came on the line. 'Guv, it's Jimmy Crack. I've got the address. I'm going to wander over there now and see if I can house him.'

'Be careful.'

'Of course. You got the Ninjas on standby?'

'They're doing a Recce as soon as he's housed.'

'Good. I'll see what I can do then bell you back.' Jimmy hung up and got out of the car.

He made his way through a parking area to the metal-railed fence that bordered the canal, then checked the letter on the block. C. That meant K was much further down away from the motorway flyover. He walked along the bank, hands in his pockets and noted two hopeful fishermen on the far side of the bank. Sunlight glinted on oil-coloured water and Jimmy wondered what on earth they hoped to catch. But they were there and if needs be that would be his observation point till it got dark at least.

K block was the second from the far end before the complex ended and 1930s' terraces took up the remainder of the street. As he moved between the parking areas he noted two black men fixing a car, further on a white man in a jogging suit coming out of the main door to G block. K block was silent. Jimmy felt his heart beat gather pace in his chest as he moved to the front door. Security locked. He had to get inside. He waited, looked up at the window of the first-floor apartment and wondered. Flat 2 would be upstairs, one on the ground floor and another above. He moved back to the bank once more. And then a man came out of the front door to K block, middle-aged, white. He carried a black dustbin liner full of rubbish to the bin and walked back again. Jimmy caught hold of the door as he was about to close it. The man looked at him and grunted. Jimmy grinned and followed him inside. He disappeared into Flat 1 on the ground floor. Jimmy unclipped his phone from his belt and started up the stairs. He paused at the landing and saw a second short flight and then another front door. He dialled Young Young's mobile number and waited. And then he heard it ringing in the flat above his head. He started down the stairs

once more. He was outside when the phone was answered.
'Yeah.'
'Joey?'
'Naw.'
'Sorry, man. Wrong number.'
At his car Jimmy got back on the phone to Keithley. 'Got him, Guv'nor. He's housed. Flat 2, Block K, Hillington Road.'
'You sure?'
'Absolutely positive. I called his mobile from the stairs and heard it ringing in the flat upstairs. Young Young answered it.'
'Brilliant. How d'you want to play it?'
Jimmy glanced at the fishermen on the far bank of the canal. 'I want an OP with a fishing rod opposite K block now.'
'Sorted,' Keithley said. 'If he doesn't move we'll hit him tomorrow morning. If he moves we'll take him out on the street. I'll ring Old Street now.'

The briefing took place at Hackney. The Specialist Firearms Officer team from SO19 had been briefed already and had carried out their Recce. The Hackney brief was to impart the tactics of the attack.
Keithley and his AMIP officers were gathered in the canteen, together with 3 Area Territorial Support Group. The SFO team mingled in their black one-piece coveralls. The team leader stood at the front with Keithley and the duty officer from Hackney. The team leader was a sergeant named Graves, tall and slim, his age indeterminate as his head was completely shaved and eagle-blue eyes inspected the room over a hooked and broken nose. His sleeves were pushed up, revealing tight sinewy arms. Vanner sat down next to Jimmy Crack. 'The men with many pockets,' he said and nodded towards Graves. 'Now if he asked you to stand still you'd take root wouldn't you.'
'Instant tree, Guv'nor.'
Vanner smiled. 'Cuddles.'
'What?'
'It's what they call him.'
'You know him, Guv?'
'Was in D11 when I was. They don't move them on when they've been there as long as he has. He's fifty years old, Jim.'
White boards were standing unfolded on the windowsill at the front, and resting against the legs of a table upturned on

another. The men moved about the room, firearms officers in black one-piece coveralls re-acquainting themselves with friends from the past. Cigarette smoke drifted as part of the atmosphere, blending with the strong smell of coffee rising from plastic cups. Two SFOs at the front handed out briefing papers.

Vanner caught Graves's eye and nodded. He turned to Jimmy once more. 'Young Young definitely housed?'

'Put to bed, Guv.'

'Someone else with the fishing rod then?'

'3 Area Surveillance. They left when it got dark.'

'Who's there now?'

Jimmy looked sideways at him. 'Couple of lovers in a car. And a body on the far bank – the other side of the bushes. We've got a rubbish truck ready to move later on.'

Vanner nodded. 'Eilish McCauley's on her way home from Belfast.'

'Deal go down?'

'We think so. Antrim Road Drug Squad had a body on her all the time she was there.'

'We giving her a tug?'

'Only if we can link her directly to the man, which somehow I don't think we will.'

'Right.'

Vanner looked at him. 'If this one went okay it'll happen again. We'll have more time to set up a plot. Slippery's snout can give us the inside track from Kilburn.'

The hubbub of conversation had risen an octave or two and Graves moved to the floor in front of the white boards. Vanner folded his arms and watched him.

'Right,' Graves said. 'Good morning ladies and gentlemen. My name is Sergeant Graves from SO19.' He turned to Keithley. 'For those of you who don't know – this is DI Keithley from 2 Area AMIP. My team and myself are here to assist DI Keithley in the arrest of Colin Robertson – more commonly known as Young Young – IC3 male, currently resident in Flat 2, Block K, Hillington Road, Hackney, opposite the Kings Park Estate. Young Young is wanted in connection with the murder of Jimmy Carter, snooker hall proprietor in Kilburn. DI Keithley will give you the full background. When he's imparted that information I shall explain the method of tonight's operation. There are four innocents on the premises, a woman and three children under ten.'

He turned to Keithley then who stepped forward and explained once again the full background to the night of Carter's murder and the reasons for arresting Young Young. He passed out photographs and gave them a full description, ending with the fact that Young Young was believed to be armed with an Uzi 9mm machine pistol. When he had finished he looked over at Jimmy Crack.

'What's the latest on the OP, Jimmy?'

Jimmy stood up and recounted the events of the day. Young Young had not come out since he had telephoned him. A woman had left the premises at three in the afternoon and returned with three young children. She had gone up to Flat 2. Since then nobody had come in or gone out. The last word from the OP was that all the lights were out by 1 a.m.

Jimmy sat down again next to Vanner and Keithley turned to Graves. Graves pushed himself away from the table he leaned against and looked at the white boards.

'Okay,' he said. 'We've looked at the premises earlier today and it's a first-floor maisonette-type occupying the upper half of what at first appears to be a tall, narrow town house. It's approached from the river walk abutting the canal by a panelled painted door in a small recessed porch at ground level. This leads to a steep staircase split by a landing which ascends to a second front door and the living accommodation.

'The premises is of semi-detached construction and therefore has openings on three sides. The red side has two window openings as does the black. There's a small, enclosed rear garden divided in two but with no direct access from the target premises, apart from a fire ladder. The roof is pitched with a loft space which may or may not connect to the next-door premises. The accommodation consists of two bedrooms, lounge, bathroom and toilet with a kitchen at the front.' He paused and pointed to the table behind him. 'There's a drawn plan available in case you haven't already seen it.

'The rear garden is fenced to shoulder height and has a gate leading to a square or parking area shared by several houses arranged similarly around it. The red side of the premises abuts a walkway and they appear on either side of the pairs of houses around the square. The square itself has pedestrian and vehicular access to Hillington Road. Again there are drawings available and if you have any questions please leave them till the appropriate time later on.'

He paused then and checked the papers in front of him on the table. Vanner shifted in his seat next to Jimmy. The two officers in coveralls who had conducted the Recce put their heads together for a moment and then Graves continued.

'Our intention tonight,' he said, 'is to covertly contain the premises with SFO officers and an ARV crew. We'll breach the door and call Young Young out, arresting him in a safe, controlled way. Having done so we will hand him over to the AMIP team from 2 Area.' He broke off, looked each of his men in the eyes and repeated his words exactly.

When he had finished Vanner caught his eye and a smile passed between them. Keithley rested on the edge of a table and drank coffee. Graves cleared his throat and continued. 'At the conclusion of this briefing we'll load up the respective vehicles and assemble in convoy order in Lower Brixham Road facing toward Wallace Street.' He tapped the map behind him. 'The lead vehicle will be the ARV with DI Keithley on board. Next will be the two SFO kit vans followed by the dog van, the rest of the AMIP team, ambulance and the TSG troop carrier. I ask that you ensure the next vehicle behind maintains the convoy and communicate any problems to me. The convoy will turn right against the flow of traffic into Wallace Street and travel via Hometown Road and Marsh Avenue till level with the Kings Park Estate. Here we turn right into Hillington Road. At Marsh Avenue all lights will be extinguished and pagers and phones switched off.'

He turned and indicated the Rendezvous Point marked on the white board behind him. 'At this designated RVP in Hillington Road the ARV will stop and the convoy form up close behind. Turn off all engines immediately. Do not slam doors and speak very quietly.' He stopped talking and turned to the Hackney Duty Officer. 'I'll then ask DI Morris to institute his cordons. These will be either end of the road and the canal bank. The team will form up and move forward as planned.' He stopped again and his eyes glinted. 'There will be some shouting and disturbance. No uniformed or AMIP officer will enter the firearms scene nor any other person unless directly called to do so by me.' He paused again. 'As my team move forward the arrest team will wait at the Form Up Point until called. Assuming a successful outcome the cordons will remain until the SFO team withdraws.'

He pushed his sleeves back once more and sipped from a plastic cup. 'Right,' he went on. 'Contingencies. If there is a shooting SO19 will control the situation. No other intervention unless invited. In that event armed officers involved will go to Tower Hamlets police station and I will ask DI Keithley to nominate a liaison officer. Nominated hospitals are Wanstead for police and New Hall for others.

'If the target is non-compliant we will drop into siege mode and negotiate. If there is a breakout, jumper, whatever, SO19 will deal with it. If he manages to do a runner SO19 and the dogs will deal.'

Jimmy Crack glanced over his shoulder at one of the dog handlers seated behind him with his lead stretched bandolier style across his shoulders.

Graves looked at them once again. 'Debrief is here at Hackney. Comms are back to back, local PR channel and mainset channel 11.' He turned then to Keithley. 'PACE is not complied with. *You* will have to caution him.'

Keithley nodded and stepped forward. 'Okay. This is armed operation number A/74-3.'

Graves looked at his watch. 'The time now is 03:15. We load up at 03:30.'

At exactly 3:55 on Friday morning the attack vehicles took up their positions at the Form Up Point in Hillington Road. Keithley was in the lead Armed Response Vehicle, Vanner and Jimmy in the TSG troop carrier and the rest of the Murder Squad in an unmarked car.

Vanner felt the muscles tighten in his face with the rush of building adrenaline. Ulster years ago, dark nights in West Belfast or the Creggan Estate at dawn. Strangely he thought about Ellie and then his father lying in his bed in Norfolk. This evening he would visit him.

Outside the SFO team moved silently into position. A stillness had settled on the street like the calm before a storm. No wind. No cloud, just streetlamp-yellow and silver stars and a sickle moon over the canal.

The SFO team entered the square around K Block, no sound

from rubber-soled boots. One man bearing a long kevlar shield shouldered his MP5 carbine and drew his Glock from its holster. Alongside him, the burly thick-set Method of Entry man carried the battering ram. Behind him a third officer backed them up, MP5 in his hands, and alongside him a fourth openly carried his baton in one hand and a small fire extinguisher in the other. A dog handler, Alsatian silent at his side, tightened his grip on the lead. Two more men for prisoner handling moved into position.

Graves took up his position with a vantage point from the fence by the canal. One by one he checked radios with a click from his transmitter. Each time three clicks answered him until every one had called in. Graves lifted the handset to his mouth. 'Stand by,' he said. 'Stand by.' He paused. 'Attack,' he said very quietly.

The MOE man smashed the front door and the SFO team sprinted up the stairs. At the top they were shouting. Again the battering ram crashed wood and the front door to the flat flew inwards. From inside a dog was barking.

'Young Young,' the MOE man shouted. 'You are surrounded by armed police. Come out with your hands over your head.'

The growling grew louder and louder and then a small black dog rushed the opening. With one step the stick man lifted the fire extinguisher and sprayed foam into its face. The dog yelped, twisted in the air and landed on its side. It wriggled to its feet and the stick man sprayed it again.

The MOE man shouted: 'Young Young. Call off your dog or we'll shoot it.'

A bedroom door stood open and torchlight from the back-up man shone on the bed, a woman, sitting up half-naked, breasts swinging free, her hands to her face, mouth open with no sound coming from it. Then she started screaming. The dog yelped again, frantically trying to scrape the foam from its face with its paws. A man rolled across the floor of the bedroom, long and black and naked. An officer switched on the mainlight and levelled his carbine at Young Young. 'Armed police. Stand still.'

Young Young was up. From the other bedroom children were crying. Young Young pivoted on the balls of his feet.

'Stand still or I'll shoot you.' The carbine was pointed directly at his chest. The baby mother was screeching.

Young Young stared, mouth hanging open. 'What you fuckin' . . .'

'Shut up.' The officer with the carbine took one step towards him. 'Do exactly as I tell you. Walk towards me. Do it now.'

Young Young stared at him. 'You . . .'

'Do not speak to me. Do exactly as I tell you. Walk towards me. Now.'

Young Young moved towards the door.

'You in the bed,' the officer said. 'Call the dog.'

The woman stopped screaming and stared at him.

'Call your dog. Now.'

The woman leaned over the side of the bed and called to the dog. It looked round, foam in its eyes, foam in its nose and wobbled across the floor to her. She took hold of its collar. Young Young rushed the door.

Instantly the stick man moved in, ducked a punch and rammed the end of his baton into Young Young's gut. Young Young buckled, a cry stopped up in his throat. The woman cried out, dog barking. From the bedroom the children were screaming.

Young Young writhed on the floor, tried to get up and the stick man hit him across his shoulders, flattening him again. The MOE man dropped his knee into his neck and hauled his hands behind him. A third officer knelt down and slipped plastic handcuffs over his wrists. When he was secured they stood up. The first officer looked at the baby mother. 'Put some trousers on him.'

Vanner and Jimmy Crack were outside when they brought him down and handed him over to Keithley. Young Young stared in Jimmy's face and a flicker of recognition passed over his eyes. The AMIP arrest team led him away and secured him inside the troop carrier. A number of people had gathered in the carpark, some in doorways, others leaning out of their windows and hissing at the police like snakes. The SFO team led the woman and her children down the stairs and over to the arrest car.

When they were inside and out of the way the AMIP team moved in to search the premises. Graves moved alongside Vanner.

'Hello, Cuddles,' Vanner said.

Graves grinned at him and nodded to Jimmy.

'Nice one.' Jimmy shook his hand.

'You guys want him too eh?' Graves said.

Vanner lit a cigarette, offered the pack and Graves shook his head. 'We want a word, yeah.'

'All yours then.' Graves walked back to his men.

Vanner went home to shower. It was six thirty and Ellie was still in bed. He paused in the bedroom and watched her sleeping for a moment, peace on her face in the moonlight. He stood by the bed and sniffed the scent of her clothes, then he walked down the landing to the bathroom.

Weariness picked at his skin as the water spread over his face. It drifted into his mouth, his nostrils and he ducked his head to breathe. Thoughts criss-crossed themselves in his head. Ellie asleep in his bed, his father in some other bed in Norfolk. Young Young in custody in Hackney and three frightened children cowering helplessly with their mother.

In the kitchen he brewed tea and carried a tray to the bedroom. He set it down by the bed, the tails of his dressing gown flicking about his calves. Ellie stirred, lifted her head and rubbed her eyes.

'What time is it?'

'Almost seven.'

'What're you doing?'

'I've come home for a shower then I'm going back to Hackney. We took out Young Young this morning.'

'Any trouble?'

Vanner shook his head. 'Unarmed. He must have dumped the gun somewhere.'

She looked at him then. 'Do many policemen carry guns, Aden?'

'Some do yes.'

'You?'

Vanner looked down at her and shook his head. 'No.'

'Did you ever?'

'Why?'

She hunched her shoulders into her neck. 'Did you?'

He poured out the tea and sat down next to her. 'I'm licensed to carry a sidearm if I ever had cause to,' he said.

'Did you ever shoot anyone?'

He opened his mouth, closed it again and looked away from

her. 'Why d'you want to know this now – you never asked before?'

'It's important to me, Aden.'

'Why?'

'It just is.'

He sipped at his tea then replaced the cup on the tray. Getting up, he shook his packet of cigarettes from his jacket pocket and stood by the window smoking.

'In 1989 I shot and killed a man called Christian Tate,' he said. 'I was relief at D11, that's the forerunner to SO19. Tate was an armed robber who blasted at me with a shotgun.'

'He was armed.'

'Of course he was armed. That's why I shot him.' He stared at the gathering light outside. Ellie slipped out of bed and her arms were round his waist and he could feel her nakedness pressed close against him.

'I'm sorry.'

He dropped his cigarette in the ashtray he was holding and turned to her. She stepped back and her nipples wrinkled under his gaze. He looked in her eyes. Reaching up, she stroked his face. 'Make love to me, Aden.'

Eilish spoke to Stepper-Nap on the telephone from her house. She had got home half an hour ago and almost immediately Mary-Anne had come round to see her. She was supposed to contact Stepper as soon as she got home.

'You're late,' he said. 'Everything okay?'

'Fine.'

'You got all the money.'

'I've got twenty-five grand.'

'What? Kilo and a half is forty-five.'

'You forgot. Jimmy Carter's cut.'

'Jimmy Carter's dead and his cut was supposed to be five.'

'His friends.'

Silence for a moment. She could hear the agitated rasp of his breathing. 'You put it where you should.'

'Of course.'

'Anybody follow you?'

'Belfast for a while maybe. But they were probably interested in who I was meeting rather than me.'

'You sure?'

'Yes, I'm sure.'

'Okay. We'll talk later.' Stepper hung up and Eilish settled the receiver back in its housing. She turned to Mary-Anne who lit two cigarettes and handed one to her. 'I hope you know what you're doing, lady.'

Eilish looked at her then. 'Oh, I know all right,' she said.

A key turned in the lock and James came in. Eilish got up and went out into the hall.

'You're back then,' he said.

'Aye, lover. I'm back. Kids all right are they?'

'Kids are fine, Eilish.' James could smell Mary-Anne's cigarette from the living room.

He looked at his sister. 'How's our ma then?'

'Better.'

'Is she?'

'Aye. She is. Much better.'

'Did she ask about me?'

'She did. She wanted to know how you were and what you were doing. I told her you were fine and looking for a job now.'

James nodded. 'She's not dying or anything then?'

'No, Jamie.' Eilish placed a hand on his chest. 'She's not dying or anything.'

Mary-Anne came out into the hall. 'I'll be away now,' she said. 'I'll phone you this evening, Eilish. We can have a natter then.'

When she was gone Eilish picked up her bag and started up the stairs. 'James, will you be a love and make us some tea?'

He brought the tea up to her. She was taking a shower and he waited until the fall of water had ceased and she came through in her robe, a towel wrapped about her hair. She touched him lightly on the shoulder and took the proffered cup. He stared at the bag by the bed.

'You unpacked yet?'

'Not yet. No.'

'Want me to do it for you?'

She looked at him and shook her head. 'I can do it,' she said. She sat down on the bed and the robe slipped up her thigh, her tattoo *Cumman na mBan* was blue against the white of her skin. As if she sensed his gaze Eilish covered it over again.

'Girls get to school all right did they?'

'Yes.'

He moved himself back on the bed, crossing his legs underneath him. 'The police were here, Eilish.'

She stopped, the teacup halfway from the tray to her lips. 'Why?'

'They were looking for Young Young.'

She looked round at him now.

'They found his car by the park. They thought he might've come here.'

'Why did they think that?'

James stared at her. 'I don't know. But they must know he does or they wouldn't have come. They know you hang out with him, Eilish.'

'What did you tell them, James?'

'Nothing.'

'Nothing at all?'

'I said he hadn't been here.'

'That night or never?'

'I could hardly say never, Eilish. They knew.' James slid to the edge of the bed.

Eilish took a fresh pair of jeans from her drawer. 'Did they ask anything else?'

'They wanted to know where you were – when you'd be back.'

'Did you tell them?'

'Of course I told them. What was I supposed to do. Young Young killed someone, Eilish.'

Eilish shrugged and took her underwear off the radiator. 'Leave me alone now, James. I want to get dressed.'

Webb and DCI Westbrook stood in the investigating officer's room at the Hendon. Weir sat across the desk from them, Ryan leaned against the wall.

'Then we're back where we started again.' Weir raked his fingers over his scalp. They had just told him that their final suspect was alibi'd.

Ryan looked at Webb. 'How is she alibi'd?'

Webb looked disinterestedly at him. 'Come on, Slips.'

Ryan shook his head and looked back at Weir. 'I'll get back on the phone then, Guv'nor.'

Westbrook sat down. 'It is PIRA, Frank,' he said. 'They just made a mistake that's all.'

'And you've run out of nominals?'

'For the moment. Inquiries go on.'

'So who *were* they after? Come on, Westy – you can tell us that much.'

Westbrook looked at Webb, then he sighed. 'They've lost a lot to us over the years, Frank. With the ceasefire ending they're active again. Their one big fear is snouts.'

'Snouts.' Ryan folded his arms.

Westbrook nodded. 'Some of them are women. Some of them are over here. That's where we're looking. We can't tell you any more than that.'

'Really helps doesn't it.' Ryan moved to the door. 'The lover is something to do with this. That's who we need to find.'

Webb shook his head. 'Won't help you, Sid. It's a mistake. Jessica was the wrong target that's all. Who she was with is irrelevant. He's probably married, kids maybe. Would you come forward?'

'What about the dummy?' Weir said. 'What about the New Forest, someone in the back of the car.'

'Coincidence or somebody conning you, Guv. Your man Case. Lives on his own, no girlfriend. He probably made it up, chased her for the hell of it and then when somebody killed her he got scared, came to you before you got to him.'

Weir shook his head. 'You haven't interviewed him, George. I think he's telling the truth.'

Westbrook sat forward then. 'The dummy is theatre if it happened at all. PIRA don't do theatre and they shoot their targets, not people attached to them. They're fighting a propaganda war as much as anything else. They don't need the publicity of killing innocent women. Wouldn't help their fund raising would it.'

Again Weir shook his head. 'I don't think it's that simple. I think there is a link. Somehow we're missing something.'

'I agree,' Ryan stood by the door. 'If it's okay with you, Guv, I want to talk to Case again. I'll either get him back in here or go to see him down there.'

'Whatever you want, Sid.' Weir looked at the two men from SO13. 'You do what you have to,' he said. 'Us – we'll do what we have to.'

* * *

Ellie drank tea with Anne, the cleaner. Somehow their breaks seemed to coincide these days.

'The man you told me about,' Ellie said. 'The one in Ireland. Has there been anyone since him?'

Anne shook her head.

'No-one?'

'I loved him, Ellie. How could there be anyone else?'

Ellie put down her cup. 'That must be awful.'

Anne lifted her eyebrows. 'To love just one man. Why?'

'I didn't mean that. I meant to love him and lose him – like that.'

'Shot. Killed. Murdered.'

The words hit Ellie like bullets, spat from Anne's mouth with a bitterness she could almost taste. 'You've never got over it have you.'

'No. I haven't. It's been twelve years, Ellie, but you don't recover from something like that. I saw him lying in the road, no jacket on, just his shirt and his tie and his trousers, lying on his side with blood in the gutter and the rain soaking into him.'

'You saw it?'

'Yes.'

'Oh, Anne.'

Ellie sat back, looked up at the clock; it was almost time to go back to work. 'How did it happen exactly? I mean, I'm sorry. I don't mean to pry. You don't have to tell me if you don't want to.'

Anne lifted a palm. 'It's all right,' she said. 'It does me good to talk. I hate the thought of ever forgetting him.'

'Maybe you should though – you know – move on.'

'You think so?'

'Don't you?'

Lines cut deep into Anne's brow then and she pushed at her hair with red-nailed hands. 'I think I'd betray him if I ever did that – betray our love – everything we went through.' She pushed her cup away. 'The worst of it was we'd had a fight. He stormed out and by the time I went after him it was raining hard. He was walking, too much to drink I think. He never took his jacket. The police ambushed him. They claimed he was a terrorist but he wasn't. He didn't even have a gun. They said he didn't do what they told him. They said he went for a gun but one was never found.'

'The police?'

'Yes.' Anne looked at her then. 'I think there was a soldier too.'

'A soldier?'

'Yes.' She leaned forward then. 'I've looked into it. Well, you can imagine. Anyway, I discovered that when the police went out like that there was usually a soldier with them. Almost always I think.'

'What happened to the men responsible?'

Anne opened her hands. 'Nothing,' she said. 'Absolutely nothing.'

Vanner and Jimmy Crack drove over to Hackney, Vanner driving, Jimmy next to him, Vanner smoking, the window wound down a fraction.

'Keithley wants him over at Hendon asap,' Jimmy said.

'When're they moving him?'

'This afternoon.' Jimmy stared out of the window. 'What happened with Eilish?'

'Spoke to Steve Riley this morning. They picked her up at South Mimms and followed her back from there.'

'Where'd she go?'

'Uxbridge. The barber's shop.'

'She didn't meet Stepper then?'

Vanner shook his head.

'Next time.'

Vanner looked at him. 'We'll give her a tug in Belfast, Jim. Get the Antrim Road boys to pull her with the gear. Then you and me can fly over, see if we can't get her to lay down. She's got kids. She won't want to lose them.'

Vanner pulled off the road and parked beside an idling TSG troop carrier. Downstairs the custody sergeant greeted them.

'Interview room 1,' he said. 'And rather you than me.'

'Frighten you does he?' Jimmy said.

'Bloke's a headcase, mate. Loco. He's been sat in there since you nicked him and threatened just about every copper in London. The things he's going to do to the Ninjas when he finds out who they are.'

Vanner shook his head. 'Let's get his arse shifted eh.'

The sergeant moved around the desk and picked up his keys. He walked to Young Young's cell and dropped the visor.

Vanner peered through. He sat on the bench along the wall with his hands in his lap. The sergeant opened the door and still he sat there, then he looked up slowly and stared into Vanner's eyes.

'Who the fuck are you?'

'Drug Squad, Young Young. Here to do you a favour.'

'Fuck off.'

The sergeant took a step into the cell. 'You watch your mouth,' he said. 'And get up. We haven't got all day.'

Young Young sat where he was and the sergeant stepped closer. Young Young round-housed him, a swinging arc of a punch which caught him behind the ear and knocked him against the wall. Vanner balled his fists, then suddenly Young Young charged, fists out in front of him, both arms. He hit Vanner like a battering ram, sending him back through the open cell door and into the far wall. Vanner dropped to one knee, the wind knocked right out of him.

Young Young was loose in the custody suite. He started for the stairs but Jimmy lifted his fists like a boxer and stepped into his path. Young Young stopped and his eyes suddenly shone.

'Oh fuck, a fighter. Come on then, you bastard.'

Two uniforms appeared on the exit stairs as Young Young came for Jimmy. He spat on the floor and lifted his own fists in mockery. 'I could fuckin' eat you.'

Jimmy looked in his eyes. 'Come on then, pussy.'

Young Young swung at him. Jimmy dropped his shoulder, riding the punch then ducked in close and hit him with an upper cut to the sternum. Young Young dropped like a sack.

He lay on the floor, both arms about his middle, his eyes bulging as if they were going to explode. Vanner grabbed him by the collar and the sergeant fastened plastic cuffs on his wrists. The two constables were staring at Jimmy who stood over Young Young like a fighter back in his corner. Vanner glanced at their faces. 'Lafone,' he said. '1988. Light heavy.' They got Young Young to his feet and Vanner grinned at Jimmy. 'Still got that punch then, you bastard.'

Jimmy smiled wickedly. 'Took down a few trees since you, Guv.'

In the interview room Young Young slumped in the chair, still trying to right his breathing. Vanner leaned against the wall and lit a cigarette. Then he moved to the chair, scraped it back and sat down. 'My name's Vanner,' he said. 'And I don't like you.'

Young Young looked cautiously at him and even more so at Jimmy. 'Take the cuffs off, man. I ain't gonna hit no-one.'

'Fuck you,' Vanner said. 'You know what – that's two assaults to add to the murder.' He leaned across the table so his face was close to Young Young's. 'We don't like people who hit coppers, Young Young. We don't like them at all.' He sat back again and blew a steady stream of smoke in his face. 'Six feet six and taken out with one punch. Some hardman you are.'

Young Young snorted phlegm into his mouth. 'I'd've taken him.'

'What – from where you lay on the floor?'

Jimmy Crack took his mobile phone from his belt and laid it on the table. He unfastened his watch from his wrist and laid it next to the phone. 'Ten minutes, Young Young. You behave yourself that long and we'll take the cuffs off. You misbehave after that and we'll give you the hammering of your life.'

Young Young eased his face back, looked from one to the other of them and nodded.

'Good.' Vanner crushed out his cigarette. 'We understand each other. Now, do you want a lawyer?'

Young Young did not reply.

'We're going to ask you some questions, Young Young,' Vanner went on. 'It's your right to have a solicitor present. Do you want one?'

'No.'

'Good.' Vanner leaned in his elbows. 'What did you do with the gun?'

'Don't have a gun.'

'Bullshit. You carry an Uzi 9mm. Think you're the fucking Terminator.'

'He's a white pussy bitch.'

Jimmy sat forward then. 'Later on today the Murder Squad will roast you about Jimmy Carter, Young Young. They got a match on the bullets you sprayed into the snooker hall when you broke Holden Biggs's head. They've got your car and your car's paint on the bumper of another car. You broke a tail light didn't you.'

'Nothing wrong with my car, man.'

'You're a liar, Young Young. You should've got them to put the rusty screw back. There's a shiny new one now.'

Young Young bit his lip.

'They've got two witnesses,' Vanner said harshly. 'One is the bouncer. He picked you out, pal. You're going down the line.'

For a few minutes they sat in silence, Young Young looking at the table top. After a while he lifted his face and his eyes were small, black and darting. 'How come you knew where to find me?'

'We're clever.' Vanner tapped his fingertips on the table. 'We're Drug Squad, Young Young. The Murder Squad comes later.'

'I don't do drugs.'

Jimmy smiled at him. 'Stepper-Nap, you were his body armour. Pretty Boy, looking to take over the Brit-Boy Massive. Am I right?'

Young Young did not say anything.

'Yeah, I'm right. Bigger Dan. Little Bigger, your half-brother. Carmel Connolly. Eilish McCauley. The list goes on and on.'

Jimmy looked at Vanner then and Vanner squinted at Young Young. 'Stepper set you up, Young Young. Jimmy Carter. You know that – your Daddy set you up. Shooting up Carter's snooker hall. That was dumb. Dumbest thing I ever saw. Dumbest thing Stepper-Nap ever saw. He was doing a deal with Carter. You went and blew it for him. Why'd you go and do that?'

Young Young sneered at him. 'Don't know what you're all talking about, man. Don't mean nothing to me.'

'Liar.' Vanner stood up. 'I knew you were stupid. I just didn't know how stupid.'

Young Young stared at him. 'Don't call me stupid.'

'Better than pussy isn't it?'

Young Young's eyes flashed.

'That's what Biggs called you didn't he. Bad-mouthing a bad man like you. You couldn't let that happen so you walk into Carter's place with your gun and make a mess of the ceiling. But Carter's a *bad bad* man, Young Young. Much worse than you. He wanted your head. Stepper wanted a deal so you took a beating instead. Trouble is – you went and spoiled it by killing him.'

Jimmy Crack shook his head. 'Why'd you do that, Young

Young – shoot the Irishman? Jimmy Carter of all people. Don't you know about the Irish? I thought all you black boys knew about the Irish.'

'Don't scare me, man.'

'No?' Vanner laughed in his face. 'They will when they get you inside. They never ever forget. I was a soldier, Young Young. I can tell you they never forget. When you go down you're history.'

He stood up and paced to the wall, leaning one hand against it. 'You should've kept hold of your gun – let the firearms team shoot you last night. At least that'd be quick. When the Irish get you inside – and believe me they will – they'll make you sweat for a while and then one day they'll come for you. But they'll make it really slow. You ready for slow, Young Young?' Vanner moved round behind him then and took off the cuffs. 'Nine minutes. I'm doing you a favour.'

Young Young brought his hands out in front of him and massaged his wrists. Jimmy leaned towards him and offered one of Vanner's cigarettes. Young Young glanced briefly at Vanner then lit one.

'We can help you, man,' Jimmy said.

Young Young frowned. 'How?'

'Keep you away from the Irish.'

'How?'

'Easy. A word in the right ear when they decide where to put you. Make sure it's a block full of brothers. They'll love you for taking on the Irish. But if you ended up with any of them—?' Jimmy shook his head. 'I wouldn't want to be you.'

Young Young snorted then and shook his head. 'You think I'm an arsehole? I talk to you and I get fucked by the brothers. I don't talk and I get fucked by the Irish. Maybe I'll take my chances.'

'Wrong.' Vanner sat down. 'We don't expect miracles. You talk to us *some* and who would ever know.'

'I don't know jackshit.'

'We think you do.' Jimmy looked evenly at him. 'We know about the doctor, Young Young.'

Young Young's eyes flickered.

'We know about Eilish and Stepper-Nap. We know she's running for him. We know about Pretty Boy's plans.'

'I ain't talking to you.'

Vanner looked at him and moved to the door. Jimmy got up from his chair. 'Fine,' Vanner said. 'Then it'll be the Irish. Watch your arse when you sit on the crapper.'

He had his hand on the door.

'Wait.'

Vanner turned once more, aware of the tension in his chest and his arms. He looked back at Young Young.

'You can really do what you said?'

'Yes.'

'Put me with my kind? Keep them Irish away from me?'

'With a word in the right ear.' Vanner moved back to the table. 'But we don't do it for free.'

Young Young seemed to ponder then. Vanner gave him another cigarette. Young Young looked up at him. 'Motherfucker stiffed me didn't he.'

'Big-time.'

Young Young nodded. 'I don't know much. I got paid to hit people is all.'

'We know that,' Jimmy said. 'Who washes the crack and where, Young Young? They'll never know you told us.'

Young Young looked at him, looked away again and chewed his lip. He rolled the cigarette around the edge of the ashtray. 'There's a small hotel in Neasden. Hill Lane by the park. Stepper's got the owner in his pocket. Crack gets washed there.'

'Who by?'

Young Young pursed his lips. 'White guy,' he said slowly. 'Hangs out in the National on Saturdays. Ginger Bill. Got red hair he has.'

They took him back to the custody suite and the sergeant accompanied by two other uniforms escorted him back to his cell. At the door Young Young paused and looked at Jimmy. He raised a fist, broadside. 'No-one ever hit me like that. Respect, man. Respect.' Jimmy nodded once.

Eilish sat in the passenger seat of Stepper-Nap's car. They were parked on the wasteground off Oakwood Lane. Stepper was staring out of the window and frowning. 'Young Young got nicked this morning.'

'I heard it on the news.' She looked at him. 'Was bound to happen.'

Stepper made a face. 'Wanted the Irish to take him. Cleaner that way.'

'Young Young won't yap.'

He looked sideways at her. 'You don't reckon? Never could figure that fucker. Law unto himself.'

She shook her head. 'He hates Old Bill worse than he hates you, baby. He isn't going to talk.'

Stepper looked at her then, arm across the back of the seat. 'So how come they took so much?'

She shrugged.

'We promised Carter five.'

She nodded. 'That was before he got shot. They figured you owed them, Stepper.' She smiled then. 'If they figure you owe – you pay – you know what I mean?'

Stepper wrinkled his mouth into a line. 'Nobody stiffs me, Eilish.'

Eilish laid a hand on his arm. 'Tell you what, lover. Why don't you fly over and argue?'

Stepper started the engine and they drove back toward Harlesden. 'Old Bill came to my house,' she said. 'When I was away. Apparently they found Young Young's car by the park.'

'He come to see you?'

She shook her head. 'They talked to James, though. Murder Squad.'

'What did the little shit tell them?'

'He's my brother, Step.'

'What did he tell them?'

'Only that I was in Ireland visiting my sick mother. It's no bother. They've got him now haven't they. I won't see them again.'

Stepper chewed his fingernails, looking at her as he drove through the lights. 'You were fucking him weren't you.'

Eilish looked out the window.

'Weren't you.'

Still she did not answer him.

'Why d'you do that, baby? Why you do that to me?'

She looked round at him then. 'His dick was bigger than yours.'

She got him to drop her half a mile from her house and she walked the rest of the way, crossing the park by herself. The house was empty, another hour until the children got home.

James was out somewhere, the job centre or someplace. Eilish plugged the kettle in and then went up to her bathroom. From under her bed she pulled out the travel bag and opened it. From inside she took a heavy paper bundle and unwrapped it. She counted fifteen thousand pounds that Cahal Barron had given her, onto the bed. Poor Stepper-Nap, she thought. He was such a fool.

From the kitchen she took a roll of clingfilm and went back upstairs. In her drawer beside the bed she kept a small screwdriver which she took with the money through to the bathroom. She closed the door and locked it, then squatted down on the floor and piled the money into two bundles. These she wrapped in clingfilm, round and round and round. She pasted the edges flat then held each bundle under the cold tap and watched the water roll off in globules. Towelling each one of them dry she set them down and began to unscrew the side of the bath. When this was done she maneouvered the panel away and placed the cash in the space by the plumbing. Then she replaced the panel, re-set the screws and went back downstairs. The children came home at four.

Late afternoon and Vanner and Jimmy Crack drove the length of Hill Lane until they came to the hotel. 'There,' Jimmy said without pointing.

'Seen it.' Vanner looked over his right shoulder as he drove. A small block of flats rose in two storeys directly opposite. It was built on four concrete stilts with space for car parking beneath.

Jimmy was busy with a pad and pencil, writing down the number of the VW car parked outside the hotel. Vanner drove the length of the road and then turned. 'What about the flats opposite for a plot?' he said.

'Go and ask shall we?'

They parked underneath and could see the front door of the hotel opposite. It was no more than two semi-detached houses, built in the thirties and knocked into one. It advertised bed and breakfast. Vanner got out of the car and they went inside the flats. A dirty chequer-board floor led to concrete steps with a metal banister.

'Which one?' Jimmy asked.

Vanner shrugged. He could smell the remnants of

somebody's curry as he started up the first flight. Two doors at either end of the landing. They went up the second flight and found two further doors. Jimmy looked left and right, moved his shoulders and knocked on the right hand door. Nobody answered.

They waited then Vanner moved to the other door and knocked again. No answer. They were about to go back down when they heard a crash then a man's voice cursing from inside. The next moment the door was answered and Vanner looked at a man in his forties, tanned face, thinning hair and gold on his wrist. He was wearing a tight-fitting white bathrobe.

'Yes?'

Vanner smiled at him. 'Police,' he said. 'Could we have a word?'

The man looked at him then grinned broadly and rubbed a palm across his jaw. 'Ye might as well –' Irish voice – 'I was all done anyway.'

Jimmy squinted at Vanner and they followed him inside.

In the hallway they came across a fallen bicycle and the man showed them into a spacious lounge with wooden floors and a white rug in the middle of it. Glass-topped table by the window with two fading couches in white leather. A sound lifted from another room then a plump-looking, middle-aged woman came through in her dressing gown.

'Iris,' the man said. 'My wife.'

'Look,' Vanner said. 'I'm really sorry. We had . . .'

'Forget about it. We were finished.' The man grinned broadly. 'Tommy Mac,' he said, offering a hand. 'What can we do for you?'

Vanner showed him his warrant card and then explained what they wanted. For a moment the man was silent, chewing at the back of his hand. He glanced at his wife then his face cracked in a smile.

'Surveillance is it – what cameras and everything?'

'One camera. Video.' Jimmy pointed. 'In the window there. They won't see anything.'

Tommy went to the window and half-lifted the net curtain. He squinted at the road and looked back at them. 'You know you're lucky you knocked on this door,' he said. 'I own this flat. The rest of them are leased.' He jerked a thumb across the road. 'Your hotel man. He owns them all.'

The Irish couple agreed to have a video camera set up in their window. Jimmy told them that he would set it up himself rather than have the Technical Support Unit stomping all over the place. 'It'll be nothing,' he said. 'Brown boxes. Look like I'm delivering a TV or something.'

'Fine.' Iris's eyes were shining. 'Just like Cagney and Lacey.'

Ellie sat in Vanner's house in the darkness. She could not get Anne's face, Anne's words out of her mind. Everything had been so simple before she spoke to Anne. Why did it make such a difference?

Vanner. She remembered the first time she had seen him. Valesca, her friend, had told her about him on their break. This tall, black-haired policeman with thirty-odd stitches in his back. He had woken up and called a woman's name. Ellie had had a glance at him while he was unconscious. Valesca pointed him out. His face had been grey and lined, black hair, whitening a fraction at the temples. Delirious for a time, calling out and then silence. She had not seen him again till that night in the pub when he came in with Sid Ryan.

Again she thought of Anne, a strange, lost sort of woman. They talked so much these days and yet a few weeks before she had never set eyes on her. Why did it make such a difference?

Vanner never talked. Tonight he would drive up to Norfolk. She had to work, wanted to work and yet wanted to go with him. And in the same breath she did not. What if his father died? What would that do to him? Could she be there for him? All at once she felt very young.

Vanner came in at seven. Ellie got up from the couch and met him in the hall. 'Where've you been? I thought you were going to see your father.'

Vanner rubbed his eyes. He had had no sleep since Wednesday. 'I am,' he said. 'I'll get a coffee and go.'

'You can't, Aden. You're exhausted. Go in the morning.'

He thought about it then. 'Today went on and on,' he said. 'Got a result this morning. Young Young, the one who killed Jimmy Carter. He gave us the wash house. We're setting up surveillance.'

Ellie took his jacket. 'Go in the morning. I'll get you up very early.'

She lay alongside him, her hand on the flat of his stomach,

feeling the rise and fall of his breathing. He lay still as death, eyes closed and sunk back in his head. She stroked his face and watched him. It was hard to believe he had killed somebody once. And then she rolled onto her side. She was twenty-five years old. Somehow it mattered. What would there be between them? He never talked of futures or families or anything. He just was. And yet a few weeks ago none of it would have mattered.

Fifteen

Vanner went to Norfolk in the morning. They woke early, made love and he left. The roads were empty and he drove north quickly, up through Stoke Newington and Tottenham and Walthamstow to the base of the M11 and then two lanes and no cars, he pressed his foot to the floor.

Time on his hands as he drove, too much time to think and look back and perhaps to wonder what might have been. He could smell Ellie on his skin. This morning had been soft and warm and full of the gentle loving that he had grown used to of late. But then he wondered at her questions – why now all of a sudden? And yet she was twenty-five, nearly fifteen years between them. What was she thinking – what sort of a future they might have together? And if she was – perhaps she was wondering what sort of a past there had been.

He shook the thoughts away however as the road unfurled into the flat lands around Mildenhall and beyond. Field and forest spilling away from the tarmac on either side, early-morning lorries thundering south on the other carriageway. He thought of yesterday and Young Young and the result with the wash house and none of it seemed to matter.

It was not yet nine when he hit Norwich so he ploughed through the centre of the city instead of skirting the ring road. As he passed the Norfolk and Norwich Hospital thoughts of his father's condition lifted inside him once more. A doctor stood by the gates, white coat flapping about his knees, stethoscope draped from his neck, smoking a cigarette.

Vanner drove quickly down Grapes Hill and right and left up Aylsham Road and then out of the city towards the coast. He smoked a cigarette, drank briefly from a bottle of water and drove on.

At nine thirty-five he pulled off the road and parked the car on the gravel drive behind his father's Metro. The air was clear and crisp and he could smell the sea in it. Sky blue, flat to the horizon, the wind took his hair as he stepped out of the car. He stood a moment and looked at the house, the sycamore tree beyond it and the squared spire of the church.

Anne met him as he got to the door and he kissed her. To think once he had avoided her eye. She took his bag and led the way into the echoing, wooden floored hall, with the banister rising sharply.

'How is he?' Vanner asked.

Her face was thin and grey and the lines showed against the skin for the first time since he had known her. Vanner laid a hand on her shoulder. 'Hard on you,' he said.

She smiled and touched his hand with hers. 'I'm all right, Aden. Come through, I'll make you some tea.'

Vanner followed her into the flagstoned kitchen where already she had a fire burning. She looked round at him as he warmed his hands. 'Central heating's so inadequate,' she said. 'Big house like this.'

Vanner nodded. 'How is he, Anne?'

She frowned. 'So so.'

'Worse than when I phoned?'

'About the same.'

'What does the doctor say?'

'He's old and his heart is weak.'

Vanner looked away from her.

She poured tea and passed him a cup which he held between both his palms, steam rising into his face as he sipped. Outside the wind chased itself through the branches of trees and he was reminded of the past, his youth and the cottage by the cliff he had not visited for a year.

'Is he asleep?' he asked her.

'Why don't you go and see.'

He took his tea with him and went down the hall to his father's study where the bed was made up. The old man's favourite room, with his weathered teak desk and ancient leather chair which had occupied many a tent in the desert. Books lined the walls from floor to ceiling, theology, mythology, philosophy. Novels: Greene, Hemingway, the plays of Arthur Miller. Vanner recalled reading *Death of a Salesman* in his teens and wondering if that might be his worst nightmare. His father lay on his back, hands by his sides under the blankets that were pressed and creased around him as if he had not moved so much as a muscle during the night. His face was white dust and his hair was very thin now, tousled on the pillow in wisps rather than waves. His eyes were closed and for one awful moment Vanner thought he was dead. He drew closer and as he bent he could make out the scant rasp of his breathing.

He sat on the arm of the chair and looked down at his father, long and thin in the bed. His face was leathery still although the flesh was weaker now and the ever-present tan of his days in the tropics was replaced by a wan and wasted look accentuated by age. Vanner sipped tea and watched him.

He did not wake up, seemed to be sleeping peacefully. For an hour Vanner sat and then a noise at the door made him look up. Anne gripped the handle in one hand and smiled at him.

'Still sleeping,' Vanner said.

She nodded. 'He does a lot of that.'

'I hope he goes like that, quietly, peacefully.' He looked at her. 'He deserves it.'

They went back to the kitchen and she dished him up a plate of bacon and eggs. He ate it although he was not hungry. When he was finished she poured more tea and he sat by the fire and lit a cigarette, exhaling stiffly into flames that curled about the logs in long lips of red.

'How's Ellie?'

He looked up at her. 'She's very young, Anne. I'm not sure we want the same things.'

'No?'

He shook his head. 'Having said that I wouldn't know what she does want.' He grinned. 'Never asked her.'

'What d'you think she wants?'

'I don't know. Husband, home, children.'

'And you?'

He sat forward and flicked ash into the fire. He looked at the end of the cigarette. 'Shouldn't be smoking in here.' He threw the cigarette into the flames and sat back. 'I've got the job. It's always been everything.'

'You don't think about Jane any more?'

He looked at her and smiled. 'No,' he said. 'I don't. Finally left her behind. Took me long enough.'

'That's good.' She patted his hand. 'Maybe you could start

again. Somebody young and fresh like Ellie. Get it right this time.'

'I've thought about it.'

'But?'

'I don't know.' He rubbed his eye. 'Just lately she's been different – or maybe she hasn't and it's just me being paranoid.' He glanced at her. 'Feels different though.'

'Has she said anything?'

'Wants to know about the past. She talked about guns. Don't know why. I don't think she was aware that policemen carried guns.'

'I didn't know myself.'

'Some do. Not all of the time.'

'You did.'

'Once upon a time. I'm still licensed.' He took his wallet out of his pocket and showed her his pink ticket. 'Glock,' he said. '9mm. Used to be a Browning. Don't know why I kept it up really. I just sort of did.'

'All those years in the army.'

'Yes,' he said. 'I suppose.'

'Why's she so interested in guns?'

Vanner shook his head. 'I haven't got a clue.'

His father woke at noon and Vanner sat with him for an hour or so. They talked sporadically but he was weak and his voice was thin and Vanner was filled with the terrible sense that he was fading. And with him a great chunk of his own life faded and for a moment or two he was terrified of where it might leave him. As the afternoon waned his father slept and Vanner just sat there watching him. In the evening he drove to the cottage.

He could hear the sea crashing against the groins on the beach as he left the car in the lane. He walked, as he had often done, the short distance to the drive and the chalet-styled cottage which was black against the horizon. Clouds had drifted in with the evening, rolling into smoky barrels under the stars which still glinted here and there where the cumulus was weakest. Gas-rig lights mottled the horizon. He stood at the end of the lawn and looked out. Somebody walked on the beach, he could make them out by the light of a torch. A dog barked and barked again. Vanner looked back at the cottage.

Inside it was very cold and the wood by the hearth was damp. He would not light a fire. He would not stay. Just to be here once more. He moved to the small room, which in times past had been his bedroom when they holidayed here, just the two of them. Cabin-style bed, hewn out of rough wood by his father and fitted into the alcove like a bunk from some ancient sailing ship. Many nights he had lain here, listening to the wind and rain pressing against the glass as if calling to him from some far and distant future. Here he stood now looking back down the shadow of the past and he was not sure of anything.

He sat for a while in an armchair, chilled through lack of use, his coat buttoned, fingers pushing into the fading arms while the single lamp glowed dull. He used to watch his father from this chair, watch him read, half-rimmed silver glasses clutching the end of his nose; chin high, lips compressed in concentration. He could see him now through half-closed eyes and the thin fog of memory.

James McCauley listened to his sister in the bath as the children got ready for bed. Mary-Anne Forbes was downstairs again. Eilish saw a lot of her lately. He did not mind. It kept Tommy's memory alive.

He sat on Caran's bed while she put her clothes away and he thought about the holdall in his sister's room. Empty now, but what had it contained before? Young Young, a murderer in their house. He looked at the girls and wondered what would become of them.

He tucked them in and the bath emptied and Eilish came through and kissed them goodnight. James switched the light off and followed Eilish into her bedroom. She tightened the cord of her dressing gown and caught the look in his eye.

'What is it, James?' she asked him.

He shook his head.

Eilish frowned, rubbed at her hair and looked at him quizzically. 'Come on, little brother. I know that look. What's on your mind?'

James lifted his hands. 'Young Young.'

'Gone, James. Over.'

'He slept with you.'

'I didn't know he killed people.'

'Stepper-Nap, Eilish.'

'I know what I'm doing, James.'

'Do you? What was in the bag you brought home?'

'Clothes.'

'The other bag.'

'James!'

James looked away from her. 'You're going to carry on seeing him – Stepper-Nap, I mean?'

'I see who I like, James.'

'Tonight. Are you going to see him tonight?'

'I'm going for a drink with Mary-Anne.'

'What does she do these days?'

'She's a cleaner.'

'Nothing else?'

'What d'you mean?'

'Nothing.'

'James.' Eilish laid her dress on the bed. 'Stop worrying. Have I ever let us down?'

'The children, Eilish. I worry about the children.'

'And you think I don't.' She fisted a hand on her hip. 'Who pays for them, James? Who feeds and clothes them?'

'You do.'

'Exactly. So stop telling me you worry about them. They're my responsibility.'

She sat down on the bed. 'Sometimes you know – you get too heavy. Christ, I thought our ma was bad . . .' She looked up at him again. 'I go my own way, James. I have my life.'

'What about Tommy?'

'Tommy's dead.'

'You loved him?'

'Of course I loved him. You know I loved him. I've never loved anyone like Tommy.'

'Stepper-Nap? Young Young?'

'That isn't love. I just use them.'

'And they use you.'

'Life, little brother. Life.'

She looked beyond him then. 'James, Tommy was special. Very very special. But he's been gone a long time. People move on. They don't forget but they move on.'

'Like you and Mary-Anne.'

'And you, James.'

He looked at the floor again. 'I might go away, Eilish. I've been thinking about it.'

'Where?'

'I don't know. I might go home. It's time I did something.'

She looked more softly at him. 'Yes, I think it is. I love having you here, but you can have a life too you know.'

'I know.' He shrugged. 'I just wanted to tell you. I'm thinking about it.'

'I think you should. Do you good. Get yourself out in the world.'

He grinned then. 'What would you do for a babysitter?'

She laughed. 'I'd manage, lover.'

Jimmy Crack set up the Observation Point over the wash house while Iris watched him and asked questions about international drugs dealers and what he would do when they caught them. The TSU had supplied the equipment but he had set it up himself to save time. When he was finished all that was visible from outside was a silver disc in the window.

'We'll leave it for a couple of weeks,' Jimmy told Vanner when he got back to Campbell Row. Vanner stood by the window in his office, staring down into the street. 'You okay, Guv?'

Vanner looked round at him and nodded.

'How's your dad?'

'Dying.'

Jimmy left him then and went back downstairs to brief his DI in the Area Intelligence Unit. Vanner sat at his desk and looked at the unwritten reports for Morrison. Ellie was in his head, Ellie and his father and Anne. They had spoken again before he left. Ellie was in bed when he got home. He wondered what sort of a future he could offer her.

After work he met Sid Ryan for a pint in the Irish pub on the High Road.

'What's new?' he asked as Vanner sat down on a stool alongside him.

'Your snout was right, Slips. Eilish McCauley's a donkey. She was clocked in Belfast when she was supposed to be in the south visiting her mother. She never got near the border.'

Ryan licked the paper on a cigarette, twisted the end and handed it to Vanner. 'Coalman was always good.' He rolled a second cigarette. 'Did Webby give you a bell?'

'Your man from SO13, yes.'

'He know her?'

'No.'

'But he might get to know her.'

'I daresay they'll give her the once-over. Come up with anything on your job yet?'

Ryan blew out his cheeks. 'Nothing they're telling us, Guv. I'm looking for the lover. Interviewed Case again, you know the fella who reckons he saw someone get in her car.'

'Lifting your leg?'

Ryan shook his head. 'I don't know. Feels right when he tells it. I've asked him three times now. I reckon he's on the level.'

'Hell of a coincidence then.'

'That's what I keep telling Webby. But as he says – *PIRA personal protection weapon. PIRA-type hit.* Only she had bugger all to do with PIRA.' He sat back and lit his cigarette. 'Doesn't make a whole lot of sense.'

'How's Frank Weir?'

'Tearing his hair out. What's left of it anyway.'

Vanner sipped Caffreys. 'Eilish is a player, Sid. How many black guys get to make moves across the water. Her contacts must be good.'

'Jimmy Carter, Guv.'

'Maybe.' Vanner looked sideways at him. 'I need to know when she's on the move again.'

'You taking her out?'

'We'll try and set her up. I want her to talk and then I want her to take me to the Daddy back here.'

'Just going to ask her are you?'

Vanner laughed. 'Something like that.'

'I'll have another word with the snout.'

'Will he come across?'

Ryan shrugged. 'Dunno. His contacts were with Carter. Carter's dead. Vacuum waiting to be filled.'

'He's an Ulsterman, Sid. He'll know people.'

'True. But he's not into spades.'

'He deals though, yeah?'

'Yeah, he still deals. I'll have a word. But he's not on the payroll any more.'

'Then set him up again. I'll square it with Morrison.'

George Webb was with DCI Westbrook on the fifteenth floor of The Yard. They were due at a briefing, a west London cell had gone live. The floor was sealed and SO19 were on stand-by. 'Spoke to 2 Area Drug Squad, Guv'nor,' Webb said as they walked the length of the corridor to the squad room. 'Bird they're looking at is a patsy over the water.'

Westbrook glanced at him. 'Who'd you speak to at 2 Area?'

'Vanner. DI.'

Westbrook nodded. 'Ex DCI – replaced me when I came here. What's he got?'

'Doesn't know. Coke maybe. We're having a word. Swann's over there now. First time across the water, Guv. Told him not to stand in The Crown and order a Campari and Soda.'

Westbrook chuckled and they paused outside the squad room. 'This Ealing thing is bugging me. A woman. That's a first. Two definite maybe's and two alibis.'

Webb nodded. 'Shit happens.'

'Sleeper?'

'Possible.'

'When they wake up we normally know about it.'

'We do.' Webb grinned. 'But we can't always be perfect.'

Jimmy Crack watched the first set of tapes from the wash house OP. He sat in the Drug Squad office with Sammy and China and froze the image on the screen as a black man came out with a paper shopping bag in his hands. 'Pretty Boy,' Jimmy stated flatly. 'Remember him from the party pictures? Trying to take over from the Daddy.'

'And not getting very far,' China muttered.

'To date. Young Young's history now though.'

Sammy looked at him. 'You think he's looking to make a move?'

'Maybe. Time'd be ripe wouldn't it.' He wound the tape on and stopped once again as a white man came round from the back and got into a red BMW parked along the street.

'The washer,' he said. 'Ginger Bill. Young Young fingered him.'

Vanner sat behind them with his arms folded. 'How long will the Irish couple let us keep the plot going, Jim?'

'As long as it takes, Guv. They're not going anywhere and they love it. Iris can't do enough for me.'

Sammy glanced at Vanner and winked. Jimmy elbowed him in the ribs. Vanner got up and moved in front of them. 'Eilish McCauley's the key to all this,' he said. 'Stepper-Nap's expansion policy.' He paused for a moment. 'Playing patsy to Belfast's a dangerous game. She must be very sure of herself.'

'Either that or she's stupid.'

Vanner glanced at Sammy. 'Somehow I don't think she is.' He looked at the pictures from the party pasted up on the wall. 'I spoke to Slippery again last night. His snout is good. Hopefully, and I stress – hopefully, he'll be able to give us the nod when she moves again. He's still got connections across the water. When she moves we'll send a team as far as the ferry. Antrim Road will pick her up and give her a tug with the gear on her. Then Jimmy Crack and me'll go across and see if we can't get her to lay down.'

'That's a hell of a long shot, Guv'nor,' China said.

'Got a better idea?'

China looked at the floor.

'If we take her out over there and she goes for it – Stepper won't know much about it. He'll be pissed off but there won't be much he can do.' He glanced at Jimmy. 'The Irish won't be dealing with the Brit-Boys direct. No contact. No names. Eilish'll be their connection. He'll still have to use her if only to co-ordinate. It might work. You up for it, Jim?'

'Whenever you're ready, Guv'nor.'

Ryan took the call from the Coalman on his mobile in the incident room at Hendon.

'The Coalman, Mr Ryan.'

'How you doing?'

'Not bad. Not bad at all.'

'You got something for me?'

'Your wee girl. She's on the move again.'

'That's a bit sudden isn't it?'

'Can't tell ye the why's and wherefore's, Mr Ryan, only what I hear.'

'When?'

'Two weeks tomorrow.'

Ryan switched off the phone, lifted the receiver on his desk and called Vanner.

Eilish lay in bed with Stepper-Nap. James was out, early afternoon, the children were still at school. A kilo of uncut crack lay wrapped in plastic on the floor beside the bed. Stepper lay back with an easy smile on his face. 'So they can't make it themselves?'

'Obviously not.'

He half-closed his eyes. 'This is going to be good. Very good. Better than I thought it would be. They ain't gonna stiff me this time.'

'Told you my contacts were good.' Eilish looked at the sandwich box on the floor. 'I didn't want to go again so soon though, Step.'

Stepper glanced at her, then took her arm gently, wrapping his fingers all the way around. The heavy gold chain fell forward on his neck as he bent towards her. 'You'll be fine.'

'But it's only been a couple of weeks.'

'So what did you expect? The last batch was for starters – first contact. Now we begin to supply.'

'I've got two kids, Stepper.'

'So. You've got a brother.'

'That's not the point.'

Stepper took her chin between his fingers and tilted her head to his. She looked into the black of his eyes. 'Your mother's not well,' he said. 'A friend phoned. She needs you.'

Eilish jerked her face away from his grasp. 'Don't tempt fate.'

He looked coldly at her then. 'I don't believe in fate, girl. Just opportunity. This keeps us ahead of the game.'

Eilish got out of bed and wrapped herself in her dressing gown. She moved to the window, eased the net aside and looked out.

'Nobody's watching you, babe.'

She ignored him, looking out over the street. Stepper swung his legs over the bed and moved behind her. He wrapped heavy arms about her and drew her back against him.

'The last time. After this I get a gopher.'

Eilish turned and faced him. 'Who?'

'Who cares? There's plenty of Irish who'll do it. I'll ask Ginger Bill to find someone.'

She looked up into his face. 'Ask him now. I don't want to go.'

He shook his head. 'Not enough time. You have to go. There's nobody else I can trust. I'll get on it, today. But you have to go this time.'

Eilish tugged at her lip with her teeth and wriggled herself free from his grasp. 'I get paid a lot this time.'

'Course you do, baby.' He drew her towards him again. 'Course you do.'

Vanner phoned Jimmy Crack on his mobile. Jimmy was at the wash house OP, changing tapes. 'I've checked with the ferry company, Jim. She's on the night boat tomorrow.'

'We got a plot set up?'

'Surveillance to Liverpool. Level 1 UC on the boat. Antrim Road at the other side.'

'Sorted then, Guv.'

'Thus far. Be tricky in Belfast though.'

'You mean if she doesn't go for it.'

'She'll go for it. She's got her kids to think about. The timing – Antrim Road'll want to know who she meets.'

'It's our deal, Guv.'

'Yes, but it's their patch.'

'So we just have to trust them?'

'No other choice. Make sure you've got a bag packed.'

The following morning Eilish prepared to travel. Her bag was packed and ready, lying on its side on the bed. James hovered in the doorway like a spectre from the past hanging over her. She had her back to him, but felt his presence like a weight on her shoulders. After a moment she turned. 'She needs me.'

He did not reply, arms at his sides, fingers curled. He looked at her, shallowed his gaze then turned and went down the stairs. Eilish glanced at the bag on the bed, shook her head and followed him.

He sat in the living room, face to the floor. 'The girls don't understand any of it, Eilish.'

'Yes they do. I've spoken to them. Their granny's not very well. Of course they understand.' He stared at her then, wrinkled his lip and looked away. 'When will you be back?'

'Just as soon as I can.' She went up to him and kissed the top of his head. 'I have to go. It's a long drive and I'm tired before I begin. Look after the girls for me.'

Vanner and Jimmy Crack watched from their car on the slip road by the park. Eilish pulled onto the main road in her blue Sierra and headed north. She did not see them, hands fast about the wheel, concentrating on the road ahead. On the other side a motorcyclist pulled on leather gauntlets, checked his mirrors and followed her. In the doorway of her house her brother stood with his hands in his pockets. Briefly he reflected on the grey of the sky, squared his shoulders and went back inside. Vanner looked at Jimmy. 'You know something,' he said. 'I get the impression m'laddo over there knows what's going on and isn't happy about it.'

Jimmy nodded. 'Plays mummy and daddy to those kids doesn't he.' He shifted himself in the driver's seat. 'Sister shagging two blacks who deal crack for a living. Can't be very good for him.' He started the car and looked at Vanner. 'Let's hope Antrim Road do their stuff.'

Morrison was in the kitchen at Campbell Row, drinking coffee with the skipper from the Firearms Inquiry team. Vanner climbed the stairs, nodded to Morrison and went into his office. He took the card Ryan had given him and dialled the pager service. He gave them the number then hung up. Morrison stood in the doorway behind him.

'How's it going, Vanner?'

'Fine, so far.'

'Results?'

'Maybe.' Vanner glanced at him. Morrison stood with one hand jangling change in his pocket.

'Good take-out with SO19 the other night.'

'Not bad,' Vanner said. 'Young Young gave us the wash house and the cleaner.'

'Ginger Bill.' Morrison smiled. 'I read your report, Vanner.' He moved into the office. 'This Eilish McCauley's the key?'

'We think so, Sir.' Vanner sat down at his desk. 'She was into Young Young *and* the Daddy. Daddy had the money. Young Young had the dick.'

Morrison smiled and shook his head. 'Nasty.'
'What?'
'Young Young.'
'They're all nasty, Sir.'
The phone rang on Vanner's desk and he picked up the receiver. 'Vanner.'
'George Webb, Guv. SO13.'
'Hello, George.'
'You paged me.'
'Yeah. Eilish McCauley. Just gone walkabout.'
'Our turf?'
'Will be tomorrow morning. You wanted to know when she moved. Got to tell you though – we're planning to pull her in Belfast.'
'Thanks.' Webb hung up and Vanner put down the receiver.
'George?' Morrison said.
'Webb. SO13.'
'Gets about. Accounts manager for our Ealing hit.'
Vanner smiled. 'How's that going, Sir?'
Morrison shook his head at him. 'Don't, Vanner,' he said.
He moved to the window and looked out. 'What's the plan with your plot?'
'Antrim Road are going to lift Eilish before she makes her connection. As soon as they do Jimmy Crack and me'll fly over. We're going to try to set her up, get her in front of a magistrate and not oppose the bail. When she gets back we're going after Stepper-Nap.'
Morrison raised his eyebrows. 'You think she'll want to play?'
'I don't know, Sir. She's got two kids. I doubt she wants to lose them.' He made a face.
'We've been on this deal one way or another for almost two years. This is our best shot yet. Eilish is close to the source. He can't do anything over the water without her. If she wants to play we'll have him.'
Morrison looked thoughtfully at him. 'Back in Belfast for you then?'
Vanner looked up at him. 'For a night at least, yes.'
'Old times, Vanner.' Morrison winked and went back out to the landing.

Eilish found her cabin, went inside and closed and locked the door. Customs were so slack on ferries. She laid her bag on the bed, unzipped it and rummaged beneath her clothes till her fingers came up against the plastic sandwich box with the crack squashed inside it. She half-lifted one corner, replaced it, and zipped up the bag once again. In the bathroom she brushed her teeth and swilled water about her mouth, staring at herself in the mirror.

The bar was quiet, few people gathered yet. She found a stool, ordered a vodka and lit a cigarette. A group of Irish lads in Glasgow Rangers football shirts drank pints of lager and played cards at a table. One of them had UDA tattooed in blue and red on his forearm. His head was shaved and he crunched peanuts as he laid down his cards. Catching Eilish's eye he leered at her. She curled her lip as if something in her mouth had gone bad and looked away from him. One man sat on his own on a couch. He was reading a folded copy of *The Independent*, a briefcase by his knees. For an instant their eyes met and then he looked back at his paper.

Eilish drank three vodkas and smoked two cigarettes. One of the football fans tried to chat her up so she finished her drink and went back to her cabin. The man on his own scoured the pages of his paper.

Alone again with the unsteady swell of an oil-black Irish Sea, Eilish lit another cigarette and lay down on her bunk, staring at the patches on the low ceiling above her. The sound of diesel engines rumbled in her head. She finished the cigarette, sat up and reached for her handbag. From her purse she extracted a small colour photograph. A man's face, wild black hair and laughing green in his eyes. James did not know she had kept it.

And now she remembered as if it was yesterday. Brindley Cross, a small flat overlooking the patch of grass that served as a village green. Across the road the pub, its sign flapping on rusty hinges whenever the wind blew hard. She had been nineteen, her brother barely fifteen and their mother and father separated. Father gone, England or Australia or wherever else he had fled to when their mother found out about his affairs. *Her* at Mass every day, safely tucked out of sight with her sister's family, back in the south where she came from. Eilish and James could have gone with her, but Eilish reckoned she could pay the rent so she took over the flat without the council ever knowing and James had remained with her.

And that night, twelve years ago when Tommy came riding his motorbike through the rain. Water falling in floods against loose-fitting window panes and the wind howling in off the sea. She heard his motorbike, rattling its way through the gale which flattened the grass by the pub. James in bed already, she just risen from a bath, her flesh pink and steaming from the heat of the water. She heard the old Moto Guzzi cough and stutter then stop and start again and he came winding down the street following the ragged line of his half-hearted headlight. She could almost feel the drink swilling inside him as he faltered from one side of the road to the other. Where he had been drinking she did not know but his manner told her he had had a skinful already. She watched from the window as he rolled down the slope, one foot on the back brake, tyre sliding behind him. He had the visor of his helmet half off his eyes so he could see through the rain in his face.

He stopped in the yard by the broken-down cars and lurched off the machine. He stood a moment, head down, supporting the bike with his weight as he fumbled with his foot to get the side stand down. He stepped away gingerly as if he was not sure it would remain upright and rain rolled off the black leather of his jacket. He stumbled against the fence, extending one gloved hand to steady himself then lifted his face to the window. He flapped a hand then staggered towards the door.

Eilish could hear every drunken step, the clump clump of ill-fitting boots. If he did not shut up he would wake Mrs McAvoy and all hell would break loose. Eilish, robe tight about her now moved to the hall, checking briefly at Jamie's silent bedroom before undoing the chain on the front door. Tommy stood there, helmet still on, water rolling off his clothes into a puddle at his feet. Eilish grabbed wet leather and pulled him quickly inside.

She helped him off with his helmet and he shook loose his hair, water flying in a fine spray across her face. He laughed then, made a grab for her but she caught his hand and squeezed, lifting a finger to her lips as she did so. 'Will you be quiet,' she hissed.

He aped her words, a sloppy grin on his mouth, one gloved hand wavering in front of his face. Then he tried to kiss her and she pushed him around and marched him through the living-room door. He tried to kiss her again. Outside, a heavy vehicle moved slowly up the road, pausing briefly outside the pub before moving on again. Eilish could make out the flood of its headlights through the ill-fitting curtains.

She pushed Tommy down into a chair and unfastened his jacket. He smiled, touched her hair with free fingers and lolled his head back. She could smell the stink of beer on his breath. 'You should smell yourself, Tommy.'

'Cannot.'

'Just as well eh.'

She helped him out of the jacket. Beneath it his shirt and tie were sodden. He looked into her face. 'She kicked me out, Eilish.'

Eilish loosened his tie. He worked in the post office as a clerk and obviously had not been home or had not yet got changed. She started at the buttons of his shirt and he made another drunken play for her. His jaw rasped against hers, beer and stale cigarettes in her face. She pushed him back. 'What d'ye mean she kicked you out?'

'What I say, Eilish? She knows about us. She's away to tell the priest and everything.'

James stirred across the landing. Eilish hushed Tommy, then she got up and switched off the light. Darkness in the room save the orange glow of street lamps through the window. She went to pull the curtains tighter, glancing briefly over the street as if she expected to see the wronged wife and her three brats marching on her with the priest. But there was nobody, nothing out there save the wind in the trees and the rain, falling in angular lines against the wall of the building. Behind her Tommy was hauling his soaking shirt over his shoulders. Eilish went to the bathroom for a towel.

She dried his naked flesh, feeling sinewy muscle in his arms. Black hair crusted his breast and belly to disappear in a mat at his trousers. Freckles on his shoulders and arms, bunching now with muscle as he shivered uncontrollably. She rubbed at his hair till it sprang back from his head. Fingers reached for her robe, tugging loose the tie. She felt a little shiver break through her and gooseflesh rode on her thighs. He bent to her belly and tasted her skin with his tongue.

She unbuckled his trousers and helped him out of them,

then they lay side by side, naked on the rough carpet and he looked deep in her eyes.

In the hallway James stood by the door. Eilish could sense him, as she always could but tonight she had felt sure he was sleeping. His footfall gave him away though and she could make out his shadow through the crack of the door.

She knelt in front of Tommy now, the robe on the floor beside her, both of them were side on to the door, which started to open a fraction. Eilish could see it moving little by little out of the corner of her eye until the gap was some two inches. Tommy was too drunk to notice. Eilish pulled him down to her then and he laid her on her back on the carpet. His breathing was thick in his throat, burring through his nose as he moved on top of her, eyes bunched, wrinkled into knots of flesh at the edges. Eilish held his back, fingernails pressing his flesh, her legs locked about the base of his spine. Beyond him, beyond the crack in the door she could see the darkness of her brother, watching them.

Tommy grunted deep in his throat, face twisting and then he let out a low groan which rose and rose until Eilish clapped her hand over his lips. He rolled off her and lay on his back, flaccid now and breathing hard, his chest rising and falling. Eilish lay for a moment longer, aware of her brother still hiding on the landing. Pushing herself to her elbow she took Tommy's tobacco from his jacket and rolled herself a cigarette.

He fell asleep. She sat and watched him, listening to the rain and smoking the cigarette. James had gone back to bed, one telltale floorboard betraying him. About midnight she heard a vehicle come by again, very slowly like the last one. Moving to the window, she looked out on a grey armoured Landrover, which had slowed to almost a stop alongside Tommy's motorbike. It moved on again and she watched the rain broken up in its headlights.

Tommy was snoring, loudly now like a pig. Eilish put her dressing gown on and shook him.

'Wake up.'

He grunted and rolled onto his side.

'Come on, Tommy. Wake up.'

He lay a moment longer and she prodded him with her toe. He sat up, rubbing his back.

'What's going on?' he mumbled.

'You got to go, Tom.'

He took the cigarette from her and scratched his groin. 'Go where exactly?'

'Home.'

'How can I go home? She threw me out so she did.'

Eilish looked beyond him to the door. James was out of his bed again. 'You can't stay here,' she said.

'Why not?'

'Because I don't want your wife banging on my door in the morning.'

'Nobody'll know I'm here.'

'So they will. Your bike's downstairs isn't it. I'm not having that bike outside my house in the morning.'

'Oh, be quiet woman.' He rubbed his belly and farted. 'Have you not got anything to drink?' He got up then and wandered, naked, into the kitchen. Opening the fridge he found a can of beer and flipped off the top. Froth bubbled over his fingers. Eilish tied her robe more tightly about her and went through after him.

'You can't stay here, Tom.'

'Where else can I go?' His voice was sharp and his eyes flashed. He drew his hand over his lips and drank again from the can.

'What about Danny?'

'Danny lives miles away. I'm too pissed to ride that far.'

She snatched the can from his hand. 'Then sober up first.'

He took it back from her. 'It's pouring wi' rain, Eilish. You want me to catch my death.'

'You can't send him out in this, Eilish.' Both of them started and looked round. James stood in the doorway to the lounge, in his pyjamas. He looked down at Tommy's nakedness and coloured.

'Jamie. What about ye?'

'I'm fine, Tom. Just fine.'

'Your big sister seems to think I ought to be riding my motorbike over to Danny's.'

'What's wrong with your place?'

Tommy grinned at him. 'Threw me out so she did.'

'Is that a fact?'

'Aye. Told me never to come back. Straight on to see the priest so she was.'

He looked at Eilish then at the rain on the window. 'How can she send me out in weather like this?'

James looked at his sister then. 'She can't. You can't, Eilish.'

'I can.' Eilish folded her arms. 'He can't stay here, Jamie. You know he can't.'

Tommy still stood naked between them, one ankle crossed over the other, sipping from the can of beer.

'Fetch us my fags, Jamie,' he said.

Jamie picked up the tin where it had fallen on the floor and handed it to him.

'Good lad.' Tommy took a paper from the tin and filled it with tobacco. Eilish was at the window. 'The rain's stopping.'

'No it's not.' Tommy looked beyond her. 'Pissing down so it is.'

'Let him stay, Eilish.'

Eilish whirled round. 'You go to bed, little boy.'

'Hey.' Tommy touched her arm. 'Don't talk to him like that.'

'Don't you tell me how to talk to him.' Her eyes smarted then, flaming suddenly against the white of her cheeks. 'You know fine you can't stay here, Tommy. We rent this flat on the quiet. Our mam's still the tenant as far as the council's concerned. If they find out they'll kick us out.'

'How can they find out?'

'Because the neighbours are just looking for an excuse to get rid of us. If they see your bike out there in the morning that's all the excuse they'll need.'

'I'll go and shift the bike.'

'No you won't. You'll go home.'

'I can't go home. How many more times, woman?'

'Then you'll go to Danny's. Shit, you're sober enough. You made it this far didn't you?'

Outside the wind blew rain against the window in a wash which rattled the pane. Tommy looked into the gloom, shook his head and picked up his underpants from the floor.

Eilish woke up with the boat pulling into the docks in Belfast. She got dressed quickly and stuffed her night things into the bag, which she zipped up tight. Then she went outside.

Gulls swooped over the deck where an old grey-haired woman was tossing up scraps of bread. Eilish watched her and thought of the mother she had not seen since Christmas.

* * *

Vanner packed an overnight bag. Ellie was still in the shower. For a moment he stood at the bathroom door and watched her through the opaque sheen of the glass. She must have glimpsed his shadow for she suddenly flicked water at him over the top. 'Bugger off, you old lech.'

Vanner grinned to himself and took his bag downstairs to the hall. In the kitchen he made coffee and then he phoned Sammy at Campbell Row.

'Any word from Belfast, Sam?'

'Boat's about to dock, Guv. We've got two lads from Antrim Road on the plot.'

'You spoken to Jimmy Crack?'

'No.'

'I'll bell him. See you in an hour or so.'

Vanner put the phone down. From upstairs he could hear the whirring of Ellie's hair dryer. When he went up with the coffee he found her kneeling on the floor, naked, with her head bent right forward and her hair flipped over her face. She tossed her head back and grinned at him, nipples hardening under his gaze.

'Don't, Aden.'

'Don't what?'

'Look at me like that. I've just had a shower.'

He bent and kissed the back of her head. 'I've got to go.'

'When will you be back?'

'I don't know.'

'You'll be all right?'

'Of course I will.'

'Phone me.'

'If I get a chance.'

She stood up then and reached for her knickers. Vanner caught her up in his arms and held her for a moment. She kissed the end of his nose, then his chin and his neck. He pushed her away. 'I've got to go,' he said.

'Right now?'

'You've just had a shower.'

'I could have another.'

'I've got to go, Ellie. I'll call you okay.'

'You make sure you do. And, Aden,' she said, as he was halfway through the door.

'What?'

'Be careful.'

At Campbell Row Sammy spotted him coming up the stairs. He stood at the top, leaning both hands on the banister. 'Got a call from Belfast, Guv. They're tailing her now.'

'Good. Is Jimmy in?'

'Downstairs, talking to his Guv'nor.'

Vanner went into his office as the phone was ringing. 'Vanner.'

'Morrison, Vanner. What time are you leaving?'

'Don't know yet, Sir. There's no point in going till RUC make their collar.'

'Just you and Jimmy Crack?'

'Yes.'

'What kind of a deal are you looking to make?'

'Depends, Sir. But she can give us everything.'

Morrison was quiet for a moment. 'One thing, Vanner.'

Vanner sat down. 'What's that?'

'Don't promise anything you can't deliver.'

Vanner said nothing.

'You still there?'

'Yes. I'm still here.'

'Did you hear what I said?'

'Clear as a bell, Sir.'

Vanner put the phone down and went through to the squad room. China was watching video tapes.

'Wash house?'

China wound the tape through with the remote control, the image flickering at fast-forward. 'Nothing so far, Guv. A couple of faces. The one Jimmy calls Thin Hand.'

'Thin Hand Billy,' Vanner said. 'Not seen much of him. No sign of the main man?'

'Not a whisper.'

'Clever fucker isn't he.' Vanner left him to it.

He found Jimmy Crack talking to David Starkey from Financial Investigation, who was doing some work on the Western Union money smurfed out to Jamaica. Starkey nodded to him and Vanner waited till they had finished their conversation.

'Any word on the cash?' he asked Jimmy.

'Nothing we don't know already. What about Belfast?'

'Sammy's monitoring it.' Vanner looked at his watch. 'It's early yet.'

'I've got us provisionally booked on the seven o'clock from Heathrow.'

Vanner grinned at him. 'Bit of a while to wait.'

Eilish drove through Belfast city centre, passing the Europa Hotel where Bill Clinton had stayed, at one time the most bombed hotel in the world. At twelve noon she pulled over by The Crown and lit a cigarette, watching her mirror for anyone watching her. On the corner a motorcycle courier talked into his radio.

Four cars back two Drug Squad officers from Antrim Road watched her in their door mirrors. Eilish moved off again, leaving the city centre and heading for west Belfast. Behind her the Drug Squad officers followed.

She left the centre, driving slowly along Divis Street. The first phone box she came to she stopped and got out of the car. The Drug Squad officers pulled over behind. Eilish was dialling, money in her hand, her back to the road and her car. The officers checked through the windows and spotted her grey, flat, travel bag. They exchanged a short glance then stepped up to the phone box. Eilish put down the receiver and looked into their faces. 'Oh shit,' she said.

Vanner sat in his office, smoking a cigarette. His bag packed and ready at his feet. Jimmy was in the squad room making phonecalls. The phone rang on Vanner's desk. For a moment he stared at it then lifted the receiver to his ear.

'Vanner.'

'DC Killiner, Antrim Road. Your runner's in custody.'

'Gear?'

'Crack. Over a kilo. We've sent it off for emergency analysis.'

'We'll be there.'

Vanner put down the phone, picked up his bag and went through to the squad room. Jimmy was talking to China. He looked up as Vanner walked in.

'Antrim Road, Jimmy. Only it's not coke it's crack.'

Jimmy frowned. 'They obviously don't have a wash man.'

Sammy drove them to Heathrow, Vanner on the mobile organising their change of tickets. There was a flight at four thirty. They would be on it. As the plane took off Vanner wondered what would come of the trip. Eilish McCauley was looking at a ten-year stretch for intent to supply. The best he could hope for her was information in mitigation with the judge. He wondered if it would be enough.

They were met at Belfast International Airport by DC Killiner from the Antrim Road Drug Squad. He placed their bags in the boot of his Rover and then drove them towards the city. Vanner sat in the front and looked out on a landscape he had not seen in twelve years.

The city lay in a valley, the airport to the north. They could see the sprawl from the road that drifted down from the escarpment.

'Been over here before have you?' Killiner asked them.

'I haven't,' Jimmy said.

Killiner glanced at Vanner. 'Sir?'

'Yes.'

'Job?'

Vanner shook his head. 'Parachute Regiment.'

Killiner lifted his eyebrows. 'I reckon you know the form then.'

'I reckon.'

Killiner scratched his ear. 'Big deal is it – back in London?'

'The biggest,' Jimmy told him. 'Been working on it for almost two years. Team working out of Harlesden, British blacks with connections in Jamaica.'

Killiner grinned. 'You know this is the biggest haul we've had over here. My bosses are delirious.'

'I bet they are,' Vanner said. 'How is she – Eilish?'

'Very pissed off. Redhead. Spits like a tiger. Doesn't want to tell us who she was meeting.'

'Now there's a surprise.'

Killiner stopped at red traffic lights and tapped out a rhythm on the steering wheel. He looked at Vanner. 'Something came up in the strip search, Sir.'

'What's that?'

'Tattoo.' Killiner touched his thigh. 'Here.' Again he looked at Vanner. '*Cumman na mBan.*'

Jimmy leaned over the seat. 'What does that mean?'

Vanner looked back at him. 'Women's wing of the IRA,' he said.

Killiner's mobile rang where it lay on the dashboard. Vanner reached forward and handed it to him. He pressed SND and fixed it to his ear.

'Killiner,' he said. 'What?' His eyebrows arched then. 'You're joking aren't you?' He paused again. 'Right. No, they're in the car with me now.' He switched off the phone and sighed. Vanner stared at him.

'What?' he said.

'We've got a problem. The crack.'

'What about it?'

'It's melted down candlewax.'

Eilish McCauley smoked white-filtered cigarettes one after the other in the interview room at Antrim Road. A woman RUC constable was with her, standing by the door with her hands behind her back. Vanner closed the door, Jimmy moving to the table. Vanner glanced at the WPC who smiled. He looked over at Eilish, long red hair and green eyes like a cat. She sucked her cheeks in hard and blew a steady stream of smoke. Vanner moved to the vacant chair. Jimmy was already seated. The tape machine was switched off.

Vanner sat down slowly and held Eilish's stare with his own. 'Hello, Eilish,' he said. 'I'm Detective Inspector Vanner. Northwest London Drug Squad. This is Detective Constable McKay.'

She looked from one to the other of them. 'Long way from home aren't you.'

'So are you, Eilish.'

She sat back and folded her arms.

For a moment Vanner did not say anything. He glanced at Jimmy Crack who leaned both elbows on the desk and steepled fingers under his chin.

'You've been arrested with a kilo and a half of crack cocaine in your possession, Eilish. Intent to supply. If you're convicted – which you will be – you'll go away for ten years.' Vanner looked at her then. 'That'll make your kids all but grown up when you get out.'

Eilish did not say anything. Her eyes betrayed no emotion, but she lit another cigarette.

Vanner cast his eyes over the gathering butts in the ashtray. 'I'm going to tell you a little story, Eilish, and when I've finished I want you to think long and hard about those ten years.' He took out his own cigarettes, lit one and snapped closed his lighter. He laid it on top of the cigarette box on the table.

'In Harlesden there's a black man called Stepper-Nap. He's married with three kids and he's on the dole. Funny thing is he drives a green Mercedes with a personalised number plate.'

Eilish was not looking at him. She sucked on the cigarette and blew smoke over his head.

'Pretty Boy,' Vanner said. 'He's part of the team and he's got takeover plans. That's probably why you're sitting there. Stepper-Nap used to have some body armour called Young Young. Trouble is Young Young's a bit wayward, likes to put it about a bit. Carries an Uzi because it makes him a hardman like his father. His father got killed in a knife fight. Young Young's got a half-brother called Little Bigger. Then there's Bigger Dan, and Thin Hand Billy and Jig. There's a tame doctor in Neasden. Stepper-Nap takes his patsies there when they swallow. The doctor gives them suppositories. Am I making sense?'

'You tell me, lover.'

Vanner smiled and put out his cigarette. 'Young Young didn't like a Jamaican illegal called Holden Biggs. Biggs called him a pussy so Young Young took his gun into Jimmy Carter's snooker hall in Kilburn. He whacked Biggs and shot a few holes in the ceiling. That really pissed Carter off. It really pissed Stepper-Nap off – so you went to see Carter and made a deal for Stepper.' He looked her up and down. 'I bet you make good deals, Eilish.'

She did not say anything.

'Stepper let Carter's mob beat seven bells out of Young Young. But you don't do that to Young Young. You either kill him or leave him alone. When he got better, he went to see Carter again – only this time he decided to shoot holes in him. He also shot the bouncer. The bouncer gave him up. You used to sleep with Young Young didn't you. I bet that really wound old Stepper up.'

'I don't know what you're on about.'

'No? That's up to you, Eilish. I'm just telling you how it is so you can think about your ten years some more.' He glanced at Jimmy Crack. 'Stepper has a little hotel on Willesden Lane where he gets a white guy called Ginger Bill to wash coke into crack for him. Stepper's got a brother in Jamaica who owns a nightclub where deals go down with men from Miami. The men from Miami know men from Colombia and they sell coke to them. The coke goes to Jamaica and then it gets on aeroplanes to Heathrow and Gatwick and that's where Pretty Boy comes in. Making sense, Eilish?' His voice was harder now, an edge to it, reflected in the black of his eyes. 'Ten years, Eilish. Your children won't know who you are.'

Eilish lit another cigarette and snapped the spent match in two. Vanner saw that her hands were shaking just a fraction.

'You can help yourself, Eilish,' Jimmy said softly. 'That – believe it or not – is why we've come all the way over here. Do you really want to go away for ten long years?'

'Your children will be taken into care,' Vanner said. 'You know what happens to little girls in care.'

'Shut your mouth.' She spat the words at him and squashed her cigarette in the ashtray.

'It's a fact, Eilish. You know it is. They'll never let you see them again.'

'My brother can look after them.'

'For ten years? No chance. Their mother a convicted drug trafficker. Probably runs in the family. You really believe the social services'll let James look after them? Grow up, Eilish.'

She bit down on her lip, hands trembling now. She looked at Vanner's cigarettes on the table. Her own pack was empty. Vanner picked up his packet and placed it in his pocket. 'We're going to put you back in the cell now, Eilish. Then we're going to hang around for an hour. If you don't ask to see us by then we're going home – and you – lady – are history.' He swivelled round in his seat and nodded to the WPC by the door.

Downstairs in the canteen they drank coffee. Jimmy shook his head. 'They must've ripped him off,' he said. 'The first time. He wouldn't do this otherwise.'

'Bloody stupid to do it at all,' Vanner said. 'You think she'll go for it?'

'If she doesn't she's walking anyway.'

'Yeah, but she doesn't know that.' Vanner looked at the clock on the wall. They had been sat there for fifteen minutes. 'If we play this just right Antrim Road might yet get her contact.'

'You mean give her back the box – let her make the deal?'

'Why not?'

'Risky. What if they figure it?'

'The wax is wrapped in clingfilm. If the contact is good

enough they'll pass over the funds and walk.'

'Yeah, but what about later – when they find out it's not crack?'

Vanner pursed his lips.

'Word'll get back to Stepper, Guv. Then it'll get to her.'

'Not necessarily.'

'It will. They only contact him through her. If that happens we've lost her.'

Vanner sighed. 'Delicate.'

'I reckon we ought to leave it, Guv. Keep the box. Let her go thinking we own her life. She won't know procedure. She'll tell Stepper she was busted.'

'But he knows it's just wax.'

Jimmy made a face. 'Then we need something from her now.'

They sat in silence for a few minutes then Jimmy said, 'That tattoo – you reckon she's a player?'

Vanner pursed his lips. 'Maybe once upon a time.' He sat forward. 'Who knows, Jimmy. A lot of them go through the phase. Tattoo is a statement. No-one on the fifteenth floor knows her.'

A man walked through the swing doors in plain clothes. Vanner bunched his eyes as he looked at him.

'You know him, Guv?' Jimmy asked.

Vanner thought for a moment. 'Yes,' he said. 'I do.' He stood up and wandered up to the counter where the man was looking at the specials on the blackboard.

'Billy,' Vanner said.

The man turned, tall with thin blond hair and pale eyes. He squinted. 'B'Jesus. Vanner.'

They shook hands. 'How are you, Billy?'

Billy Callaghan. Vanner knew him from his days as an army intelligence officer with 90 Section, just before he resigned his commission. Callaghan was B Squad Special Branch. They sat down at a table, Vanner glancing once more at the clock.

'What're you doing here?' Callaghan said. 'You were out last time I heard.'

'I am out, Billy. The army that is.' Vanner showed him his warrant card. 'Old Bill,' he said. 'Northwest London Drug Squad. Your boys lifted a patsy I'm after.'

'Well there you go – small world isn't it.'

Vanner nodded. 'What're you doing these days?'

'Ex-branch, now. Other duties.' They looked at one another and Vanner nodded.

'How're the boys?'

'Boys?'

'Yeah. The ones I used to know.'

Callaghan sipped coffee. 'You don't know?'

'Should I?'

'Dave Quigley got shot in Morne.'

Vanner's face furrowed. 'When?'

'1994. July. On holiday with his family. Close quarter. Tokarev .62mm.'

Vanner stared at him.

'They found him floating in Spelga Dam.'

Vanner was suddenly cold. 'You said Tokarev?'

'That's right.'

'You get them?'

'Nope.'

Vanner sat back again and took out his cigarettes. He offered the pack to Callaghan.

'We've got a shooting with a Toky in London.'

'I know,' Callaghan said. 'Same gun, Aden.'

Vanner stared at him once more. 'You sure?'

'Course I'm sure. Lambeth sent it over here for checks. The cartridge cases that is. They matched Quigley's murder. Ejection marks, firing pin, the works.'

Vanner looked at the clock. Half an hour. He glanced at Jimmy who made a face. Again he looked at Callaghan. 'The others okay?'

'Others?'

'You know what I mean.'

'Tim Phelan's disabled. Got blown up in '88.'

'Bad?'

'No legs. One arm. Lives on your side now. Yorkshire.' Callaghan sat forward. 'Funny thing that – DPOA took a call from him a while back. Reckoned he was being looked at. Woman in the park by his house. Three times she was there. No kids with her.'

Vanner bunched his right hand in a fist. 'What happened?'

'DPOA phoned SO13 and they sent a couple of lads up to

see him. Found nothing though. Reckoned it was just the cracks.'

'You heard from him again?'

'No.'

Vanner looked at the clock, then glanced over his shoulder as the WPC from the interview room came into the canteen. She spotted Jimmy Crack and went over to him.

Vanner scraped back his chair. 'Got to go, Billy. You got an address for Tim?'

'I can get it.'

Vanner peeled a card from his wallet. 'Phone Campbell Row. Ask for Sammy McCleod and give it to him will you?'

They shook hands and he went over to Jimmy's table. 'Result, Guv'nor,' Jimmy said. 'I think she wants to play.'

Eilish was back in the incident room. Vanner took out his cigarettes and handed the packet to her. 'Okay, Eilish?'

'Have to be don't I.'

'What can you tell us?' Jimmy said.

'What can you tell me?' she replied.

Jimmy glanced at Vanner who blew out his cheeks. 'If you play ball, Eilish,' he said very carefully. 'You can walk out of here, collect your car and go home to your kids.'

The relief stood out in her eyes.

'It's not quite that simple though.'

Her eyes clouded again.

'You see we're in Belfast and this is the largest haul of crack they've ever had over here. They think it's a right result. Does morale no end of good. The two guys who nicked you – they're on cloud nine.'

'So?'

'So you have to prove to us you can really help us big-time. I mean all the way help us. Otherwise we'll never convince them to play.'

'But I will be released.'

'Police bail. You mess up once and your ten years become twelve.'

She sat back in the chair, face white, bags beginning to draw under her eyes. She scratched at her hair with long-nailed fingers and smoked for a while in silence.

'What d'you want to know?' she said finally.

Vanner looked at her and smiled. 'I want to know everything

that you know about Stepper-Nap, Eilish. I'm going to talk you through what we have and I want all the gaps filled in. When we've done that we'll work out how you can help us nick him.'

Sixteen

Ellie was still up when Vanner got home the following night, the lounge lights burning at one in the morning. He thought it odd when he parked his car. She greeted him in the hall, face pale, red about the eyes as if she had been crying. Vanner looked at her. 'What is it?'

For a moment her lip trembled. 'Your father's dead,' she said.

Vanner looked down at his father's face, upturned toward him in the coffin. The silence of the room gathered about him. No breath. He stood with his hands in his pockets, the wall lights bright all at once against his eyes. His father's face had colour, eyes closed, hands resting on his stomach. For the first time in his life Vanner noticed his fingernails. His hair was combed, shirt black, priest's collar very white at his throat. He would have wanted to be buried that way.

Outside the chapel of rest he lit a cigarette and walked through the city. The funeral would take place at the cathedral, a mark of his days at the school. It would be the first time that Vanner had set foot in the place since he had left twenty years ago. He walked towards it now, aware of the echo of his footsteps on the pavement. So many thoughts to contend with, so many memories and yet at the same time an emptiness in his mind he would not have expected. He had seen death before many times. But his father. Ever since Ellie had told him of the heart attack he had thought about this time, the first moments alone when he would know he was gone for ever.

And now it was here he could not put words to it. He walked along the towpath towards the bridge by the station. A pair of swans traced patterns in the water, one after the other, feet moving soundlessly beneath the graceful weight of their necks.

He watched them, seated on a bench. Father gone. Alone now. He thought momentarily of Ellie, back at the house with Anne and he realised how little he knew her.

They buried his father on Maunday Thursday. The cathedral was full. The school choir sang. Anne cried. Ellie cried. Vanner helped lower the coffin into the ground and long after everyone else had left he stood alongside with the wind twisting the roots of his hair. Eventually the presence of the gravediggers broke in on lost thought and he turned and walked away.

When he got back to the house all the guests had gone. Anne and Ellie sat in the twin rocking chairs by the kitchen fireplace. Easter weekend stretched before them. Vanner put his head around the door and caught Ellie's eye. 'Going to make a phonecall,' he said.

In the hall he dialled Jimmy Crack's mobile. 'What's happening?'

Jimmy seemed surprised to hear from him. 'You okay, Guv?'

'Yes.'

'Funeral was today, wasn't it?'

'Just got back. What's happening?'

'Eilish has met with Stepper-Nap.'

'You spoke to her?'

'Yeah.'

'And?'

'He knows she was lifted.'

'What did he say?'

'Not a lot. He didn't tell her the crack was candlewax.'

Vanner thought for a moment. 'We'll need to keep an eye on her.'

'Thought occurs to me, Guv,' Jimmy said.

'What's that?'

'Old Stepper might think we switched the wax for crack. Her prints were on the sandwich box weren't they? It'd be all we'd need.'

Vanner bunched his eyes. 'Either that or Irish coppers are stupid. He's got something to think about, Jim.'

'He should be busy anyway,' Jimmy said. 'Rafter's baby mother's coming in with gear. We've got the plot set up.'

Vanner was quiet for a moment. 'I'm going away for the weekend, Jim. Few days to myself. You've got my number if you need me.'

'I'll try and leave you alone.'

'Thanks,' Vanner said and hung up.

Ellie touched his hand as he sat down beside her. Anne was making tea. She looked pale but collected. Vanner watched her move about the open kitchen and for the first time in a long while he was reminded of his ex-wife.

'You okay?' Ellie asked him.

He nodded, looked at the snakes' tongues of the fire and saw his father's face in them. 'You want to come away with me, Elle?'

'When?'

'This weekend.'

Ellie looked at Anne.

'Don't worry about me,' she said. 'I've got friends coming over. Do you two good to spend some time together.'

Ellie looked at Vanner. 'Where?'

'Yorkshire.'

'Why Yorkshire?'

Vanner sat back, resting his hands on his thighs. 'There's someone I need to see up there.'

'Who?'

He glanced at her. 'Just an old friend. Besides, I'm in no mood to go back to London.'

'You want me with you?'

He looked at her again. 'Do you want to come?'

Tension between them, he knew she felt it but could do nothing about it.

'Maybe you need to be alone,' she said.

Anne looked at him then. 'Do you think you should be alone, Aden?' she said. The concern stood out in her eyes. Vanner smiled, then clasped Ellie's tiny hand in his. 'No,' he said. 'I don't.'

They booked into the Nags Head Hotel in Pickhill, busy, an early season cricket team in the bar. The landlord apologised for the noise and Vanner told him not to worry about it. He and Ellie had a room in an annexe away from the hubbub of the main building. The room was small but neat with an en suite bathroom. Vanner lay on the double bed and watched the TV, mounted on the wall while Ellie took a bath. Ben Hur, Charlton Heston in a chariot race and lepers and the death of Christ and water. Vanner watched listlessly, trying not to think about his father. Ellie came through wrapped in a towel. He turned the sound down on the TV while she dried her hair.

They ate in the bar that night, Vanner glad of the noise and the distraction of men drinking loudly. It reminded him of the past; fondly, with his father. Later, after they had made love he lay in the darkness with her alongside him, warm yet distant against his flesh.

On Saturday morning Ellie took the car and went shopping in Bedale, just a little further up the A1. Vanner had coffee in the bar and smoked a cigarette and then he walked the short distance to the green and Tim Phelan's bungalow that overlooked it. He paused on the road outside and looked up. A large, particularly low window dominated the front of the house. From where he stood Vanner could see the flickering images of a TV set. He went up the drive and rang the doorbell.

Half a man in a chair answered it, thin black hair and overlong moustache, perhaps grown to take your eyes from the bits of him that were missing. Legs gone at the knees, stumps barely extending over the edge of the chair, one arm gone and half the shoulder. Vanner looked down at Phelan. Phelan did not say anything. It was twelve years since they had seen one another. He drew up his eyes at the corners as if memory eluded him and then his face softened and recognition slowly settled.

'Vanner.'

'Hello, Tim. I've come to buy you a drink.'

Vanner walked alongside the electric whirr of the chair as Phelan guided it across the road to the door of the pub. There was a step that Vanner helped him over and they went into the public bar with the flagstone floor. A fire burned in the grate and one or two of the cricketers looked as though they were embarking on a pre-match session. Phelan settled his chair to the right of the fire and Vanner went to the bar for drinks. One man, tall, a pint of bitter in his hand stood in his whites with no shoes on. Vanner looked him up and down.

'Bit early for cricket isn't it?'

The man grinned. 'Annual event,' he said. 'Touring side. We always come here for a match before the season starts.'

'Where you from?'

'Nottingham. Playing the pub team.'

Vanner nodded and glanced at the green and yellow hooped cap on the bar at the drinker's elbow. The insignia looked like a bird with a club and a ball. Vanner lifted an eyebrow.

'Cuckoos,' the man explained. 'What we're called.'

'No nests.'

'What?'

'Cuckoos,' Vanner said. 'Use other birds' nests.'

'Exactly.' The man made an open-handed gesture. 'We've got no home ground.'

Vanner bought the drinks and took them over to the table.

'Cricket match,' Phelan said.

'First of the season. Be bloody cold this afternoon.'

'Where they playing?'

'Masham.'

'How far is that?'

'Couple of miles.'

'I'll take you if you want.'

Phelan's eyes lit up. 'You got a car?'

Vanner grinned. 'How else d'you think I got here?' He sipped his beer. 'Girl I'm with is shopping in Bedale. She'll be back later. I'll take you over to watch.'

Phelan raised his glass to Vanner and drank. He set it down again and wiped froth from his moustache. Vanner looked at him. 'You don't get out much then?'

'No.' Phelan looked down at himself. 'Seem to spend all my time in front of the box.'

'What about your mates?'

'All across the water. DPOA are good, mind. They keep in touch.'

Vanner nodded. 'Billy Callaghan told me you had a visitor.'

'Visitor?'

'In the park.'

'Oh her.' Phelan drank again, a longer draught this time and looked at the beer in the glass. 'Felt a bit of a prat about that. Three times mind, the same woman. I don't know.' He shook his head. 'Two fellas came up from London.'

'SO13?'

Phelan nodded. 'Good lads. Soon as I got in touch with the DPOA the call went out.'

'Look after our own, Tim. Always did.'

'Aye.'

Vanner offered him a cigarette and lit it for him. 'Tell me about the woman.'

Phelan twisted his lip. 'What's to say. Youngish. Thirty maybe. Black hair. The thing that bothered me was – she sat in the park opposite my place on three separate occasions. She had a good look at me, I know, and there were no kids with her.'

'Tell you what,' Vanner said quietly. 'I'd've called someone too.'

'Yeah?' Phelan looked hopefully at him, eyes broken up at the edges. 'You don't think I'm a fool then. Not just the cracks beginning to show?'

Vanner looked closely at him then. 'Tim,' he said, 'if anyone had good reason for the cracks to show it'd be you.'

'Aye, maybe right enough.'

Vanner shook his head. 'Only they aren't.' He leaned on the table. 'Quigley got shot in Morne.'

'I know. Just before the ceasefire.'

Vanner licked his lower lip. 'What about the others?'

'Priestley's dead. Heart attack. Just after he retired last year.'

'Kinane?'

'Don't know. I think he's over here somewhere.' Phelan cocked his head to one side.

'You think something's going on, Aden?'

Vanner sat back and pressed his shoulders into his neck. 'Don't know, Tim. But Quigley was killed with a Tokarev. That's PIRA PPW. Right?'

'Yeah.'

'The same gun was used to kill a woman in London on February 12th this year.'

Phelan stared at him. 'Who was she?'

'Name was Jessica Turner. There's an ongoing murder investigation with SO13 involved. But the victim had nothing to do with Ulster.'

'PIRA wouldn't use the same gun with the same shootist, Aden. You know that.'

'I know. They also don't have girls doing the close-up stuff. But the killer in London is female. They found size-seven shoe prints from an ESLA lift, a false fingernail and long black hair.'

Phelan was very still after that. 'Nobody got lifted for killing Quigley,' he said.

'I know.'

Phelan tasted the beer on his lips and looked at Vanner's cigarettes. Vanner passed him another one.

'Could be nothing,' he said.

'Probably is.' Vanner sat back again and looked at the cricketers as they filed out to their cars. 'Nobody's had a go at me.'

Phelan squinted at him then. 'You'd be hard to find.'

'And it's been twelve years.'

'But you thought you'd check.'

Vanner nodded. 'Would anyone back home have an address for Kinane?'

'I imagine so. I'll make some calls when we get back.'

Vanner drove back to London with Ellie on the Sunday night. In his pocket he had Raymond Kinane's address and telephone number. He intended to call him when they got home. Ellie watched the taut lines in his face. 'You okay, Aden?'

He nodded.

'Why did you want to see that man?'

Vanner looked sideways at her. 'No reason.'

She stared at him then. 'Don't be stupid. We went all the way to Yorkshire to see him.'

'No we didn't. We went to Yorkshire to spend a few days together. Tim was only part of it.'

'You wanted to see him, Aden. I don't understand why you won't tell me why.'

He drove on, traffic becoming more bunched as they got closer and closer to London. 'It was just something that came up when I was over the water. You don't need to worry about it.'

She folded her arms. 'Don't need to worry about it. Jesus, you never talk to me. Your father died for Christ's sake and you've not said a word about it. Am I part of your life or not?'

The words stung him, tinged with the memory of other

voices. He ground his teeth together. 'Not now, Elle. Please.'

She shook her head very savagely and stared out of the window.

Vanner phoned Sid Ryan when he got back. 'Me, Sid,' he said when Ryan answered.

'Hello, Guv. Sorry about your old man.'

'Yeah, thanks. Listen, Slips. What's happening with your Ealing inquiry?'

'Same as before. Nothing.'

'What about your man with the dummy and the body in the back of the car?'

'Same story.'

'Nothing else?'

'No.'

'SO13?'

'They don't tell us anything, Guv'nor. You know that.'

'But they think your body was a mistake. Right?'

'Yeah. Why the interest?'

'Not sure, Slips. Just something I picked up when Jimmy Crack and me were over the water. I'll let you know if it comes to anything.'

'Whatever.' He heard Ryan move the phone from one hand to the other. 'What happened with the donkey?'

'She thinks she's looking at a ten stretch for intent. Kilo and a half of crack.'

'And is she?'

'Hardly. Crack was melted-down candlewax.'

Ellie went back to work the following morning. Vanner's silence, although something she had seen before, disturbed her. The death of his father; no words, no tears, just that little bit more silent than before. It plagued her all morning, how little she knew this man and – how quickly it seemed now – she had abandoned her home for his.

She went about her duties in a daze and at twelve o'clock she went down to the canteen for her lunch. Anne, the cleaner, was sitting at a table on her own, apron on, drinking a cup of coffee and looking out of the window. Ellie watched her from the queue at the counter, black hair, hanging over her face, a sort of lost air about her. She was not really in the mood for her company after the events of the previous week, but Anne always sat at a table on her own and if she did not speak to her then who would. She took her tray and sat down opposite. Anne smiled at her, replaced her cup on the saucer, lipstick marking the rim.

'How are you?' she said. 'You look tired.'

'I shouldn't be. I went away for the weekend.'

'With your boyfriend?'

'Yes.'

'Anywhere nice?'

'Yorkshire.'

Anne nodded. 'I always liked Yorkshire.'

'Bedale's nice. I went shopping in Bedale.'

'Where did you stay?'

'Place called Pickhill.'

'Don't know it.'

'Aden wanted to see somebody there.'

'Aden?'

'Aden Vanner. My boyfriend.'

'Of course. I'm sorry.'

Ellie started her lunch and then pushed the plate away. 'I don't know what's the matter with me,' she said.

Anne looked at the food. 'You should eat you know.'

'I know. Just can't face it.'

Anne touched her hand then. 'What's the matter?'

Ellie looked at her. Her lover, boyfriend, whatever, shot dead by policemen. She thought of Tim Phelan then and the reality of what had happened to so many people over so long came home to her.

Her pager sounded and she unclipped it from her belt. Lifting it to the table top she looked at the face. CALL ME. 0973 883721.

'What is it?' Anne asked.

Ellie showed her the message. 'Aden,' she said. Anne looked at the face of the pager.

'Mobile?'

Ellie nodded.

'Everyone carries one these days.'

'Yeah. Except me, Anne.' Ellie stood up. 'I need to find a phone.'

In the corridor she phoned Vanner's mobile. 'It's me, Aden.'

'You at lunch?'

'Yes.'

'Sorry.'

'It's all right. What did you want?'

'I'm going to be very late tonight. I've got to go down to Bournemouth to see someone.'

'Shall I cook?'

'No, don't worry about it. I'll pick up a carryout somewhere.'

'Okay.'

'Listen,' he said. 'I'm sorry if I'm distant. It's just my way . . . my way of dealing with things.'

'It's okay, love. I understand.' Ellie held the phone very close to her ear. 'See you when you get in.'

Back at the table Anne was preparing to leave. 'Everything all right?' she said.

'Yeah. Just going to be very late that's all. Got to go to Bournemouth or somewhere.'

Anne looked at her and smiled. 'Lucky he bothers to tell you. Wouldn't occur to most men.'

Vanner sat in his office in Campbell Row and telephoned Ray Kinane's home number. He looked at the clock on the wall. Four thirty. No point in going all the way down there if he was not in. He waited as the phone drilled in his ear. Four rings, five, six. Then a woman's voice answered.

'Mrs Kinane?'

'Yes.'

'Aden Vanner. Friend of your husband. Is he in?'

'Not right now.'

'Will he be back later?'

'Should be. He's normally home by six thirty.'

'I haven't seen him for a while, Mrs Kinane. We were colleagues in Belfast years ago. Can you tell him I phoned? I'm in your area tonight. I'd like to see him, a drink or something maybe.'

'I don't think he's going out, Mr Vanner. I'll tell him. Can he call you back?'

'I'll be on a mobile. Tell you what – I'll call him.' Vanner put down the phone and went out to his car.

He drove south west along the M3, traffic very thick at the

junction with the M25. He listened to PM on the radio. Habit of his father, the five o'clock news every afternoon on Radio Four, whether he was driving or not. Politicians, newscasters, letter writers, their words drifted through his head until they became just a babble and he switched the radio off and drove on in silence. The past grew up in his mind amid the red and white of car lights. Quigley, Phelan, Priestly, that left Kinane and himself. Probably nothing, he told himself. Probably just coincidence.

Kinane lived at Three Legged Cross, more Verwood than Bournemouth, on the edge of the New Forest. Vanner left the M27 and headed west on the A35 before calling again from his mobile. Kinane answered almost immediately.

'Hello.'

'Ray, it's Aden Vanner.'

They met at a pub. Kinane seemed keen that Vanner did not come to the house. His voice had been just a little bit agitated and when Vanner put the phone down he could feel the hairs on the back of his neck. Kinane was waiting for him, two dark pints of Guinness set before him on a rough wooden table in a corner. Vanner recognised him instantly, tall and well built with thick black hair, oiled away from his face. Kinane stood up, not as tall but broader. They shook hands for the first time in twelve years.

Vanner sat down and lit a cigarette. Kinane toyed with a beer mat, tearing off the edges and rotating it in his hand like a spinning wheel. 'Couldn't quite believe it when the wife said Aden Vanner had phoned.' Kinane grinned but there was no merriment in his eyes.

'How you doing, Ray?'

'I'm doing fine, Aden. Making money.'

Vanner nodded. 'You always said you would.'

'When I left the job.'

'Made a bit when you were there though eh?' Vanner drew on his cigarette. 'All that overtime.'

'Aye. I did right enough.'

'You got kids, Ray?' Vanner asked him.

Kinane nodded. 'Two boys. You?'

Vanner shook his head.

'You were married though yeah?'

'Once. Not any more.'

Kinane toyed with the beer mat again. 'Surprised you joined the Met, Aden. I'd've thought it would be small fry after what we went through.'

'Same game, different rules.' Vanner shook his shoulders. 'Only thing I knew.'

They looked at one another. 'This isn't a social call is it,' Kinane said.

Vanner shook his head.

'And you weren't just in the area?'

'Drove here just to see you, Ray.'

Kinane narrowed his eyes. 'Why?'

'We need to talk.'

'I haven't set eyes on you in a dozen years, Aden. Why do we need to talk?'

'Tim Phelan.'

'What about him?'

Vanner pushed out his lips. 'I saw him this weekend. A few weeks back he thought somebody was having a look at him. Somebody from the past, Ray. Bad enough for him to bell the DPOA over the water.'

Kinane frowned. 'Who was it?'

'Black-haired woman on her own. Watching him from the park.'

'Did he know her?'

Vanner shook his head. 'DPOA took it seriously though. They got a couple of lads from the Anti-Terrorist Branch to drive up and see him.'

'Anything come of it?'

'Not so far.'

Kinane looked a little bemused. 'So what's the significance?' He scratched the back of his hand. 'You've lost me, Aden.'

Vanner sipped Guinness. 'You know Priestley's dead.'

'Yeah. Heart attack. That was before I came over here.'

'What about Quigley?'

'What about him?'

'You don't know then?'

'Know what?'

'He was shot in the head at Spelga Dam in July '94. Close quarters. Tokarev PPW.'

Vanner looked in his eyes. 'They never caught anyone.'

Kinane sat forward, took a long pull at his drink and set down the empty glass.

'I'll get some more,' Vanner said.

He could feel Kinane's eyes on his back as he waited for the girl to pour the fresh drinks. When he turned with them he was still staring at him. He sat forward as soon as Vanner set the glass before him.

'You want to tell me something don't you,' Vanner said quietly.

Kinane blew out his cheeks, rubbed fingers through his hair and licked his lips. 'Been driving me crazy. Now I know why.'

'What has?'

Kinane scanned the drinkers about them, nobody near enough to hear him. 'Will it go any further?'

'Depends on what it is.'

'I need to know.'

'You know the game, Ray. You played it long enough.'

'We both played, Aden.'

Vanner held his eye. 'Different rules now.'

'Is it?'

'You know it is.'

'Aw sod it.' Kinane clasped his hands together and stared at his fingers. 'February 12th of this year,' he said. 'Sunday night. A woman called Jessica Turner was murdered.'

'I know,' Vanner said. 'Close-range shooting with .62mm Tokarev.'

Kinane nodded.

'The same gun that killed Quigley, Ray.'

Kinane's eyes balled.

Vanner leaned close to him. 'The shootist who killed Turner was a woman. Long black hairs were found at the crime scene.' He paused. 'You were the lover weren't you?'

'What?'

'AMIP. Hendon Murder Squad. They're looking for whoever was with Jessica that weekend. It was you wasn't it, Ray.'

Kinane looked at the floor, sighed once and nodded.

Vanner sat back, lifting his knee so it rested against the table and lit another cigarette. 'Why didn't you come forward when they made their appeals?'

Kinane opened his hands. 'Over the side, Aden. Wife. Two kids. I had a lot to lose.'

Vanner looked away from him. 'And she was dead already.' He pushed out a cheek with his tongue.

'What would you've done?'

Vanner shrugged. 'I don't know, Ray.'

The silence opened between them then. Vanner pursed his lips and sipped at his Guinness.

Kinane took one of his cigarettes and lit it. 'What're you going to do?'

Vanner squinted at him. 'I don't know yet.'

Ellie felt strange, lying in the bath in Vanner's house listening to the sound of the silence. She had been here alone before, many times in fact, but tonight, she did not know why, she felt odd. The bathroom door was open. Why had she done that? Left it open. She never did that. She shook her head, told herself not to be so stupid and lathered her legs with soap from the dispenser.

Across the road in the car the woman sat very still. Rain fell in harsh lines across the windscreen. A couple left the Greek restaurant on the corner and ducked into the pub. Scaffolding poles rose like mechanical arms to embrace the building opposite his house. She was parked between two yellow rubbish skips, piles of rubble protruding from the one directly in front of her. Beside her on the seat was a holdall. Inside the holdall, a black automatic pistol.

Ellie got out of the bath and towelled herself dry. Vanner's shaving things stood on the windowsill by the sink. His toothbrush beside hers in the glass. The glass needed cleaning. She ought to take it down to the kitchen and bring up a fresh one. She moved, naked still, from the bathroom to the bedroom and passed before the window.

In the car outside the woman looked up at the lights, saw someone cross the glass, and curled her fingers into fists. She sat a moment longer, then pulled the hat closer down against the back of her neck and stepped out into the rain.

Ellie put on her dressing gown and sat down to brush her hair. Again the strange sensation overtook her. She looked to the open bedroom door as if she half-expected somebody to walk through it. The rain whipped against naked glass. She got up to pull the curtain. A figure stood in the rain beneath the scaffolding poles across the road and stared up at her. Ellie jumped back, hand to her mouth. For a moment she stood there, fear beginning to grip her. Then she moved to the window again. The figure was no longer there, but she peered and thought she could make out somebody in the car between the skips. Smoke flared from the exhaust pipe and the car lurched out into the road. Ellie stepped back, then looked again. The car disappeared round the corner.

Vanner got in late, slept for four hours and left again. He drove to Campbell Row and sat brooding at his desk. The past becoming the present. Wasn't that what his father once said to him. The past becoming the present or something like it. He could not remember. But he sat there now, thinking hard with ghosts rising that he thought had been banished forever. He heard somebody outside and Sammy poked his head round the door.

'You're early, Guv.'

'Thinking, Sam. Couldn't do it at home.'

'Sorry about your father.'

'So am I.' Vanner looked at the wall. Now he could really do with him, to talk, the non-judgemental wisdom of an old man. He had gone though and there was still so much to be said. He had always known there would be.

When Sammy had gone he picked up the phone and dialled Ray Kinane's home number.

'Kinane.'

'Ray, it's Vanner. We have to talk.'

'I know. I've thought about it. What d'you want me to do?'

'Just make yourself available. The Murder Squad will want to talk to you.'

'Can we do it at work?'

'Yes.'

'What about the family?'

Vanner thought for a moment. 'I'll do what I can, Ray. But I don't have many brownie points round here.'

'Okay. Whatever. If she's going to find out just make sure somebody lets me know so I can tell her myself.'

'Sure. Somebody from AMIP'll contact you.'

Vanner put the phone down and was about to pick it up

again when Jimmy Crack came in. 'Picked up the tapes from the wash house last night, Guv.'

'And?'

'Pretty Boy carrying a bag and Ginger Bill coming out just after.'

'No main man?'

'Nope.'

'What about Rafter's woman?'

'She didn't show. Still in Kingston.'

Vanner made a face. 'You want to give the wash house a spin?'

Jimmy shook his head. 'Not yet. I want to wait for Eilish.'

'She given us a time and a place yet?'

'No.'

'Remind her what she's looking at.'

Jimmy Crack closed the door and left him alone. Vanner picked up the phone and dialled.

Ryan answered.

'Vanner, Sid.'

'Hello, Guv.'

'You in a briefing?'

'About to start.'

'SO13 be there?'

'Not this morning.'

'Who's giving it – Morrison?'

'Frank Weir. Morrison's tied up today.'

Vanner nodded. 'Tell Weir I want to talk to him. I'll see you in a minute.'

Ryan and Weir were waiting for him when Vanner got down to the Hendon incident room. Ryan stood up from his desk and glanced through Weir's open door as Vanner came into the room.

Vanner went straight into Weir's office. Weir sat behind the desk and looked up at him. Ryan came in behind him and closed the door. Weir nodded to a chair and Vanner sat down.

'You got information on my inquiry, Vanner?'

'I've found your missing lover.'

Weir looked at Ryan, then behind them both to the hubbub of the outer office. 'Forgive me for looking confused,' he said.

'It's a long story.' Vanner glanced at Ryan. 'His name's Ray

Kinane,' he said. 'He works as an operational consultant for CableTech Security.'

'Paul Johnson,' Ryan said.

Weir looked at him.

'Jessica Turner's contact at CableTech.'

'Not her only one obviously,' Weir said. 'What do you know, Vanner – and how come you know it?'

'I'll tell you what I know. How I know it – I'll tell to somebody else.'

Weir's eyes smarted.

'Kinane's ex RUC, Frank.'

Vanner was back in his office when Morrison telephoned him. 'I've just spoken to Frank Weir, Vanner. He told me what happened.'

'And?'

'And I want to know what's going on.'

Vanner chewed his lip. 'Who's your liaison with the Anti-Terrorist Branch?'

'What?'

'I want to know who at the Yard you're dealing with.'

'Vanner, I'm your Divisional Superintendent. Anything you want to say you can say to me.'

Vanner was silent. 'I'd rather talk directly to SO13.'

Morrison stifled a shout. Vanner could feel it reverberate down the phone.

'I want you in Hendon now, Vanner.'

Vanner put the phone down and sat for a moment. Darkness swamped the window. Rush-hour traffic building up on the High Road outside. He sat forward and picked up the telephone once more.

'New Scotland Yard,' the voice on the other end informed him.

'This is Detective Inspector Vanner of 2 Area Drug Squad,' he said. 'I want to talk Sergeant George Webb of SO13 Reserve.'

He sat back again and waited for the phone to ring. He would have paged Webb himself if he could find the number that Ryan had given him. He waited. Jimmy Crack knocked on the door and put his head around. 'I'm off for a couple of days, Guv. Leave owing. Wanted to let you know.'

Vanner looked up at him. 'Anything I need to know?'
'All's quiet.'
'How long d'you figure before Eilish gets word that the crack wasn't crack?'
'Depends on the Daddy, Guv.'
Vanner nodded. 'I might be a little busy myself, Jim. Can you make sure Sammy's fully briefed?'
Jimmy nodded and closed the door. The phone rang on the desk before him and Vanner picked it up.
'George Webb, Guv'nor.'
'George. Thanks for calling me back.'
'What can I do for you?'
'Your Ealing close quarter. I've got some information for you. Secret and delicate, George. You understand?'
'Who d'you want to talk to?'
'Superintendent, I guess.'
'Okay. I'll sort it and call you back.'
'Ring my mobile. I've got a meeting with Superintendent Morrison and AMIP in Hendon.' Vanner gave him the number. He rang his house and got no reply so he rang the nurses' station at the hospital. Ellie answered.
'Me, love. Listen, I'm going to be late tonight.'
'Again?'
'Yes, again. I'm sorry. I've got a meeting at Hendon, then I have to go to The Yard.'
'Aden, there's something I wanted to tell you – about last night. It might be nothing but . . .'
'Can it wait, Elle? I'm in a hurry now.'
She was quiet.
'Ellie?'
'Yes, it can wait.'
'Good girl. I'll speak to you later.' Vanner collected his coat and went out to his car.

It took him half an hour to get from Wembley to Divisional Headquarters at Hendon. Morrison was in his office, waiting for him with Weir. Vanner had a touch of déjà vu as he pushed open the door. Last year, the Denny drugs inquiry when an informant got killed and Morrison wanted Weir to be his investigating officer. Vanner had won that round. He knew he would win this one as well.

Morrison's face was the colour of white stone. Weir stood with his hands in his suit pockets, chewing gum.

'Sit down, Vanner.'

Vanner glanced at Weir and sat.

'Now,' Morrison said, clasping his hands together. 'What's going on?'

Vanner looked him full in the eye. 'I told Frank here that I've spoken to Raymond Kinane. Ex RUC now working in security for CableTech.'

'What's he got to do with you?'

'Not important, Sir.'

Morrison slapped his palm on the desk, making papers jump. 'I'll decide what's important, Vanner. This is my inquiry. If you have information you give it up. Do you understand?'

Vanner flared his nostrils, aware of the beginnings of a pulse at his temple. 'With respect, Sir, it's also an SO13 inquiry. What I have to say I will say to them and them alone.'

Morrison cocked an eyebrow at him and sat back. He traced the line of his lips with his tongue. 'Their Super's been on the phone, Vanner.'

'Then you know I'm going to see him.'

'*We're* going to see him.'

'Fine. Do you want to drive or shall I?'

Weir drove, Morrison in the passenger seat, Vanner hunched up in the back. Weir had the driver's seat pushed right back so Vanner had no room for his legs. Morrison leaned over the back as they cut their way through the traffic towards Victoria.

'This is all to do with the past isn't it, Vanner.'

Vanner stared out of the window.

'Isn't it?' Morrison's eyes pierced and Vanner turned to look at him.

'Secret and delicate, Sir. My perogative to talk only to the security services.'

'I'll bet.' Morrison shook his head. 'If this is what I think it is.'

Vanner looked away again.

George Webb met them in the foyer at the Yard and took them up to the fifteenth floor.

'Operation just gone live,' he explained. 'Floor should be sealed.'

'Somebody active are they?' Vanner asked him.
'Something like that.'
Webb led the way along the corridor to the senior officers' rooms. The Commander's was empty. Westbrook was coming out of the DCI's room with a folder under his arm.
'Vanner. What're you doing here?'
'Westy. How're you?'
Westbrook glanced at Weir and Morrison, lifted his eyebrows and shifted the folder to his other arm.
'Here to see Robbo', Guv'nor,' Webb explained.
Westbrook nodded. 'He's in the squad room. I'll let him know you're here.'
Webb showed them into Superintendent Robertson's office and gestured to vacant chairs. Vanner moved behind the desk and looked out over the lights of London. Webb went to fetch coffee.
They waited ten minutes and then Robertson came in with Westbrook. Robertson had grey hair cut very close to his scalp. His tie was undone and his sleeves pressed against his elbows. He looked directly at Vanner.
'You're DI Vanner?'
'Yes.'
Robertson glanced at the others. 'This is to do with the Ealing close-quarter shooting am I right?'
Vanner nodded.
'Sorry to have kept you waiting but all hell's breaking loose round here.' He placed a stack of papers in his top drawer, locked it and pocketed the key. Then he placed both hands palm down on the desk.
'Sir,' Vanner said. 'The information I have is secret and delicate. I'm only talking to you and DCI Westbrook.'
Morrison started to speak but Robertson quashed him with a downturned palm. 'His right, Andrew. If the information is pertinent to AMIP you'll know about it. Webb'll show you downstairs.'
For a moment Morrison sat where he was. Weir looked uncomfortable and he rose first. Vanner stared at Morrison who held his eye, lips compressed, a bloodless line in his face. Webb held the door open for him.
When they were gone only Robertson, Westbrook and Vanner were left. Robertson shook his head as he sat down. 'Politics,'

he said. 'Can't bloody stand them. Any coffee going anywhere?'

Westbrook went to the pot that Webb had brought in and poured three cups. He handed one to Vanner.

'Now,' Robertson said. 'What's this about?'

Seventeen

Vanner sipped hot, black coffee and looked at Robertson and Westbrook in turn.

'February 1984,' he began. 'I was a captain in the Parachute Regiment.'

Robertson looked at him over the rim of his cup. 'Go on.'

Vanner placed his cup and saucer on the edge of the desk. 'I was part of an intelligence operation,' he said. 'Joint military and RUC Special Branch.'

Robertson looked at Westbrook.

'90 Section intelligence officer,' Vanner went. 'We were looking at a nominal in Brindley Cross, South Armagh. Thomas Michael Quinlon. Part of an ASU responsible for explosions in Newry in '82 and '83.' He paused then, remembering, a rain-filled night and the pub sign swinging on rusty hinges. 'Quinlon got killed,' he said quietly.

Robertson sat back. 'And?'

'The SB squad was comprised of four men,' Vanner told him. 'Priestley died of a heart attack. The others were Ray Kinane, David Quigley and Tim Phelan.'

'Phelan?'

Westbrook sat forward and looked at Robertson. 'Webb and Swann paid him a visit in Yorkshire last month, Sir. DPOA gave us a call from Belfast.'

'Phelan thought he was being looked at,' Vanner said. 'Woman in the park. Three days on the trot. No kids with her. His bungalow looks over the green. He's got a specially lowered window because he's very disabled.'

'Black-haired woman,' Westbrook said.

Vanner nodded. 'Your Ealing subject was shot with a Tokarev. The same gun killed Quigley in Morne in 1994.'

'And Quigley was part of your team,' Robertson said.

Vanner nodded.

'And Kinane?'

'He's the lover who didn't come forward when AMIP made their appeal through the papers.'

Westbrook lifted his eyebrows.

'He works for a security firm,' Vanner went on. 'Clients of Jessica Turner.' Robertson's pager sounded and he looked down at it. 'We'll have to leave it there, Vanner. I'll speak to you as soon as I can. Right now we're going to be busy.'

Weir drank Bacardi with ice but no Coke. Morrison sipped at a pint of bitter.

'*Shoot to kill,*' Weir said. 'Vanner was involved in shoot to kill?'

'He was an army intelligence officer attached to RUC Special Branch for six months, Frank.'

Weir made a face. 'You mean *this* is about Vanner?'

'I'd say so wouldn't you?'

'Why Jessica Turner?'

'I don't know. Maybe they were really after Kinane. They'd already killed Quigley.'

Weir sipped Bacardi. 'If they were after Kinane they'd've got him.'

'Maybe. We'll talk to him, Frank. This is still our inquiry.'

Weir nodded. 'I'll take Ryan with me tomorrow.'

'Don't take Ryan. Take somebody else. Ryan was Vanner's minder in the Drug Squad.'

Weir looked at him. 'Ryan's sound, Andrew.'

'Even so. Take somebody else.'

Vanner took the phonecall from Ray Kinane on his mobile. Kinane told him that he had been contacted by Frank Weir who was coming down to interview him. Vanner was in traffic, on his way from Camden Town to Victoria Street.

'Just talk to them, Ray,' he said. 'You know the form.'

'But my family?'

'Tell them how it is. Maybe they won't need to know.'

He heard Kinane sigh.

'What can I tell you, Ray? You should've come forward at the time.'

'Yeah Yeah. See you, Aden.' Kinane hung up. Vanner switched his phone off and tossed it onto the seat next to him.

He was met by DCI Westbrook, who showed him into his office. There were three DCI's on the branch, the other off-duty that morning. They had the office to themselves. Westbrook brought in coffee and sat opposite him. 'Myself and George Webb have been working on the Ealing killing with AMIP, Vanner. The old man wants me to work on it with you. I'd like Webby's input too if that's okay with you.'

'Anybody else?'

'DS from the SB cell.'

'Fine.' Vanner drank coffee. 'Where's Webb now?'

'On his way in. We were busy last night.'

'Result?'

Westbrook smiled. 'You didn't read about it did you?'

They waited for Webb to arrive before they began in earnest. DS King from the Special Branch cell joined them and they used the DCI's office as a briefing room.

'It's got to be connected,' Vanner was saying. 'Quigley was part of our intelligence unit, so was Phelan and so was Ray Kinane. Quigley was killed with the same weapon as Jessica Turner.'

'That bit doesn't make a lot of sense,' Webb said. 'Not in normal PIRA terms anyway.'

'You mean same gun – different killers.'

Webb nodded.

'We don't know that they weren't different killers,' King said. 'We've no witnesses for the Morne shooting.'

Webb stroked his moustache. 'I'd put money on the bird in the park in Yorkshire being the same as the one in the Turner house.'

'But PIRA don't use women for stuff like that,' Vanner said.

'No. You're right. They don't.'

They were still for a few moments then Vanner said. 'Any definite maybe's?'

Webb looked at King. 'We had two,' he said. 'Both are alibi'd for February 12th.'

Vanner steepled his fingers. 'Nobody claimed the Turner killing.'

'No,' Webb said.

'Which generally means it's a mistake.'

Webb nodded.

'Only in this case it wasn't a mistake,' Vanner said. 'They meant to kill her.'

'Then it isn't authorised PIRA,' Westbrook stated.

'I agree.' Vanner half-smiled, looking at each of their faces in turn. 'It's revenge.'

'After twelve years?' Webb arched his eyebrows. 'That's a long time to get round to it.'

Vanner squinted at him. 'Depends where you've been I guess.'

The Special Branch sergeant made notes. He scratched his ear with his pencil. 'I still don't get it,' he said. 'Quigley makes sense. Somebody looking at Phelan makes sense. I guess they saw how bad he was already and decided he wasn't worth it.'

Vanner nodded.

'But what about the Turner woman? Surely they'd go after Kinane.'

Nobody spoke. After a while Vanner said, 'You're right. It doesn't make sense.'

Webb got up from his seat and wandered to the window. 'We need to narrow this down now. We can't assume that it is pure revenge, or that we're looking at only one shootist.' He looked back at Vanner. 'Quinlon,' he said. 'We need chapter and verse.'

Vanner drank with Sid Ryan in Camden Town. Ellie was working late. They had a meal in the Greek Taverna and went across the road to the pub. Vanner bought beer and they sat in a booth near the door.

'Weir spoke to Kinane?' Vanner said.

Ryan nodded.

'What did he say?'

Ryan made a face. 'Not a great deal, confirmed the story that Michael Case gave us so at least we know he was telling the truth. Apparently there was a dummy in the road but nobody ever found it.'

'You looked for it though, Sid?'

'Course we did.' Ryan rolled cigarettes.

'Why didn't one of them report it,' Vanner said, 'the body in the back of the car?'

Ryan lifted an eyebrow. 'They were both playing away, Guv. Get a life.'

'Yeah. Right. Sorry.'

Vanner sipped at his beer. 'You're quiet tonight, Sid.'

'Not sure what to say, Guv'nor. You're teamed up with SO13 now aren't you. I mean *I* thought I was paranoid until I saw Morrison yesterday.'

'Morrison's got his own agenda, Slips.'

'Yeah.'

'You know then?'

'Half-know. Weir wouldn't take me to interview Kinane. I think that was Morrison's idea. Party politics. He took Braithewaite instead. What I'm telling you is second-hand.'

Vanner lifted his foot to the other seat and rubbed his knee. 'I'll tell you, Slips. Morrison thinks I was involved in a shoot-to-kill policy in South Armagh in 1984.'

'That's what this is all about then?'

Vanner nodded.

'Then why kill Jessica Turner?'

Vanner scratched his head. 'I don't know. The rest makes sense, but the pattern breaks there. Why go after her and not Kinane? He was the guilty party in their eyes.'

'Revenge then?'

'I don't think PIRA are behind it. It's their methods and it's their weapon. But a Toky is not what they'd normally use for a hit. It's a personal protection weapon at best. The killer is probably a paid-up member but PIRA aren't officially behind it.'

'Lone wolf then?'

'I'd say so, yes.'

'That doesn't tell us why they shot Jessica Turner.'

'I know.' Vanner finished his beer and got up to get more. When he came back Ryan was looking thoughtful.

'What're 13 doing now, Guv?'

'Looking for nominals.'

'Again? They've done that already.'

'They didn't know then what they do now. They're dragging files from RUC. They should be over in the morning. Then maybe we'll get somewhere.'

Ryan nodded, looking at him with a strange light in his eyes. 'Thought occurs to me, Guv.'

'What's that?'

'If this is about revenge – someone's looking at you.'

* * *

Eilish McCauley sat in Stepper-Nap's Mercedes on the Chalk Hill estate in Wembley. From the paper shopping bag on her lap she took doughnuts and two cans of Coke. She handed one of each to him.

He stared coldly at her. 'So what did you tell them, little girl?'

Eilish stopped, her teeth embedded in the doughnut. She sucked sugar from her lips. 'Who?'

'The Irish coppers. Who else?'

She shook her head. 'I didn't tell them anything.'

Stepper laughed then, a cruel sound, from way back in his throat. 'Don't dis' me, girl. Nobody walks away from a kilo of crack.'

'I did.'

'Yeah. But why?' He laid a cold hand on her shoulder and squeezed fingers into the muscle along her collar-bone. 'Must've given them plenty to walk out of that one.'

Eilish was cold now, his hand alien on her flesh. She laid the unwanted doughnut in her lap. 'I didn't say anything, Stepper. They gave me bail.'

'Signed papers did you?'

She looked at him.

'Did you?'

'No.'

He forced air from between his teeth. 'Oh, Eilish, Eilish. You know what I do to people who stiff me. You ever seen what happens to people who snitch?'

She was shaking now. 'I swear, Stepper. They let me go because I've got kids.'

'Bullshit, girl.' He was staring at her now, coal-black eyes. 'I'll tell you why you walked shall I?'

She did not reply.

'Shall I, Eilish? Shall I?'

'Go on then – why?'

'Because there wasn't any gear.'

Now she stared at him. 'What d'you mean – no gear? I carried a kilo of crack for you.'

'No you didn't. You carried a kilo of candlewax.' He leaned across the seat, face so close that she felt his breath on her face. 'Nobody rips me off, Eilish. Not you or any of your kind.'

She stared at him, mouth open, mind working. Vanner and McKay and the Belfast Drug Squad. She forced her lips together.

'When I sell for forty-five grand I get forty-five grand. Jimmy Carter's cut was five grand at best. Nobody steals from me, Eilish. I don't care who they are. They get in touch with you – you tell them no deal. They want do deal with Stepper-Nap – they pay first. You dig?'

She had her hand on the door. 'You mean you got me to go over again, to leave my kids again, for a lump of fucking candlewax.'

'That's exactly what I mean.' Again he leaned toward her. 'When you sleep with me, babe – you sleep with me – not some two-bit bum who works for me. You dig that, honey?'

She opened the door but Stepper caught her hand. 'When I find out what you said – I'm going to peel your skin off.'

'Thomas Michael Quinlon,' King, the Special Branch DS said aloud. Webb sat next to him, watching the computer screen as he scrolled.

'Active 1980 to 1984, wanted for causing explosions in Newry in 1982 and Londonderry RUC station in 1983. Also suspected of shooting an Orangeman in Ballymena in July 1981.' He pushed his chair back and looked at Webb. 'Shot dead by C 1-2 in 1984 at Brindley Cross. Unarmed and on foot. Running through a roadblock.'

Webb stroked his moustache and looked him in the eye. 'Shit happens,' he murmured.

The DS looked back at the screen. 'He worked with Seamus Malloy in Armagh. Never came over here.' He sat forward then and stared at the screen. 'Look at this,' he said.

'What?'

The DS tapped the screen. 'Female cell member, put away right after Quinlon got shot. Nine years for conspiracy to cause explosions. Got out in '93.'

'Mary-Anne Forbes,' Webb said. 'Picture?'

The DS pressed a button on the keyboard and a digitised image spread over the screen. She had long black hair.

Vanner sat in the squad room, drinking tea with Jack Swann. 'Phelan seemed like a good man,' Swann said. 'Webby and I spent a couple of days up there just to make sure nothing was happening.'

'And it wasn't?'

Swann shook his head. 'We'd have known if it was.'

Webb stuck his head around the door. 'Guv'nor?'

Vanner looked up.

'Going for a beer. You want to come along?'

Webb and Vanner took Webb's car to the Spanish bar in the West End. Webb drove.

Vanner glanced behind at the bomb gear strapped in a bag on the back seat. 'Always carry that stuff with you?'

Webb nodded. 'Boot's full too. First call out if something goes bang.'

Vanner shifted the magnetic blue light by his feet and dropped the window a fraction. The traffic was thick round Victoria station, buses and taxis clogging up the carriageway.

'Never drink near the Yard then?' Vanner said with a grin.

'Would you?'

Vanner shook his head. 'Wouldn't have a Christmas party either.'

'Just gatecrash everyone else's.' Webb pulled into the outside lane and overtook the taxi in front of them. 'Westy's going to join us later,' he said. 'Thought we'd chat over a beer instead of back at the Yard. Too much going on.'

'You're busy then?'

'We're always busy, Guv.'

They parked outside the bar and wandered down the steps. The barman grinned at Webb and started setting up some tapas. Webb ordered Spanish beer for both of them and settled himself on a stool.

'Local then?' Vanner said.

'Been drinking here for years.'

Vanner nodded to the staff. 'Know what you do?'

'Yeah.'

'Look after you then?'

'They do.'

They drank out of brown bottles and Vanner picked at the tapas. 'We've got a possible,' Webb said quietly. The bar area was empty save the two of them and the barman polishing glasses. Vanner lit a cigarette and broke the match in two. His mobile sounded on his belt and he unclipped it.

'Vanner.'
'Jimmy Crack, Guv.'
'What's happening?'
'Just spoke to our girl.'
'Eilish?'
'Blown out, Guv'nor. She said if she ever hears from me again she'll make a formal complaint.'
'Ah,' Vanner said. 'Cottoned on at last.'
'Spitting blood. Stepper's threatened to skin her.'
'Then tell her to give him to us and we'll put him away.'
Vanner put the phone away. Webb was eating potato pieces with a cocktail stick.
'Eilish?' he said.
'McCauley. Remember her?'
'Oh yeah.'
'Women's wing of the IRA tattooed on her leg.'
'Non-player, Guv. Somebody's patsy that's all.'
Vanner nodded. 'The gear she was carrying turned out to be candlewax.'
'Somebody on a wind-up.'
'Harlesden posse. Jimmy Carter was involved.'
Webb lifted his eyebrows. 'Nasty.'
Vanner ordered more beer and tucked into the potatoes himself. 'Possibles, Webby?'
'Oh yeah, right. SB got some information this afternoon. I was checking it with the DS while you were talking to Swann.'
'Likely?'
'Definite maybe.' Webb leaned closer to him and dropped his voice to a whisper. 'Mary-Anne Forbes.'
Vanner thought hard, the name was familiar. Then he remembered. 'Quinlon, the Newry bombs.'
'Right.' Webb wiped his fingers on a serviette. 'She was arrested three months after Quinlon's death. Did nine years for conspiracy. She got out in '93.'
'I remember her,' Vanner said. 'But she had auburn hair.'
Webb shook his head. 'It's very black now.'
Vanner felt the hairs rise on his neck.
'She's over here, Guv. We've got Box taking a look at her.'

Eilish had a drink with Mary-Anne in the Drop Inn bar attached to the National. She sucked hard on her cigarette. 'The big black bastard. Thinks he's something special. There's some over there who'd eat him for breakfast and not spit out the bones.'

Mary-Anne looked at her. 'You want to watch him, Eilish.'

Eilish sat back again. 'I know. I'm thinking of moving on, Mary-Anne.'

'Yeah – where?'

'Home maybe. Either that or the south.'

'Home's not what it was.'

'How would you know? You only saw it from a cell.'

Mary-Anne crushed her cigarette in the ashtray.

'Why'd you come over here?' Eilish asked her.

Mary-Anne made a face.

Eilish cocked her head to one side. 'Working again are you?'

'Sort of.' She sipped at her drink. 'Bit of this, Eilish. Bit of that. Brings in a few quid now and then.' She put her glass back on the table. 'If he threatens you again – tell me eh. I know a few people.'

Morrison chaired the meeting with Westbrook and Webb and Vanner. Frank Weir was there as was Ryan and DS Braithewaite from AMIP.

'We interviewed Raymond Kinane,' Morrison said. 'His story bore out all that Michael Case said. There was a dummy and there was a body in the back.'

Webb looked at him. 'There was a dummy, yes. Kinane had that from Turner. But we don't know about the body in the car. We've only got Case's word for that.'

Morrison shook his head. 'No,' he said. 'We've got Kinane's. They cleaned her car on the Saturday morning. Traces of mud in the back. There was somebody there all right.'

'It's irrelevant now,' Westbrook stated. 'So the shootist tried in the New Forest first and failed. She succeeded back in London. The result is the same.' He looked from Morrison to Weir and back again. Vanner sat silently with his arms folded.

'It's an SO13 deal now, Sir,' Westbrook went on. 'There's no point in two investigations.'

Morrison was quiet after that. He looked at Vanner and then at Weir. Ryan spoke first. 'So we've wasted a couple of months then. Well there you go.'

Weir looked at Westbrook. 'So what you're saying is you want to run this from the Yard now.'

Westbrook nodded. 'I think it makes sense. Information's there. Vanner has clearance to be there. Simpler that way.'

Weir stared at Vanner. Vanner did not say anything.

'I'm sorry,' Westbrook went on. 'The way things work out that's all.' He looked from Morrison to Weir once more. 'We're all on the same side after all. So long as we get a result.'

'Yes,' Morrison said. 'So long as we get a result.'

The meeting broke up, Vanner got up to leave and Morrison called him back. 'I don't know what I did to deserve you, Vanner. Every time I turn around you're there to plague me.'

Vanner looked down at him.

'I never did trust you. I don't trust you now. Did it ever occur to you that an innocent woman is dead because of your activities twelve years ago?'

Vanner folded his arms. 'I think you're getting confused, Sir.'

'I don't think so.'

'I didn't kill Jessica Turner.'

'No. But you killed Thomas Quinlon.'

Vanner did not say anything.

'Unarmed, Vanner.'

'Is there anything else, Sir?'

'Just one thing.' Morrison stepped up close to him. 'When this is cleared up. Get yourself a transfer. We take bachelors in the Cayman Islands.'

Webb was waiting for him downstairs. 'Doesn't like you – your Guv'nor.'

'Can't have it all can I?'

'Always piss him off did you?'

'Always.' Vanner lit a cigarette and looked at the sky. 'Any word from Box?'

'Not yet.'

Vanner glanced at him. 'She in London?'

'Hammersmith.'

'Figures then.'

'Looking more likely isn't it?'

'Anything else I can do?'

'Not right now.'

'Good. I'll go home then.'

Ellie came in after him, looking weary. Vanner was preparing food downstairs, music on, a glass of red wine at his elbow. He got her a Coke from the fridge and poured it into a glass.

'I need a holiday,' she said, sitting down at the table.

'Tell me about it.'

She took a long pull at her Coke. 'Have you spoken to Anne?'

He shook his head.

'Shouldn't you?'

'Probably.'

'Will you?'

'When I'm ready.'

She got up and went to the stove. 'What's cooking?'

'Chicken.'

'Smells good.'

'Don't worry. There's no vegetables.' He caught her up in his arms then. 'You know for somebody in the medical profession you have a shit diet.'

She pushed him away. 'No I don't. I have all the vitamins I need.'

'Right. Out of a bottle.'

'Listen, Vanner. With your track record for nicotine and alcohol you're in no position to comment.'

Vanner laughed then and tried to catch her again. 'Take me upstairs and fuck me,' he said.

She shook her head. 'Too tired. I'm going for a bath. Call me when dinner's ready.'

Later, Vanner left the food to simmer and went upstairs to the bathroom. The door was open and steam drifted onto the landing. Ellie lay back in the water, bubbles over her belly, the red of her nipples just rising above the water. She looked at him where he stood at the door.

'You haven't told me what's going on. How come you're spending so much time at the Yard?'

Vanner looked at her then and considered. He opened his mouth and closed it again.

'Secret is it?'

He made a face. 'Delicate.'

'Too delicate for me?'

'Maybe.'

'Why don't you try me?'

He leaned against the wall and sipped his wine. 'It's to do with the murder in Ealing in February.'

'The one Sid's working on?'

He nodded.

'So how come you're involved now? I thought you were doing a crack deal or something.'

'I am. I was. I'm sort of seconded.'

'To whom?'

He thought before answering. 'It doesn't really matter, Elle. It'll be sorted soon.'

'Oh for Christ's sake. Talk to me, Aden. If I can't share your job what can I share? You don't have anything else.'

He sighed and looked at the floor. 'All right,' he said. 'I'm working with the Anti-Terrorist Branch. The Ealing shooting wasn't in isolation. There's other people involved.'

'Like you.' Her face was suddenly very serious.

He nodded.

'How?'

'That's not important. Basically whoever killed her has Irish links, possibly PIRA links, hence the Anti-Terrorist Branch.'

'And you used to be a soldier – is that it?'

'Sort of.'

She shook her head. 'Sort of. Maybe. God I love these conversations, they're so open and honest and normal.'

Vanner went to the door. Ellie called him back. 'There's something I've been meaning to tell you,' she said.

'What?'

'The other night when you were out late I . . .' She broke off. It seemed so silly now. 'Oh it's nothing really. I was having a bath and felt a bit weird. When I went through to the bedroom a man was watching me from outside.'

Vanner looked down at her. 'Who?'

'I don't know do I. When I looked down he left.'

Vanner shook his head. 'Probably knows you get undressed with the curtains open, Elle. Shut them next time eh.'

George Webb phoned him three days later. He was in his office in Campbell Row, his mind anywhere other than the crack investigation which with the loss of Eilish McCauley had all but ground to a halt.

'Guv'nor, it's George. Can you get over here right away? There's something I want to show you.'

Vanner put the phone down, got his coat and went out to

his car. At the Yard he showed his warrant card to the gateman and was ushered into the underground carpark. Webb met him as soon as he got out of the lift.

'What you got, Webby?' Vanner asked him.

'Two things, Guv.' They walked to the DCI's office. 'Number one Mary-Anne Forbes is alibi'd. She was in Belfast the weekend of the 12th. Box snout spotted her at a christening party. She didn't come back to London till Tuesday morning.'

'So we're back to no-one again.'

'Not quite.' Webb pushed open the door to Westbrook's office. Westbrook was at his desk, leafing through a selection of photographs.

'These came in from RUC this morning,' Webb said.

Vanner sat down and Westbrook passed him the pictures. Vanner laid them flat on the desk before him and began to peruse. Thomas Quinlon, long black hair and wild green eyes. He remembered him vividly. He moved on, Quinlon with Mary-Anne Forbes with auburn hair scraped back from her face. The next one, Quinlon and a youth he did not recognise. Quinlon had his arm around the boy's shoulders, pointing at something in the distance. Vanner moved on. Quinlon with two others he did not recognise. Then Quinlon with a lean, thin-faced man with weak hair and narrow eyes. Cahal Barron the informant.

'Barron,' he said. 'I know him.'

'Yeah. Double-sided player. Lucky to survive as long as he has.'

Vanner nodded. 'That what you wanted to show me?'

'Keep going.'

Vanner turned the next picture up. Quinlon with the youth again and on the other side a girl. Young, much younger than Quinlon, pretty white-skinned face and long red hair. For a moment he did not recognise her. Then all at once it dawned on him. 'That's Eilish McCauley,' he said.

Webb snaked his tongue across his lips. 'Is it? I wasn't sure.'

'I am.' Again Vanner looked at her face. Two weeks ago he had been seated across the table from her at the Antrim Road RUC station. She was older, but the features had not altered and her hair was still long and very red. Webb came alongside him.

'Look at what she's wearing,' he said.
Vanner looked and frowned and looked again.
'The sweater,' Webb said. 'It's pink.'
Vanner laid the pictures down very deliberately.
'AMIP lab liaison found a piece of pink angora wool at the crime scene in Ealing,' Westbrook said.
Vanner stared at him. 'Quinlon was married with three brats. We always thought he was over the side with the Forbes girl.' He looked again at the photos. 'Who's the lad?'
'Box don't know. They can only identify Quinlon.'
Vanner looked at the young face of the boy. 'I suppose it could be her brother.'
Webb sat down again. 'Think about it, Guv. McCauley. You had her pegged as a donkey for your crack team in Harlesden. Irish connection. Crack in Belfast or whatever. *Cumman na mBan* on her thigh. If she was running gear over what was she bringing back?'
Vanner looked at him. 'Shagging Tommy Quinlon?' He made a face. 'Why twelve years?'
'I don't know. But I think we ought to ask her.'

Eilish lay asleep in her bed, alone tonight at least. James was restless. The moon bright against his curtains, normally hidden under the crackling of false light from the streets. He lay on his back, aware of the time ticking on and on and sleep a million miles from him. Since Eilish had got back from Ireland he had seen none of the gang. He did not know what had happened, only that she had been nowhere near the border. He had phoned the Liverpool Ferry on a whim and discovered his sister was booked on the Belfast crossing. He remembered the holdall from the last time. Maybe something had gone wrong. The phonecalls since she got back, another male voice. *Tell her Jimmy called.* Who the hell was Jimmy?
A noise outside. He rolled onto his side, pushing his weight up onto his elbow. Footsteps. Moving to the window he drew aside the curtain and looked out. His eyes balled. Cars at the park end of the road. Four of them, men in black suits running towards the house. The next thing he knew the front door crashed and men were in the hall, shouting. James dashed onto the landing.
'Stand still. Armed Police.' Torchlight in his face and behind

him Caran's voice crying out. He wanted to call to her to tell her it was all right but he could not. Two black-suited men in gas masks were on the stairs, machine guns pointed at his chest.

'Lie down. Now. Lie down on the floor.'

James fell forward to his knees. The first man was at the head of the stairs. The light came on in Eilish's bedroom and she appeared at her door. James looked helplessly at her.

He sat in the lounge with both the children on his knees, their arms about his neck, their cries ringing in his ears. Vanner looked down at him. 'Make them be quiet,' he said.

James stared into his face. 'Oh yeah. And how am I going to do that?'

'Think of something.'

Vanner stepped back into the hall, past the SO19 men who secured it. Outside a hire car had been brought up, paper over the seats and polythene sheets over that. Webb and Westbrook stood in the hall in coveralls, plastic booties over their shoes. Sterilised completely, both of them.

In the kitchen, a female Anti-Terrorist officer also in blue overalls assisted Eilish with the paper suit she had unwrapped from sterilised plastic. Eilish stared beyond her at Vanner. 'What the hell is this about?'

'Shut up, Eilish.'

'I've a right to know what this is about. Coming into my house in the middle of the night.'

Vanner just looked at her.

'You,' she hissed. 'You're a lying bastard.'

Vanner folded his arms and leaned against the door.

'Candlewax,' she said. 'Fucking candlewax, you lying cheating bastard.'

Vanner nodded to the clothing. 'Put the suit on, Eilish and be quiet eh?'

In the bedrooms clothes lay on the beds, drawers were open and the contents laid out on the windowsills and the carpet and on Eilish's dressing table. One officer was rummaging through her wardrobe. He stopped as his eye caught something, then he lifted it out. Vanner stared at a pink wool sweater.

The officer handed the sweater to him and Vanner turned it over in gloved hands. He checked the back, the front and the sleeves. At the elbow of the left one the wool pattern was fractured. Vanner handed it back to the officer, then a thought struck him and he went into the bathroom. He flicked through the contents of the shelf above the sink, then opened the medicine cabinet. A flat cardboard box caught his eye. He lifted it down. Hair dye. Raven-black.

Downstairs Eilish was guided between Webb and the female sterilised officer to the back of the waiting hire car. James sat dumbfounded in the living room. Westbrook was talking to him.

'Is there somewhere you can take the children?' he said.

James looked bug-eyed at him. 'What are you doing with my sister?'

'Arresting her.'

'Where's she going?'

'Paddington Green police station.'

'I want to talk to her.'

'You can't.'

The children started crying once more.

'Is there anywhere you can take them?' Westbrook repeated. 'We're going to turn this house inside out.'

'What the hell are you looking for?'

'Is there anywhere you can take them?'

James blinked and blew out his cheeks. Caran nuzzled his neck like an animal. 'The priest,' he said, 'Father Joe Sheehan. Willesden Green.'

'Phone him.'

Sheehan arrived fifteen minutes later in his car. Eilish was gone already, the crime scene team were beginning to strip the house. James watched from the doorstep, holding both the girls close to him. Westbrook stepped up to the priest. 'I'm Detective Chief Inspector Westbrook,' he said. 'Eilish McCauley has been arrested and her brother says that you might look after the children.'

The priest stared at him, then at James. 'Please, Father,' James said.

'Of course.' The priest beckoned him. 'Come on,' he said. 'Come with me.'

When they were gone Vanner stood in the hall and surveyed the work of the crime scene team. They left nothing to chance, every chair pulled inside out, every piece of furniture all but taken to pieces. The carpets started to come up, the loose linoleum in the kitchen. They worked quickly and efficiently. Westbrook grinned at him. 'Very good aren't they?'

Eighteen

Eilish McCauley sat in the interview room at the high security cell block at Paddington Green police station. The paper suit rustled as she crossed one leg over the other. Westbrook and Webb sat opposite her. Vanner watched through a two-way security mirror. He could hear every word that was said.

'I'm allowed a phonecall,' Eilish said. 'I know my rights. I'm allowed one phonecall.'

'You're right. You're allowed one phonecall.' Webb stood up, winked at Vanner through the glass and left the room. He came back a few moments later and plugged a phone into the socket in the wall by the door. Unwinding the cord, he set the phone before her.

'Who're you calling?' he said.

'A friend.'

'Who?'

'Her name's Mary-Anne.'

Webb nodded slowly. 'What's the number?'

She gave it to him and he dialled. A woman's voice answered and he passed the phone to Eilish.

'Mary-Anne. This is Eilish. You'll never guess where I am.' She stared in Westbrook's eyes as she said it. 'Paddington police station. I've been arrested by the Anti-Terrorist squad. Yeah, me. Stupid fucks eh. Get me a lawyer, Mary-Anne. Wait a minute.' She held the receiver away from her ear and looked at Webb. 'Where's my kids?'

'Your priest has them. Your brother took them there,' Westbrook told her.

'Father Sheehan's, Mary-Anne. Check on my kids will you? Tell them Mummy loves them and she'll see them very soon.' She put the phone down and looked straight at Westbrook. 'Very soon,' she said.

Westbrook smiled, rubbed his palms together and sat forward. 'Well let's hope so eh.'

Eilish sat back. 'I'm not talking to you till my lawyer gets here.'

Webb looked at her. 'Mary-Anne Forbes. That's a good start, Eilish. I bet she knows some great lawyers.'

Eilish stared at him, uncertainty showing in her eyes for the first time since she had been brought in.

'Worked with Tommy didn't she?'

'Tommy who?'

'Come on, Eilish. Tommy.'

'Quinlon. You're talking about Tommy Quinlon?'

Vanner watched through the glass, Jack Swann sitting next to him. 'She's good, I'll give her that,' Swann said. 'Not your average volunteer.'

'Thomas Michael Quinlon,' Webb was saying. 'Shot dead by security forces in February of 1984.'

'Murdered.'

'What?'

'Murdered by security forces. Shot in cold blood, mister. Unarmed man. He wasn't even wearing a jacket.'

Vanner frowned. The dummy in the road. Ray Kinane's statement. A store mannequin, male, trousers, no jacket, lying in the rain in the road. He half-closed his eyes. A man lurching down the hill to the ford, shirt plastered against his flesh by the rain. And shots ringing out. He sat forward in his chair and looked closely at Eilish.

'That night,' Webb was saying. 'That's what all this is about isn't it, Eilish?'

'All what? I don't know what you're talking about.'

'Course you don't. You don't know anything about Jessica Turner either or David Quigley for that matter.'

Eilish looked blankly at him. 'You're right,' she said. 'I don't. Now, why don't you take me back to that nice little cell until my solicitor gets here.'

Webb came into the room where Vanner and Swann were sitting. 'Get all that?' Webb said.

Vanner nodded. 'Thinks she's a hardcase. It was the same when we interviewed her in Antrim Road.'

'One phonecall and it's Mary-Anne Forbes.'

Vanner turned his mouth down at the corners. 'Not a very bright thing to do.'
Webb grinned at him.
'The dummy,' Vanner said. 'Beginning to fit.'
'How's that?'
Vanner thought carefully before replying. 'That night at Brindley Cross – it was raining very hard, Quinlon was only wearing a shirt. Turned out later he was pissed.' He paused then added: 'Friday the 12th it rained. The dummy in the road had no jacket on.'
Webb scratched his chin. 'Bit deep isn't it?'
'Twelve years,' Vanner said. 'Lot of time for someone to think.'
'It's a long time generally. Why wait a dozen years?'
Vanner shrugged. 'Maybe it took that long to find out who we were.'
'*You* maybe, but not the RUC boys. That would be easy enough if you had the right PIRA contacts.'
'Ask her,' Vanner said.
'I intend to.' Webb opened the door. 'Want to see what the Exhibits boys have come up with?'
They went upstairs to the evidence room. Webb nodded to his colleagues, who were laying plastic bags on the table.
'What you got, boys?'
One of them looked up at him and nodded to the bags. 'The sweater,' he said. 'Piece missing at the elbow. Waiting for the sample from Hendon then I'll get it down to the lab.'
Webb stared at the table and picked up a bundle wrapped in plastic. 'What's this?'
'Fifteen thousand quid, Skip. We found it behind the bath.'
Vanner looked at the cash. 'Fifteen thousand,' he mused. 'Now that is very interesting.'
'Drug money?'
'Could be.' He looked at Westbrook then. 'What're the chances of me having a chat with her?'
Westbrook made a face. 'If we've got the right body – you were her next target.'
'So?'
'So, I don't know. Leave it for now. Let Webby and me handle it. If we get nowhere then maybe we'll see.'
The phone rang and one of the Exhibits officers offered the receiver to Webb. Webb took the call, spoke for a few minutes

and then hung up. 'Lawyer's going to be late,' he said. 'In court this morning. We'll have to wait till this afternoon.'

Westbrook took a breath. 'You want to try again without?'

Webb shook his head. 'You saw her, Guv'nor. She isn't going to talk.'

The door opened and two more Exhibits men came in. One of them carrying a plastic bag with something heavy and black inside it. For a moment Vanner's heart pumped.

'Not a Toky,' the man said as he laid it down with a thump. 'Uzi machine pistol.'

Vanner picked up the package and inspected it. 'Where'd you get this?'

'Coal bunker. It wasn't in use, full of concrete and bits of wood.'

Webb took it from him and turned it over in his hands. 'Hers?'

Vanner shook his head. 'I don't think so,' he said.

At Hendon, Morrison was in the Superintendent's office with Weir. Vanner walked past the door on his way to the stairs. Morrison called him inside.

'Shut the door, Vanner.'

Vanner looked briefly at him then did as he was asked. Weir stood with his hands behind his back.

'What's happening?' Morrison asked him.

'Waiting for Eilish McCauley's lawyer.'

'She's made a complaint against you, Vanner. Formal one. Funny how many people do that.'

Vanner shook his head. 'What's she saying?'

'She's saying that you and Jimmy Crack lied to her over a consignment of crack in Ulster.

She reckons you told her she had a kilo and a half and unless she co-operated she would be looking at ten years.'

'Antrim Road verified it?'

'Not yet.'

Vanner shook his head. 'Crack turned out to be candlewax, Sir. Don't know what she's on about.'

Morrison leaned on the radiator and looked disparagingly at him. 'What else is happening?'

'SO13 found fifteen grand stashed behind the panel of her bath.'

'Anything else?'
'Yes. Young Young's Uzi.'
Morrison looked up. 'Carter's killer.'
Vanner nodded. 'His car was found at Roundwood Park. That's over the road from Eilish's house.' Vanner looked at him then. 'Do you want me to tell Keithley?'
'I'll do it,' Morrison said.

Outside Vanner phoned Jimmy Crack and told him about the find in the coal bunker. 'Eilish is gone as far as Stepper-Nap's concerned, Jim. But at least Young Young's history.'
'Something I guess. Doesn't give me who I want though, Guv.'
'Can't win 'em all, Jim.'
'It's not over, Guv. We've still got Rafter's baby mother.'
'Any more on that?'
'Me and Sammy are going down to have another word with him. She's still over in Kingston. He says he needs money for phone cards.'
'Give him all he wants.'
'I intend to. What's happening your end?'
'Getting there, Jim. You seen Slippery?'
'No.'
'Probably arguing with himself somewhere. If you see him tell him to bell me would you?'
'Sure. See you, Guv.'

Vanner got in his car and drove back to Willesden. He parked outside Eilish's house where the front door was still cordoned off with tape. Inside SO13 officers were putting back the carpets. Vanner showed his warrant card to the uniform at the door and stepped inside. He spoke to the nearest man. 'You finished in here?'
'Yep.'
'Got everything?'
'Never been known to miss.'
Vanner nodded. 'Family can come back then, brother and that.'
'I reckon. You better check with the Guv'nor.'
'Explosives?'
'Not a trace.' The man grinned again. 'Believe me we'd know.'

'I believe you.'

Vanner went into the lounge and leafed through the phone book until he came to Father Sheehan's address. He wrote it down and then went back to the car. The house was a small two-up two-down built alongside the Catholic church off the High Road. Vanner parked and locked his car then walked up the path. It was opened by a woman of about fifty, grey-white hair fastened with a silver pin.

'Father Sheehan please.'

'And you are?'

'Detective Inspector Vanner.'

Sheehan was in his study talking to James McCauley who sat in a low armchair, gripping the arms with stiff fingers. The children were nowhere to be seen. Vanner showed his ID to the priest. 'Where're the kids?' he asked.

'School,' Sheehan told him. 'We thought that would be best. Take their minds off last night.'

Vanner did not say anything. He looked at James. 'You okay?'

James snorted. 'What kind of question is that? You burst into our house at four o'clock in the morning, waving machine guns and terrifying the children.'

Vanner looked evenly back at him. 'Your sister is a suspected terrorist, James. What d'you expect us to do?'

'Terrorist?' James stared at him, then he laughed, almost brutally. 'She's no more that than I am.'

Vanner looked again at the priest. 'Would you give us a minute please?'

Sheehan looked doubtfully at James. James looked at Vanner, then at the floor. 'It's all right,' he said.

'Okay,' Sheehan said. 'I'll be in the kitchen if you need me.' He looked at Vanner as he passed him. 'You know you ought to consider your methods,' he said.

Vanner smiled. 'Believe me we do.'

He closed the door and then sat down in the swivel chair by Sheehan's desk. 'They're almost finished at your house,' he said. 'You'll be able to go home soon. You can pick up the kids from school.'

'And my sister?'

'Your sister's in custody.'

James bunched his eyes at the corners.

'It's very serious, James.'

'What d'you want me to do about it?'

'Nothing. Look after the kids that's all.'

'Been doing it all my life.'

Vanner leaned his chin in his palm. 'Wild is she your sister?'

'I don't think I want to talk about her.'

'Why not? You might be able to help her.'

James sat silently then and Vanner considered his words. 'You knew Young Young didn't you?' he said quietly.

James looked up at him.

'I'm with the Drug Squad, James.'

'Why last night then?'

'Long story. It's not important right now.' He sat up straighter in the chair. 'Young Young used to come over to your house didn't he? Sometimes he slept with your sister.'

James looked at the floor.

'And Stepper-Nap. The big fat one who drives the Mercedes.'

James looked at him then. 'I hated them,' he said. 'I don't know what she's doing with them.'

'I'll tell you what she was doing with them, James.' Vanner's voice was sharper. 'She was running drugs for them. How many times has she crossed the water lately. Two, three times? What did she tell you – visiting your mother?' He paused then. 'Why don't you ring your mother, James – ask her when last she saw Eilish?'

James gaze clawed at the carpet around Vanner's feet. 'I don't need to,' he said. 'Besides, she's not on the phone.'

'Convenient.'

James did not reply.

'You know what Stepper-Nap is don't you, James? He's a crack dealer. He sells misery for a fat profit and kids on the street look up to him.'

'I told you. I hate the fat bastard. Eilish should never've hooked up with him.'

'I'd like to get him off the street, James. I thought Eilish might help me but she won't.'

James chewed the end of his finger.

Vanner sat back again. 'Tell me about Mary-Anne Forbes.'

'Don't really know her.'

'Eilish does.'

James shrugged.

'Mary-Anne did time in Northern Ireland, James. Terrorist activities. Did you know that?'

'Yeah.'

'And she's a good friend of your sister.'

'They know each other that's all.'

Vanner laughed. 'Come on, James. Eilish was allowed one phonecall from custody. She called Mary-Anne. She wanted Mary-Anne to get her a lawyer. How d'you think that looks?'

'Don't know.'

'Course you do. You're not stupid, James. It looks bad. I mean it looks really bad.'

'Why're you telling me all this?' James's voice had risen a fraction. He looked Vanner in the eye now.

'Tell me something, James. When Eilish went across the water, not just now, in the past. Did she ever bring anything back?'

'Like what?'

'I don't know. A bag maybe – box or something?'

James shrugged.

Vanner sat back again. 'Tell me something else, James. When did you last see your mother?'

'Ages ago.'

'When exactly?'

'July.'

'Last year?'

James shook his head, watching Vanner carefully. 'The year before.'

'1994.'

'Yes.'

'Was Eilish with you?'

'We all went.'

Vanner stood up. 'Thank you, James. By the way, it's okay to go home.'

James nodded.

'And look after the children.'

'I always do.'

Back at Paddington Vanner sought out Webb and Westbrook. Eilish's legal representation had arrived and was talking with her in the interview room.

'I spoke to the brother,' Vanner said.

'When?' Westbrook looked across the desk at him.

'Just now. I told him he could go home soon.'

'He can go now. We've got everything there is to get.'

Vanner nodded. 'July 1994,' he said. 'Eilish was in Eire visiting her mother. She lives just across the border.'

Webb and Westbrook resumed their interview with Eilish. The lawyer was a woman in her late twenties, black two-piece suit over a white high-collared blouse. Webb smiled at her.

'You're a solicitor are you?'

'Yes.' Irish accent. Webb smiled again.

'I mean a real one.'

The woman frowned.

'What he means is,' Westbrook cut in, 'are you a solicitor or a solicitor's clerk?'

The woman coloured. Eilish cast a glance in her direction.

'Well?' Webb went on.

'I'm a legal executive.'

'Not a solicitor then?'

Again she coloured.

'A clerk,' Webb said, nodding to himself.

'Legal executive. I'm empowered to do this, officer.'

'Fine.' Webb smiled again. 'But you're not technically a solicitor.'

The woman tapped the end of her pen on the desk. 'Not technically. No. But I can do this. I do it all the time.'

'You're fully conversant with The Prevention of Terrorism Act,' Westbrook said.

'Yes.'

Webb smiled. 'Just so long as we all know.' He looked at Eilish. 'How often d'you dye your hair?'

'I don't.'

'No?' Webb looked at Westbrook. 'Then why is there black hair dye in your bathroom?' He lifted the plastic bag in front of him. 'We found it, Eilish. Raven-black. Nice colour. Must look good with your skin. Sort of Morticea style.'

'That's ancient. I haven't used it in years.' Eilish looked at the box. 'See for yourself. I bought it years ago.'

'Like to change your hair colour do you?' Westbrook said. 'Different look, different style.'

'I told you. I haven't used it in years. I think I bought it for a party about three years ago.'

'Witch were you?' Webb said.

The legal executive looked sourly at him. 'Cheap joke, sergeant.'

Webb rocked back on the legs of the chair. 'How come we found a 9mm Uzi in your coal bunker?' he said.

Eilish stared at him.

'Not well hidden but hidden.'

Eilish said nothing.

'Yours is it?'

'I don't know anything about it.'

'Funny thing is,' Westbrook cut in, 'we didn't find the Tokarev.'

Again Eilish said nothing.

'What did you do with it?'

'I don't even know what it is.'

'Yes you do, Eilish,' Westbrook voice was quieter. 'You used it to kill Jessica Turner. Why did you do that? And why the dummy? Bit theatrical wasn't it?'

Eilish opened her mouth, closed it again and shook her head. She looked sideways at her solicitor. 'I don't know what he's on about.'

'Jessica Turner, Eilish. February 12th of this year. Sunday night, very cold. On the Friday you followed her down to the New Forest and laid a dummy out in the road. Then you got in the back of her car and you would have killed her there if another car hadn't followed you.'

Eilish stared at him. 'You're making this up aren't you? Belfast all over again.'

'Belfast?'

'Yeah. Fucking candlewax.'

Westbrook made a face. 'Why her and not her lover? It was him you really wanted.'

'You're talking shit.'

'Ray Kinane, Eilish. Jessica Turner's lover. Ex RUC Ray Kinane. Special Branch. He was there when Tommy jumped the roadblock.'

Eilish stared at him now, lips thin in her face. 'Tommy didn't jump any roadblock. He was shitfaced. He was on his way home to his wife. He was shot dead just for being there.'

'Is that how you see it?' Webb said. 'Is that what this is all about? Why twelve years though? Why did you wait so long?

Did you need Mary-Anne to help you – is that it?'

'I don't know what you're talking about.'

'So where were you on February 12th?'

Eilish shrugged. 'I don't know. I'd have to check.'

Vanner watched, stony faced through the security mirror. Eilish facing him yet not seeing him.

'Come on,' Westbrook said. 'It wasn't that long ago.'

'I said – I'd have to check.'

'You were in Ealing, Eilish,' Webb cut in. 'Sitting in your car with your little black gun. How'd you get that – bring a bag back on one of your trips home?'

Eilish said nothing.

'Why've you got a PIRA tattoo on your leg?'

Eilish touched her thigh through the paper suit. 'I did it when I was a kid. Kids do things like that.'

Webb placed both hands behind his head and crossed his legs underneath the chair.

'Eilish, we found a pink wool sweater in your house.'

'That old thing. I haven't worn it in years.'

'A piece of the elbow is missing. When we match it to a piece we found at Jessica Turner's house on the night she was murdered that'll place you at the crime scene.'

For a moment fear showed in Eilish's face. 'Wait a minute,' she said. 'When was February 12th?'

'What d'you mean when?'

'What day, stupid?'

'Sunday.' Webb sat forward again. 'You still haven't told us why you shot Jessica Turner. You killed Quigley. Why not Kinane? You had him there on the Friday.'

'And Tim Phelan, Eilish,' Westbrook cut in. 'What stopped you killing him – some sort of warped compassion? Maybe you figured he'd had enough already, not having any legs or anything.'

Eilish looked him in the eye. 'I don't know what the hell you're on about. I don't know anyone called Quigley and I don't know anyone called Phelan.' She thought for a moment and then a light sparked in her eyes. 'And on February 12th I was at a party in Brighton.'

Behind the security mirror Vanner suddenly stared at her. Webb was talking, but Vanner did not hear him. He stared at Eilish, the clarity sudden but there in her eyes. February 12th

– a party in Brighton. Brighton by the sea. Getting up from his chair he went out to his car.

His mind was racing, all the way back to Campbell Row. He had thought of ringing Jimmy Crack instead of going himself, but he would still be on his way back from Winchester.

China was the only one in the squad room. 'Where's everyone?' Vanner asked him.

'Plaistow, Guv. Amphee plot.'

Vanner nodded. He went to the Exhibits cabinet at the back of the room and opened the second drawer. Jimmy Crack's photographs were bound by a rubber band and sealed inside a clear plastic sleeve. For a second Vanner stared at them. China was watching him, a quizzical expression on his face. Vanner took the pictures through to his office, where he opened them. His heart sank as he looked at the date inscribed electronically on the bottom as the camera took the photograph. 12.2.96.

He looked very carefully at the picture of Eilish standing between Young Young and Stepper-Nap. Stepper had his left hand draped over her shoulder, hand all but across her breast. On his wrist was a big fat rolex. Vanner thought for a moment and then took the picture downstairs to the Financial Investigation Unit. Dave Starkey was sitting at his desk. He smiled as Vanner walked in.

'Hello, Guv. What can I do for you?'

'The microscope thing, Dave. The one you use for checking notes and stuff. Is it about?'

Starkey took him through to the mini lab in the back office and Vanner handed him the picture. 'The watch,' he said. 'I want to know what time it says.'

Starkey played around with the focus and then bent closer to the lens. 'Ten to twelve,' he said. 'Have a look for yourself.'

Vanner went back upstairs and for a long time he sat in his chair. Eilish with Young Young and Stepper-Nap, dark, the lights of the pier and the sea in the background. She couldn't have killed Jessica Turner. The phone rang on the desk and he picked it up. Jimmy Crack, voice interrupted by the hiss and rattle of the mobile line.

'Jimmy. Where are you?'

'Just left Winchester. She's on the move, Guv. We'll tag her all the way and hope that customs don't stop her on the way back.'

'Can't we make sure they don't?'

'The way they're acting at the moment – you must be joking.'

Vanner was silent.

'What's happening your end?'

'It isn't Eilish, Jimmy.'

'No?'

'Can't be. The night of the party with the Brit-Boy posse. The photos remember? February 12th, Jim. Eilish was in Brighton.'

Vanner put down the phone, looked at the pictures once more then scooped them into a pile and thrust them back in the envelope. Getting up, he placed them in his jacket pocket and went back to his car. On the way to Paddington he phoned George Webb. 'What's happening with the suspect?'

'Sticking to her story about Brighton, Guv. Reckons she was there until Monday.' Webb laughed. 'Trouble is she can't give us a single name who'll verify it.'

Vanner put his mobile down and drove. Of course she couldn't. They were all crack dealers. But that did not change the fact she was alibi'd.

Webb and Westbrook were both in the canteen when Vanner got back to Paddington. He found them at a table drinking tea, bought himself a cup of coffee and sat down.

'You look happy,' Webb said.

Vanner produced the photographs from his jacket pocket and laid them out in front of them. He tapped the date at the bottom right-hand corner. 'Eilish McCauley's alibi'd,' he said.

Webb stared at the pictures. 'A party,' he said. 'Is it Brighton?'

'That's the pier.' Vanner looked again at the one with Stepper-Nap and Young Young. 'That's the Daddy from the Harlesden crack team I've been working on,' he said. 'His watch reads ten to twelve. The tall, skinny one is Young Young. He shot Jimmy Carter.'

Webb put down the picture. 'No wonder she can't produce a witness.'

'Doesn't have to does she?' Vanner took out cigarettes, looked up at the no-smoking sign and cursed under his breath.

'So not Mary-Anne Forbes and not Eilish either.' Westbrook pushed a hand through his hair.

Vanner looked him in the eye. 'PIRA don't use women shooters. Never have.'

Webb leaned on his elbows. 'But the pink sweater matches. We've had the report back from Lambeth.'

'Somebody else with access. Somebody who might wear false fingernails.' He paused. 'And maybe a wig.'

'The brother,' Westbrook stated.

'What about the prints from the ESLA lift?' Vanner looked at Webb.

'Could fit a man's foot. Although he was wearing flat-soled women's shoes. There's always a margin of error.'

'It has to be James,' Vanner said. 'Who else could get in her wardrobe?'

Webb stroked his moustache. 'But why?'

'I don't know.' Vanner stood up. 'Let's pick him up and ask him.'

On the landing Westbrook paused. 'He's armed.'

'There was no gun in that house except the Uzi in the coal bunker,' Webb said. 'If it is him he's got the Toky stashed someplace else.'

'SO19?' Vanner said. 'We could get an ARV over there.'

'We've got pink tickets,' Westbrook said. 'We can get weapons from here.'

'Do it then. Save time.'

They took Vanner's car and headed west towards Willesden. 'You want to give Old Street a bell just in case?' Webb said. 'See if they've got a Trojan in the vicinity?' They were close to Roundwood Park. Vanner looked at Westbrook. 'We'll be all right,' he said. 'He'll have the kids with him.'

'Better get hold of a social worker then, unless we release Eilish.'

'Not yet,' Vanner said. 'Not till we know exactly what we've got. We can get a plonk out from Harlesden nick in the meantime.'

They pulled up outside the house. No lights showed round the curtains. Vanner looked at Westbrook. 'They should be back by now. I gave him the all clear hours ago. Kids finish school at three thirty.' He got out of the car and they followed him up the path to the front door.

'I'll take the back.' Webb checked his Glock 9mm pistol and holstered it again. 'Give me a minute.'

He disappeared around the back of the house and they waited. Then Vanner lifted his fist and knocked. No answer. He knocked again. Still no answer. He knocked again, then peered into the gloom of the hall through the letter box. He let it flip closed and straightened up. 'House is empty,' he said.

Webb came round the path and made a face. 'No-one home?'

'The priest's,' Vanner said. 'Maybe they're still there.'

They drove to Father Sheehan's house and he answered the door himself. Vanner looked him in the eye. 'Is James McCauley here?'

Sheehan looked flustered. Behind him, from the kitchen they could hear the sound of children's voices.

'Is he here?' Vanner asked again.

The priest shook his head. 'He collected the children from school and then brought them back here. Said the house was still upside down.'

'The house is fine,' Vanner said. 'What time was this?'

'About four.'

'Where did he go?'

'Said he was going to check on his sister. I haven't heard from him since.'

Vanner glanced at Westbrook then back at the priest once more. 'Will you be okay with the children?'

The priest raised his eyebrows. 'For how long?'

'I don't know. The house is fine, Father, and James has been nowhere near his sister.'

'It's very important we find him,' Westbrook put in. 'If you can't handle the kids we can get a social worker.'

'Social worker? I don't understand.'

Vanner leaned against the door frame. 'James isn't coming back, Father. And at the moment Eilish is still being held.'

'I'll look after the children. I've got my housekeeper to help me.'

Westbrook took out his business card and handed it to him. 'We'll notify social services. If you need anything just call.'

They left him then and drove back to Paddington. 'How'd you want to play this?' Vanner asked them.

'James has gone walkabout,' Webb said. 'I'll get back to the Yard and do some digging with SB. See if I can't come up with a background. He was only a kid when Quinlon was shot, couldn't have been more than fifteen.'

Vanner stared at him then. 'Twelve years to grow up.'

Webb took his car back to Scotland Yard and Westbrook and Vanner went down to the interview room.

'What's his motive?' Westbrook said musedly. 'We've nothing on file to suggest he's a player.'

'Maybe his sister can tell us.'

'You want to let her know she's clear?'

'Not yet. If she thinks she's walking we're nowhere.'

'She knows she's alibi'd.'

'No she doesn't. She knows she didn't do it. But she also knows that nobody from the posse'll come forward and say so.'

Eilish was brought back to the interview room with her solicitor. She saw Vanner and curled her lip at the corner. 'Mr Candlewax. What're you doing here?'

'Sit down, Eilish.'

'I'm not talking to you.' She looked at Westbrook. 'Where's your little mate? I'm not talking to him.'

'Sit down,' Westbrook repeated.

She sat, arms folded, legs thrust away from her under the table. Her solicitor sat down and unfastened her briefcase. Westbrook switched on the tape confirmed the time and sat back. 'You say you were at a party in Brighton on the night of February 12th.'

'I was.'

'But nobody can verify it. Why not?'

Eilish pressed her lips together and looked at him.

'Why not?'

'Because I hardly know them.'

'But you stayed all night.'

'Yes. I told you that already.'

'So where did you stay exactly?'

'Friend's house.'

'So the friend can verify it?'

She shook her head. 'Not my friend. Friend of a friend.'

Vanner lit a cigarette. 'Complicated isn't it?'

She ignored him.

'Eilish,' Westbrook continued. 'We've got a pink wool sweater from your wardrobe with stitching missing at the elbow. The missing piece of wool was found at the scene of a murder which took place on Sunday 12th February. How do you explain that?' He said it openly, an easy expression on his face.

Eilish rubbed a hand across her mouth. 'I don't know.'

'Who else had access to your clothes?'

'Nobody.' She stopped. 'Well the kids I suppose and James.'

'Your brother,' Westbrook said.

'Yes.'

'Tell us about James,' Vanner said.

She looked at him then, again curling her lip. 'I'm not telling *you* anything.' She turned to Westbrook. 'I want him out of the room.'

'He stays.'

'Then I'm not saying anything else.' She folded her arms once again.

Westbrook glanced at Vanner who scraped back his chair. He walked out of the room and into the next one, then settled himself behind the mirror.

Westbrook sat forward in his seat, elbows resting on the table. 'See,' he said. 'Gone. Now – what's he like – your brother? How come he lives with you?'

She shrugged. 'Always has.'

'Since when?'

'Christ, I don't know. What's it matter? Since our parents split up.'

'Where's your father?'

'Haven't got a clue and I don't give a toss.'

'Mother?'

'Ireland.'

'Where?'

'Little town just south of the border.'

Westbrook sat back again. 'You were there in July of 1994,' he said.

'Was I?'

Westbrook nodded. 'You all were. You, your kids and your brother. Holiday was it?'

'Must've been.'

'Did you go north?'

'Don't remember.'

'Day out – to Morne maybe?'

'I've been to Morne. But we didn't go that trip.'

Westbrook cocked his head at her. 'Spent the whole time together did you?'

'I can't remember.'

He leaned closer to her. 'Eilish, on July 17th 1994 a man called David Quigley was shot dead at Spelga Dam. The gun the killer used was the same gun that killed Jessica Turner on February 12th of this year, the night you claim you were in Brighton but your pink jumper says otherwise.' He looked very keenly at her. 'That's two killings, Eilish. Two murders.'

She opened her hands at him, eyebrows arching. 'I don't know anything about either of them.'

Westbrook toyed with the pencil he had laid out on the pad before him. 'You're a member of the Provisional IRA aren't you?'

She looked him full in the eye. 'No,' she said. 'I'm not.'

'Then how come you've got that tattoo on your thigh?'

'I told you earlier. I was young when I did that. We all do stupid things when we're young.'

Westbrook shook his head. 'We think you're active, Eilish. We think you bring things back from your drug smuggling trips.'

'I don't smuggle drugs.'

'Where'd the fifteen grand come from then?'

She stared at him. Through the mirror Vanner watched the expression in her eyes. 'What fifteen grand?'

'Come on, Eilish.' Westbrook shook his head. 'You really think I'm stupid. We found it behind your bath. Used notes, fifties and twenties. Wrapped up in clingfilm.'

'Coke money, Eilish. Crack money. That's what Vanner thinks.' He slanted his eyes then. 'Or is it other money?'

She looked at the floor between her legs.

'Where did you get the gun?' Westbrook asked.

'What gun?'

'The Tokarev you shot Jessica Turner with.'

'I never shot anyone.'

'What about the Uzi?' he went on. 'That yours too?'

'What Uzi?'

'We told you. The one we found in your coal bunker.' Westbrook looked at the notes Vanner had made for him. 'Young Young had an Uzi didn't he, Eilish. Did he get the Tokarev for you – or did you bring it back in a bag you weren't supposed to open?'

Eilish looked at her solicitor. 'I'm not answering any more questions.'

'Fine,' Westbrook said. 'We've got enough evidence anyway. Fifteen thousand pounds you can't account for. We've got your sweater at a murder scene when you claim you were elsewhere but can't produce a single person to prove it.' He stood up. 'We don't need any more.'

Westbrook looked at the solicitor. 'You better tell her about the thirty years. She'll be a grandma before she gets out.'

Vanner went home. The house was empty. A message from Ellie telling him that she had gone back to Shepherds Bush for the night. He stared at the note on the table, an emptiness opening inside him that he had thought he could not feel any more. He sat down at the kitchen table and re-read the message. She had not been home for even one night in the past two months. All at once he thought of his father, but now his father was dead. Picking up the phone he dialled her flat and got her answermachine. He did not leave a message.

Upstairs he stood for a long time under the shower. The emptiness of his house seemed to echo in his head above the hiss and rush of the water. He leaned both hands against the wall and bent his head to the torrent. He stood there until the shower ran cold, then he got out and dried himself.

Downstairs, he made a cup of coffee, lit the umpteenth cigarette of the day, thought about quitting and smoked it in silence. James McCauley's face in his mind, young and vulnerable, incongruous with the venom of his flame-haired sister. He recalled the first time he had seen him, in the park with those two half-caste girls. He wondered who their father was.

Ray Kinane's story of the dummy, shirt and tie and no jacket, lying in the road with rain falling all over it. Jessica must have given him a very graphic description. The dummy had never been found. James McCauley in the back. Who else had access to Eilish's wardrobe? Who could have got the sweater except perhaps Mary-Anne Forbes who had been active with Quinlon in the eighties. But Mary-Anne Forbes was alibi'd, spotted in Belfast the night of the shooting. He thought of Tim Phelan, broken into pieces in a chair amid the silence of his Yorkshire village. Why Jessica and not Kinane?

He took his coffee through to the lounge and sipped at it. Cold already. He thought about making a fresh one. Instead he poured himself a shot of Bushmills and swallowed hard before pouring another. The darkness of the street pressed against the uncurtained window. When he looked sideways he could see his face in it. He lit another cigarette, smoked half and crushed it in the ashtray. He thought of Eilish in the cell and her children with the priest, wondering what on earth had become of them. Checking the phone book, he found the number and dialled. The priest answered and Vanner asked him if James had been in touch. The priest said that he hadn't. Vanner asked him if there was anywhere else he might be. The priest said he didn't know. Westbrook had set up an OP at Mary-Anne Forbes's place in Hammersmith but so far they had seen no-one.

He looked at the telephone, wondering again whether he should phone Ellie a second time. He wanted to, but what was the point. Her distance of late, too much too soon. Three months of intensity and then maybe reality settling in. Guns, why had she started asking about guns?

He picked up the telephone and rang her. Again the answer machine. 'Elle, it's me. Pick up the phone if you're there.'

Nothing.

'Ellie. I mean it. Pick up the phone. It's important.'

Nothing.

Getting his coat he went out.

She did not answer her door. Fear and frustration rose in his chest. He rang again and still she did not answer. Friends, he thought. Who were her friends? The other nurse, the one who had patched him up that time. Valesca. He rang Sid Ryan at home.

'Sid, it's Vanner.'

'Hello, Guv. Cracked it yet?'

'What?'

'My AMIP deal.'

'I'm not in the mood, Sid.'

'No. Neither am I.'

'Listen, Ellie's mate – Valesca.'

'The other nurse?'

'That's right. You don't have her number do you?'

'No. Should I?'

'I just wondered.'

'I'm a married man, Guv.'

'When it suits you.'

'What's the panic?'

'Oh, nothing. I can't get hold of Ellie that's all. I just thought you might know.'

'Dumped you has she, Guv. Not before time.'

'Not funny, Sid.' Vanner switched off the phone.

As he drove off a woman watched from a car across the road. She had painted nails and long black hair. Her make-up was a touch too heavy.

Vanner lay awake most of the night, thinking about his father. He thought of Jane again and some of the old pain revisited him. In the morning he tried ringing Ellie again and got the answer machine. He did not leave a message.

Westbrook and Webb were waiting for him at the Hendon incident room. They had been briefing Morrison and Weir. Ryan was there looking sullen. Vanner walked in and Westbrook nodded to him.

'How long can you hold Eilish McCauley?' Morrison was asking.

'Seven days. Fourteen if we have to.'

Morrison nodded. 'She obviously hasn't seen a set of the pictures.'

'Obviously,' Vanner said without looking at him.

Webb took him to one side. 'You okay, Guv'nor? You look knackered.'

'I am. No sleep last night.'

'James McCauley,' Webb said. 'We've had word on him.'

'Already.'

'Snouts who remember Quinlon are wound up, Guv'nor.'

'Good – your information is it?'

'What do you think? We'll talk back at the Yard.'

Vanner sat at Ryan's desk and picked up the phone. He dialled the nurse's station at the hospital and breathed a silent sigh of relief when Ellie's voice answered.

'Ellie, it's me.'
'Hello you.'
'You stayed away last night.'
'Yes.'
'Why?'
'I just needed my own place.'
'I know. It's all right. I was worried about you that's all. I called you but you were out.'
'Drinks with the girls. Blow the cobwebs out. I've let myself go stale.'
'You don't drink, Elle.'
'Coke.'
'Right.' He paused, lost for what to say. 'You coming home tonight?'
'Not sure.'
'Okay. Whatever. I need to talk to you though.'
'What about?'
'Not on the phone.'
'Tomorrow? I'm going out again tonight.'
Vanner sucked breath silently. 'Fine. You'll come round?'
'Yes.'
'Good.'
'Okay.'
'Elle.'
'What?'
'I . . .'
'What?'
'Nothing. See you tomorrow.'
'What were you going to say?'
'Nothing. It doesn't matter.' He put down the phone.

Nineteen

Eilish sat in her cell at Paddington Green police station and thought about her children. No word, nothing from anybody to tell her that they were all right. She stared at the wall, hating Vanner for his lies in Belfast and hating Stepper-Nap for setting her up like he did. All at once she thought of her mother and a loneliness that she had not known before descended like a weight inside her.

She got up from the bench that served as her bed, trying to work out exactly how long she had been in this sterile, lifeless place where time had no meaning and meals were pushed through a crack in the door. Apart from Vanner, she had no idea who the men were who interviewed her. Nameless faces from across the table. Thoughts of the children plagued her. What would she do without them? Thirty long years stared her in the face and there was nothing she could do about it. The only person alive who could help her was the leader of a crack gang who had threatened to skin her alive.

Her mind wandered and she began to think back to how she had got herself into this mess in the first place. Fun originally, a life other than that which she had known, when all there was was James with his sombre face, tugging at her emotions like a son she had never borne. And then Stepper and Young Young and the countless others. She could not even look her children in the eye and tell them who their fathers were.

Lying down again she closed her eyes and a night long past, now resurrected in a terrifying way, lifted once more in her head.

Tommy reaching for his underpants, naked until that moment with her watching him and her brother watching him too. He pulled them on, trembling slightly, unsteady still on his feet. Eilish stood with her arms folded and watched him.

'Get him his trousers, Jamie.'

James did not move. He stared at her, something like hatred standing out in his eyes.

'You know he can't stay here,' she said.

James picked up the trousers, held them a moment then passed them to Tommy. He took them without speaking, thrust one foot in and almost fell. He shook his head and laughed. 'You can't send me out now, Eilish. I can hardly stand never mind ride my bike.'

'You can't stay.'

He shook his head at her then buckled his trousers and reached for his shirt, tie still held in place by the button-down collar. He pulled the shirt over his head and stuffed it into his belt.

'Gi's my boots, Jamie.'

James passed them to him as he sat in the chair and he worked his feet into them. Then he sat with his hands resting on his thighs and looked up at Eilish.

'Don't, Tommy,' she said. 'I'll lose the flat. You know I will. Ride on over to Danny's.'

'It's pissing wi' rain. How'm I gonna make it to Danny's?'

'You drank the beer. Nobody forced it down your neck.'

'For Christ's sake, Eilish.' James looked imploringly at her.

She rounded on him then. 'Go to bed, Jamie. And keep your mouth shut. This is nothing to do with you.'

'But, Eilish.'

'If you want a place to live – go to bed now.' She fisted one hand on her hip as if daring him to defy her. He looked at Tommy who winked.

'On you go, son. Don't worry about me.'

For a moment James stood where he was, then he turned and went back to his bedroom.

Tommy looked up at Eilish from where he still sat in the chair. 'Tell you what, lass,' he said. 'You make me leave now and I won't be coming back.'

Eilish trembled slightly. 'That's up to you, Tom. But you know I'm right about the flat.'

'I know you're a bitch is what I know.' He stood up then and faced her. She flared her nostrils at him, standing her ground. He took one step towards her, features stiff all at once, a coldness in the flat of his eyes.

'Get out,' she said. 'Get out of here now.'

Still he stood there, hands loose at his sides. For a moment she thought he was going to hit her, but all he did was lift a palm to his face and rub the line of his jaw. She called to him as he opened the front door. 'Your jacket.'

'You wear it.' The door slammed and she heard him crashing down the stairs. She closed her eyes then, hating herself and fearing the noise and Mrs McAvoy's mouth in the morning.

Rain washed the glass as she peered out of the window. Tommy was beside his motorbike, trying to get the kick start down. He sat astride it, shirt plastered against his flesh, hair thick and black like oil over his head. He kicked the starter over and the bike coughed but did not respond. He tried again and again and still nothing. Then he got off, lost his balance and watched as the bike crashed into the grass on its side. Lifting his head to the window he stared at Eilish before lurching off down the street. Far in the distance she could see the pale wash of headlamps.

She was sitting in the armchair he had just vacated when James came back through from his bedroom. She could still smell him, cigarettes and alcohol and the sweetness of sweat after love. She closed her eyes, opened them again and looked at her brother. He was fully clothed, accusation large in his eyes.

'Go to bed, Jamie. He's a big boy.'

'You shouldn't have sent him away, Eilish. Where's he going to go?'

'He's got a wife hasn't he?'

'Not any more. You took him away from her.'

Again she closed her eyes. 'Shut up, Jamie. You don't know what you're talking about.'

He turned for the door. She opened her eyes again. 'Where you going?'

'After him. I'm not staying here with you.'

Eilish stared at him then. 'You little shit,' she said. 'Tell me something, Jamie. When you play with yourself while we're screwing – is it me you're watching or him?'

James dropped his gaze, a redness on his face like a rash creasing the skin. For a moment she thought he would cry, then he turned and stalked into the hall.

'James.'

The door slammed shut for the second time in as many minutes.

She sat up on the bunk and looked at the wall of her cell, eyes wide now, staring at a dirty mark on the paint. Much later, when he came back in floods of tears he had told her what happened.

James ran through the rain, away from the flat, away from the pub, to the end of the village and then down the road to the ford where the army set up roadblocks. He ran hard, feet slapping through puddles broken up with rain. He could not see Tommy. He was that drunk he could not have got very far. Halfway down the hill he thought he heard a shout and he paused, straining his ear to the wind. A second shout, definite this time. He looked back up the road suddenly very unsure of himself. He looked back down the hill and as he did so three shots rang out in quick succession. He had heard gunfire before. He knew what it sounded like. And then he was running, blind panic, and as he rounded the bend before the ford he saw headlights and dark figures moving. He shrank into the bushes that bordered the tarmac.

He was barely a few yards away when he saw two men with torches move across the brimming ford to a figure lying in the road. James stifled a cry. It was all he could do to keep it in his chest. Torchlight and a body, lying askew with one arm hunched underneath him and the other splayed out like a half a crucifix. He could see the massed black of his hair.

Eilish got up from the bench and banged on the door. 'Open this up,' she cried. 'I've got things I want to say.'

Webb and Westbrook went down to the interview room. Her legal counsel was not there yet but all of a sudden she wanted to talk. Vanner sat behind the security mirror and watched her sitting in the room before Webb and Westbrook arrived. She was hunched, dwarfish and lost in the chair, one knee to her chest, both her arms wrapped around it. The WPC stood against the door with her arms folded.

Webb and Westbrook came in and Eilish almost jumped at the sound. She looked round, glancing between their faces in quick succession.

'Cigarettes,' she said. 'Have you got any cigarettes?'
Webb looked down at her. 'We don't smoke.'
'Somebody must have some. Get me some will you.'
A moment later Webb stuck his head round Vanner's door. 'Guv'nor . . .'
Vanner held out his packet.
Eilish smoked, sucking hard, cheeks narrowing and then inhaling with a hiss through her teeth.
'You don't want to wait for your lawyer?' Westbrook asked.
She shook her head. 'Lot of good she did me.' She sat forward, tapping the cigarette end on the edge of the tin-foil ashtray. 'If I help you what'll happen to me?'
Westbrook made a face. 'Don't see how you can, Eilish. We've got you at the scene – your pullover. Remember.'
'I wasn't there.'
'So you keep saying.'
Eilish drew savagely on the cigarette and exhaled in a stiff stream of smoke. 'My children,' she said. 'I can't lose my children. They're all I have in the world.'
'You will lose them.' Webb stuck his face into hers. 'Terrorists do their time, Eilish. Every single day of it.'
She shook visibly, dropping ash over the table. 'My brother's gay,' she said.
Webb looked at Westbrook. 'That supposed to mean something to us?'
She bit her nail then, eyes on the floor as if unsure how to go on. Westbrook clasped his hands together. 'What are you telling us, Eilish?'
'I'm telling you I was at a party in Brighton on February 12th. I can't verify it because I was there with a crack gang from Harlesden. I was sleeping with the leader. He's not going to come down here and tell you himself so I'm fucked.'
Westbrook looked at her. 'Go on,' he said quietly.
'James was home on his own that night. Both the girls were staying over at friends. James was home all weekend in fact.'
'What're you saying – your brother killed Jessica Turner?'
Eilish stopped then. 'Look,' she said. 'If I tell you this you've got to let me go. I can't lose my kids.'
'You ran drugs to Northern Ireland.'
She shook her head. 'It was candlewax. Stepper-Nap tried to stiff them.'

'Who?'

'I don't know names. Okay, I admit I thought it was crack but it wasn't so I can't get done for that. Look,' she said. 'I'm telling you the truth. I really am.'

'So far you're telling us nothing.'

'James,' she said. 'He used to stand outside my room and fiddle with himself when I was with men. It started with Tommy and I thought it was just him, some sort of stupid boyish crush. But he did the same with Young Young and Stepper-Nap.' She paused and licked her lips. 'James saw Tommy the night the police shot him. He was lying in the ford at the bottom of the hill in Brindley Cross.'

'Quinlon was PIRA wasn't he?'

She bit her lip and nodded. 'He was unarmed. Pissed as a fart. Couldn't even start his motorbike.' She looked Westbrook in the eye. 'They shot him down and James saw them do it. He blamed me because I wouldn't let Tommy stay.'

'Why not?'

She shook her head. 'It was my ma's flat and she had gone south and we hadn't told the council. I was terrified the neighbours would create. Tommy was married to a good Catholic girl and I was the floozy who screwed up her life.'

She bent her head then and through the glass Vanner saw her shoulders convulse and for a moment he thought she would cry. She gathered herself though, lifted her head, lit a third cigarette and went on.

'James was distraught. I've never seen him so lost. He blamed me. Tried to hide it but he couldn't. He kept asking me what I was going to do about it. I was a nineteen-year-old girl for Christ's sake. It was fun with Tommy, but I never had anything to do with what he did. I knew Mary-Anne but I didn't know what she did until she was sent down in Belfast.' She broke off, coughing suddenly.

'James started seeing men. Stupidly, in the toilets, that kind of thing. He loved Tommy Quinlon. He watched us together. He took up with any stranger that looked at him twice after Tommy was killed. He was only fifteen for God's sake. I couldn't stand it so in the end we moved back to our mother's and then we came over here.' She looked up again then. 'I only got the tattoo done because I felt so guilty. I did it for Jamie more than for me.'

'You were never a member?'

She shook her head. 'I was a good-time girl. I screwed some of them. I was good at it. James,' she said, 'when he was sixteen he tried to join the youth wing – Oglaidh na hEireann.' She pinched up her face. 'I felt so desperately sorry for him. They knew what he was like. They laughed and sent him away.'

Webb and Westbrook were silent. Eilish sat with her head bowed. Westbrook said, 'When you visited your mother . . . July 1994. Did he go off on his own?'

'For two days yes.'

'Did he say where?'

'Walking, he told me.'

Webb scratched his chin. 'Where did he get the gun, Eilish? If he was turned down – where did he get a Tokarev? It's a PIRA weapon.'

She did not answer him.

'Where, Eilish?'

Still she did not answer.

'Come on. If you want us to believe this you have to tell me.'

'It's true. Every word I've said. Ask Mary-Anne Forbes. She knows what he's like.'

'The gun,' Webb persisted quietly. 'How did your brother get his hands on a Tokarev?'

Eilish bit her lip. 'Once,' she said. 'Only once. I brought over a bag.'

'From Belfast?'

She nodded.

'What was in it?'

'I don't know. I knew enough about Tommy's mates not to look.'

'When was this?'

'January '94.'

'Where did you take it?'

'Victoria station. I left it in a locker.'

'So what're you saying?'

She looked keenly at him then. 'It was in my house overnight.'

Vanner sat with Webb, Westbrook and Chief Superintendent Robertson in the DCI's office at Scotland Yard. Vanner had one ankle crossed over his knee, staring at Westminster Abbey through the window. Westbrook was briefing Robertson on how James had got the Tokarev. 'Pretty simple really – whoever picked up the bag was just another gopher.'

'She had no comeback.'

'No. Quarter Master couldn't have known what he was getting.'

'Happens,' Webb said.

Vanner was only half-listening. The phone rang on his belt and he pressed it against his ear.

'Vanner.'

'Feel my pain.'

He sat up straight. 'Hello, James,' he said.

'Feel my pain.' The phone went dead in his ear.

Vanner switched off his phone and laid it on the desk. For a long time he did not say anything. Robertson stared at him. 'James McCauley?'

Vanner nodded.

'What did he say?'

Vanner glanced up at him. 'Feel my pain.' And then he knew for certain why Jessica Turner had been killed and not Raymond Kinane. He went a little cold as suddenly he recalled his flippant remark when Ellie said there was a man looking up at the bedroom window. Reaching across the desk he picked up the phone and dialled the nurses' station. It rang four times and then somebody else answered.

'Ellie Ross please.'

'She's with patients.'

Vanner let go a breath. 'When she's free. Get her to ring Aden Vanner on his mobile. It's very very important.'

He put down the phone and looked at them. 'Jessica Turner was killed because killing Quigley was no good.'

Webb looked puzzled.

'Three shots and dead. No more. Nothing.' Vanner stood up. 'For ten years McCauley lived with his teenage memories of Quinlon dying. PIRA blew him out. His sister failed him. So when he got the gun he went after Quigley. But it was no good.' He stopped. 'That's why he killed Jessica Turner – so Kinane could feel his pain. Only Kinane didn't come forward because he had a wife and two kids. Phelan was a possible but what good would it do him to shoot a man blown up already.

Priestley's dead. That only leaves me.'

'You're a target, Vanner,' Westbrook said.

'No I'm not. My girlfriend is.'

The phone rang and Vanner picked it up. 'Ellie?'

'What do you want that's so important?'

'Do not go back to your flat tonight.'

'Why not?'

'Just don't. Wait for me at the end of your shift. Stay inside the hospital and I'll come for you. Do not leave without me. And do not go outside.'

'Aden, you're scaring me.'

'Good, then you'll stay inside.'

He put down the phone and looked at Robertson. 'Her name's Ellie Ross. She's a nurse at Barts. She's going to need a safe house.'

He drove to the hospital, watchful. He was early. Ellie not yet down. He stood in the foyer, wondering what exactly he was going to say to her. People moved about him, buying papers, sweets and chocolates. Visitors. Vanner saw a man coming out of the florists with a bouquet under his arm. He stared at the shop window, thought for a moment and then walked inside. The girl behind the counter smiled at him. He nodded briefly and looked about him. A stack of single roses wrapped in polythene with red bows on them stood in a bucket by his feet. Tightly curled buds, just beginning to flower. He felt the girl at his arm.

'Can I help you?' she asked him.

He looked round at her, muttered something about waiting for someone and looked again at the roses.

'Visiting?'

'What?'

'Are you visiting someone?'

He shook his head, glanced at his watch then looked out into the foyer once more. 'I'm waiting for a nurse,' he said.

'Oh.' Again she smiled. 'Roses are very nice.'

He looked at her, grinned and looked at the floor.

'Special is she?'

He made a face.

'Course she is.' The girl lifted a single rose from the bucket and held it out to him. 'Make her feel special,' she said.

He had never bought roses. The only time he could recall being in a florist's was when he bought a wreath for his father's coffin. He glanced through the open doorway and saw Ellie walking down the corridor with another woman he did not recognise. 'Another time maybe,' he said, and walked outside.

Ellie spotted him and came over. Vanner looked at her across the fifty yards that separated them. The woman she was with was a little older, dark hair, lots of make-up. Ellie said her goodbyes, the woman glanced at him briefly and then went outside. Ellie came up to him.

'Who was that?' he asked her.

'Anne,' she said. 'Just a cleaner. I have my tea with her now and then.'

Vanner nodded.

'What is it, Aden? What's going on?'

He took her arm and led her out to the car, gaze shifting across the faces of those coming into the hospital entrance. An ambulance pulled past them and they waited before walking up to his car. He had parked it on double yellow lines, the Met warrant book stuffed against the windscreen.

He drove, Ellie sitting next to him, her coat over the back seat. 'How come you went home last night?' He glanced briefly at her as he said it.

She stared through the windscreen. 'I don't know. Missed my own space I guess.' She touched his arm. 'What's going on, Aden? Why all the fuss?'

'I'll tell you when we get home.'

He parked outside his house and glanced briefly at the scaffolded building still being renovated across the street. The workmen were all but finished now and soon the poles would come down. He looked up and down the road for cars that shouldn't be there.

Inside there was a message to phone George Webb. Vanner paged him while Ellie made coffee. Webb called him straight back.

'Got her?'

'Yes.'

'Good. Safe house is ready. How'd you want to play it?'

'Give me the address. I haven't told her yet.'

Webb was quiet. 'Better if somebody else took her, Guv. Bring her in and we'll sort it from there.'

'You got a PROT set up?'

'On standby.'

'Good is he?'

'They're all good, Guv'nor.'

Vanner thought for a moment. Ellie came up from the kitchen with two mugs of coffee. 'I'll bell you back in a little while. She's safe with me for the time being.'

'Don't leave it too long.'

Vanner put down the phone and went through to the lounge. She was standing in front of the window, one arm cupped round her waist, staring out into darkness.

'Come away from the window, Elle.'

She looked round sharply at him. 'Why?'

'Just do it. Please.' He moved beyond her and pulled the curtains. She sat down in the chair against the far wall. Vanner sipped coffee and lit a cigarette.

'What's going on?' Her face was fearful. For a moment he did not look at her.

'There's something going down,' he said after a moment. 'It's a long story and I'm afraid it might involve you.'

'Involve me? You're not making any sense, Aden.'

He held up his hand. 'Bear with me. Question of where to start.'

She looked irritated. 'Why don't you try the beginning?'

Vanner sat back, drew on his cigarette and exhaled. 'You know I was a soldier,' he said.

She nodded. 'A long time ago.'

'A very long time ago.' He looked at the floor, remembering, a dark street, a ford full of water with raindrops caressing the surface. He swallowed coffee and looked up at her. 'I served time in Northern Ireland. Captain. Left in 1984, resigned my commission and joined the job.'

'I know all that.'

He nodded. 'For the few months before I came out I was an intelligence officer assigned to RUC Special Branch. One night . . .' He tailed off, drank more coffee and went on. 'One night we were out. Five of us, four police officers and me. That was how we did it. Always an army presence on an intelligence job.'

'Armed?'

He looked up at her. 'Yes. I was always armed over there.'

Ellie's face was still. She sat upright in the chair, hands cupping the mug in her lap. 'Go on,' she said.

'We were after a particular target. IRA man, working with a cell in South Armagh. We knew he was responsible for at least three deaths and we had word that he was about to go active again.'

'How did you know that?'

'Doesn't matter. We know things. We get to know things. Information, intelligence gathering. That's how wars are fought.'

'What happened?'

Vanner sighed. 'This man. We came upon him or rather he came upon us at a place called Brindley Cross. It was raining. We were parked by a ford in the road – bottom of a hill.'

She was staring at him now. 'What happened?'

'He broke a roadblock. We shot him.'

She chewed her lip and watched him. 'Who shot him?'

'We did.'

'Who exactly?'

'I don't remember.'

'Yes you do. Who shot him, Aden?'

'What does it matter, Ellie?'

She was bug-eyed now, face set very hard. 'It matters to me.'

Vanner could not look at her.

'He was unarmed wasn't he?'

'As it turned out, yes.' He looked away from her. 'We weren't to know.' He looked up again. 'In those situations you don't take any chances.'

'What was his name, Aden?'

'Quinlon,' he said. 'His name was Thomas Quinlon.'

Tommy. Anne's words from the hospital. Ellie was shaking. 'What's this got to do with me?'

Vanner told her then, everything about Eilish McCauley and James and the deaths of David Quigley and Jessica Turner. 'That crippled guy we met in Yorkshire. He was part of the squad. The killer went looking for him but he was all blown up already.'

Ellie still stared at him. 'Who killed Quinlon, Aden?'

'It doesn't matter.'

'You did didn't you?'

He looked at the fireplace, then deep in her eyes. 'No, Ellie. I didn't.'

Then she hugged herself. Vanner made to get up but she held up a palm as if to keep him away. 'I'm all right.' She gathered herself. 'So this James is after me now?'

'I think so. Just before I phoned you he phoned me on my mobile. God knows how he got the number.'

Ellie stood up and walked toward the window. She checked herself and looked at him. 'He dresses up as a woman?'

Vanner nodded. 'We think he took his sister's clothes the night he shot Jessica Turner.'

'Why does he dress as a woman?'

'He was in love with Quinlon. Quinlon was sleeping with his sister.' He moved his shoulders. 'I don't know, Elle. Maybe in some warped way being a woman makes him acceptable to Quinlon.'

Ellie sat down again. 'Aden, there's something I've got to tell you.'

'What?'

'There's a woman at the hospital. Anne.' Her eyes widened then. 'Jesus, you saw her.'

Vanner bunched his eyes. 'The cleaner?'

She nodded. 'She told me her lover, boyfriend whatever, was shot by policemen in Northern Ireland.'

Vanner stared hard at her.

'She was with me,' Ellie went on, 'once when you paged me. Your mobile number flashed up on the screen.'

Vanner stared at the wall. Black hair. Too much make-up. 'How long's she been working there?'

'A month or so.' She made an open-handed gesture. 'She just turned up one day. Cleaners come and go so much.'

'Employed by the hospital?'

She shook her head. 'That was all contracted out ages ago.' She bit her lip then, blinked hard and tears filled her eyes.

Vanner stood up, went over to her and crouched down in front of her. 'Look,' he said. 'I know this is bad, really bad.' He took her hands, but they remained limp in his grip. 'Can you handle it?'

'What do I have to do?'

'Nothing. But you can't stay here. He phoned me, Elle. He

told me I'd *feel his pain*. That means he's after you. He shot Jessica in the hope that Ray Kinane would feel his pain, but Ray didn't come forward. He needs the visibility of it. He's waited a long time. He's grown up with this.'

'You mean he wants to kill me?' Her eyes filled with tears then, no sound, just rolling over her cheeks. Vanner brushed them away.

'I've arranged for you to go to a safe house,' he said quietly. 'That's a police premises where you'll be looked after and guarded by a Close Protection Officer.'

Her eyes balled again and she squeezed his hands with hers.

'They're the best, love. Trained. But you'll have to stay inside.'

'A prisoner.'

'Safe, Elle. Just until we get him.'

'Will you kill him?'

He shook his head. 'We'll arrest him. The Anti-Terrorist Branch are dealing with it. They do it all the time. They're very very good at it.'

She looked at him then. 'If he can't get to me he'll go after you, Aden.'

'Probably.'

'What're you going to do?'

'I don't know yet. But you don't have to worry. I've been here before, Elle. Just stay safe until this is over.'

She pushed him away then, gently, and stood up. She hugged herself once more. 'I'm not sure I want a life like this, Aden. Guns and killing and everything. I'm only twenty-five. I want a normal life.'

And then he knew he was losing her. He bit down on his lip and stood up. 'I know,' he said. 'It's all right.'

In the hall he stood a moment by the phone, one hand fisted, knuckles pressing into the wall. He phoned George Webb. 'I'm going to bring her to the Yard now. You can sort it from there.'

At Scotland Yard they were met by a Special Branch Close Protection officer and a WPC. They took Ellie away in an unmarked car. Vanner watched them pull onto Dacre Street. Webb was at his side.

'Hard on her.'
'She's not that tough, George.'
'Who is?'
Vanner looked at him then and they took the lift to the fifteenth floor. 'I want to be armed,' Vanner said.
Webb stroked his moustache. 'They won't go for that.'
'I've got my ticket.'
'You know the game, Guv. They won't allow it.'
Vanner scowled at the floor. 'What's happening with Eilish?'
'Released. Back home with her kids. We've set up an OP over the road and we're wired into the phone. If her brother contacts her we'll know.'
'She knows she's clear then.'
Webb nodded.

Upstairs Westbrook and Robertson met them. 'Everything sorted?' Robertson asked.
Vanner nodded.
'Go home, Vanner. Get some rest. We'll figure out what we can do in the morning.'
Vanner looked at him. 'As soon as he knows he can't get to her he'll come after me, Sir.'
'Probably.'
'I'm up for it. I want to be a target.'
'I'm speaking to SO19, Vanner. We'll talk about it tomorrow.'

Vanner went home to his empty house and sat in the bedroom with the light off and Ellie's chemise in his hands.
His mobile rang at three o'clock in the morning. He was dreaming of fishing with his father when he was a child. Ellie was there, watching their boat from the bank. Vanner woke up feeling the ringing inside his skull. He switched on the light and held the phone to his ear.
'*You* are going to feel my pain.'
Vanner sat up. 'Who is it – Anne or James? Who're you tonight, you faggot?'
Silence. Breathing. 'She's safe, James. No-one's going to feel any pain but you.'
'I'm coming for you.'
'Good.'

'You won't know where and you won't know when, but I'm going to kill you, Vanner.'

'Look forward to it.' Vanner switched off the phone.

Twenty

Vanner was on the fifteenth floor at eight o'clock the following morning. He had not gone back to sleep after James McCauley telephoned him. Robertson and Webb were on their way in, Westbrook was at his desk in the DCI's room.

'He phoned me,' Vanner said. 'In the middle of the night. Little bastard's enjoying himself.'

'Say the same thing?'

'That and the fact that he's coming after me.'

Westbrook grinned at him. 'Say when and where did he?'

They got coffee and waited till Robertson arrived. He came into the DCI's office and sat down. 'Ellie Ross is in a safe house,' he told Vanner. 'We use a couple of flats. She's got A squad protection round the clock.'

'Where?'

'Better you don't know.'

'Can I talk to her?'

'She can call you.'

Vanner looked at the silent phone on his belt. He sat back and folded his arms. Westbrook told Robertson about Vanner's midnight phonecall.

'I want to be visible,' Vanner said. 'As visible as I can be.'

Robertson nodded. 'I'll square it with Special Branch to assign two PROT's to you. Twelve-hour shifts. They're used to it.'

Vanner looked him in the eye. 'I'd rather have a gun, Sir.'

Robertson grinned. 'I'm sure you would.'

'I've got my pink ticket.'

Robertson shook his head. 'No-one would sanction it, Vanner. Who's going to take responsibility for you bearing firearms twenty-four hours a day. I certainly wouldn't.'

Vanner finished his coffee and tossed the plastic cup in the bin. 'You mean I have to sleep with them?'

'Not in the same bed,' Westbrook said.

Webb came in. 'Sorry I'm late,' he said. 'Had to check something.' He grinned at Vanner, standing with his hands on his hips. 'You okay, Guv?'

Vanner told him about the phonecall.

'Itchy then. You tell him your bird was away?'

'Yes.'

Webb nodded and looked at the senior officers. 'PROT then.'

'Yeah.' Westbrook stood up. 'I'll wander upstairs. Get somebody allocated.'

'What about an SFO team?' Webb said.

'On standby. Fully briefed. If it comes to it they'll work out a rolling plot, but we're more likely to need the Gunships.'

'Are they up to speed?'

'I've spoken to their Skipper and briefed them as much as I can,' Westbrook said. 'But we don't know who we're looking for. A man dressed as a woman.'

Vanner stood up. 'I'm going back to work,' he said. 'I've got a crack team to nail.'

'Wait till the PROT's sorted out.'

Vanner shook his head. 'I'm going to drive from here to Wembley. I'll be fine.'

Robertson looked at Westbrook. 'Get SB to send their man to Campbell Row.'

Vanner was watchful all the way across London, particularly at lights and zebra crossings. Jimmy Crack met him at the Drug Squad office.

'Rafter's girl's coming home,' he said. 'And I've got Pretty Boy at the wash house.'

'What about the Daddy?'

Jimmy shook his head. 'Eilish was our best bet there. You know I'd never have figured she'd give up her brother.'

Vanner lit a cigarette. 'She had no idea we knew she was alibi'd did she. As far as she was concerned the only person who could save her was Stepper-Nap and that wasn't about to happen. Thirty years concentrates the mind, Jim. Especially when you've got two young girls to think about.'

Jimmy nodded. 'Paddington Green doesn't help. Like a world all of its own.'

'Timeless,' Vanner said. He sat back and rested the sole of

his foot against the edge of the desk.

'What's happening with you, Guv?'

Vanner told him that James McCauley was looking for him. He told him that Ellie was safe but he was going on with his work as normal. 'They've assigned me a PROT,' he said. 'He'll be here any minute.'

'So you've got a shadow.'

Vanner made a face. 'At least he's armed, Jim.'

The phone rang and Vanner picked it up. 'Vanner.'

'Morrison, Vanner. I want to see you in Hendon.'

Vanner let go a breath. 'Sir, I've only just got here and there's a pile of papers to sort.'

'I don't care. Robertson's just been on the phone from SO13. He told me what's going on. You're under my command, Vanner, in my division. Your actions might jeopardise other officers.'

'I can work on my own.'

'Don't be ridiculous. Just get yourself over here.'

Vanner squeezed the phone a little more tightly. 'I've got a PROT on his way here, Sir.'

Morrison went quiet. 'As soon as he gets there then.'

Vanner put down the phone and gestured with his middle finger. 'You should've seen his face, Jimmy; Morrison, when I told SO13 that I wanted positive vetting. He still doesn't know what this is about.'

'What is it about, Guv?'

Vanner slowly shook his head. 'Get me some fresh coffee eh. Then brief me on Rafter's girl.'

The Close Protection officer arrived and sat with Vanner in his office while Jimmy updated him on the movements of the Brit-Boy posse. The PROT's name was Michael Wilson. He was Vanner's height, tall and thin, a Special Branch DI. He sat in the chair under the window while Vanner and Jimmy talked. 'I want to view the wash-house tapes,' Vanner said, 'and I want to lean on Eilish.'

Jimmy looked unsure. 'That a good idea, Guv?'

'Yes. She might give us something on Stepper and more importantly it might flush out her brother.' He squinted at Wilson. 'You up to speed on this?'

Wilson nodded.

'What are you carrying?'

Wilson eased his jacket back to reveal a brown leather shoulder holster.

'Glock,' Vanner said. 'Good weapon. Light.'

Wilson nodded.

Jimmy Crack stood up. 'You want to view the wash-house tapes now, Guv?'

Vanner shook his head. 'No, I'd better go and see Morrison.'

He drove, the PROT next to him watching every car that passed them, eyes all over the road. 'Black wig,' he said.

'That's been the form so far.'

'I knew David Quigley,' Wilson said quietly.

Vanner glanced at him and drove on. 'Dave was a good copper.'

'One of the best,' Wilson smiled at him. 'This might get a bit personal.'

Morrison was in his office. Vanner saw Ryan in the corridor downstairs, chatting to a uniformed WPC.

'Leave the plonks alone, Slippery,' Vanner muttered as he passed him. 'They don't know where you've been.'

He knocked on Morrison's door and went in. Wilson went with him. Morrison was behind his desk, blotting ink on a page. He looked up and took off his half-rimmed spectacles. 'Special Branch?' he said to Wilson.

Wilson nodded.

Morrison flicked at the door with his glasses. 'Wait outside.'

Wilson hesitated.

'Who's going to have a go at him here? Go on. Wait outside.'

When he was gone Morrison gestured for Vanner to sit down. Vanner sat, looked at him and crossed his ankle on his knee. They regarded one another warily, like two old-time alley cats from the street. Morrison spoke first.

'I'm not sure I want it like this, Vanner.'

'Think I should sit it out at home do you?'

'The thought had occurred to me. You're putting people at risk.'

'I'm flushing out a killer.'

'Yes you are aren't you.' Morrison cocked his head at him. 'Eaman Farrell and Cahal Barron and Brindley Cross all over again. I knew it wouldn't rest, Vanner. Those things never do.'

Vanner folded his arms.

'You noticed how the past comes back to haunt you? How many lives have you trodden on? I can count half a dozen at least.'

Vanner sat forward then and when he spoke his voice was very cold. 'Has this conversation got any bearing on what I'm doing, Sir? Because if it hasn't I've got things to do.'

'Who shot him, Vanner?' Morrison rested both elbows on the table and clasped his hands together. 'Who killed Thomas Quinlon?'

Vanner started to get up.

'Sit down.'

'I don't think so.'

'Sit down, Vanner.' Morrison's eyes smarted like green fire. 'I'm your senior officer, Vanner. You'll sit there as long as I want you to.'

Slowly Vanner sat.

'You shot him didn't you.'

Vanner did not reply.

'Come on. You can tell me now.'

'Anything else, Sir?'

Morrison sat upright, pushing his weight back in the chair, hands pressed against the edge of the desk. 'Liability. I always said it. First time you get a woman who cares about you you put her life in jeopardy.'

Vanner stood up then. 'You want to watch your diet, Sir. All that bile's not good for you.'

'Vanner.' Morrison stopped him. 'You wearing a vest?'

'Of course I'm wearing a vest.' He turned then and went out. Wilson got up from where he was sitting on a chair in the corridor. Vanner ignored him, turned to his right and trotted down the stairs.

'Where to now?' Wilson asked as they got back in the car.

'Willesden,' Vanner said. 'I want to see the sister.'

He phoned Webb on the line they had opened. 'Anything from the phone tap at the sister's?' he asked.

'Not a whisper.'

'What about Ellie – she okay?'

'So far. She hasn't called you?'

'No.'

'Free access to the phone, Guv.'

'You trying to tell me something?'

Vanner switched off the phone and plugged it into the cigarette lighter to re-charge it. Then he drove down through Cricklewood, turning off at Chiselle Road toward Willesden. He phoned Jimmy Crack on his mobile. Jimmy said he would meet him at Eilish McCauley's.

They parked in the slip road by the park with no sign of Jimmy Crack. Vanner wound his window down and lit a cigarette. Wilson got out of the car and checked the immediate vicinity. A few minutes later Jimmy drove up and parked behind them. He climbed into the back of Vanner's car.

'Had word from Sandra, Guv.'

'Who's Sandra?' Vanner glanced at him in the rear-view mirror.

'Snout who housed Young Young for us. Eilish is out of the game as far as the posse's concerned. Stepper knows her gaff was turned over.'

Vanner leaned his elbow on the windowsill, the sun peeking from behind the clouds, warming his face. He let smoke drift from his nostrils. 'Wonder how she'll fare with just her dole cheque for company.'

Jimmy looked across the road toward the brown, pebble-dashed house. 'Got to play mother now.'

Vanner looked back at him. 'I'm going over, see if I can't wind her up a little bit.'

They all got out. Vanner led the way across the main road and up past the school.

'She doesn't know about the photos?' Jimmy said.

Vanner shook his head. 'All she knows is SO13 let her go. She's grateful enough for that.'

'Why're we going round?' Jimmy asked.

'I want to look in her wardrobe. Find out what baby brother is wearing.'

He rang the bell, Wilson standing between him and the road, watching. Nobody answered. Vanner rang again and saw a figure coming down the stairs through the glass in the door. Moments later Eilish stared in his face. Spittle seemed to form on her lip. 'What do you want?'

'I want to talk to you.'

'Well you can't.'

Vanner put his foot in the door so she could not close it. 'I can,' he said, 'and I will.'

Inside, she stood in the lounge staring at him. She eyed Wilson and Jimmy then looked back at Vanner. 'Thought you were bloody clever in Belfast didn't you.'

'Shut up, Eilish. What clothes are missing from your wardrobe?'

She stared at him. 'You want me to take them out one by one, lay them on the floor?'

'Let's just go and look.'

She led the way reluctantly upstairs and into her bedroom. The bed was unmade and she dragged the covers over the rumpled mess of the sheet. Vanner indicated the wardrobe.

'Take a look,' he said, 'and no bullshit, Eilish.'

She opened the doors wide and stared at the clothes, bulging at her from the hangers.

'I don't know.' She placed one hand on her hip.

'Look,' Vanner said.

She looked, thumbing through the clothes and back again. 'Black jeans,' she said.

'He can get in them?'

'He's small.' She looked at him. 'You've seen him.' She looked back at the clothes. 'Blue sweat top and a shirt. White one with little flowers on it. And he's got my red jacket.'

Downstairs the phone rang. Vanner stared at Eilish. 'If that's him I want to know.'

She picked up the phone. Jimmy and Wilson moved past her. Vanner sat on the stairs.

'Hello,' she said.

'What did you tell them, Eilish. And why are they in the house?'

Eilish stiffened. 'What d'you mean?'

Vanner went very still, watching her, face away from him, leaning against the wall.

'What did you tell them, Eilish? How come they're looking for me?'

'I didn't tell them anything.' She steeled herself. 'But Tommy's dead, Jamie.'

'I know he's dead, you bitch. All these years he's been dead and you did nothing about it.'

She sighed. 'What did you want me to do?'

'Something. Anything. You sent him out to them. Why didn't you let him stay?'

'Jamie . . .'

'Just get them out of the house.' The phone went dead and Eilish settled the receiver.

Vanner's mobile rang.

'Webb, Guv. He's just phoned the house.'

'I know. I'm here.'

'He knows you're there. That means he can see you.'

Vanner stared at Wilson. 'Outside. Now.'

Wilson was at the front door. He opened it a fraction. Vanner looked at Eilish. 'Where's the nearest phone box?'

'I don't know.'

'Think?'

'Up the street. The other side of the road.'

Vanner was on his feet, pushing past Wilson at the door. He looked up the street. Wilson got to him, hand on his arm. Vanner looked left and right, then spotted the phone box further up on the left hand side of the road. He could see that it was empty.

He phoned Webb from the car. 'Missed him.'

'Cheeky bastard isn't he.'

'Some of her clothes are missing. Red jacket, black jeans, and a blue sweatshirt. You want to relay that to Old Street?'

'Will do. Where you going now?'

'I don't know,' Vanner said. 'But I want this bastard.'

'Take it easy, Guv. He'll give you the runaround. You'll broke up his party remember?

Vanner went back to the Drug Squad office and watched the video tapes from the wash house. At seven o'clock he drove home. Wilson had a drink with him across the road while he waited for his relief to arrive. Vanner did not relish the thought of a night with a stranger in his house.

Three days, four days, five and nothing. Ellie phoned him once, ice in her voice as she spoke to him. Vanner was helpless. He could feel her drifting away from him.

'What can I say, Elle? At least you're safe.'

'Safe. I'm a prisoner and I haven't even done anything.'

He said nothing. There was nothing he could say.

'Talk to me, Aden. You got me into this.'

'It'll soon be over.'

'You're right,' she said. 'Over.'

On the eighth day, Monday, late in the afternoon he was driving with Wilson towards the West End, the street lights casting a musty glow over the gloom of rain-washed tarmac. Two cars behind them a black cab trundled with a single occupant in the back.

James had not phoned his sister again. Ellie had not phoned him. Vanner pulled over to the side of the road and looked at Wilson. 'Going to get cigarettes,' he said. Wilson looked at the double yellow lines. 'Parking here are you?'

'I'm Old Bill. I can park where the hell I like.' Vanner got out of the car.

The cab pulled over and a woman stepped out, paid the driver and moved towards the entrance to the tube station.

Vanner bought a packet of Marlboro and some matches. When he came out of the shop a woman moved towards him from the entrance to the tube station, black jeans and red jacket. For a moment he stared at her. Black hair and too much make-up, hand in a zip-up bag off her shoulder.

Wilson stepped in front of him, reaching into his jacket for his weapon. He had no time to draw it. The woman pulled a short black pistol and fired. Wilson crumpled like sack on the pavement. People screamed. Vanner stood for a moment, waiting for more shots, unarmed, helpless. For a second the woman stared at him, then she was gone, disappearing inside the tube station. Vanner dropped to one knee, fumbling for his phone. Wilson was breathing heavily, holding his leg at the thigh. Blood jerked in little strings from his fingers.

'Vanner,' he said as the phone was answered. 'High Street Kensington, outside the tube station. PROT down, leg wound. Target. Black jeans, red jacket. Black wig. Ran into the station. Get me an ambulance. Now.'

He dropped the phone onto the pavement, shouting at the crowd of shoppers to move back and give Wilson some room. Wilson lay on the ground as rain fell on him, head resting against a shop window. Blood covered his hand now, forming a dark pool on the concrete. Vanner checked the wound. 'Just the leg?'

'Yeah.'

'You sure?'

'Yes. Jesus.' Wilson's head rolled against the glass, eyes balling, colour draining from his face. Vanner pulled out his handkerchief and pressed it against the wound. Wilson cried out with the pain.

In the offices of the Anti-Terrorist Branch Webb was on the phone to Old Street. He got Graves. 'Operation Zero hour. Gone live. PROT's been hit, Vanner's with him. Target got away. Last seen entering High Street Kensington tube station. We've got uniforms on the move and the BTP's been informed.

'Right, we'll roll. Any ideas where we might put him to bed?'

'He might go to his sister's but I doubt it. Keep a rolling plot till we have a location. We've got street camera control on the sixteenth floor. Best place for your Scene Commander.'

Webb put down the phone and went with DCI Westbrook up to the sixteenth floor. At the control desk he flicked on the radio with which he could speak to any officer's back to back anywhere in the city.

'All officers BH, BS, PH, PP. This is Sergeant George Webb SO13 Reserve. We have a terrorist suspect last seen entering High Street Kensington tube station. Armed. Female. ICI wearing black jeans, red jacket. Approach with caution. All sightings report Code 33 – 40 channel.'

He put down the set and looked over at Westbrook who was punching the keys of the computer which gave him control of every traffic camera in the city.

The ambulance bumped up onto the kerb and Vanner moved away from Wilson. He was losing blood fast. The wound was close to the groin, and the level of blood told him a main artery had been severed. He had done his best to stop it but Wilson was growing weaker. The paramedics jumped out, green suits, plastic cases in their hands. Vanner opened his warrant card and clipped it onto his jacket pocket.

'Gunshot,' he told the paramedic as he knelt beside Wilson. 'Hit in the leg close to the groin.' He stopped talking. Seventy per cent of all groin shots were fatal.

He stood back as the paramedics began to work. Traffic had almost stopped on the street with rubber neckers. The pavement crawled with onlookers. He saw one Japanese man with a video camera. His mobile rang and he flipped it open.

'Vanner.'

'Webb, Guv. What's happening?'

'Ambulance is here. Top of the thigh, Webby. Almost the groin, pissing blood like there's no tomorrow.'

'SFO's on standby.'

'Lot of fucking use. We don't know where he is.'

'How'd he get to you?'

'I don't know. Must've followed us from Wembley. Cab maybe. Whatever.'

'Description's out to every copper on the manor. Stay with Wilson. Go with him in the ambulance. Safest place for you.'

Vanner looked down at the stretcher levelled in the puddles with the blankets and the straps thrown back. The two paramedics were lifting Wilson onto it. When he was laid out they covered him with blankets and strapped him. The amateur cameraman stepped closer. Vanner moved in front of him, up-ending his camera with a palm. 'One more step and I'll push that through your face.'

Wilson was in the ambulance. Vanner climbed in beside him and the driver closed the doors. Seconds later they were threading through the traffic, with all sirens blaring.

'Where we going?' Vanner asked the paramedic.

'Chelsea Royal. Straight down Sloane Street.' The paramedic had the straps off Wilson and was easing his clothing from him. His hand came up against the shoulder holster and he pulled out the gun.

'Diplomatic protection,' Vanner told him.

'I don't want to know. Here. You look after it.'

Vanner took the Glock, held it, fingers tightening about the handle. He slipped it into his pocket.

He phoned Webb. 'What's happening?'

'SFO rolling. Scene Commander's just arrived. We're covering every traffic light in the city.'

'We're going to Chelsea Royal.'

'Right.'

'I want to know when you find him.'

Vanner switched off the phone. They were almost at Sloane Square tube station when it rang again.

'Vanner.'

'Where are you, Vanner? I'm at Victoria station, waiting for you.' The phone went dead.

Vanner shifted up the cramped aisle to the driver. 'Stop the van.'

'What?'

'Stop it, I have to get out.'

The driver pulled over and Vanner opened the back doors. He looked at Wilson, oxygen mask across his face, very blue in the lips.

Rain fell on his head, harsh heavy spots that slapped against his scalp. He ducked inside the tube station and called Webb. Downstairs he could hear the thunder of a train arriving.

'Vanner. Target just called me. He's at Victoria station. Where's the SFO?'

'Wait a minute.' Webb put his hand over the phone then spoke in his ear once more.

'Miles away. We sent them to Eilish's.'

'Webb, listen to me. Tell the Guv'nors. I'm instantly armed. Paramedic gave me Wilson's Glock to look after.'

Webb was quiet for a moment.

'Log it,' Vanner said. 'Instant arming.'

'Will do.'

'I'm in Sloane Square tube. Train's coming. I'll be in Victoria in two minutes.'

He raced to the bottom of the steps and jumped the eastbound train just as the doors were closing.

On the fifteenth floor Webb spoke to Graves, the Scene Commander from SO19.

'Victoria. Target just called Vanner. He's at the station.'

From where he sat, Westbrook looked sideways at him.

'Vanner's armed,' Webb said. 'Got Wilson's Glock. He'll be there in two or three minutes.'

Graves stroked his jaw. 'SFO's off the patch,' he said. 'Give me the radio.' He narrowed his eyes as he spoke into the handset. 'This is Bronze Commander Graves – SO19. All Trojans respond. 511 location?'

The radio crackled and a thin voice came over the air waves. 'Bronze Commander from Trojan 511 – location Shaftesbury Ave.'

'Trojan 541 respond.'

The call came back. '541 stationary. Lambeth.'

'Operation 13, armed terrorist. Rendezvous Point – Victoria station. Respond and contain. Bronze Commander out.' He turned to Westbrook. 'Nearest nick?'

'Belgravia.'

'Get me the duty DI.'

Webb was on another phone speaking to Jack Swann downstairs. 'Sterile car, Jack. Victoria station. Sterile arrest team. Now.'

'Moving,' Swann said in his ear.

Vanner jumped off the tube train, pushing passengers out of the way; a white skinheaded youth stepped into his path.

'Don't.' Vanner pushed him against the wall and sprinted along the tunnel. He came to the first set of escalators and raced up them, brushing people aside. A briefcase blocked his ascent and he kicked it against its owner's legs. Then he was running again, the second set of stairs, up the middle flight, three steps at a time. He got to the main entrance hall and paused.

He stood for a moment, breathing hard, the gun cold in his grip, hand in the pocket of his jacket. With sharp, experienced eyes he scanned the hallway for a black-haired woman in a red jacket. No-one. Nothing. He moved out into the open, walking slowly, eyes everywhere, on everyone's face. Nothing. He stood a moment and paused again. Then he looked left to the main entrance which was humming with people as the rush hour began. Taxis hissing diesel fumes, buses pulling in and out of the coach station. He looked at his watch. Thirty-five minutes since Wilson was shot.

Again he looked about him, eyes on stalks. No-one. He moved to the main entrance. People bunched to get out, long-distance travellers just in from the airports pushing trolleys loaded with luggage.

Outside the rain fell in grey sheets, washing across buildings and traffic and people. Vanner stepped to the edge of the pavement and stared across at the bus terminal. On the far side in front of the office building taxis pulled up. His eyes fixed on a black-haired woman handing money over the seat. He tensed, gun still in his pocket and watched as she climbed out on the far side of the cab. Red jacket. Rain fell on black hair. Vanner took out his gun.

Forty feet away from him. Buses moved into his line of vision, blocked it then passed. People bumping behind him, the noise of trolleys crashing together as they were discarded. People climbing into cabs to escape the rain. Across the road the woman opened her black shoulder bag. Vanner lifted the gun. For a moment she looked up and their eyes met. Thirty yards. Vanner could hear nothing save the blood in his ears. He could smell sweat and diesel and then the traffic broke in.

'Armed police,' he bellowed.

She looked at him, beyond him, at him again. People stepped back from him. A bus driver thumped his horn which blared out through the rain. Black bag, red coat, black hair. Vanner tensed, lifting the gun, two hands now, finger in the trigger guard, blood cold in his veins.

Still her hand was in her bag, fumbling. Traffic noise. Had she heard his shout? Their eyes locked.

'Armed police. You in the red. Stand still.' Vanner shouted again and as he did so a trolley crashed into the rack behind him. The woman drew something black and slim from her bag. Vanner tensed and fired.

Three shots. She buckled, body flicking back in sharp, ragged movements. Sirens in his ears. For a moment she stared at him. Women screaming. Men shouting. Only her eyes on his. She fell back, bag opening, the slim black weapon falling from her grip.

Vanner stepped across the road and as he did so a feeling of dread stilled the breath in his lungs. He got closer, twenty feet, fifteen, ten. Out of the corner of his eye he saw a blue light flashing.

511 Trojan jerked to a halt and the three officers got out. Three 9mm pistols. Two MP5 carbines.

The driver was on the radio. He saw Vanner with a gun and a body lying on the road by the bus stop. People milled everywhere. Cars were arriving from all sides. The wail of sirens filled the air.

An armed officer moved towards Vanner from the car, short black rifle extended like part of his arm.

'Armed police. Stand still.'

Vanner heard him. He looked again at the woman. Not James

McCauley. No gun, just a large open handbag and a small leather encased umbrella, the kind that springs open at the press of a button.

He half-turned toward the officer.

'Stand still.' The command split the air. People stared at him. He half-turned again.

'Do not look at me.'

'I'm D . . .'

'Do not look at me.' The officer was ten feet from him now. Vanner could almost smell the adrenaline through the rain.

'Keep your hands away from your body and look straight ahead of you. Do not move. Do not turn around. If you look at me I will shoot you.'

Vanner bit down on his lip, then turned his head to his left and stared into the eyes of a young, dark-haired man wearing black jeans and a sweatshirt on inside out. He carried a bag over his shoulder. His face was reddened and his hair tousled and as he stared Vanner realised he was smiling.

'Keep your hands away from your body.' The command came again.

Slowly, with no jerky movement, Vanner extended his arms at his sides, the right one heavy with the gun. He was still looking to his left and stared deep into the dark eyes of James McCauley. Not a woman, No wig now. No red jacket, only short dark hair and a smile creasing his lips. The woman he had shot was an innocent. *Feel my pain.* The words rang in his head.

'Now.' The ARV man was speaking again. Vanner could do nothing. Say nothing. Nothing he said would make any difference. He was an armed man and there was a woman bleeding to death on the kerbside. The crowd grew larger, easing away from him like the leper he had become.

'Do exactly as I tell you. Do it only when I tell you. Do not move sharply and do not look at me. Keep your hands well away from your body.'

Vanner lifted his arms higher still and stared at James McCauley. McCauley stared at him. From the corner of his left eye he could see a second ARV with officers training their weapons on him.

'Now.' The officer behind him was talking again. 'Right leg. Kneel down slowly.'

Vanner did as he was commanded.
'Place the gun on the ground. Place it. Do not throw it.'
Vanner put down the gun. James McCauley looked as though he was laughing. Vanner's gaze twisted to the woman he had shot. Another ARV officer was on one knee with a first-aid kit in his hands. Vanner saw a box of tampons lying open, spilled from her handbag. The officer tore the paper off one with his teeth and plugged the hole in her chest. Vanner knew the pad would expand and soak up the blood.
'Stand up.' The armed officer was talking to him again.
He stood.
'Now. Step away from the gun.'
Vanner stepped back.
George Webb got out of his car on the other side of the bus terminal for Heathrow and quickly took in the scene. He saw two ARVs and he saw Vanner in front of him. An ARV man was tending an injured woman before him.
Vanner spotted him, opened his mouth to call out and closed it again. The ARV officer was moving closer to him. Webb caught his eye and Vanner flicked his gaze towards McCauley, who was watching it all with his arms folded, black bag hanging from his shoulder. Webb frowned. Vanner flicked his eyes again and Webb tried to follow them.
'Right leg again,' the ARV man commanded. 'Kneel down.'
Vanner hesitated.
'Do it.'
He dropped to one knee. Webb was scanning the crowd. He saw James McCauley in profile.
'Left leg. Kneel down.'
Vanner did as he was asked, puddles under his jeans, the cold soaking into his flesh.
'Now. Fall forward onto your palms and lie flat.'
Vanner looked one last time at Webb, then fell forward, face twisted to his left. Now James McCauley was looking straight down at him.
He could feel the weight of the people. Pressmen and amateur photographers and tourists getting a taste of London they never dreamed they would see.
Vanner thought of Ellie in the safe house. He stared at McCauley's face. He could feel the armed officer right behind him now. George Webb was moving through the crowd.

'Place your hand, right palm upward into the middle of your back.' The command came, less loud now, but close and chilled, clipped tones, the sort of voice you listened to.

Vanner moved his arm and stared into McCauley's face. McCauley smiled down at him. There was perhaps twenty feet between them.

'Left hand, palm upward into the small of your back.'

Vanner did as he was asked.

'Now, interlock your fingers.'

Vanner entwined them and then felt a knee in his neck. One hand gripped both of his, imprisoning him completely. He wondered how many times he had completed the procedure himself in his days with D11. He felt the rush of blood as plastic handcuffs secured him.

George Webb moved towards the second ARV where the Duty DI from Belgravia had assumed command. Webb took his warrant card out of his pocket and flipped it open over the breast pocket of his jacket. He stepped up to the driver of the Armed Response Vehicle.

'Detective Sergeant Webb,' he said. 'SO13 Reserve. Man in black jeans, blue sweat top and black bag.' He saw the driver glance, scan and see him. He looked back in his eyes. 'He's Provisional IRA, armed with a .62mm Tokarev. The man you've just detained is DI Vanner of 2 Area Drug Squad.'

The driver's face fell.

'Doesn't matter,' Webb went on. 'Nothing you can do about it now. Safest place for him is in the Trojan.'

He looked round then and saw McCauley moving away from the arrest scene towards the station entrance. He thought for a moment. 'Bronze Commander Graves,' he said. 'SFO Blue team is here somewhere. This is his operation.' McCauley was almost inside the station. 'Take this number down.' Webb gave the driver his mobile number. 'I'll keep the target under surveillance. Keep this phone line open.'

Twenty-One

Webb followed James McCauley into the station. McCauley walked briskly now, cutting his way through the crowds to the ticket office, where he fished in his pocket for money. Webb stood behind him, one person between them and watched as he bought his ticket. McCauley moved off again, bag across his shoulder, hand in one pocket and wandered to the information boards that hung above the concourse. He looked up at the departure information and then moved off in the direction of platforms 15-19. Webb's mobile rang.

'Hello?'

'Westbrook. What's happening?'

'I'm following McCauley. He's no longer in disguise, wig and make-up gone. Carrying a black bag. He's still armed.'

'Where's he going?'

'Don't know yet. He's heading for one of the platforms between 15 and 19.' Webb watched McCauley striding out ahead of him now. '18,' Webb said, then McCauley moved right. '19. He's boarding a train at platform 19.'

'Okay. Keep with him, Webby. We've got the SFO team on the way. Graves is here. He's with the BR people now. I'll let you know what we decide to do.'

Webb switched off his phone and followed McCauley onto the platform.

Vanner sat in the back of the first ARV. He rubbed his wrists and accepted the cigarette from the man who had secured him.

'Sorry about that, Sir,' the officer said.

Vanner stared ahead of him. 'You were doing your job. You saw a man with a gun.'

'Yeah.' The officer ducked out of the car again and spoke to the driver. Vanner was watching the paramedics lifting the prostrate form of the woman he had shot into the back of an ambulance. He wondered who she was, who her family were, whether she would live or die.

Westbrook came over to the car and looked in at him. 'You okay?'

Vanner did not reply, He sucked hard on his cigarette and exhaled stiffly. Then he looked at Westbrook. 'What's happening?'

'McCauley's on a train bound for the coast.'

Vanner looked forward again. 'It was raining,' he said. 'Noise. Traffic everywhere.' He looked into Westbrook's face. 'I shouted a warning. Twice. I shouted at her twice. She didn't listen, kept on inside her bag.'

Westbrook straightened. 'We're interviewing, Vanner. There's bound to be people who heard you.'

Vanner nodded grimly.

Sergeant Graves, the SO19 scene commander was at the British Rail Rendezvous Point he had set up, talking to the controllers of the station. He looked at his wristwatch. 'How long till the train leaves?'

'Three minutes.'

Graves nodded. 'Now many coaches?'

'Eleven.'

'Right.'

'Do you want us to delay it?'

Graves considered for a moment, then he picked up the phone and called Webb.

Webb was seated in a carriage three seats back from McCauley. They faced each other, both occupying seats on the aisle. The phone rang.

'Yes.'

'Graves. You got him?'

'Yep.'

'How crowded?'

'All the seats are taken.'

'Standing?'

'Not yet.'

'What carriage are you in?'

'Fourth from the front.'

'Good.'

'What're you going to do?'

'I'll let you know.'

Graves put the phone down and looked at the BR executives. 'Delay the train,' he said.

'How long?'

'Ten minutes. Tell them it's signals or something.' He stood up as a man in a black coverall suit came in. 'Blue team's here, Sir.'

'Good. Green?'

'Two minutes.'

Graves nodded. He walked across the office and looked at the layout of the track on the wall. 'First stop is Clapham Junction,' he said.

The BR man nodded.

'He's in the fourth coach from the front. I want you to wait ten minutes then roll the train out. I'm going to get my men to Clapham Junction. I may need you to stop the train on the tracks to give me more time. Can you do that?'

'We can.'

'Then do it.'

The BR man issued the orders. Graves went out to his men.

On the train Webb waited and watched McCauley sitting easily in the seat ahead of him. His eyes were closed, the bag held loosely across his knees. Webb wondered if he could move past him and take the bag. The gun would be in the bag. McCauley opened his eyes, looked at him and hunched the bag closer to his chest. Webb stared out the window.

Vanner got out of the car and walked over to Westbrook. 'What's going on?'

'SO19 deal now, Vanner. Scene Commander's working on it.'

'What can I do?'

Westbrook laid a hand on his shoulder. 'If I were you I'd sit back in the car.'

Vanner drew in a breath, filling his chest and letting the air out slowly. He stared about him. Uniformed officers were taking statements from witnesses at the entrance to the station. He looked again to the bus terminal stand where she had lain a few minutes earlier.

'Is she dead?'

'Don't worry about it now.'

'He stood and watched me. McCauley.' He shook his head very bitterly. 'Got what he wanted didn't he.'

Westbrook looked him in the eye. 'You're a good copper, Vanner. This is his fault not yours.'

Vanner looked beyond him then and saw Superintendent Morrison moving towards him from the entrance to the station. He went back to the car.

Graves spoke to Webb on the telephone. 'We're going to let the train out of the station. I want to take him at Clapham Junction. If there isn't enough time for us to get there we'll stop the train on the track, signal failure.'

Webb spoke with his face averted from McCauley. 'He's still armed. Carriage is full now.'

'Okay. Listen carefully. We've deployed two SFO teams, and three ARV units to Clapham. When you get there we'll have cleared the station. BR will announce that the train is going to terminate there. A second train will be waiting on the next platform. The passengers will be asked to transfer. Where's he sitting?'

'Forward end of the carriage,' Webb said, 'aisle seat on the right-hand side as you look from the back. Four seats from the end.'

'Next to him?'

'Girl.'

'And across?'

'Can't see. Both seats are occupied though.'

'You armed?'

'No.'

Webb switched off his phone again and checked the battery. McCauley was staring into space now. Webb checked his watch. The train was ten minutes late. And then it moved under him, pulling slowly out of the station. He felt the adrenaline begin to build.

Vanner looked into Morrison's face. He was sitting in the back seat of the ARV once more.

'What happened, Vanner?' Morrison's face was stiff.

Vanner pursed his lips. 'You don't know?'

'I want to hear it from you.'

Vanner stared through the windscreen and flared his nostrils. 'I shot the wrong party.'

'How? Why were you armed?'

'PROT got shot in Kensington High Street. In the ambulance the paramedic gave me his gun.' He looked at Morrison. 'By the book, Sir. Instant arming. It was logged with SO13.'

Morrison nodded. 'And he lured you here?'

'Phoned me on my mobile. Sloane Square tube. I was here in three minutes.'

Morrison looked across the road where the traffic was jammed up solid with the police activity. People filled every space imaginable though the rain still fell in torrents.

'Same clothes, same hair, same bag. I was thirty yards away,' Vanner said. 'She got out of a cab. Went for something in her bag. I shouted the warning twice, Sir.'

'And then you shot her?'

'She was bringing something black from the bag. Eye contact. She ignored me.'

'She didn't hear you.' Morrison leaned on the roof. 'Too much noise. Too many people.'

Vanner thinned his eyes. 'You believe me then?'

'Of course I believe you, Vanner.' Morrison straightened. 'What's happening now?'

'SO19 are looking to take him out. He's on a train. George Webb has him eyeballed.'

'Well let's hope they get the bastard.'

'CIB on their way?'

Morrison looked back at him. 'Not yet but they will be.' He paused and looked Vanner in the eye. 'I may not like you, Vanner. But you have my word – if there's witnesses who heard you – I'll back you to the hilt.'

Vanner looked at him and nodded. 'Thank you, Sir,' he said.

The train crossed the bridge and rumbled along the open track towards Battersea power station. Webb looked down at his telephone, then again at McCauley. McCauley was watching him. Webb looked away, ignoring the urge to eyeball him. When he looked back McCauley was staring out of the window.

Just before the power station the train shuddered to a halt. Webb stared at McCauley who lurched forward in his seat, almost losing his grip on the bag. The passengers were restless. One man next to him got up and looked out of the window. Webb felt sweat on his forehead. McCauley was looking at him. His eyes were dull, a puzzled expression on his face. His right hand was on the zip of the bag. Webb felt his heart jar in his chest.

Just then the Tannoy crackled and the passengers were informed that there was a signal fault on the line. The train would be delayed a few minutes and would have to terminate at Clapham Junction. A second train would take them from there to their destinations. Webb licked his lips and watched McCauley's face. He looked agitated, a tick starting just under his eye. The phone rang and McCauley looked directly at him. Webb looked away casually, grinned and spoke into the phone.

'Hello?'

'What's happening?' Graves's voice.

'Nervous.'

'Yeah?'

'Yeah.'

'We've got the teams on the move but you'll be sat there for a few minutes yet. We need to clear the station. When you get there let him off the train before you, we'll keep this line open now and you'll have to identify him for us.'

Webb thought for a moment. 'Lot of people getting off the train. Get somebody there who can identify him from your end.'

Graves was silent. 'Who knows him?'

'Vanner.'

The driver of Vanner's Armed Response Vehicle took the call on his PX radio. He spoke quickly then looked over his shoulder at Vanner.

'They're taking him out at Clapham Junction,' he said. 'Commander wants you there to spot him for us.'

Vanner stared in his face. 'Let's get moving then.'

They drove very quickly, the driver swinging the wheel through his hands, staggered sirens howling overhead, blue lights flashing as they cut a path down the middle of the road at eighty miles an hour. Vanner sat in the back, rocked from side to side feeling the sweat gather on the palms of his hands.

George Webb let out a silent breath as the train moved off once again. In front of him James McCauley's eyes darted from one window to the next, his hand inside the shoulder bag. He watched the faces of the people closest to him, and then he stared at Webb.

The British Rail staff cleared Clapham Junction station. The first Specialist Firearms Officer team had arrived and were swiftly assessing the layout of the station for positions. Graves commanded, the open phone line in his hand. He directed two men to enclosed steps which led up to the other platform and the exit. Further along the platform a second set of steps led down. He deployed two men halfway down them. A red control room squatted in the middle of the platform. Two other officers crouched inside. Graves deployed further men on the other side of the tracks and stationed five more in the five-coach train that had been shunted onto the opposing platform. When all were positioned he checked in with each of them. The train approached slowly along the tracks. Graves moved inside the control room and took up a position, a BR jacket over his bullet-proof vest.

Vanner walked down the steps to the platform with the officers from 511 Trojan. He spotted Graves inside and moved to the door.

'Where'd you want me, Cuddles?'

Graves looked at him and considered. 'Just here inside the door.' He put the phone to his ear. 'You there, George?'

'Live and kicking.'

'What's he doing?'

On the train Webb watched McCauley's face. McCauley stared right back at him, hand still inside the bag. 'Right now he's watching me.' He touched his lips with his tongue. 'He's very very nervous.'

The train drew slowly into the station. Across the other side of the platform the second train stood waiting with all its doors open. The Tannoy sounded again, the driver apologising for the inconvenience and instructing the passengers to move directly to the other train. Webb watched McCauley. McCauley was looking at the girl alongside him.

In the platform control room Vanner stood with Graves while Graves spoke into his PX handset. 'Stand by,' he said. 'Stand by.' Vanner watched as the first carriages rolled past. One, two, three, and then the fourth. It rolled beyond the window and came to a halt just before the stairs.

On the train Webb stroked his moustache. 'Train stopped,' he said quietly into the phone. 'First passengers getting off. He's not moving. He's still not moving.' McCauley got up as the girl in the window seat moved past him. He pressed himself close to her and looked up and down the carriage. His eyes alighted on Webb. Webb lowered the phone and stood up. McCauley was looking out of the window. Webb spoke again. 'Moving, almost on the platform, black jeans, blue sweatshirt. He's got a girl very close to him. Possible Yankee.'

In the control room Vanner stared at the doors of the fourth carriage. Graves was speaking to his men. 'Stand by, possible hostage situation. Caution. Stand by. Stand by.'

Vanner saw McCauley step off the train, the girl in front of him. 'There,' he said to Graves.

'Steps,' Graves said. 'Colin. Jimmy. Your man. Stand by.'

Webb stepped off the train. 'He's behind the girl, black jeans, blue sweat top.'

'Eyeballed,' Graves said in his ear.

All at once McCauley looked right and saw two armed policemen on the steps. He grabbed the girl by the throat and dragged her against him.

'Yankee,' Graves said.

McCauley had dropped the bag and as he did so he brought up a gun and pushed it against the girl's cheek. He stared straight at the two policemen.

'Back off,' he shouted.

The rest of the passengers were moving towards the other train. Some of them looked round, a woman screamed and people started running.

'Shit,' Graves said and stepped onto the platform.

The SFO men were speaking to McCauley. 'Put the gun down, James. There's nowhere for you to go. Armed police everywhere.'

James was looking about him, sweat on his face, lips drawn back from his teeth. George Webb stood fifteen feet from him and their eyes met.

'Put it down, James,' Webb said. 'Let her go.'

McCauley stepped back toward the train. 'Back off. All of you. Back off or I'll kill her.'

The two SFO men had their carbines trained on his head. Graves was watching them, watching him. The girl was silent, tears on her face, hair pushed up against McCauley's chest, his arm locked about her throat, shielding his body with hers.

'Put it down, James,' Webb said. 'It's over.'

McCauley lifted one foot behind him seeking for the step to the train; the girl almost fell but he held her. Vanner watched from the door of the control room. He saw James McCauley and he saw the girl and he saw an innocent woman bleeding on the pavement in the rain. He touched Graves on the shoulder and stepped past him.

'Stand by,' Graves said into the radio.

Vanner walked slowly towards McCauley. Webb saw him and squinted. Vanner walked on, fists balled at his sides. McCauley had not seen him. He was pushed back into the doorway of the train. Vanner walked on, aware of his footfall, twenty yards, fifteen, ten.

'JAMES!' he suddenly shouted. James saw him and stumbled and as he did so the girl half-pulled away from him. From the bottom step the armed officer shot him.

He fell back, face exploding, the girl was spattered with warm blood and now she screamed a high-pitched wailing sound that lifted and lifted. McCauley fell against the train and bounced off the door before crumbling onto the platform. The gun rattled off concrete and settled.

Vanner turned away. He could hear the screaming; the screams of men, the screams of women. He saw the woman he had shot falling away from him and people diving for cover in the rain. He crouched, fingers pressed into the concrete. From his pocket he took a cigarette and lit it with wavering hands.

The smoke burned his throat. Somebody moved alongside him.

'He's dead, Guv'nor,' Webb said.

'So is she, George.' Vanner spoke without looking up.

Vanner stood in the living room of his empty house listening to the rain on the window. He leaned against the empty fireplace with a glass of whiskey in his hand and stared at the photograph of his father. CIB had interviewed him. There were witnesses. They had heard his shouts, but an innocent woman was still dead and he knew all about James McCauley's pain. Ulster and a rain-filled night and the members of C1-ZG Squad all about him. Lights and blue tape and Quinlon dead in his shirt sleeves with his face buried in water. The past. The present. The future. He stared at his father again, wondering how he would face things without him. Not a gun but a slim leather-bound umbrella half in, half out of a bag. Rain and people and traffic. The clothes were the same, the hair. And then McCauley looking down on him while he lay prostrate in the rain with his face pushed into concrete.

A car drew up outside and he went to the window. George Webb got out and came around to the passenger side. He opened the door and Ellie got out with her bag. She looked drawn and pale in the fall of light from the street lamp. Vanner felt something tear inside him.

His heart began to thump as she climbed the steps. He looked at Webb. Webb looked at him and then got back in the car. Her key in the door, the terrible ache in his gut. The whiskey was suddenly sour in his mouth and he placed the glass on the mantelpiece. The front door opened, closed again and then silence. He stood where he was and then looked up as she appeared, tiny and frail and frightened in the doorway. The bag looked heavy in her hands. He looked at her. She looked back at him. He did not speak.

'They told me what happened,' she said.

He nodded.

'Is she dead?'

He nodded again.

She sighed then very heavily, closed her eyes and leaned her head against the door frame.

Vanner looked at the glass he had placed on the mantelpiece.

'What'll happen to you?'

'I don't know yet. But I shot an innocent woman.'

'George said you shouted the correct warning.'

'I did. But it didn't make any difference. Maybe she didn't hear me.'

'But if you shouted you did the right thing didn't you?'

'Yes.'

'Then . . .' Her voice tailed off.

'We'll have to see, Ellie.'

Still she stood there. Still she held the bag, then she straightened and turned and went out through the door. Vanner heard her feet on the stairs. He followed her into the hall.

'Ellie.'

She stopped on the first landing and looked down at him.

'Are you going to pack your things?'

She stared at him, face very still. 'No,' she said. 'I'm not.'

Inheritance

Keith Baker

When retired RUC officer Bob McCallan is killed in a gas explosion in a caravan in Donegal, his son Jack inherits an unexpected fortune. He also inherits a key to the past.

The violence in Northern Ireland has been over for two decades, but there are still secrets that could shatter the foundations of peace. Secrets that Bob McCallan's untimely death threatens to bring to the surface. Secrets that some people would do anything to keep buried.

'A gripping read' Michael Dobbs

'Breathtaking . . . if you buy no other thriller this year, buy this one' *Irish Times*

'Gripping' *Belfast Telegraph*

0 7472 5235 1

Guilt

John Lescroart

Mark Dooher has it all. A prosperous law practice. The respect of his peers. A healthy wife and family. But he wants more. He wants young lawyer Christina Carrera to be his lover – and his new wife.

Killing Sheila, after twenty years of marriage, is tough. But Dooher's used to tough decisions. It's what comes next that's hard. The unremitting scrutiny of a head of homicide who, with a terminally ill wife, is fixated on catching Sheila's killer. The hints of suspicion from his best friend and defence lawyer. And worst of all, in the mind of the woman for whom he's jeopardised everything, the woman who's soon to have his baby, there's a growing suspicion of his guilt . . .

'Lescroart has brought so much more to the novel than simply courtroom dazzle . . . first-rate . . . raises the drama to an unusually sophisticated level . . . cracking legal drama' *Publishers Weekly*

0 7472 5457 5